THE
KINGDOM OF
THE WIND

The Kingdom of the Wind

THAMES RIVER PRESS
An imprint of Wimbledon Publishing Company Limited (WPC)
Another imprint of WPC is Anthem Press (www.anthempress.com)
First published in the United Kingdom in 2014 by
THAMES RIVER PRESS
75–76 Blackfriars Road
London SE1 8HA

www.thamesriverpress.com

Original title: *Kaze no Okoku*
Copyright © Hiroyuki Itsuki 1985
Originally published in Japan by Shinchosha
English translation copyright © Meredith McKinney 2014

Printed and bound in Sweden by ScandBook AB.

A CIP record for this book is available from the British Library.

ISBN 978-1-78308-129-5

This title is also available as an ebook.

This book has been selected by the Japanese Literature Publishing Project (JLPP),
an initiative of the Agency for Cultural Affairs of Japan.

THE KINGDOM OF THE WIND

HIROYUKI ITSUKI

Translated by Meredith McKinney

THAMES RIVER PRESS

Plough no furrow
Belong to no nation

Live in no place
Have no self

PART I

PART I

PART I

A sudden raucous voice blared behind him. A red light was flashing in his rear view mirror.

"The white car with the Shinagawa number plate! You there, pull over to the left!"

Taku Hayami stepped on the brake. He had been aware of the patrol car tailing him for some time. But he couldn't think why he was being pulled over.

"Damn." He put on his turn signal and slowly drew the car to a halt beside a utility pole. The patrol car swerved ahead of him and pulled up. It bore the name of the Osaka Police Department. A helmeted policeman emerged and strode over. Another remained in the car.

"Your license," said the cop. He was young, with a boy's face. Taku pulled his license out of his back pocket and handed it over.

"You're from Tokyo?"

"Yes." Taku turned on the interior light so the policeman could see his face.

"Thank you, that's fine." Returning the license, the cop stepped back a few steps. "Turn off your lights and step on the brake please." He spoke in a local Kansai accent.

"The brake?" Taku raised his right foot and lowered it onto the brake pedal.

"There, you see?" said the policeman, pointing to the rear of the car. "The left brake light's out."

Taku stepped on the brake again, and the policeman shook his head. "No, it doesn't come on."

"Right. I'll fix it right away." Taku glanced at the clock. Eleven fifteen. Nothing to worry about. There was still plenty of time until midnight, when the group would gather.

"I'm going to impress you by changing the bulb inside one minute," he announced. He turned off the engine, and took from the glove compartment a black box containing various spare bulbs. Then, from the toolbox under the dashboard, he drew out a Phillips-head screwdriver. He stepped out and around behind the car.

The policeman trained a flashlight onto the rear of the car. "This is a Mercedes 4WD, is it?" he said in surprise.

"That's right." Swiftly, Taku removed the brake light cover. He changed the bulb, then carefully screwed the plastic cover back into place. If you tightened too much, it tended to crack. The policeman helpfully shone his torch on Taku's hands as they worked.

"You're registered as a normal sedan car, I see. Unusual for something this size."

"That's right. That's the beauty of this car." Right on the minute, he gave the screw its final twist and all was completed.

The policeman was no longer trying to hide his expression of youthful fascination with cars, and this one in particular. He was round at the door ahead of Taku, peering in. "I'll try the brake and see if it's working now. Okay?"

"Sure, sure, go ahead."

The policeman opened the door and twisted himself into the driver's seat, checked to see where the brake was, and put his foot down on it. The brake light flashed.

Taku held up his hand. "That worked. Thanks."

"This car has no free-wheeling hubs, eh?" the policeman asked.

"Yes, I guess you don't want to stop the car when there are bullets flying at you, say, or cause a breakdown in the desert or something. Besides, it's not the kind of car that has an issue with noise."

"You use it in the military too, do you?"

"Yes, Daimler Benz developed this car in collaboration with the weapons company Steyr-Puch, you see. Apparently they were put to pretty big use by the Argentine side in the Falklands War. A different type from this one, of course."

"Wow." The policeman was still sitting in the driver's seat, disinclined to move. "So this is the transfer control lever? And what's this round one?"

"You use that to independently lock the front and rear diff."

I was just like this when I was his age, Taku was thinking. No, probably not like this really. I would've done whatever it took to get my hands on the steering wheel and do a lap around the block.

"Actually, I'm planning to get myself a Jimny 1000 sometime," the young policeman revealed a little shyly. He climbed out of the car, bowed politely, and turned back to the patrol car.

"Er, just a moment," Taku called to him as he was sliding into the driver's seat of his Benz. "Could you tell me if I'm on the right road for the Nintoku Tomb?"

"You mean the burial mound of the ancient emperor?" The policeman nodded, and gave him succinct directions. "If you end up in the area round the back, it's full of love hotels, you know. Drive safely."

He was about to go, but suddenly he stopped and cocked his head to one side quizzically. "Is something going on there tonight? At the mound, I mean."

"Why do you ask?"

"Some others were asking the way there just a while ago too."

Taku forced a smile. "I'd guess they were just a bit shy to ask how to get to a love hotel in so many words."

"Those guys didn't look like the type, really."

"Well, thanks." Taku Hayami raised his hand in farewell, pressed lightly on the accelerator, and turned the key. The five-cylinder diesel engine started at what seemed a single touch, spinning into action with a metallic cry that resounded confidently through the quiet night. The loud beating of his heart seemed to echo it. He released the hand brake, throwing his weight behind the gesture, and headed the car towards the Nintoku Tomb.

Turning left at the traffic light as instructed, Taku found himself in a wide, empty street. Imperial Tomb Avenue, said the sign. Not a soul was in sight along the dark road. On his right soared a high tower, while a black row of trees lined the stretch to his left.

This was his first visit to the tomb mound. He'd double-checked its location with the aid of a map before he set off, and found it on GSI 1:2500 map 4 for the Sakai area of Osaka, at N1/53/15/9/2. The address was number 7 Daisen-cho, Sakai. A large number of other ancient imperial tomb mounds, the most famous of which was that of emperor Richu, dotted the surrounding area known as the Mozu Tomb Collection, a place of great archaeological significance. On his way here, he'd dropped into a book shop in Kobe and snatched a look at a guidebook of the area, which said that it was one of the two great imperial mound regions in the Kawachi area, rivaling the famous Furuichi Tomb Collection in importance.

Can it really be bigger than a pyramid? he wondered. Taku recalled the great pyramid of Pharaoh Khufu that he'd seen when he went to Giza, at about the same age as that young policeman.

Seven or eight years had passed since his trip to Egypt. He'd been a young man in his early twenties back then, temporarily employed as a driver by a Japanese company in Cairo—an impetuous, car-loving youth, bursting with the urge for adventure. Now he was a tired man past thirty who still lived alone. He was no longer as fascinated with driving cars. These days, his only love was walking.

In no time, he saw a small open area on his left. He slowed as he passed it. To its right stood a building that might be some sort of administrative office. A single light burned softly above the door. Taku could make out a set of stone posts strung through with a chain indicating a parking lot, a gravel area, and a black metal fence surrounding the whole space. Beyond stood the dark shape of a shrine gate. To either side of it, two dense rows of tall shrubs stood blackly, as if to obstruct the gaze from what lay beyond.

So this was the Nintoku Tomb.

Taku drove on for a while, keeping his eye on the row of trees that continued on his left.

Yes, it was big all right.

He finally came to a halt some distance beyond the plaza. It took both hands to pull up the heavy handbrake. Then he cut the engine, which stopped with a thud that shook his shoulders. He guessed there were so few passersby in these parts that he could safely leave the car parked here for a while without attracting complaint.

Taku tugged a haversack from the back seat and got out, slinging it over his shoulder. He didn't lock the doors. First he must survey the plaza. He set off at a leisurely pace, adopting a casual air. Just before the plaza, he paused and peered through the darkness. No sign of anyone there yet.

Taku now stepped off the pavement, and moved around to the front of the building that stood at the edge of the plaza. A large wooden notice board hung there. He ran his eyes along the brush-written words on it: "Imperial Household Agency Documents and Monuments Department Furuichi Surveillance Area Mozu District Office." Apparently this gravelled plaza was open for public visiting. The area beyond, surrounded by a series of dark moats and a stone fence, would be sacred ground to which entry was forbidden.

Suddenly from the depths of memory he recalled the fact that this imperial mound was the world's largest tumulus in the peculiar elliptical shape characteristic of those in the region. He remembered seeing a marvelous bird's-eye view of it taken from the air in some photographic magazine.

He was not particularly interested right then in the ancient imperial tomb itself. It was just that he'd been impressed by how much grander and more beautiful it had looked in comparison to the other tumuli in surrounding photographs.

He stood there for a while, gazing as if entranced at the vast shape of the burial mound that rose before him in the darkness.

Suddenly, an odd feeling gripped him, as if something was calling to him from the mound. Presently, he grew aware of a strange, unanticipated emotion beginning to stir deep inside him. The sensation made him slightly uncomfortable.

It was feeling he had never before experienced, a delicate mixture of peculiar nostalgia and unidentifiable sadness. What's more, it was unquestionably emanating to him like sound waves from somewhere within the shrine gate that stood beyond the moats, penetrating deep inside him. He felt rising slowly within him like a tide the urge to rush to the ancient tomb that lay in there in the darkness, fling himself down onto its earth and wail and sob aloud.

"Something's wrong with me this evening," he thought, shaking his head, and he raised his left hand as if to block the invisible waves flowing out to him from the tomb, and checked his watch.

In another half circle, the glowing blue minute hand of his titanium waterproof watch would coincide with the hour hand. The last Saturday of March would soon be over. A long day, and one he would never forget.

Yes, this Saturday would be remembered as the day he had met with the most shocking thing in his ten and more years of roaming.

But was the thing I saw this afternoon up there in the mist of Nijo Mountain real? he asked himself. And will that "flying woman" appear again here?

Calm down. There's still some time to go, he told himself, and he set off walking slowly across the road, away from the plaza, toward the park opposite.

Taku Hayami settled himself into the shadows behind the bushes of the park, and from this hidden spot he watched the plaza.

"Will they really come?" he wondered.

Across the road and facing the park, not a soul was in sight. A chill breeze carried the faint scent of the sea.

Suddenly Taku was hungry. He searched in his haversack, and pulled out a paper bag—a packet of dried sweet potato slices he'd bought in the greengrocer outside his apartment the night before as he was setting off.

He'd loved these things since he was a kid. "Popeye likes spinach, Taku like dried sweet potato!" his older brother Shin'ichi used to tease him. But, aside from the question of calorie count, he did prefer these to other dried foods such as beef jerky, which was so salty that it gave you an awful thirst.

Working to bite off a piece of dried sweet potato with his front teeth, Taku laughed silently. He was suddenly recalling the time three years earlier when he'd trekked for two weeks through a Nepalese valley, walking from village to village.

They were a party of three men and an animal—himself, an elderly Sherpa guide, a young porter, and a skinny donkey. His three companions had completely fallen for the dried sweet potato slices he'd been sent from Tokyo, and he was remembering now their humbly expectant expressions as they waited for him to dole out this precious preserved foreign food at every tea break on the trek.

The donkey had particularly adored them, and by the end of the trip his ears would stand straight up at the cry of "*Imo!*", the Japanese word for sweet potato.

The trip was a failure, thought Taku, but it was fun nevertheless. He hadn't managed to meet the Lung-gom-pa, the holy men who levitated as they walked, that he'd heard about; still, he'd learned a great deal about walking from his guide and porter. And from Chunjun the donkey, whose spindly legs looked likely to snap but were in fact astonishingly tough.

The sweet potato was too hard even for his strong teeth to break. The packet must have lain gathering dust in the greengrocer for a long time.

He drew a small knife from its sheath, an elegant little thing with a hardwood handle. He usually carried nothing more than a worn old cheap pocket knife, but as he was preparing to go on this research trip his brother Shin'ichi had convinced him to take this one.

Shin'ichi was a year older, and a complete gearhead. He wasn't one to be satisfied merely with collecting knives. His first step was to take over the underground garage of the house, installing a specialty belt grinder, a small lathe, a sclerometer and so forth, trying to make knives out of sheet metal himself.

Before long, however, he'd realized that making good knives was in fact a professional job worthy of deep respect, not something an amateur with nothing more than an interest in it could perform. He had now given up on blades, and instead was enjoying himself by making knife handles and sheaths.

The knife he'd asked Taku to take along was one of the "backpack handle" knives that were his latest creation. It was an unhilted drop point, the small blade just a little over five centimeters long, but the semi-hollow grind finish made it perfect for a utility knife. He had painstakingly carved the dark green Micarta handle in a beautiful curve that seemed to draw the fingers into it.

The rock-hard sweet potato chips peeled away as smoothly as butter under the Hitachi ATS34-strength blade.

"Poor fellow," murmured Taku, recalling his brother's clean-cut profile, his face tanned brown from the artificial sunlamp. But no, perhaps he wasn't so poor after all. No, no matter how weird his way of life seemed, at least his older brother wasn't alone. He was living with a woman he really needed. That was for sure.

In the darkness, Taku's thoughts shifted to picture the older woman, a flat-chested singer with skin through which the veins showed.

Suddenly he felt he heard the sound of singing from somewhere.

Do not point the finger, pray.
There goes another fellow-man...

It was the song she herself loved best, though of course this gloomy ballad never became any kind of hit.

Instantly another woman's image came back to him, like a stab to the heart.

It was the face of the "flying woman," speeding towards him astonishingly fast through the mist. Suddenly, his heart was beating loudly.

To recover his composure and turn his mind to other matters, he looked up at the sky. The air was cold, and remarkably clear and dark for a city skyscape. Yes, he recalled suddenly, this was the right moment to search for the Arc to Arcturus. Pleased by the idea, he focused his eyes on the northern stars.

The Arc to Arcturus, so named by Dr. Suzuki, is famous among amateur sky watchers as one of the main nocturnal events in the spring skies, together with the so-called Spring Triangle. Unfortunately, however, the air at this time of year tends to be humid and overcast, far from ideal conditions for stargazing. But since childhood Taku had had a fondness for staring up at the lonesome sky of spring.

The winter heavens, so sublime with their vast throng of jostling constellations against a lacquer-black frozen sky, were unquestionably an incomparably more impressive sight, it was true. Yet Taku had an odd love too for these forlorn little spring stars that shone so hesitantly above the swaying atmosphere, and found them somehow warm and nostalgic.

Taku first located Mizar, the first star at the point where the Big Dipper's handle bends around. Right next to it should be visible a little fourth-magnitude star by the name of Alcor, like a child hidden away behind its mother. Long ago, the Arabs used to select their warriors by testing the strength of their eyesight by distinguishing its faint light.

He focused his mind intently on the sky for a while, and finally gave up. There was no point in trying to find Alcor at this season, and in such a place. He went back to Mizar and mentally drew a gentle curve out from it into the southern sky, till he came to the first-magnitude constellation of Arcturus, burning there flame red.

Next was Spica. His eye followed a further mental arc, and there it was, glittering coldly along the line. Taku took a moment to breathe before sliding his eye directly across from Spica back towards Arcturus and then to Mizar. The majestic Arc to Arcturus had just perfected itself above his head.

"That went well," he thought. "She'll come for sure. No question."

With a quick nod he lowered his face to gaze once more across the road at the dark plaza.

As he did so, he saw a number of black human shapes suddenly gathered there, like crows newly alighted on the ground.

Taku checked the time once more. Five more minutes and it would be midnight.

There were five figures in the plaza now. They soon swelled to ten, then very soon from fifteen to twenty. Finally, he counted twenty-five black shapes.

"There'll be more," he thought. "Thirty, probably even more."

The human forms appeared from the left and right of the road, as if erupting out of the darkness. Each one wore a wide-brimmed

conical hat like the sedge hats of ages past, and short traditional
happi coats. They resembled the pilgrims one still sees occasionally
in Shikoku walking the round of the eighty-eight Kannon temples,
but something was different. Their hands were without the
traditional hand covering, and they held no pilgrim's staff.

Their coats and leggings looked black in the night, but in fact
must be dark blue. The rule for pilgrim's garb was white traveling
clothes, with a white *sanya* haversack on the shoulder, plus a rosary
and little bell.

They were silent. There was not even a hint of speech or
laughter. All that could be heard was the soft tread of those
approaching along the road, and the slight crunch of feet on gravel
from the figures already assembled at the place of worship. About
half seemed to be women. There were also a few smaller figures
who might be youths.

Some rested themselves on the stone posts, some leaned against
the iron railings, some squatted, shifting about on their haunches.
All exuded an air of extreme exhaustion. A few were sitting on the
gravel, legs thrown out before them, visibly breathing hard.

At length, a single car approached slowly from the left, a plain
grey station wagon that cruised past Taku with only the fog lights
on, then turned left just before the plaza and drew up. The hazard
lights were left flashing as the doors opened, and out stepped three
men, a silver-haired ancient, and behind him a tall woman.

The three men dragged themselves along as if they might fall
at any moment. They staggered towards the park, the old man
walking ahead and the woman taking up the rear. The old man was
extremely small and thin, but his step was firm. None wore sedge
hats, only the coat and leggings.

The woman walked quite soundlessly. Just as she was about to
turn into the plaza, she glanced around for a moment as if quickly
checking the area, and the street light illuminated her face.

"It's her!" Taku almost leapt impetuously to his feet, but he
restrained the urge and stayed low, peering hard.

Darkish skin, thick eyebrows. The stern line of her lips, like
something carved from steel, followed through to the curve of a
pointed chin. Her short-cropped hair was like a boy's. She would

be perhaps a little over 160 centimeters tall, and weigh less than fifty kilograms.

"A woman like a Damascus knife," thought Taku.

When they'd passed this morning, up there on the ridge of Mount Nijo, he'd been too astonished to take in her face and figure. He had only stood staring at her retreating form, stunned by her extraordinary walk, almost as if she flew.

Now in the night, the momentary glimpse he had of her pierced his heart with a literally physical pain. He remembered that up there on the mountain path in the mist, too, his first meeting with her had sent a kind of electric shock through him that set his heart fluttering. This time, however, it was his whole body that reverberated, with what was in part a kind of masochistic sexual thrill.

As the group, led by the old man, approached the plaza, all the dark shapes already gathered there stood to silent attention in a row. There would have been altogether more than fifty of them.

The old man slowly approached the line. The young woman, together with the three staggering men, suddenly melted in among the waiting people. Taku found himself regretting that he hadn't brought along the little pair of lightweight bird watching binoculars his brother had pressed him to take when he set off on his journey. He couldn't get a good look at the old man's expression from where he stood hidden.

There were no passersby walking along Imperial Tomb Avenue at this late hour, and only an occasional car drove by, oblivious to the figures gathered there.

A chill crept over Taku. The temperature seemed suddenly to have dropped. He kept his eyes trained on the plaza opposite, desperately suppressing the urge to sneeze.

The old man seemed to be talking quietly, telling the assembled people something. Though Taku couldn't hear what he said, his skin registered the strangely reverent atmosphere emanating from the listeners.

He concentrated all his attention, straining to catch the words. He believed that humans could reclaim powers that transcended the accepted levels of modern civilized man, and become again like the Bedouin men he had met in the Sahara, who could hear the shift of sand dunes with a sensitivity beyond that of normal men, or like the old religious ascetic he'd fallen in with once on a mountain path in Kyushu, who told him he could hear the autumn leaves changing color if he closed his eyes. This was the only thing he'd learned from his ten and more years of wandering, and the urge to verify it provided him even now with the only meaning in life.

He steadied his breathing and gazed at the old man's dark mouth. His whole body became ears trained on the plaza. Suddenly, there was a breath of wind, like the distant song of the sea, and for a moment he seemed to faintly hear the voice. It could have been an illusion, or an auditory hallucination. Yet he felt in his heart that he had heard it, really heard it.

And so we must never forget those who are buried here...

These were the last words the old man spoke. Finally, he turned to face the dark, sacred ground beyond the stone fence. His knees bent slowly, until he was sitting formally on his heels on the gravel. All those lined up standing behind likewise sank to their knees. In the glow from the street light, he could vaguely make out the word "Gods," printed in white and enclosed in a circle on the backs of the coats they wore.

The old man raised his hands aloft, then prostrated himself deeply on the ground. All did likewise. Then he returned to a seated position, and for the first time Taku heard his voice clearly.

"AU AU AU..."

The almost animal cry was swallowed by the dark inner recesses of the tomb. The old man prostrated himself twice more, throwing himself forward onto the gravel, and the fifty shapes behind him did the same.

Watching from his shadowy vantage point in the park across the road, Taku felt a peculiar compulsion stir and surge up again deep within him. This archaic scene of worship performed by people who looked like pilgrims but were clearly different from the usual kind did not strike him as weird. It wasn't that. No, it was a strange and inexplicable surge of feeling, the urge to rush over and prostrate himself on the gravel among them.

"AU AU AU..."

The old man's cry, which came to him as both a wail and a kind of summons, continued to reverberate in his heart after it had died away. It felt branded red-hot into him.

He heard the crunch of gravel. They were on their feet again. The line of black shapes was preparing to wordlessly depart. Taku watched as the crowd flowed past him.

By the light of the street lamp he could read the words that were written in white on their dark blue coats: "Company of Fifty-Five" and "Tenmu Jinshin Group Religious Organization."

The group of elderly people was the last to leave the plaza. The tall woman accompanied the old man as they walked towards the car, together with the limping men. They moved through the half-lit darkness like pantomime shadow figures.

Now the "flying woman" was walking quite calmly past his eyes. The old man's step was still firm. They made no sound as they walked. The woman's gait was particularly lithe and beautiful. Her legs swung forward precisely balanced, the elastic knees absorbing the impact of the road; he could imagine the thirty bones that made up her lower limbs all operating in unison as smoothly as a twin-cam engine. This way of walking, smoothly shifting the center of gravity forward in a motion like the strong flicking of a thumb, was more impressive than any he'd come across before.

It was unlike the walk of the short-bodied and long-legged races of Europe and Africa, however, and this further stirred his curiosity.

The legs were very slightly, almost imperceptibly, turned in, which in fact gave her lower body a greater sense of stability. When first born, all humans have legs in the shape of an O, the result of pressure from the womb walls. But when the black and white races grow, they often develop overextended knees or curved legs, a body type known as "X legs," or in the common parlance "giraffe legs." They look good, but they're generally not very useful for hard walking.

The woman now walking away from him through the darkness, however, had an irrefutably beautiful Asian body type. This moved him. He wanted to leap into the road and tell her so. And he also longed to speak to this woman about that extraordinary "walk" he'd encountered up in the mountain mists.

Yet he was nailed to the spot. Something told him that the weird ceremony he had just witnessed strictly forbade the approach of any third party.

He heard the car doors close. The engine started, the red rear lights began to move away, and then the car was swiftly swallowed by the night. The crowd of dark figures, too, was drawn into the darkness and away. He was surprised again by the quickness of their pace, watching them flicker away like a skip-frame film.

And now Taku was left alone in the park. Before him rose the black shape of the ancient burial mound. The wind was cold. There in the northern sky, Mizar had shifted west by ten degrees.

"I'm going to find her," he murmured in the darkness. "Come what may, I must meet her again…"

Then once more the weird cry of the old man—AU AU AU— rose clearly within him.

Taku Hayami was driving along the Osaka Ring Road headed for the Matsubara Interchange. Late as it was, the roads were empty. On his right from time to time he could see the black silhouette of Mount Nijo. The dark ridge line of the Katsuragi Range and Mount Kongo too stood faint against the sky.

At length, he saw on his right the hump of the thickly wooded ancient burial mound. This was the Otsukayama Tumulus. There was a bizarre contrast between the dark shape lying quietly in the darkness, and the gaudy lights of the huge spaceship-like pachinko parlor nearby.

He paid his money at the Matsubara toll, and set off along the West Meihan. This freeway would take him to Tenri, about thirty kilometers away. From there, he could take the relatively traffic-free Meihan highway, which ran on through a steady series of hills and valleys—first the steep Yamato Aogaki National Park, then on to Iga Ueno and Kameyama—until it joined the East Meihan.

He could choose to stay on this road all the way to Nagoya, but he had another route in mind. He'd leave the East Meihan at Kuwana East, and drive for a while beside the Nagara River along Route 258. Then all he had to do was join the Meishin freeway at Ogaki, and settle down to calmly follow the phalanx of night transport trucks. It was rather a long way round, but a less tiring route if he felt like taking it easy.

This way, he'd reach his brother Shin'ichi's house in Yokohama at around nine or ten in the morning. There he would hand over this lump of 4WD metal he was driving, and half the purpose of his little trip would be achieved. He also had the Kongo sand he'd picked up on Mount Nijo, which his brother wanted for sharpening his blades, and, more importantly, a headful of tales he wanted to tell Shin'ichi.

Mount Nijo still hovered on his right, though now seen from a different angle. The needle of the small tachometer stood still precisely on 4,000 RPM. His gaze fixed on the narrow beam of the headlights, Taku suddenly winced. He had the feeling that Mount Nijo was staring at him through the darkness.

"What on earth has done this? What's made me feel so connected to that mountain?" he wondered.

Nijo and himself. The woman in the mist. And the Nintoku Tomb in the night.

He began to summon to mind, one by one, all the things that had happened around him in the last few days, as if in an attempt to untangle a knotted bundle of grey thread.

2

Taku had first heard the name Mount Nijo three days earlier. Given that he was a professional travel writer who worked for a magazine, he should be expected at least to know the names of Japan's major mountains, but in fact he had more knowledge of the geography of other countries than his own. More than ten years ago, at the age of eighteen, he'd set off southbound with a cheap air ticket to wander the world, and since then he had spent almost half his time abroad.

Nijo might be a name well known to scholars, but Taku had never been interested in classical Japanese literature or in historical facts, and besides, Nijo wasn't really a popular mountain compared to the other mountains of Yamato or nearby Yoshino. He must have at least heard the name before, but it had completely slipped from his mind.

When the call had come that day from Meteor Publications, Taku had still been in bed.

"There's a job we'd like you to do. Come right now," said the voice on the other end. "If you don't make it here inside fifteen minutes, you're fired. Don't even think of walking. Grab a taxi. Got it?"

It was Goro Hanada, the man in charge of publications. This was how he always talked. He looked forthright and he was. His pushy, impatient style was not unpleasant, but these days he was a rather old-fashioned editor type. Mind you, he seemed to be not unaware of his own behavior.

"I'll be there in twenty minutes," Taku said, and put down the phone. He always enjoyed seeing how much he could undercut the twenty-minute walk between the Meteor Publications building in

Toranomon and his apartment on a street behind the main shopping district in Azabu Juban.

A glance at the clock told him it was 10 a.m. He got up, dressed, and five minutes later he was striding along the pavement.

By the time he arrived at the door of the Meteor Publications building, Taku had worked up a sweat. It had taken him nineteen minutes and thirty seconds. He leapt straight up the stairs to publications on the fourth floor.

"The chief is waiting for you in the upstairs reception room," a part-timer informed him. Taku threw up his hands and set off, this time more slowly, to climb to the next floor.

He lowered his head in a bow as he entered. "Sorry to keep you waiting."

"Ah, there you are. That was quick, eh?" Hanada thrust his chin forward and tugged at his crinkly hair.

The reception room was a simple affair. A glass-framed ancient Inca fragment hung on the wall. Atop the table's vinyl centerpiece was an aluminum ash tray. On the bookshelf, beside a catalog listing all of Meteor's publications, stood twelve or thirteen carved wooden *kokeshi* dolls. However you looked at it, the room struck the viewer as somewhat incoherent. Tokyo Tower was visible beyond the window.

There was another guest already in the room, a man probably in his mid-fifties, wearing metal-framed glasses. He was pale, with well-groomed reddish hair that immediately told you it was dyed, and he wore a dark blue pencil-stripe suit. A gold bracelet glinted against the wizened skin of his wrist.

This was Hideyuki Nishihaga, a university professor who was often seen on NHK's educational TV programs. His field was classical Japanese literature, and he was well known as a very active essayist as well.

Taking an audible sip of the tea that had been set on the table before him, he examined the new arrival from under his brows.

"This is the fellow I was telling you about," said Hanada, pointing to Taku. He spoke as if appraising a bull at a market. "Over thirty, but still footloose and fancy free. He looks fighting fit though, don't you think? He should be quite useful to you."

"I'm Nishihaga," the professor said with a bow, without putting down his tea cup.

"Yes, I know." Hayami ducked his head in greeting. "I've seen you on television."

"On television?" Nishihaga's voice was cross. He pushed his glasses up his nose with a forefinger. "You don't read many books then, eh?"

"Er, well…"

Nishihaga looked sullen.

"Well, well, sit down" Hanada said soothingly, doing his best to mediate. He pushed a chair towards Taku. "Actually, professor, it's not just this fellow, I have to say. Youngsters these days generally don't have a lot to do with the printed word, you know. They're brought up reading, ah, comic books, you know, illustrated stories, that sort of thing. They don't even have a clue about basic classics such as the *Hyakunin Isshu*, let alone more esoteric things like the ancient *Man'yoshu* poems. But that's exactly why, you see, your essays on the classics, the kind of thing even young girls could read, are so necessary in journalism today. I understand your latest book, *The Lights and Shadows of Yamato*, has sold over eighty thousand."

"It's *The Road to Yamato – Its Lights and Shadows*," Nishihaga corrected him irritably. "Do get the book's title right, please. And you speak only in terms of sales numbers, but I'd like you to know I don't just write simple books for the general public."

"Oh yes, quite so, quite so," Hanada nodded, pushing the cup of cold untouched tea in front of him towards Taku. "Have this, would you? I haven't touched it."

"Thank you." Taku casually helped himself to some milk. Hanada pulled out a cigarette and put it in his mouth, but noting Nishihaga's undisguised frown, he put it back in his pocket.

"This chap, er, what's his name?…" muttered Nishihaga, looking at Taku over his glasses.

Taku introduced himself, and Nishihaga nodded. "Taku Hayami, eh? You're a freelance writer then, are you? Or are you a real employee in the editorial department here?"

At a loss, Taku looked over at Hanada, who nodded and said, "He's not really either. He's a sort of part-timer, you might say.

We pay for his apartment plus a bit of a salary. He also makes ends meet with this and that, fees for a monthly column, help with overseas material, conducting the Asian tours we run and so on, or so I understand."

Hanada seemed to be pretending not to know about the moonlighting he also did for other companies, thought Taku as he listened. Hanada had been providing him with work ever since Taku's long years of wandering abroad had come to an end about eighteen months ago and he'd come back to Japan. But thanks to the recent "Outdoor Lifestyle" craze, other companies had begun to call on him from time to time to write something for them as well.

Recently, with the fading of the vogue for jogging and its replacement with a sudden enthusiasm for walking tours, backpacking and camping holidays, and mountain walking (as distinct from mountaineering), a recognition of the significance and attraction of walking itself had slowly begun to emerge in Japan, and orders had begun to flood in from advertising and sports magazines and the like.

Most, of course, were in the form of anonymous explanatory articles, tests for gear, or guide maps. But occasionally there was a young editor who requested a piece along the lines that really interested him—the art, philosophy and history of walking. Recently, in fact, he'd been finding life quite busy, albeit he still wrote anonymously.

"I've heard from Hanada here how you've spent quite a long time abroad," Nishihaga said. "Many have a hard time re-adjusting to life in Japan if they've lived elsewhere for too long, scholars included. You're the kind who's managed to settle back down at the right time in life, eh?"

"Yes."

"Well I wouldn't call him exactly settled," Hanada cut in. "I met him when I'd got involved in a nasty accident in Morocco and was in a real fix. Had passport plus all my money taken, actually—the lot. I didn't know where to turn. Five years ago it would be now, I think."

"Six," Taku said.

Hanada nodded. "Right. And we've known each other ever since, so I know you can trust him. He's strong, too."

"You seem to be very keen on emphasizing how strong he is," said Nishihaga. "But in my opinion, this job doesn't require strength so much as sensibility."

"Naturally, naturally." Hanada gave a painful grin and brought his big arm down on Taku's shoulder with a thump. "Eh there, Taku? A healthy sensibility in a healthy body, no? You're fine in that department too, right?"

"But just what am I being asked to do?" asked Taku.

Hanada had begun to take his cigarettes out of his pocket, and regretfully slipped the packet back as he replied, "Climb Mount Nijo, that's what we're asking."

"Nijo? Where in heaven's name is that?"

"Let me explain," said Nishihaga, drawing over his leather case as he rose to his feet. "Is there some way to project slides in this room?"

"I'll set things up for you."

With a private shrug to Taku, Hanada went out. His back was broad and heavy. Every time Taku saw it, he was reminded of the astonished expression on Hanada's face when he'd come across him six years earlier, tossed out on a street corner in Marrakesh in nothing but his underwear.

He's a good man, Taku thought. I probably wouldn't have ever had the chance to settle down back here if it weren't for Hanada.

As if breaking in on Taku's moment of tender feelings, Nishihaga abruptly got to his feet again, crossed to the window, and addressed him with his back turned.

"You don't seem to have heard anything about this job from your boss."

Taku affirmed this, and Nishihaga nodded. Staring out the window, he began to talk.

"Meteor Publications is going to be publishing a twelve-part series on travel. It will be a double feature of luxury collector's item plus general publication "mook." The title will be *Japan—Its Lights and Shadows*. Distribution to start this fall. We've already lined up twelve top-notch photographers for the illustrations. But my plan isn't to provide a conventional travel guide."

Taku listened in silence.

"What I want to focus on is actually the 'shadow' side of the 'lights and shadows' formula," Nishihaga went on. "This has been touched on in ancient histories and travel journals, of course, but never more than in passing. My plan is to prioritize these 'shadow' areas. Now I've already done a lot of the field work, going to places such as Ushikubigawa in the Hakusan Range, where the descendants of the defeated Heike warriors settled in the twelfth century as you'll no doubt remember. I've visited the site of the Iwai Revolt in Tsukushi, the villages in Kyushu's Kirishima Mountains where the proscribed believers of the *nenbutsu* cult hid, and so on. I can start the writing up any time now. However…"

Nishihaga paused, and nervously tapped the window with his fingers. "The thing is, the person who holds the actual power in this company is the operations managing director, Shimafune."

Taku remained silent.

"And," Nishihaga continued with an ironic grimace, "this Director Shimafune has now stated that the first in the series is to be the Yamato book. It seems he's adamant. And he came out with this a mere two or three days ago."

I see, thought Taku as he nodded. So I'm guessing Mount Nijo is in Yamato. But what the hell is he asking me to do?

"Of course the Yamato area is my speciality," Nishihaga continued. "I can pick up a pen and write about it any time. But it needs no pointing out that the 'shadow' side of Yamato is not the morning sun of the old Yamanobe Road to the east that we all know so well from poetry, but the somber evening world to the west, the Katsuragi Way. That area, often referred to as the Old Katsuragi Road, is a kind of hidden underground stream that carries two thousand years of dark Yamato history secreted in its misty valleys. The route that runs along the western edge of the Nara plain, from the southern base of Mount Nijo along the foothills below Katsuragi, on to Kongo and finally to Kaze no Mori Pass, could be said to be a kind of Yamato 'Narrow Road to the Shadows,' to borrow a phrase from the haiku poet Basho—a route that holds all manner of ancient sites and legends. Being a journalist, I imagine you're familiar with all this."

"Well, I'm afraid I'm not as well up as I should be..." Taku mumbled. "So just how high is this Mount Nijo?" he went on.

He regretted the question immediately. What a stupid thing to ask, he thought. I'm obviously not cut out for this particular job. He sat there hunched as Nishihaga replied.

"The mountain has two peaks, Odake and Medake, the male and the female peaks. The Odake, the male one, is the higher—515 meters, I seem to remember."

"Is that all?"

"Yes, just 515. Medake is lower, perhaps around 474 or 475. You're disappointed?"

Nishihaga turned to look at Taku, his expression stern and tense.

"'Is that all?' you said. And it's true, Nijo isn't high. However..." he clamped his lips as if momentarily hesitating. After a pause he went on in a low voice. "However, that mountain is a special one. The area above ground is 515 meters, it's true, but beneath the earth its roots go down beyond human calculation. One could say that Nijo is Yamato's house of the dead. You know the old song, 'Ah Futakami, house of our country's dead'? Futakami, of course, being the old name for Nijo. And I must admit, of all the mountains of the Yamato region, Nijo is the only one I've never set foot on."

As he spoke, Nishihaga clutched his hands together, and his cheeks tautened slightly.

"Yes, that's a fact, I've never climbed Mount Nijo. But I can't write the story of Yamato's shadow side without speaking of this mountain. So what do you think I should do, eh?"

"What you ought to do, I'd say, professor, is head right off for there, tomorrow maybe, and climb those two peaks. It's only 515 meters high, after all. A mere hill."

"But I have no desire to climb Mount Nijo!" Nishihaga's voice was full of suppressed ferocity, an emotional exasperation.

Taku shrugged.

"Sorry about the delay," came Hanada's sudden voice, as he walked back into the room with a young female student assistant who carried a slide projector. "Could you get that thing going for us?" he said to her.

She bowed to him and obediently began to set it up, while Nishihaga took some slides from his black bag and with a practiced hand began to slot them into the feeder.

"I'll close the curtains," said the girl. The room grew dark. The machine's cooling fan began to hum softly, and a white frame appeared on the screen. Then, with a metallic click, a blurred image appeared, and the focus was quickly adjusted. The clear image of a colored map was now on the screen.

"It seems you don't care for too much detail, Mr. Hayami, so I'll just present a brief outline. You can do your own research later if you find this interests you. All right?" Nishihaga was speaking in the darkness, his tone now that of a typical teacher.

"Sure, go ahead," Taku responded softly.

Nishihaga began. "Here we have the geography of the area covering the boundary between Osaka and the northwest section of Nara prefecture. That basin on your right there is Yamato. The plain opposite, over on the left, is Kawachi. These two areas constitute the most important region of Japan's ancient culture. Right?"

"That urban area over there is Sakai and Osaka, yes?" Hanada interposed. The professor's shadow nodded.

"That's right. In ancient times, that area was known as Tajihi-mura, and the Osaka Bay area was called Naniwa-tsu. But right now let's concentrate on Yamato and Kawachi. You can see a long, narrow range of mountains intersecting the two plains here, right?"

"Yes."

"Starting from the north, we have Mount Ikoma, Mount Shigi, then Mount Nijo, the Katsuragi Range, and Mount Kongo. This long range stands as a barrier dividing Yamato and Kawachi into two separate areas. You can't go from one to the other without crossing it. So for our ancestors, it was a matter of supreme importance to establish a connecting route between the two."

The slide was replaced with another. Nishihaga went on explaining.

"Right, now we have an aerial view of the same area. What do you think, Mr. Hayami? If you had to find a route to connect the two regions, where would you first look?"

"The lowest place between them, in other words, a river. I can see what looks like a river there between Mount Ikoma and the Katsuragi mountains."

"Precisely. The Yamato River," said Nishihaga, sounding pleased. "'The mountains many-folded' as the old poem about these beautiful mountains goes, the mountains that enclose the inland plain that is Yamato. The water that flows from them becomes the Katsuragi, Takatori, Hatsuse, Asuka, and Soga Rivers, which all meet in the Yamato River. The Yamato cuts through the Ikoma Range and runs into the Kawachi plain. It flows into the Inland Sea here at Naniwa-tsu, which was the destination for foreign ships that arrived from distant lands. So you could call the Yamato River a kind of arterial waterway in ancient times. In fact, back in 608, when Ono no Imoko came back from his official visit to the Chinese Sui dynasty, the ship is said to have landed at the port of Naniwa and continued up the Yamato River to the capital in Yamato. So, as you can see, back in earliest times, the river was for all intents a road. Of course you could come down a river easily enough, but going up it was a difficult business. Besides which, a river in its natural state doesn't provide a stable environment for transport, as the course keeps changing. The Yamato was a typical river in that respect."

"I see."

"So there was a need to develop a stable land route that would allow large numbers of people and large amounts of goods to be transported from Kawachi to Yamato. Five years after Ono no Imoko came back to Yamato up the river, in other words in the twenty-first year of Empress Suiko's reign, we get the opening of the first official road in ancient times to link Kawachi and Yamato. It's recorded in the official record of Suiko's reign, where we read, 'A great road was established from Naniwa to the capital.' This makes it clear that one of the arterial land roads passing through Kawachi and Yamato was already in existence at the time of the great Prince Shotoku, Empress Suiko's famous regent."

"That would be the ancient 'Highway One' they did a program about on NHK television, wouldn't it?" Hanada's loud voice cut in.

"So what you'd need to do," Nishihaga went on, "is connect up the Naniwa Road that begins here in Naniwa with Yoko Road that starts over in Asuka—two roads that already existed—by a road that crosses the mountains, right? But the problem is, where do you cross? It would be a huge job to cut through the mountains and make a road that way. So the clever thing would surely be to find an old 'road' of some sort that already existed, and widen it. What do you think, Mr. Hayami?"

Taku nodded. "I agree, yes. There'll always be some kind of track even in the steepest mountains as long as animals live there. Humans and animals are the same, after all, they can't survive without paths."

It was Nishihaga's turn to nod. "Correct. There were actually a number of secret tracks from way back that crossed between Kawachi and Yamato. There would have been any number of old Stone Age tribes all over the country from earliest times, who wandered freely and survived in the wild by finding nuts and fruits, hunting animals, and catching fish in the streams. And wherever they spent their lives, there would naturally be paths, innumerable paths all over those unfrequented mountains. What's known as the Takenouchi Highway is believed to be the result of an official effort to develop one of the more important of these original paths. Look, here it is."

A new slide appeared.

"Here we see two strange peaks that suddenly rise just where the Katsuragi foothills are sinking into the plain. This is Mount Nijo. The mountain road that crosses the Nanroku Pass here used to follow a number of different routes, such as the Takenouchi Road and the Taima Road and so on. Taima is the modern pronunciation, of course, but it used to be pronounced Tagima, an old word meaning very rough, mountainous country. Now, the Yamato government back then took one of these rough, precipitous old roads and developed it into the Takenouchi Highway, which became famous as a great national artery. It was set up as an official road, but actually it was far from easy traveling, and people and pack horses had a great deal of difficulty navigating it. Anyway, this Takenouchi mountain pass route connected through from Yamato to Kawachi, then on to Naniwa, and from there via the sea route to China, to the lands to the south and to the Chinese capital of the time. Most of the ancient treasures held in the famous Shosoin

Treasure House in Nara, not to mention the early missions from abroad and indeed all manner of writings and ideas from other countries, reached early Yamato via the Takenouchi Highway. And, essentially speaking, ancient Japanese culture bloomed under their influence. Right…"

A new image appeared on the screen—a white-walled farm house with yellow mustard flowers out front, and behind it, an oddly-shaped mountain, with a double peak rising like a camel's two humps. A somehow distorted yet strangely compelling shape.

"Is this Mount Nijo? Nice little mountain," Taku remarked.

"Much more than merely *nice*," Nishihaga shot back. After a moment, another slide replaced it, a breathtakingly beautiful sunset scene. The black forms of the double peak stood out on the glowing red horizon. The sun was on the verge of setting right between the two humps. A pool in the foreground blazed bright scarlet. It was an extraordinary scene, somehow not of this world. Nishihaga's voice went on.

"Mount Miwa, in the east of the Yamato Plain, is the deity of the morning sun. Mount Nijo in the west, on the other hand, is the mountain of the Buddhist Pure Land paradise, where the sun sets. The sun goes down right behind it. The corpse of the anti-government rebel Prince Otsu was buried on that sunset mountaintop. The western side of the mountain also holds a whole nest of ancient imperial tombs. Look, this gives you some idea."

Nishihaga flicked through a series of slides of the tombs of early emperors—Bidatsu, Yomei, Suiko, Kotoku. There were also photographs of the grave of the early envoy to China, Ono no Imoko, and the mausoleum of Prince Shotoku. Nishihaga explained that the bodies of all these emperors and nobles were carried along the Takenouchi Highway in funeral processions and buried in state at the back of Mount Nijo.

"In ancient times, Nijo formed the boundary between this world and the other. Beyond it lay the world of the dead. The graves of almost all the rulers and nobles from the time of Emperor Ojin down to Emperor Yuraku are clustered there. Over 2,300, and that's just the ones we know of. Mount Nijo is the western door to this crypt. We have no way of grasping the intensity of awe and terror with which the ancient inhabitants of the Yamato Plain would have gazed toward the setting sun of Mount Nijo. Whenever I try to imagine…"

Nishihaga abruptly halted. The black silhouette of Nijo loomed motionless, almost deathly, on the screen beyond him.

"I'll be honest. I don't like this mountain. In fact I could almost say it terrifies me. And yet, I don't know why, I find I'm constantly thinking about it. I've been along the Katsuragi Road numerous times, but never once climbed Nijo. Neither the male nor the female peak. I don't want to go there. I have no desire ever to ascend it. I have my own reasons, which I don't need to explain to you. But, as I said, I can't write about the shadowy side of Yamato without speaking of Nijo. So what I want is for you to climb it on my behalf, take a good look around, check it out, feel it out, and report back. This is what I'm asking of you."

A switch clicked. Mount Nijo disappeared from the screen. Nishihaga's heavy breathing was audible in the dark room.

"I see," said Taku, and nodded. This guy may look like a simple TV celebrity professor to the world, he thought, but he could just be quite a talented individual. Only people who lacked imagination knew no fear. Perhaps it was because he was a real scholar that he had the empathy to experience the emotions of ancient people as his own. "I'll be happy to accept," he went on. "I'm to walk the Takenouchi Highway, then climb Nijo, and hand in a report to you, right?"

"That's correct. I want you to tell me just what you saw and what you felt."

"Open the curtains please," said Hanada, and the room grew bright. "Is something the matter, Professor? You look a little pale," he went on, looking at Nishihaga. There was an almost cruel hint of mockery in his tone.

"No, no, I'm fine." Nishihaga shook his head and stood up. "I'll leave the arrangements to you two to decide. I'll be off now. You can keep the slides." He raised his hand slightly in farewell, nodded to Taku, and left the room, staggering slightly as he went. Hanada made no attempt to accompany this important client to the door, but simply pulled out a cigarette and stuck it in his mouth.

After Professor Nishihaga's departure, Taku and his boss stayed on together finalizing arrangements for the trip to Mount Nijo. Then on his way out Taku dropped in on the third floor's Magazine Editorial Department.

Almost the entire floor was given over to the editing of the numerous magazines produced by Meteor Publications. The big room was open plan, with everyone working on the various magazines sharing the space in a comfortable mixed-living arrangement.

Taku made his way through the areas devoted to *Life and Nature*, *Outroads*, *Traveling the Seasons*, *Camping Life*, *Monthly Hiking Notes*, and *SW Journal*, heading for the *Tramping Quarterly* desk in the far corner. It was located in what Nishihaga might call the "shadows" realm, out of the way and secluded from the light.

The chief editor, Kyoko Shimamura, was sitting at her desk reading a book, deep in a valley formed by two mountains of books, papers, paper bags, and the like that towered on either side. She was small and slightly built, like some junior high student, and her bobbed hair made her look more than ten years younger than her real age of thirty-four. She gave absolutely no impression of being the warrior walker who had clocked two three-thousand-kilometer walks, from the southern island of Kyushu to Japan's northern tip in Hokkaido. Taku always found himself relaxing with a sigh of relief when he saw Kyoko, with her habitual shy smile and her habit of pushing up the glasses that slid down her nose. It was a custom of his to drop in on her after a blasting from Hanada about something or other.

"What are you reading?" Taku asked.

Evidently embarrassed, Kyoko hastily closed the book and put it in a drawer. "Hullo there," she said in a melodic voice. "Hey, I really loved that piece you wrote for *Outroads* the other day, 'Farewell to the Dear Old Ghost Bus.'"

"Thanks, Shima. I didn't think you'd look at a mag like that. You've thrown me."

Outroads was a specialist bicyclists' monthly that Meteor Publications had begun producing about a year earlier. The intended audience of young people keen on cross-country biking had taken it up in a big way, and it apparently had a circulation of 170,000 or 180,000.

Tramping, on the other hand, dedicated entirely to walking as it was and with a serious focus on the subject as a kind of way of life, obstinately failed to expand its readership, and even after three years was still only a quarterly publication.

Kyoko Shimamura was highly critical of the 4WD and bicyclists for their lack of concern for the environment, and introduced the subject often in the pages of her magazine. Her belief was apparently that every time humans damage nature, they damage themselves.

The logo "Walking Softly on the Earth" over the title of *Tramping Quarterly* was her doing. Of course this phrase derived from the Sierra Club's call to "Walk Softly in the Wilderness," but Kyoko's message was that we humans must not only treat the natural world with care when we enter it, but must carry this "low impact" lifestyle through into everyday city life.

What made Meteor Publications special was that it was prepared to quietly leave Kyoko Shimamura in charge of this unprofitable magazine without interfering—though the recent trend for slashing staff meant that its entire masthead consisted of Kyoko plus her assistant, a young man by the name of Kohei Mamiya.

"I think you should pick up that piece where you left off and make it into a book, you know," said Kyoko. "And I also liked the piece of yours I read a while back in *Childcare Journal*. Called 'I was a Walking Angel as a Kid,' if I remember rightly."

Taku stared at Kyoko in genuine astonishment.

"Why would you read a publication devoted to childcare?" he asked.

"Well, I want to read absolutely everything you write. I'm a fan of your writing, see."

"I'm the one who's a fan of yours, actually."

A large shoulder accompanied by a haze of cigarette smoke suddenly intervened between them. It was Hanada.

"Hanging around making a nuisance of yourself here again, eh?" he said, then abruptly he laid his big hand on Kyoko's small bosom and cried in English, "*Touching Softly on the Bust.*"

"Important to be soft," Kyoko said quietly. She sat quite still and rigid, making no attempt to remove his hand.

"Yes indeed, yes indeed." Hanada blushed like a boy. Then off he went, hiding his embarrassment by crying, "Tramp! Tramp! Tramp!..." with each step.

Taku spent that afternoon cleaning his apartment, doing laundry, and writing a letter to his father back in Fukui. It was a good day— the wind was strong, but out his window he could glimpse a patch of blue sky over the neighboring rooftops.

His chat with Kyoko Shimamura on the third floor had largely soothed the unsettling impression that Professor Nishihaga had left on him, and the difficult discussion of ancient history.

"...It's been eighteen months now since I came back," he wrote to his father, "and I've finally settled into a routine with the work. I can see my way at last to gaining a steady life." The tone of the letter suggested that he wrote only rarely. In fact, he wasn't at all sure how long his present life would last. But his father still worried about his thirty-two-year-old son as if he were a little boy, from time to time slipping a few ten-thousand-yen bills in with his letters, so Taku felt he must somehow calm his fears.

Yuzo Hayami, Taku's father, had a business in the seaboard town of Mikuni over on the Japan Sea coast, selling parts for the engines of fishing boats. The business had done well in the boom economy back when Taku and his brother Shin'ichi had been kids, but these days his dad was running it alone on a shoestring. Shin'ichi had been very angry when he heard at one point that his mother had taken a part-time job with the Mikuni Speedboat Club. But it was a choice the couple had made, after all, based on their convictions.

"Work while you can and never be a burden on your children," his father often said, and though Shin'ichi sent money time and again, he refused to touch it.

"It always comes back marked 'Return to Sender,'" Shin'ichi reported incredulously. "The old man's stubborn as a mule." Shin'ichi was probably aware that his father didn't have a high opinion of his way of life. Apparently they had more or less ceased to communicate recently.

Some years back, Shin'ichi had suggested that he'd like his parents to move to Tokyo so he could look after them, and was very hurt when his father hadn't even deigned to reply. It seemed the old man didn't approve of Saera Maki, the singer Shin'ichi lived with, either.

"So Shin'ichi's some woman's gigolo," Taku had once heard his father spit out, and the words had made him wince.

"My next work assignment will take me to Nara," he now wrote. "I've been asked to climb a mountain by the name of Nijo. There's a possibility I might drop in on you for a day or so on the way back." Taku was aware of something bothering him after he'd written this, but it would be too much trouble to rewrite the letter so he slipped it into an envelope and put a stamp on it. In fact, he was half inclined to check out that northern sea again. It had been quite a while.

That evening he went off to the local bath house, then dropped in for a Chinese meal at the Lotus. He had a fondness for their Sichuan chili cuttlefish fry, and went there twice a week to have the dish. It was a tiny place where customers sat along the counter, but the proprietor, a man by the name of Cho, was a very unusual fellow. Occasionally he was off somewhere else, but today Taku found him in his usual place behind the counter.

"Have you ever heard of Mount Nijo?" Taku asked while his chopsticks were busy picking out the pine nuts scattered among the slices of cuttlefish.

"Nijo? Ah yes, that's where you find sanukite, right?' Cho replied casually, wiping the sweat from his brow with his apron. "You know sanukite, Taku?"

"I've heard of it, yes. It's what they call 'sanuki stone' in central Japan, isn't it?"

"Here, this is how you write in Chinese characters." Cho's round babyish fingers picked up a ballpoint pen and wrote three complex characters on a receipt that was lying on the counter. "It's a black andesite that people in early times used to make arrowheads and knives," he explained.

"I've seen it in photographs."

"You also find Kongo sand, or emery, on Nijo, used for sharpening blades. And Shoko rock. Used to make tombs and burial chambers for important people. Apparently it was used for the ancient Takamatsu Tumulus, and also for old Horyuji Temple down in Nara. Almost all ancient imperial tombs were made of it. And even more amazing is..." his voice dropped. "Corundum. A precious jewel second only to diamonds in value."

"Corundum? I don't know it."

"Red kind is a ruby. Blue kind is sapphire. They say you don't find sapphire in Japan, right? That's what scholars say in their books. But sapphires were found on Nijo long ago. No lie."

"Why would you find so many different kinds of stone on Nijo?" Taku asked, happy that he was the only customer.

"Nijo was once a volcano, see."

"A volcano? So what about now."

"Extinct now. But long ago, it was a fire mountain. The area round there, Yamato, that was a marsh two thousand years ago. Nijo had a huge eruption that produced a tableland and rivers, and finally it was worn to a plain. Once Nijo was the only mountain round there to spout fire, a tholoide volcano. That's why you still get lots of kinds of stone. But why do you ask?"

"Thanks for all the information." Taku paid his bill, said his farewells and left. This place is my own personal classroom, he thought to himself.

Before he went home, he did some shopping at a bookstore and an electrical goods shop.

Although this area was tucked in behind the modern centers like Roppongi and Iikura, it had a relaxed feel strangely reminiscent of the old low-lying *shitamachi* part of Tokyo. There were good grilled meat restaurants and public bath houses, and he'd heard the area had once been a thriving geisha scene. You could find amazingly cheap apartments if you were prepared to put up with a certain lack of sunlight.

He was living on the third floor above a barber shop. The first floor was shops, the second housed the families and staff that worked in them, and the three rooms on the third floor were rented out. A foreign student and a Roppongi gay bar hostess shared the floor with him.

The single room made life a bit cramped, it was true, but the feel of the area suited him, and he'd been there ever since coming back to Japan. He also liked the fact that he could walk to the Meteor Publications building.

When he got to the door of his place, he discovered the telephone inside was ringing. He opened the door and stepped up into the room without removing his shoes at the entrance.

"Is that you, Taku?" It was a woman's voice. In the background he could hear some kind of musical instrument.

"Are you recording?" Taku asked. She was probably calling from the corridor outside a recording studio. He knew from her voice that it was Saera Maki, his brother's lover.

"Shin's not there. What should I do?" She sounded scared. Taku wasn't surprised. This was how she always was. She was the sort of girl who'd phone home several times a day if she had the time. Or more than several, tens of times. Not for any reason, simply to calm herself by hearing Shin'ichi's voice. As soon as he spoke, she'd quickly put down the receiver.

But if Shin'ichi didn't answer, nothing the manager said could convince her to leave the telephone. In the end, she'd ignore even stage calls or filming schedules. This had caused trouble and grief for her management countless times.

It was kept a secret to the outside world, but in fact Saera had once spent some time in a hospital. Shin'ichi had taken her up to a place in Fukui run by a friend—needless to say, a psychiatric hospital.

"He'll be in the toilet, I'd say," Taku responded lightly.

"Really?" Saera's voice suddenly grew calm. This was a warning sign. "You ought to know that there's a telephone in every toilet at home."

"Oh yeah, that's right."

"And in the garage, the workshop, the garden, and the storeroom. Everywhere."

"Okay then, maybe he's taking a walk."

"Shin always carries a cordless phone or a pager in his pocket when he's out."

"There's a phone in the car too, right?"

"When he doesn't answer it can only mean one of two things— either he's dead, or he doesn't love me anymore."

Taku sighed. "Well then I guess he may have died, eh?" he said, and immediately regretted the tasteless joke.

"That's right." Saera's voice was now still calmer. "And if that's the case, then I'll die too."

"Miss Maki!" a man's voice was calling repeatedly in the background. It was Seta, her manager.

Gently, Taku said, "Don't go causing everyone trouble, okay? I'll search for him. Try phoning him in Yokohama again in five minutes."

"Five is too long. Three."

"Okay,"

The phone went dead. But Taku didn't dial Shin'ichi's special number. There was no way his brother would go missing.

Shin'ichi had organized his life so he could always answer calls from Saera, 24/7. The reason he didn't answer would have been because he didn't want to. Men have these moments, no matter how much they love a woman.

But Taku didn't take Saera's mention of dying as an idle threat. If she rang Yokohama again in three minutes and Shin'ichi still didn't answer, she really would be as good as dead. She wouldn't be able to speak, let alone sing. Taku didn't just dismiss her as pathologically unstable. *After all*, he thought, *it takes all sorts*.

Five minutes later the telephone rang again.

"Sorry." Her voice was warm and vivacious, the voice of a little girl who's been half way to the world of the dead and returned to life again. "He was there. He said he was just coming to pick up the phone when he knocked over a spirit lamp. He must've been heating up oil to put on his new shoes. Apparently the cushion caught fire and it was quite a job to avoid the place going up in flames. I'm sorry, Taku. I won't bother you like this ever again. Promise."

"What a relief, eh? Hope you sing well." Taku replaced the receiver.

As a singer, Saera Maki could pull in the money. In the last four or five years, she'd disappeared from the big shows, the NHK end-of-year song contest extravaganza *Kohaku*, best ten hits programs and the like, but she was still a star. There weren't that many adult singers in their mid-thirties who could command 30,000 yen a head every month at a dinner show in a top class hotel.

Though she was no longer young, her popularity sprang from the fact that her face and body were actually more beautiful than in her twenties, and besides, she had fabulous fashion sense. Over the years she'd had a number of big hits in the old urban-style popular song genre. She was absolutely the opposite of the approachable girl-next-door type currently in vogue. What her adult fans saw in her was a kind of 1920s elegance and mystique. And she was a star who could give it to them, one hundred percent. Just so long as Shin'ichi answered every phone call she made as soon as she was off the stage.

Taku didn't at all dislike this popular star who was his brother's lover. He loved her songs—they had charm, even on those days when her pitch and rhythm was a little shaky. The elderly gents and middle-aged men who made up her fanbase watched her performances anxiously, always fearing that this fragile-looking woman might not make it through unscathed that night. Young girls adored her as a fantasy projection of who they might be twenty years down the track. And her lack of any whiff of sensuality meant that women of any age could relate to her without feeling threatened.

Saera had a certain nonchalantly unconcerned air, a rare trait. Shin'ichi had encouraged her to wear Jean Louis Scherrer dresses for occasions that were a little special, while her normal choice was Sonia Rykiel knitwear, but in fact she wore things so naturally that almost no one seeing her walking towards them would notice the brand. Even professional fashion people looked up to her, and not because she had a rich store of information and a deep enthusiasm for fashion—quite the contrary. It was because she had a thoroughly unaffected disregard for it.

She was always in fine health, and even days of hard work and no sleep never affected the smooth perfection of her makeup. And she was a great deal tougher than she looked. Nor was she the type to agonize over things. Yet she somehow had the air of one who was holding back a deep unhappiness. No one knew what it might be, but her fans all sensed it, and it made them forgive her everything.

Taku believed that Shin'ichi had been wrong to take Saera off to a psychiatric ward as he'd done. Her pathological reactions didn't fit the category of psychosomatic illness that was all the rage these days, nor was it an anxiety disorder. It couldn't be called an extreme form of hysteria either. He guessed there was some inner wound that lay behind it. The throbbing ache of some trauma was what kept her pinned to the phone. He felt he could virtually see before his eyes Saera's "scarred soul" (to borrow a phrase from Françoise Sagan).

The telephone rang again. This time it would be from Yokohama, he guessed. He settled down on his back, and picked up the receiver.

"Hey, sorry, man. Saera's been bothering you again, I hear." It was his brother's voice.

Take gave a little laugh. "No, no, nothing special. You knocked over a lamp, I gather. All okay?"

"Yeah, well," Shin'ichi mumbled, and went on. "Say, can you come over tonight, Taku?"

"Maybe."

"Saera finishes work at nine. Seta was lined up to bring her back in the car, but he says he's suddenly developed a fever or something so he was going to send her back ahead. She claims she could drive herself—what do you think, Taku?"

"What's the car, do you know?"

"A new Maserati Quattroporte. It's huge."

"She's bought another has she? Why does she go through cars like this? And a Quattroporte! If she was going to buy a Maserati, why didn't she get a Kyalami?"

Shin'ichi didn't answer this. "If you don't want her to attract attention, could you bring her over in your car, Taku?" he asked. "Please."

Taku found Shin'ichi hard to resist when he talked like this.

"Where does she finish off at nine?"

"The music studio. It's in Shiba, so just down the road."

"Right."

When he heard his brother's voice, he simply couldn't say no. He knew that he was his brother's only friend, just as Shin'ichi was Saera's only mainstay in life. And besides, he was his only brother.

Once he'd hung up, he lay there for a while, thinking of nothing. A song was going through his head.

What was the second line of that song, "*Don't judge and turn your eyes away*"? He scratched his head, trying to remember. That was it—"*There goes another fellow man.*" When would he have first heard that song? he wondered, staring at the ceiling.

The big Maserati sedan spun along Freeway 1 through the Hama-Kawasaki area like a great land cruiser. New cars are still stiff to handle in every way, and besides, the suspension retained a moderate amount of awkwardness from its De Tomaso heritage. Size 225 Michelin XVX tires supported the almost two-ton weight of its frame. The steering was so heavy it scarcely seemed like power steering at all. Taku felt slightly drunk on the heady mixture of the scent of tan leather mingled with that of Saera's breath.

On their left a black canal appeared with the sea beyond it, then at length the fiery glow of the late-night factories, still powering away. Taku held the left-hand drive back at 20 KPH over the speed limit, still slow enough to be almost torture for a V8 engine that guzzled ten liters of oil.

"I love the landscape here, you know," Saera said from the passenger seat. She leaned forward, gazing at the night scene of the Keihin industrial heartland. "I think maybe I live in Yokohama just so I can see this view when I come home at night."

"Nothing but factories," Taku remarked.

"It looks too real in the daytime – I hate that." Her leaning body tilted to the left, brushing his arm. With her face so close to his, he caught a slight whiff of her feminine scent. "That was Ikegami Canal we just passed," she went on, pointing out the window. "The next one's Tanabe Canal. The one over there's called Keihin Canal. You know this?"

"No." Taku was startled. He often used this route, but he'd never realized that the black channels of water that flowed between the factories all had names.

"The narrow one over there between Nippon Steel Pipes and Showa Electrical is Minami Watarida Canal. Sakai Canal flows from

Nippon Foundry down to Mitsubishi Processors. Kawasaki Canal flows between Mobil and Toshiba. Then there's…"

Red flames spurted from the chimneys, lighting up the surrounding area. The image of the erupting Mount Nijo suddenly came to his mind.

"People are funny, aren't they?" Saera remarked, settling back in her seat. "Don't you think so, Taku?"

He didn't speak. In the right lane, a German car with a flashy arrow pattern hurtled past them. Did that young BMW driver held alert in his seat by aero-parts have any idea that this unsophisticated, homegrown-looking car could hit speeds of 230 KPH if it felt inclined?

Saera touched Taku's arm lightly. "Listen, tell me something. Just what kind of little kid was Shin'ichi?"

"What kind? I don't know, nothing special."

"Which one of you was better at studying?"

"He was."

"What about fights?"

"Him."

"And women?"

"No comment."

"Who was cleverer with his hands?"

"My brother was."

"So what about you, Taku? What were you good at?" Saera giggled, a gentle little laugh. She took off her high-heeled shoes and tucked her feet up beside her on the broad leather passenger seat.

"I was the one who helped the old man. I was crazy about messing around with the little fishing boat engines."

"Can I ask you something? It's a bit personal."

He knew what she wanted to ask. She knew that Taku wasn't Shin'ichi's real brother. She'd be wanting to find out more about the circumstances. It wasn't something he especially wanted to hide.

"Haven't you heard about it from Shin?"

She nodded. "He's told me just a little."

Taku dropped the speed back a touch. An irritable whine rose from the engine. "What did he say? Don't worry, you can tell me."

Saera's answer was a little muffled. "About all I know is that your parents died in a flood, and you were taken in and raised by the family in Mikuni."

Taku nodded. This was all quite true. He knew that she wasn't just asking out of idle curiosity. She wasn't that sort of woman.

"I don't really know the details too well myself," he began. "My real parents were working in the mines at that time. Apparently they wandered the country when they were young, but once I was born they settled down in the mining area between Toi and Amagi in the Izu peninsula."

Saera gave him an encouraging nod.

Carefully negotiating the right-hand downslope curves just before Koyasu, Taku continued. "I had a little sister. There were just us two kids, but my father really wanted more, apparently."

"Really."

"When I was around four, my parents built their first house. It was in a sunless spot up against the bottom of a cliff, mind you. Still."

"I can imagine," Saera said, her voice warm with empathy.

"Then in September 1958 came Typhoon 22. There was major flooding all through central Izu, and over a thousand people died. They called it Typhoon Kanogawa, you know. It was big news at the time."

"And your family's house was among…"

"That's right. Apparently it was destroyed in a matter of moments, with the rushing waters plus a landslide. It was on a valley floor and the ground was unstable all along, see. And it turned out that I was the only one saved. The bodies of my mother and father and sister were never found. I was sent to various institutions after that, and then when I was seven the Hayamis took me in. Formally adopted me. They had a son just a year older, who was wonderfully kind to me. Shin, that was."

Saera was silent. Taku glanced at her, and smiled. "Well, that's about it. You should ask Shin the rest."

"I'm sorry, Taku. I've brought back bad memories for you."

"No, it's all long ago stuff now."

Taku swung the car through the freeway curve in the direction of Yokohama Park. There wasn't much traffic. From Osanbashi there was the rare sight of the lights of a big foreign ship.

The home of Saera Maki and Shin'ichi Hayami stood in the center of a plateau that looked down on the city of Yokohama. On Sundays the streets seethed with young tourists wandering the area from Motomachi to the old foreigners' graveyard, but at this time of evening they were quiet and deserted.

Taku let Saera out, then took the car around to the garage. Wide though the Quattroporte was, it handled with remarkable ease. The garage contained a new Porsche Carrera that looked like a big white cake, and a subdued gunmetal blue Ferrari 400i. Taku felt that they should have been parked the other way round, but Shin'ichi had his own ideas about cars, and Taku felt he might stir up trouble if he said the wrong thing.

He managed with difficulty to slide the big sedan in beside the Porsche, then went around to the dining room via the garden.

The white building was designed to make clever use of the sloping land. At first glance the style of decor was strikingly chaotic, but Taku knew that this was precisely Saera's taste. She went out of her way to avoid a unified style.

"Here, look at this," she laughed, pointing to a round burn mark on one of the cushions on the floor. Taku noticed that she'd quickly slipped into casual clothes.

Shin'ichi emerged, also laughing. "The whole place could easily have gone up in flames," he said.

A healthy tan and close-cropped hair, trim, taut body, white teeth—Shin'ichi was the epitome of the kind of sporty, early middle-aged man you see in pictures. His feet were the same size as Taku's, but he was five centimeters taller. On his wrist was a diver's watch with a Caterpillar band. He wore corduroy pants with a Stag shirt, and black flat-soled shoes that for some reason looked uncomfortable.

"Shin says he's not even going to take these shoes off in bed tonight," Saera announced wryly. She swiftly poured some tea and put the cups on the table.

"Thanks, Taku. You've really gone out of your way for us," said Shin'ichi. "Will you have something to drink?"

"No, thanks."

"Here are some yummy rice crackers," said Saera. She felt around in her bag, pulled out a paper bag and opened it.

Shin'ichi gave Taku's knee an irritable poke. "Hey, what do you think of these shoes?"

"They look wet."

"I'm giving them a 'shakedown' right now, see. Running them in, so to speak." Shin'ichi happily proceeded to explain the specialist knowledge he'd apparently gained from some book. In order to make new leather shoes a perfect fit for your foot, you first pour hot water into them, then tip it out and wipe the shoes dry, and while the leather is still warm slip your feet in, wearing a pair of thick socks. You wear them for twenty-four hours straight, changing to dry socks every hour or so, he explained.

"You were boiling your shoes with the spirit lamp, weren't you!" cried Saera, collapsing into laughter. "Our Shin takes everything he reads in books at absolute face value and tries it all out. He's such a kid."

"So what do you think, Taku?"

"Hmm. I'd say you'll have your answer in twenty-four hours. Personally, mind you, I don't think such soft leather needs any special breaking in."

"These are Vibram soles, you know. This type without the heavy soles is starting to really catch on as walking gear. I can't imagine what those guys who walk along well-maintained trails in shoes like bulldozers can be thinking. These are just out from Florsheim. What do you say?"

Taku frowningly examined the shoes, then, by way of response, he replied, "Not too bad at all. Florsheim's a Chicago shop, isn't it? Not so surprising they put out short boots with Vibram soles, since they started off by producing hefty leather-soled shoes for businessmen who are on the move a lot."

Taku's tactful reply produced an irrepressibly delighted boyish response from Shin'ichi. "Businessmen on the move? Come on! Chicago gangsters back in the thirties loved these shoes too, man.

European shoes focus on size, but these shoes are all about width, so they suit us Japanese. But they started making casual shoes like these three or four years ago. Times are changing, eh?"

"They look pretty light."

"Sure are, 270 grams each. Remember those Church's urethane sole shoes I found last year and got you to try? Well, these are fifteen grams lighter."

"Well, well. You're displaying a worrying tendency to go light these days, I must say, Shin. Must be getting old," said Taku teasingly.

Saera sat munching home-baked rice crackers and smiling as she listened to the two men talk. Occasionally, a gust of wind could be heard outside. The weather was probably turning. Beyond the window, the lights of the Marine Tower blinked on and off.

What Taku's elder brother longed for above all else was a like-minded friend to listen admiringly to his childish bragging. Best of all would be someone who occasionally interposed an insightful criticism, in such a way as not to harm Shin'ichi's self-esteem. And the only friend who could perform this role for him was his brother Taku.

"If you start talking about age Saera won't be able to make dinner, you know," said Shin'ichi.

Saera laughed. "That's okay, I don't mind. After all, my dream is to turn forty as soon as possible so I can wear the suit I bought in the Chanel store when I was nineteen."

"She holds the record for being the youngest woman ever to have a suit made up for her in a Chanel boutique, you know," said Shin'ichi. "Can you believe it?"

"But it's true!"

"Don't the hostesses in the high class clubs in Ginza wear Chanel?" asked Taku.

Saera just shrugged and giggled. "There's all kinds of Chanel. You want to see?"

She stood up and went into another room. Before long she emerged carrying with elaborate care a navy blue suit. "This is it. I got them to add a label certifying it was made in 1966."

Then she proceeded to tell the story of the autumn when she made her first million-seller hit. Instead of a bonus, the record company had taken her to Paris. She'd taken a taxi straight to the Chanel boutique on Rue Cambon, but she was so young that at first they'd refused to believe she was a serious customer.

"Please come back again in twenty years, mademoiselle," said a lady by the name of Madame Mortaur, gently shaking her head, but she'd begged her through the interpreter. 'If you make me a dress,' she'd said, 'I promise I'll keep it safe until I'm forty and never wear it till then. Please believe me.'"

After gazing into her eyes for a moment, the lady finally smiled and nodded. "That's all right, as long as you're confident you can keep your present figure and courage unchanged for the next twenty years," she said.

"'*Ne vous inquiétez pas, madame*,' I said. You're right of course, I'm hopeless at French. It was from a *chanson* I used to love then. But look how quickly time's passed. Three more years and I'll be the age I promised. Look at me, both of you. What do you think? Will I be able to wear this suit then?"

She turned herself elegantly around for their benefit. The two men looked at each other, then applauded. Neither had seen the nineteen-year-old Saera except in photographs.

"Thank you. Okay, I'll go get us some nice boiled rice with tea. You want to show Taku your workroom, don't you Shin?"

When Saera had gone out carrying her suit on its hanger, Shin'ichi looked meaningfully at Taku. "Let's go into my room for a bit."

"Oh, let's stay here. Your storeroom exhausts me."

"Unfriendly tonight, aren't you."

For the last half year, Shin'ichi had been building a log hut for himself behind the garage. It was still at the planning stage, but Taku already knew what he had in mind. Once it was done, Taku would get his conscription orders. Shin'ichi's aim was always to get Taku to move out of his cheap apartment and come to live with them.

The northern half of the house was devoted to Saera's guests, while the southern half plus garage and basement were Shin'ichi's world. One room was crammed to the ceiling with all manner of footwear, accumulated over the years since he'd first fallen for Red Wing and Santa Rosa boots. Hundreds of leather-soled boots—from

Vibram and Galibier to Pirelli and San Moritz, sports shoes with every kind of sole, traditional Japanese workmen's two-toed *tabi* boots made by Nikka Rubber and Tsukihoshi, to the latest models brought out in Japan – all were there.

Besides all this there was also a collection of old shoes—the Nun Bushes and Frenchshriners so beloved of the Occupation Forces after the war, the object of envy for that famous band, the Yokohama Boys.

Every pair had been broken in indoors, diligently softened with oiled fingers, appropriately creased, and made ready to wear. Shin'ichi apparently chose a pair each night to wear to bed. But the problem was, he hadn't once actually exposed them to the elements, or walked in them over stony plains or along dew-soaked forest roads. At most, all he did was walk around the garden, or go for a quick trek up and down the hill around the nearby foreigners' graveyard.

For some reason Saera didn't care for the outdoors, sunlight, rain, or wind, and aside from her work, she seemed to live only for the time she spent in the house with Shin'ichi. It was as though she had a pathological fear of nature.

"Shin…" Taku began.

"What?"

"Did you really knock over that spirit lamp today?"

"Hmm…"

"Not that it matters."

"Hey, come on, don't worry. It's not as bad as it looks, we're getting on fine."

"Okay. I won't say another word."

Shin'ichi changed the subject. "How's the old man?"

"He seems fine. I'm going down to Kansai for a couple of days and I'm thinking of calling in there if I can get the job done quickly."

"Where are you going?"

"I'm going to climb Mount Nijo."

"Mount Nijo?"

"You know it?"

"Mount Nijo, eh?" Shin'ichi scratched his head thoughtfully. "I think I've heard of it somewhere."

"It's not much of a mountain, but apparently there's quite a bit of interesting stuff there."

"Tell me the story when you get back. I don't need to hear about the old man."

"I get the feeling you've never really got on with him, you know. Why would that be? You're his real son, after all."

"He never wanted the kind of son I am," said Shin'ichi. Then he was silent. Out in the port, a ship's horn sounded. Taku had a sudden sense that a moment like this had happened once before, more than twenty years ago. Their hometown of Mikuni was also a port, and suddenly he felt himself transported back to the past.

Unlike Taku, as a boy Shin'ichi constantly read books, particularly books about mountaineering, adventure stories, hunting wild animals, and archaeological excavations. He'd read stories of penniless young hitchhikers in foreign countries so often that he as good as memorized them.

Every night in bed, Shin'ichi would tell these stories to Taku, with a certain amount of embellishment.

Taku revered him, and he obeyed Shin'ichi's urgings to climb barefoot down the nearby Tojinbo Cliff right to the edge of the sea, or walk far south down the coast road in search of a place called Torikuso Rock.

It was Shin'ichi who would look at maps and decide on a place that seemed interesting. Sometimes he gave Taku the train or bus fare to get there.

These adventures were, of course, kept absolutely secret from their parents. Sometimes Taku would skip school for them. His brother in the class above him would always make up some explanation for the teacher.

One day he was sent to Yoshizaki to check out the old Noh mask that had given rise to the terrifying legend of the Mask of Flesh. It had brought him near to tears. He'd also run into big trouble when he sprained his leg investigating the ruins of the Maruoka clan fort.

Such memories still made Taku nostalgic. When he came home in one piece, Shin'ichi would welcome him like a returning astronaut, and reverently listen to all the tales of his adventures long into the night. He'd lie there shivering, or leap up from his bed in excitement, imagining that it was he himself who was climbing down the dizzying cliff face, or stuck in a cave, or face to face with a big snake.

When Shin'ichi reached middle school, he became a fan of motorbike books.

Late at night, he'd stealthily wheel his father's Honda Super Cub out of the garage and push it along the road to where Taku was waiting among the sand dunes by the sea, rubbing his tired eyes. Shin'ichi never got on a bike himself, but poured his passion into teaching Taku about the mechanics and riding techniques. When Taku fell off he was genuinely worried, which pleased Taku so much that he sometimes made a point of taking a tumble.

"Keep your knees tight," Shin'ichi would tell him. Or, "The balance of front and rear brake is important when you're going downhill."

Once out of middle school, Shin'ichi graduated to the prefectural high school. A year later, Taku went on to a private technical high. For the first time, they were leading separate lives. But they were still closer than blood brothers. Taku never felt a moment's sorrow at the fact that he was an orphan adopted into the family. His foster father Yuzo was kinder to him than to Shin'ichi, and besides, he liked the town. Nevertheless, once or twice a month he would suddenly be assailed by an inexplicable melancholy.

At such times, he would go off on his own without saying anything even to Shin'ichi and watch the motorboat races, or head off up a tributary of the Kuzuryu River and go rock fishing.

Eventually, Shin'ichi tired of bikes and instead fell in love with cars. The two of them would drive unlicensed along deserted farm roads around Kitagata Lake all night in the pick-up their father used for work, with the excuse that they were helping to keep it in good running order.

When Taku went for his license exam, Shin'ichi came along. He taught Taku everything, from the road rules to engine construction. Taku passed the exam on his second try. But, true to form, Shin'ichi never made any attempt to drive himself.

In the summer of his third year of high school, Shin'ichi was beaten up by a bar owner in the Awara Hot Spring town.

He'd become intimate with the man's daughter at Hamaji Beach. It cost him a torn left ear.

Three months later, Taku lay in wait for the man at the entrance to the motorboat races, and gave him a licking by thrusting a sharpened screwdriver into his thigh. He didn't, of course, tell Shin'ichi. For this, Taku was expelled from his high school. He found work as a temporary mechanic at the tractor parts factory in nearby Komatsu.

Two years later, Taku set off on a long journey, with the plan of hitchhiking for three years around Europe and the Middle East. It was Shin'ichi who urged him to go, and as always he provided the plan and the funds, and put himself in charge of convincing their parents to accept the idea.

And so it was that Taku came to set off in a plane from Haneda Airport. It was summer, and he was eighteen.

After they'd finished the boiled rice with tea that Saera had cooked up, the three of them settled down to watch a documentary on Bhutan on television. Saera declared that the sight of the brightly hued Joyous Buddhas painted on the wall of Donche Temple scared her somehow.

"Where did you say that Mount Nijo was?" Shin'ichi asked suddenly.

"Between Kawachi and Yamato, apparently. I plan to go via Nara Prefecture this time."

"Could you drop in to Kobe on your way back?"

"Why?"

"We've left a Mercedes 4WD in the parking lot next to the Oriental Hotel there. You'd be doing us a big favor if you could bring it back."

Shin'ichi went on to explain that Saera's manager, Seta, had taken it down there when Saera had a show in Kobe, and left it there. "The fool entertained himself driving up and down stairs in the square, apparently. Eventually the transfer lever got stuck in low. It got so jammed that even the gear lever wouldn't budge, so he gave up and left it there. That was three days ago, and the parking fees aren't cheap."

"Why not ask the dealer to pick it up?"

"Yes, I've been planning to."

"You get that problem a lot. All you have to do is give it a really good kick. People treat them too carefully because they're imported cars."

"Could you pick it up on your way back and bring it up here, Taku? Think of it as a part-time freighting job."

"What if I can't move it?"

"In that case could you arrange for repairs."

"Right."

Shin'ichi's face brightened at Taku's consent. He went off to his room and returned with an armful of objects. "Here you are, here's the car key. And could you give these binoculars a try-out for me? And there's a new knife here. Take your pick of these socks. The Harrison toed ones look pretty good. And shoes…"

"Hey, I'm getting sick of being your consumer guinea pig, Shin." Taku waved a dismissive hand. "This mountain I'm off to isn't worth carrying all that stuff for."

"Don't be like that. Just give these things a tryout and tell me what you think, okay?"

"Okay, make it just the knife then. I'll try out the shoes and socks next time. I don't need the binoculars."

"How about a camera? There's terrific film in this Minolta CLE. It's not even on sale yet.

"I hate carrying too much."

"Right, so a daypack then. Or this, an austere little improved version of the Kyoto Ichizawa Hanpu shop's Nekoda bag sewn from sailcloth. And take a look at this, a specialist Komine Kozan step-down transformer. Or if you want something big on your back, how about the Korean *chige*?"

Taku began to laugh.

"If you ever give up the singing career, Saera, you and Shin could start up a gear shop together."

Saera winked at him. "It's true. Shin even gets into a sleeping bag like some kind of chrysalis when he sleeps, you know. If I go off on tour to the provinces, he'll put up a tent in the back yard to sleep in, rain or shine. We should take him to the hospital to get him checked out, don't you think?"

"Won't you stay the night, Taku?" Shin'ichi asked.

Taku shook his head. "No, I've gotta get back. There are things I need to check out."

"Okay, I'll send Saera to see you off to the station then."

"No need. I'm happy to walk."

"Oh, come on." Shin'ichi stood up. Taku and Saera went out the front door together, and Shin'ichi went around to the garage, cleverly started up the Porsche with a single turn, and brought it round to the front of the house.

He owned three or four cars, but in fact it was always Saera's manager Seta or one of his friends who drove them. Saera occasionally took the wheel herself, but Shin'ichi focused his attention on the constant maintenance and car-washing. His version of the Grand Tour was to bring a car around from the garage to the front gate.

"Okay, take care," he said to Saera as he climbed out. Saera settled into the driver's seat with a smile. Once Taku was in, she backed rapidly down the drive, then swung the steering wheel hard, and took off at astonishing speed down the hill. The unashamedly loud exhaust note of the Flat-6 engine echoed through the suburban night.

"That's amazing," said Taku.

"What?"

"So they make a Porsche Carrera with a built-in phone, eh?"

"Call Shin for me." Saera pushed the car through the lights just as they changed from amber to red.

"You've forgotten something?"

"Just call him."

Taku pushed the dialing button. Immediately Shin'ichi came on.

"I'll take it." One hand holding the bottom of the steering wheel steady, Saera tucked the receiver under her chin. "You love me?" she said loudly, her foot going down harder on the accelerator. Then she laughed happily. "I'll be back soon. Wait there like a good boy."

A sudden inexpressible sadness rose in Taku's heart. With the ball of his finger, he gently stroked the sheath of the new knife Shin'ichi had given him.

3

Early in the morning, three days after he'd received the summons from Hanada and met Professor Nishihaga, Taku Hayami set off on his mission to report on Mount Nijo.

The walk along the old Takenouchi Highway route plus the Nijo climb could all be completed before sunset, he calculated. Then he'd head down to Kobe, take a look at Shinichi's car as requested, and, so long as he could get it going, take it straight out onto the freeway and head east. If he took the Hokuriku Highway from the Hikone Interchange, all he had to do was go on through Tsuruga and turn off at the Maruoka Interchange. After that he'd be on the route to his father's house in Mikuni that he'd known since childhood. If the car looked as if it would take a while to fix, he'd stay the night in Kobe then head straight back to Tokyo. He could visit his father some other time. This was the general plan he had in mind when he left his apartment that morning and set off.

A quick ride on the bullet train got him to Kyoto before ten in the morning. There, he changed straight onto the express to Kashihara.

There were no stops between Kyoto and Yamato Saidaiji, just outside Nara. Young women in uniform moved along the aisles handing out warm hand towels to the passengers, or selling beer and packed lunches. Taku pulled out his map and set about locating the precise position of Mount Nijo.

Before long, the large young black-robed monk sitting beside him hailed a passing girl and bought a box of sushi wrapped in salted persimmon leaves, a local delicacy.

"How do they taste?" Taku conversationally inquired as the monk began to eat.

The monk paused in his eating and considered for a moment. "Well, I myself find them quite pleasant."

Taku smiled at this scrupulous answer. If you asked this sort of question down in Kyushu you were likely to be met with an effusive response, and find yourself being urged, in heavy Kyushu dialect, to sample the food in question. Quite likely you'd end up having to buy a beer into the bargain. By comparison, thought Taku, this young monk's reply was absolutely typical of the notoriously polite and reserved Kyoto area.

He waylaid a passing girl and bought a box of the sushi for himself. Somehow, sitting there watching the scenery slip past the window provoked an urge to snack. I'll make this an early lunch, he thought, unwrapping the box.

The sushi proved very good, perhaps because while he ate he was gazing out from the upper level of the superb "viewing carriage" over the clear Kizu River to the distant Kasagi Range. He decided it would stand up well against the sea bream sushi that was the specialty of Fukui, or Toyama's trout sushi.

"Are you from Tokyo?" the young monk asked.

"Yes. I set out early this morning."

"Ah. You must be tired then." The monk had high cheekbones, manly black eyebrows, and was somehow colorlessly pale. Despite his youth, he had an impressive presence. Taku discreetly took in his bare feet in traditional wooden *geta*. The tendons at his heels stood out as though in relief carving, and strongly developed thigh muscles were evident beneath the robe. This man can walk, Taku thought.

"Pardon me, but which…?" he began, then the question died on his lips. Should he ask which sect the monk belonged to, or was it better to say "order"?

The monk evidently grasped the meaning of Taku's hesitation. "Tendai," he replied, naming one of the two major sects of the Esoteric school of Buddhism.

"Ah."

"Do you yourself happen to have any affiliation with a particular temple?"

"No, no, not really…" Taku mumbled. Then he went on, "When I was a child I visited Eiheiji Temple a number of times, you see, and I just felt that you somehow had a similar kind of air to the monks there."

"Well, Eiheiji is a Soto Zen temple, in fact, but it's true that Dogen, the founder of the Soto sect, first studied Buddhism as a Tendai monk in the great temple complex on Mount Hiei, so no doubt there would be similarities." The young monk was clearly taking pains to be comprehensible to a layman.

"I understand that Eiheiji used to be much more hidden away in the mountains than it is now," remarked Taku. "Do Tendai monks also perform their religious practice in the mountains?"

"Well, we have various forms of practice."

"I've heard the Mount Hiei monks perform a kind of religious austerity called the 'Walking Practice.' I read about it once in some book. I think it was called something like the 'Thousand-Day Mountain Circuit'…"

"Yes, we do have that."

"It's a really tough practice involving fifteen or sixteen hours of walking a day, right? That's what the book said."

"There are monks who have walked a distance that would take them several times right around the world, you know."

At this moment there was an announcement that the train was approaching Yamato Saidaiji.

Taku's evident fascination with the subject seemed to touch a nerve, for the monk now set about a quick explanation of the Thousand-Day Circuit.

It was, he said, a rare and remarkable practice still performed today at the great Enryakuji Temple on Mount Hiei, the head temple of the Tendai sect founded long ago by the saint, Saicho. A monk who was prepared to undertake this rigorous austerity donned what were called "death robes," the pure white robes and straw sandals in which a corpse was traditionally dressed for the journey into death. He must spend one hundred days over a three-year period, excluding winter, walking a prescribed route over the mountain and praying before various shrines along the way. In a single day he would walk about thirty kilometers.

Once this was completed, a further two years were spent walking the mountain route for two hundred days each year. Once this total of five years of walking austerity was achieved, he was faced at the start of his sixth year with an even more arduous practice—one hundred days of performing the sixty-kilometer-long walk from Mount Hiei to Sekisan Zen-in Temple and back.

"He walks sixty kilometers a day every day for a hundred days?"

"Yes. And it's by no means a level path."

"Walking sixty kilometers in one day isn't so astonishing in itself I guess, but for a hundred days… That's a total of six thousand kilometers."

"So far I've been speaking of what's known as the normal austerity. But he then encounters the great circuit that takes him through the city of Kyoto as well. He must do a further one hundred days walking from mountain to city, then around various temples there, and back again, all the while responding to the crowds of believers who follow him. For these hundred days, he walks an average of around eighty kilometers a day. Not so much walks as runs, really."

"Eighty kilometers from mountain to city and back? In a day?" Taku let out his breath in amazement.

The monk nodded. "That's right. Then, once he's finished the hundred days…"

"You mean there's more?"

"He finishes by performing a final hundred days doing the original thirty-kilometer circuit on the mountain. This makes a sum total of one thousand days, hence the name 'Thousand-Day Circuit.'"

"What kind of man could manage to complete something like that? No, not even man, superman."

"Well, actually, if you meet these men they seem perfectly normal." The monk reinforced his words with a firm nod. "Once I had the honor of paying my respects to such a man on a street corner during his descent into the city. His followers were sitting in the street awaiting his arrival. No sooner did the white robed figure appear in the distance in one direction than he was disappearing off in the other again, as if on wings. A young yakuza-type who happened to be passing was so astonished that his legs almost gave under him. 'A mountain spirit! That's gotta be a mountain spirit!' he cried."

Taku found himself recalling the day three years earlier in Granada, when a young Japanese backpacker had let him use his hotel bathroom. He'd borrowed a little book the young man happened to have, in which he read of the Thousand-Day Circuit. It was book about walking by Shunjiro Matsushima, brought out by Mountain and Valley Publishing, he recalled. Most of it was now forgotten, but he remembered that it described how during the hundred-day city circuit the monk rose at one in the morning, and walked continuously for fifteen or sixteen hours a day on a single simple meal. Ten men had completed the whole austerity in the last seventy years.

He must tell Shin'ichi about the book next time they met, he thought. If he read nothing but foreign technical manuals and catalogs, he was in danger of having a head stuffed with nothing but barren theory.

Once the train had passed Yamato Saidaiji, the ancient pagoda of Nara's Yakushiji Temple flashed past the window remarkably close, no sooner there than gone.

"You look as if you are quite a walker yourself," the monk remarked with a smile. "Where would you be off to today?"

"I'm going to climb Mount Nijo."

"Well, well." The monk cocked his head in apparent surprise. "What will you do there?"

"I'm just going to climb it."

"We'll see it out to the right before long. Back in the days before all these buildings covered the area, it would have been visible from all over the Yamato Plain."

He fell silent for a while. Taku gazed out the window. Beyond Yamato Koriyama Station the train began to pass a series of goldfish breeding ponds, while off to the right ran a smooth undulation of hilly terrain. There was a tender feel to the curves of that mountain country.

"Nijo is over that way, is that right?" Taku asked.

The young monk shook his head. "No, that area is what's known as Yata Hill. Mount Kongo Temple, also called Yata Temple, and Matsuo Temple are there. The settlement that's tucked into the arms of the foothills and Tomio River has the name of Ikaruga Village. First there's Horyuji Temple, then the temples of Horinji and Hokkiji. Then, if you go up the little lanes in the area around Chugu Temple you find others—Jonenji Temple, for example, or Seikoji, temples that have a somewhat different feel from the big well-known ones of the old capital of Nara."

From time to time Taku glimpsed white-walled houses, redolent of the Yamato landscape. The sky was a hazy blue, and the white undulations of the serried ranks of plastic hothouses glinted in the soft sunlight. New housing estates in the making stood out in the landscape like scars. Billboards for motels also struck the eye.

Shrewdly following Taku's gaze, the monk murmured, "Yamato's a living thing too, you see." He seemed almost to be talking to himself. Then he added, "There's a golf club in the mountain behind the great temple of Horyuji called 'Horyuji Country Club,' and I hear the local women are rushing at the chance to do part-time caddying there. Another sign of the times, you might say."

At length, a long, tapering mountain range reared up imposingly on the right. The long north-south ridgeline was smooth, but these mountains that loomed over the Yamato Plain were surprisingly steep and rugged. Those towering, dark indigo shapes could only be the famous Katsuragi Range and Mount Kongo, thought Taku.

In which case, that road underneath them must be the Old Katsuragi Road. Professor Nishihaga's words suddenly echoed inside his head. But what about Mount Nijo, then?

"That's Nijo there," said the monk, pointing. Then he suddenly murmured what sounded like part of an old poem in the classical language, although the words were difficult to catch over the clatter of the train on its rails—"*Ayashi ya tare ka / futakami no yama…*"

"What was that you said?" Taku said, surprised.

"Look at that," said the monk. "You can see it particularly clearly today. The male and female peaks look almost as if they're holding hands and smiling at each other, don't you agree? Well, what do you think?"

The two mountain peaks soared together in the western sky. One was like a flattened breast, while the other thrust strongly up at a slight angle. To their south lay the long, dark Katsuragi Range and Mount Kongo. In terms of topography, Mount Nijo was in fact just a small mountain accompanying that great range that barred the way between Kawachi and Yamato, but in reality Taku had a strong impression of Nijo as a powerful presence, brooding over the Yamato Plain with Katsuragi and Kongo in attendance beside it.

Yet the Nijo that he gazed at now from the train window looked entirely different from the image that Nishihaga had shown him, that backlit black mountain floating beyond the blood-red pool like the realm of the dead. It looked much more comically reminiscent of a humped camel, in fact.

"This is the mountain that the ancients referred to as *umashi futakami*, 'Beauteous Futakami,'" remarked the monk. Then he went on, "But it is also *ayashi futakami*, 'Uncanny Futakami,' you know. Don't be deceived by that mild look it has at the moment."

"You said something just now, some snatch of poetry perhaps..." Taku braved the question. The monk withdrew his gaze from the mountain, and turned to look at him.

"There are a number of paths up Mount Nijo. If you climb from the Yamato side, you can set off from Futakami Shrine and climb the male peak. Then there's another way, the route that goes up from Taima and follows the course of the ancient road. If you take that one, you first go to Taima Temple. Skirting around it, you climb up between Yamaguchi Shrine and Oike Pond till you come to Yusenji Temple. Here a path to Iwaya Pass goes off to the left, but on your right you'll see a little track that takes you to the saddle between the male and female peaks of Nijo. A little way on up that right-hand path you may well notice a standing stone bearing an incised poem on its face. I was reciting a bit of that poem. Yusenji Temple belongs to my own Tendai sect. Long ago an old monk by the name of Mugaku the Unlearned lived there. He was the man who made this poem. Listen to how it goes, just the sound of it."

The monk closed his eyes and, slowly pronouncing each syllable, intoned the following:

"*Namu Amida / hotoke no mina wo / yobu kotori / ayashi ya tareka / futakami no yama.*"

Taku listened, straining not to miss a thing.

"*Ayashi ya tareka / futakami no yama,*" the monk repeated again, and Taku said it softly to himself several times.

"It's in old Japanese, of course, but perhaps you can understand the meaning?" the monk inquired.

Taku shook his head. "Well, I guess I can sort of get the first part. It's something like 'Namu Amida! The small birds cry / chanting the Buddha's sacred name.' But as for the last part…"

"The first part is a kind of cliché really. It's typical of the sort of poem a monk would compose. But the last part is very odd. What could it possibly mean?"

"I don't know."

"No, you do. You undoubtedly do. You do, and yet you don't." The monk drew his dark brows together and folded his arms. His lips had closed themselves over the words, and nothing further escaped them.

Taku changed trains at Kashihara and took the Minami-Osaka Line as far as Taima Temple. He was sorry to have parted from the kind and helpful monk without even exchanging names.

"Taima," he said to himself. "I have a feeling I've heard that name somewhere." But try as he might he couldn't locate the memory.

The road up to Taima Temple was so narrow that two cars could barely ease past each other. Still, thanks to this, no big tourist coaches plied the route, and the houses that lined the road had a quiet country air.

The map alone didn't really provide a sense of the topography. Even the Geographical Survey Institute map only gave the height of the female peak. The complicated foothills of the mountain seemed to suggest any number of possible routes, not to mention the likelihood that there were traces of countless ancient paths that were no longer real tracks among the mountains.

Taku was enthralled by the words of the monk he'd met on the train. Whatever else he did, he thought, at any rate he'd start by following the route that would take him past the stone with its "uncanny" poem.

Up close, Taima Temple turned out to be a most impressive place. The grounds were extensive and the buildings grand. A magnificent three-storied pagoda towered against the mountainside as if to quell it. The Golden Hall, the Lecture Hall, and the main Mandala Hall were each in their own way splendid buildings, but somehow there seemed to be a lack of overall integration to the place. Why? Taku wondered.

He had the impression that Taima was not so much a temple backing onto a mountain as one locked within it. The bell tower and indeed all the buildings were perched on high stone foundations, making them appear oddly top-heavy and unstable. Seen from the road, the temple's entrance gate too seemed to be teetering at the top of its stone staircase.

Taku suddenly recalled the time six months earlier when he'd gone to Korea with others in the Publications Department to do a piece on Bukkokuji Temple. The main hall of the temple was very similar, he though—a precariously tall building balanced above a stone staircase.

Ah yes, his friend Cho the Chinese cook had said that there was lots of good stone on Mount Nijo, he now recalled. And he'd mentioned that the Takamatsu Tumulus and Horyuji Temple had both used Nijo stone in their construction.

Taku went straight over to the Mandala Hall at the front of the temple complex. Taking off his shoes he stepped in, joining a couple of other worshippers to gaze up at the huge painting depicting the various Pure Land heavens. As he stood taking it in, a couple of men approached, one a tall man in his forties with a badge on his lapel indicating he was from a television station, the other a well-built, amiable-looking monk. It looked as if someone from the temple was showing the producer around in preparation for filming a show. The man from the television station came to a halt beside Taku, briefly bowed to the altar, then raised his eyes to the large framed picture above it.

"So this is the famous Taima Mandala, eh? It's bigger than I expected, I must say. It'd be about four meters square, would it?"

"Yes, it's about five meters high in fact. Right up there under the top of the frame there are wonderful lacquered gold depictions of flying phoenixes with an arabesque design, but unfortunately it's very old so there's a lot of damage."

Taku casually moved away from the others so that he could overhear the conversation. The monk spoke in a lustrous baritone voice that rang out clearly in the high-raftered wooden hall.

The producer was nodding. "Yes, I can see it's very darkened with age, and it's certainly hard to make out the details. I'm just repeating what I've read here," he went on, "but I believe the arabesque style was very popular back in the eighth century Nara Period. I guess the designs in this piece might well be a lot more splendid than you find in the ancient fabrics held in the Shosoin Treasure House. The mandala itself is marvelous too. This would be a copy, right?"

"It is indeed a hand-done copy. The original ancient mandala was done over a thousand years ago, so it no longer remains. This work is known as the Bunki Mandala, and is an accurate copy of the earlier work, made around the fifteenth century."

The producer nodded thoughtfully and gazed at the picture. Then a thought occurred to him. "I've heard that this temple is rather different from the other early temples in the area in that it drew on support from the local populace rather than being merely an official temple under the government bureaucracy, is that right?"

"That is so," the monk answered with a smile. "Back in the old days, by which I mean when I was still young, I used to give sermons before this mandala to gatherings of fervent believers. *Etoki*, it was called—the picture was used to illustrate and give structure to the sermon."

The producer nodded, intrigued. "Yes indeed, I can imagine what marvelous talks you'd have given with that ringing voice of yours. All those good men and women would have listened, entranced. You must have had a great many eager fans."

"No, no, not at all really. Still, I suppose I did have a bit of a reputation." The jovial monk suddenly drew himself up, pointed to the mandala, and in a resonant voice intoned a short passage of elucidation. His voice was splendidly modulated and impressive. "There," he finished shyly. "That's the sort of thing I did." He went on to explain with a wry smile that this style was considered very old-fashioned these days.

The producer was impressed. "It's different from the old sutra-preaching puppet drama that's making a bit of a come-back lately, isn't it?" he remarked.

"Yes, of course the word 'sutra' there might suggest that it has to do with temples, but what we Buddhist practitioners perform is a sermon in the strict sense of the word, in other words, preaching the Buddhist Way."

"I gather there was something called the 'Fushidan Sermon' later on, where sermons were sung."

"That is so. A really skilled practitioner could be most impressive. He could use his fine voice plus particular ways of intoning to make his audience laugh and weep with emotion. The result was a blend of something like *naniwabushi*-style song, lecture, and *rakugo* stand-up, with a strong dose of moving Buddhist sermon thrown in. No wonder these practitioners were known as the kings of art. This temple could be said to have survived the vicissitudes of the ages thanks to the support of the worthy men and women who were such ardent fans of this sermon style."

"Fascinating," said the producer. "We must try to do a recreation of this in our program."

At length they moved slowly around behind the picture. The producer was apparently inclined to hear more of the monk's fine exposition on the subject of the "mandala sermon."

Taku remained standing there, gazing intently at what was depicted in the mandala.

"This woman gives me the creeps," came a girl's voice. "She really looks alive."

"How come? There's nothing particularly creepy about her. I like her, personally," said another girl. Both spoke in the local Kansai dialect.

"But look how red the eyes are. She looks like she's crying. It's freaky."

"This is the Chujo maiden. The heroine in that big picture over there. She's supposed to be cool."

Taku guessed they were a couple of high school students who'd dropped in to see the temple while out hiking. Jeans-clad, day packs dangling from their hands, they peered alternately at the picture and at a seated carved figure to its right as they argued. Their strong, youthful voices jarred with this calm and hallowed place.

Taku had been feeling rather overwhelmed by the vast mandala and its splendid frame, so he seized the opportunity to leave it and, with a sense of relief, moved over to see what the girls were discussing.

The sculpture of the Chujo maiden, tucked unobtrusively away to one side, did indeed have something unsettling about it. Her delicately parted lips and the faint red of her eyes produced the vivid sensation that here was a living woman. Perhaps it was the very slightly crossed eyes that created such a strange, enigmatic air. It was a wonderful image, one that suggested the name "the Mona Lisa of Yamato." Indeed there was a sense of deep mystery about her. Taku felt he could quite understand the young girl's dismay.

He stood a long while before the figure. As he gazed, he had the illusion that the lips were murmuring something.

"*Ayashi ya tare ka / futakami no yama.*" Suddenly, the young monk's voice echoed in his mind. Before he knew it, he had taken a step back from the image of the maiden. I certainly won't ever forget this face, he thought.

When he stepped out of the dimly lit Mandala Hall, the midday sun was dazzling. A cloud was slowly misting the mountain peak that loomed over the temple. Like the distant view of Mount Nijo from the station, the mountain had a calm, gentle air now too. It was steep, certainly, but it didn't look like a mountain that would have given the ancients such trouble to cross.

I can afford to take a bit of a rest before I set off, he decided. He paid the entrance fee at a small side-temple, went in and looked at the garden, then sat on the red felt mat in the temple's front room and had a bowl of green tea with tea ceremony cake. He wasn't very good at sitting correctly on his heels as required, but if you put your mind to it, he thought, it was probably useful in straightening out any leg and skeletal problems.

In came the two girls, now solemn and earnest. They seemed impressively well-versed in tea ceremony rules as they elegantly took their tea bowls from the monk who had made the tea.

The smaller of the two set about questioning the monk, in carefully polite language. Taku now realized that she must be a university student, no doubt specializing in Japanese classics.

"We've just climbed the male peak," she said to the monk. "Could you tell us why Prince Otsu's grave is constructed with its back to Yamato?"

"Well," the monk replied carefully, "There are various theories about this."

"Could it be because he was buried facing west, which would be the direction of the Buddha's Western Paradise if seen from Yamato?"

"You could interpret it like that, yes. After all, Nijo can be thought of as the sacred boundary between this world and the next, and directly west from it you find all the countless tombs of the nobles and imperial family, and Prince Shotoku himself. Some people also take the view that Otsu was buried facing the point where the sun sets into the sea. And who knows, there may have been a feeling that it would be somehow oppressive to have someone looking down on you day and night who'd been executed for rebellion, prince though he was. But it was a very long time ago. I'm sorry I can't give you a proper answer."

Taku softly cleared his throat to address the girls beside him. The monk was evidently feeling a little uncomfortable in the face of their studious questions, so Taku introduced himself to the girls, explaining that he'd been sent here by a Tokyo publisher to gather material. "You've just climbed Mount Nijo?" he then asked.

"Yes."

"I'm just about to myself. Could you suggest a route?"

"We set off from Mount Nijo Station, walked in past Kasuga Shrine, and climbed up the ridgeline to the male peak."

"How was the path down to here?"

The girl turned to her companion. "Amazingly tough, right?"

"Yeah." They looked at each other, and both confirmed that the climb down was far harder than the path up.

"It was a really narrow path, and incredibly rocky, wasn't it?"

"Yeah, and all wet and slippery. Pretty scary."

"But we did meet those awesome people, didn't we?" said the large girl with boyish haircut, touching her friend's shoulder as if to remind her. "That group of four or five who overtook us on the way down, remember?"

"Oh yeah, them. They were just like a young wolfpack. They came rushing past like the wind, running somewhere just off the path. You didn't have time to think more than 'Hey!' and they were gone. They were amazing."

"What sort of people are you talking about?" Taku asked.

"I don't know. They were kind of like out of a period drama show."

"They had like sedge hats on their backs."

"Yeah."

An elderly white-haired man had come in unobserved and was now sitting on the edge of the mat. He was dressed in a three-piece grey suit and on his knees was an old-fashioned peaked cap. "They'd be members of the Wayfarers' League," he suddenly said quietly, gazing out at the garden.

"What was that?" Taku leaned forward. "What's the Wayfarers' League? What sort of thing does it...?"

"Well, I don't really know much about it either." Legs informally crossed, the man put the little tea cake to his lips. "The name is similar to the name people used in the old days for those pilgrims that follow the Shikoku temple pilgrimage, but this isn't the same thing. I just remember my dad once telling me someone was from the 'Wayfarers' League.'"

"Was this a really long time ago?"

"I'd have still been a child. My dad and I once walked over Anamushi Pass to Upper Taishi to visit a relative of ours who was in some sort of trouble. I remember the bright moonlight. I saw a line of figures crawling along like animals in the direction of Nijo Valley from Dontsurubo. They were a really long way off, too far off to make out if they was humans or what. I told my dad and he said, 'Ah, the Wayfarers' League is back again, eh?' That's all he'd say."

"Pardon me, but are you from around here?"

"I am. As a kid I used to live in Anamushi, but these days I run a business in Nagoya."

"What's Dontsurubo?"

"Dontsurubo, the name of the mountain peak." The man wrote the characters for "Gathering Place of Cranes" in the air.

Taku nodded. "Ah yes, I noticed that name on the map. I wasn't sure how to pronounce it."

"The mountain round there is covered in white rocks. People have taken tuff for building from there for a long time. There's over thirty acres of it up there, apparently."

"Wayfarers' League, eh?" Taku muttered the name over to himself.

One of the girls gave a sudden cry. "Hey, look at the time!" Taku glanced at his watch.

It was time to climb the mountain. He wrapped the remaining cake in a piece of paper and put it in his backpack, said farewell, and left.

He climbed slowly up beside a deeply-cut stream. The path was rough but reasonably well-maintained. The mountain slope that ran down beside him bore a sorry tangle of fallen trees, presumably the result of a particularly violent flash flood. Taku began to understand the likely reason behind the high stone foundations of Taima Temple.

It had been quite a while since he'd last walked a wooded mountain path like this, but he didn't feel weary. The treads of his boot soles were nicely worn back to the point where he could feel the path's surface beneath. Stiff boots with a sharp-edged sole may be stable, but that actually produced its own kind of instability. It was like putting tires with too much traction on an old Porsche. They gripped the road perfectly, but if you got into a slide they were difficult to control. With both cars and shoes, Taku liked the kind with a natural slip to them. Once you really broke in a pair of boots, you felt like you had eyes in the soles of your feet. It was civilized man who had reduced the sole of the foot to nothing more than a mere walking tool. Feet had their own kind of radar. Once you put it to use, you should be able to walk with your eyes closed, he believed.

Arriving at the point where two paths diverged, Taku felt a fleeting disappointment when he saw that the little roofed rest shelter was replete with a drinks machine selling bottled water.

Between the two paths was a temple, which would be the Yusenji Temple that the monk in the train had mentioned. The path to the left went over Iwaya Pass to join the Old Takenouchi Highway. Taku guessed it must be the old woodsmans' path known in the old days as Taima Path. The monk had said that the right-hand path would take him over the saddle between the male and female peaks and on to Umanose. This is the one he should take if he wanted to see the poem stone.

Taku passed under the gate with its bark-thatched roof and stepped off along the mountain path. The placement of logs and stones along the track gave it a somehow refined air more reminiscent of something found in a temple garden than on a mountainside. It was wide, and the spacing of the trees on either side of the paved path added to the suggestion that it wasn't a path that had always been there. It certainly felt entirely different from the steep mountainside Taku had been imagining he'd find.

Perhaps I'd have done better to choose the path over Iwaya Pass, he began to think regretfully.

After a brief walk, he came upon a stone pillar that stood as if driven into the rock of the slope to his left. At the top, four little square windows had been carved, as if to create a stone lantern.

This must be it, he thought. The poem stone that the monk in the train had spoken of. He went over to it and with a finger traced the words carved there.

"Yusenji Temple, South Hiei Training Hall, Nijo Peak," he made out. On the side facing the way he'd come was a faded carving of a poem, in a mixture of Chinese characters and Japanese phonetic script.

"*Namu Amida Butsu,*" he read with difficulty—the chant repeated by believers in praise of Amida. "*Mina wo yobu kotori*" it continued.

But this didn't quite make sense. Looking closely, he now made out a *no* at the end of the first line but it still didn't really come together. Perhaps the characters should be read a different way.

On the next line he saw *ayashi ya*, "uncanny."

So perhaps it meant "*Namu Amida Butsu* / uncanny how the small birds chant that name"—well at least that seemed to work somehow. And then "*futakami no yama*," Futakami Mountain, the old name for Nijo. Yes, he could see that made sense.

He tried repeating it all to himself a few times, but somehow it still didn't feel quite convincing. Surely the monk on the train had told him a different version.

Again and again he turned back to gaze at the stone inscription, and now he made out, between *ayashi ya* and *futakami no yama* the letters *tare ka*.

But this threw the poem back into further confusion. It seemed to have lost all poetic rhythm. He repeated to himself the words he recalled the monk speaking, and suddenly it came home to him. Yes, you could read those first words a different way: not as the chant *Namu Amida Butsu*, but lifting the last word, "Buddha," into the following sentence. So—"*Namu Amida* / the small birds chant the Buddha's name." This followed the right rhythm, and the rest of the poem slipped into rhythm too. He could see, now that he read it this way, the monk was right when he remarked that the first half of the poem was the kind of clichéd poetic formula typical of Buddhist poetry.

Well, I don't know the first thing about this kind of literature anyway, he told himself. Yet the question of the last half of the poem still niggled. What meaning did it hold? In particular, the mysterious *tare ka*?

I'll check it out with Professor Nishihaga or Hanada when I get back, he decided.

He pulled from his backpack the trusty instant camera, and snapped four or five photos of the stone. From now on, he'd have to take photos as a kind of memo to augment the report he'd be making. He'd been in danger of forgetting Hanada's instructions. While he was at it, he added some photos of the surrounding trees and the temple below.

The end of the poem still ran in his head. *You know the meaning, yet you don't*, the monk had said. What a peculiar poem. What on earth could that *tare ka* mean?

Taku shook his head to free it from this nagging question, and set off once more along the stone-paved path.

Before long the climb suddenly grew steep. Trickles of underground water glistened down the rocks, and the forest on either side was denser. Wavering strips of sunlight filtered through the branches and lit the path before his feet. The cool, damp air felt good on his lightly sweating skin.

He climbed on without pausing. The path became steeper still, but he strode smoothly along in an unbroken rhythm.

At length, the sky suddenly opened above him. With another heave, he was standing on the saddleback ridge. He'd reached the boundary between the two prefectures, Nara and Osaka.

It was indeed like a horse's saddle, smoothly curved. The view was immense; standing there, he could make out through the hazy air the distant urban areas of Kawachi, Izumi, Sakai, and Osaka. There was a glittering river that would probably be the Ishikawa. Countless white rows of plastic agricultural hothouses stood everywhere on the plain. To the south were the wave-like folds of mountain, the Katsuragi-Kongo Range, and below him on the left he could see the bypass of the new Takenouchi Freeway under construction.

Taku decided he would climb the male peak to his right to begin with. He set off up the reddish path, photographing as he went. The summit was a mere stone's throw away, but the path was very rough underfoot. He climbed straight up without pausing, taking care where he trod.

All the guidebooks described the ridge path up the male peak as the toughest section. It was indeed steep, but not as bad as all that, Taku thought. He barely needed to catch his breath when he reached the top. If anything, the climb gave him the enjoyable sense of an easy hike.

There was a tiny flat area at the summit on which stood a little shrine surrounded by a wall of concrete blocks, an unprepossessing little prefab building that suggested a humble folk religion worship of the mountain deity more than the impressive formal shrine indicated by its elaborate name, "Seat of the Katsuragi God, as prescribed in the tenth century Engi-shiki Code." Inside the precinct, he could see an unpretentious burial area.

For all the brightness of the surroundings, this spot alone was somehow hushed and shadowed. Oddly, despite the breeze, the dark leaves on the nearby trees barely moved.

So this is Prince Otsu's grave, Taku said to himself.

Its back was indeed turned to the Yamato plain, just as the girls at the temple had described. He walked slowly over to it.

An Imperial Household notice board proclaimed this as "the Mount Nijo grave of Prince Otsu, son of emperor Tenmu." Beyond the board stood a small shrine gate, in the midst of a thick dark growth of trees. The grave felt withdrawn and hidden. Following the stone-paved path that circled the iron fence, Taku suddenly found himself looking out over the whole expanse of the Yamato plain below. The Osaka side had been hazy, but here on the Nara side the air was clear. He had no need to open the map to recognize from textbook memory the famous landscape of the ancient realm of Yamato, where the Japanese nation had been born.

And where is Mount Miwa of the morning sun? he wondered, recalling the epithet of early poetry.

He opened the guide map. Here and there on the plain, ponds glittered in the sunlight like jewels. The garish white of new buildings and factory complexes struck the eye painfully. The Western Meihan Freeway sliced through the middle of the plain and on to the city of Tenri. When he concentrated, he could make out a wide east-west road linking the area south of Taima Temple with distant Sakurai City via Yamato Takada.

That might be the route where the ancient cross-Yamato road had run, he decided.

Taku recalled the information he'd seen on the notice board earlier—the Takenouchi Highway that crossed the mountains connecting Osaka with Kawachi joined the cross-Yamato road, the old Asuka road from Taima. The three famous mountains in the Yamato Plain—Unebi, Miminashi, and Amanokagu—lay to either side of it. Following the cross-Yamato road further east brought one to the Hatsuse Road, an important route that continued on east through Iga and Ise.

He could see a gently conical little mountain rising out of the plain this side of Sakurai City, and for some reason he knew right away that this must be Mount Miwa. The north-running road that skirted its foot was probably the famous Yamanobe Road, an ancient pathway that was now a mecca for hikers. Taku recalled the little chat about Yamato that he'd had with Kyoko Shimamura before he left Tokyo, in which she'd mentioned that there was a site called Chopsticks Grave near Mount Miwa.

According to her, the story was of a strange suicide committed by a young maiden who had angered the god who lived on Miwa—she had, of all things, used a chopstick to stab herself in the genitals. Kyoko went on to say that the grave was reputedly roofed with stone cut from Anamushi, on the north side of the male peak on which he stood.

No question about it, thought Taku, Yamato abounded in bloody tales.

He settled himself down at the edge of the stone fence and let his thoughts run on while his eyes took in the peaceful plain spread below him.

The young man known as Prince Otsu who lay buried next to him here had also met an untimely end at the age of only twenty-four. It was his own stepmother, the empress, who had ordered his execution. The story was that she drove the popular and able youth to his death through her desire to see his rival, her own son Prince Kusakabe, inherit the throne. She herself later became ruler, taking the name Empress Jito, and moved the capital to Fujiwara, near Mount Miminashi, another little mountain he could see on the plain below. With what thoughts would she have watched each evening as the shape of Mount Nijo loomed black against the setting sun? Perhaps it was the agitated heart of this powerful female ruler that had led her to bury the prince she had murdered so that he faced away from the capital.

A soft breeze blew, but the air was warm and damp. And now a light mist came seething up out of the valley, moving with extraordinary speed. It crossed the saddle below him and sped on towards Kawachi.

Taku was suddenly overcome by an irresistible drowsiness. He gave a great yawn, then another. It occurred to him that he had risen at five that morning and spent the hours in the train reading maps and guide books, so he'd hardly slept at all.

Okay, just a five-minute nap then. These mini–naps were his specialty. He could set his internal clock to wake him to within a minute or so of the time he chose. It was a habit he'd acquired quite naturally in the course of his long travels abroad.

Taku slipped the haversack back from his shoulder, settled comfortably with his back resting against the wall around Prince Otsu's tomb, and felt himself almost sucked under as his eyes closed.

A wind was blowing somewhere. The damp air brushed his cheeks as it flowed over him. It was indescribably pleasant to lie there, his consciousness wavering and wandering in the pale light of the boundary between sleep and waking. Someone was walking nearby. Then the sound of the footsteps gradually grew distant.

The footsteps drew near again, and now he seemed to hear a voice. Bird song, human voice, and footsteps all approached, mingling in the half-light of his consciousness, then disappeared again.

Now came the guttural voice of a man, half singing, half murmuring. Wind singing in the trees erased it, but then after a pause it came again.

It was like a dream, and yet he felt it was no dream. For some reason, he heard again in the darkness of his mind the short passage of mandala sermon he had heard back there in the temple. The voice that intoned it and the gravelly male voice from nowhere blended and became one, and Taku was a young man standing entranced before the mandala, hearing the sermon delivered by a master preacher.

The voice flowed on like water. In the half light, he strained to listen. And now the wind changed direction, and suddenly he could hear it clearly. Drifting below consciousness, he heard the voice as the whisper of the wind.

It's a dream, he said to himself. I'm dreaming. But why such a dream...?

As if by a powerful magnet, Taku felt himself drawn down, deep into dark mist. A weird incantatory chant began, and grew slowly stronger. Some he could follow, some was incomprehensible.

And in this way
Sekenshi *flow*
between mountain and village
and the essence of
the Way of Sekenshi
is fuko isseden
fusai issoshi
a life without home
and its spirit
is isshin mushi
menme shinogi...

What? Whose voice was this? And what on earth was it saying? What was this *Sekenshi*...? The five minutes is up, he told himself. Gotta wake up...why can't I get out of this dream? God I'm sleepy. Ah, here's the voice again.

Yon mountain
be Katsuragi Kongo
Shigi Ikoma this peak
Yon river far Yamato
Ishikawa this river near
Far yonder Yoshino Iga-Ueno
Yet farther Tamba Mino Kisoji
From Hakusan Mountain in the North
To Kumano to South
Sekenshi, *a living stream,*
Flow through mountains and rivers
And the life blood springs
here on Futakami.

Yes, an old man's guttural chant. Where is he? Wait. Now it's a woman's voice. Not exactly a hymn, not a sutra either. And not that sermon chant I heard back at the temple. God, I'm sleepy. There's a wind. Can't hear the voices any more…no, here it comes again.

From the male and female peaks
Far in the distance Tajihi village
And that great mountain soaring
From out the sacred plain of Mimihara
In ages past the imperial tombs
in Mozu Mimihara
Close by Daisen Tomb
Still stands great
Its name now Nintoku Tomb
We now are gathered here
In memory of the seven
Who sleep within that mountain fastness
Bow down to the earth, and to those gone before
Tell their tale
tell now the tale of Kenshi-gari…

A young woman's voice. Ah, now a whole chorus of voices! Seems like they all repeat over each verse after she gives it. Come on, just open your eyes and check out who on earth these people are. No. I can't. Sleepy again.

Takenouchi Highway
was of old the Kenshi Road
of Futakami Mountain
and opening up that road
where Tajihi and Anamushi
and Mamushi snakes did dwell…

Then he woke, with a sensation as if floating on water. He shook his head and looked around. All was dark.

Damn. Taku checked his watch. It was only two-thirty. But how dark it was! It seemed he was almost in some different world.

When he realized it was a mist that had come boiling with astonishing speed up from the valley below, for a moment he was assailed by an indescribable alarm. More and more mist kept seething out and making its way up through the trees. The sky grew darker and darker. The layers of low-hanging cloud seemed about to brush the summit of the peak where he lay.

He stood up. He'd only been dozing for about ten minutes at most. What an extraordinarily swift change the summit had undergone!

The geography of this area made it prone to mists, he knew, but it was still astonishing how suddenly Mount Nijo had changed. There was no sense now of that benign twin-peaked mountain he'd gazed up at from the temple station.

The female peak was invisible. That smooth ridgeline that had lain beguilingly beyond the saddleback ridge, seeming almost to entice him up, was now swallowed deep in mist.

Here, at the grave of Prince Otsu, there was no sign of anyone. The grave seemed darker yet, pervaded by an uncanny atmosphere. The plains on both the Yamato and Kawachi sides were completely blanked out.

Were those voices I heard just now really a dream? he wondered.

Their sound, like running water, still reverberated softly in his head as if muffled in mist. As he made his way towards the downward path, he tried to assemble the fragmentary words, but almost nothing came to him.

Yes, it must have been a dream. He turned for a final look at the shadowy tomb, then set off down the steep slope back towards the saddleback ridge.

A word from the chant suddenly rose in his mind—*Kenshi-gari*. No, it made less sense than ever now. Taku went on down the rocky path, feeling his way blindly through the mist.

A sudden dull sound under his feet, like leather being struck, and the next instant something bird-shaped leapt up into the air, brushing his face as it passed. When it had gone, the world around him grew still quieter. And in that silence, he heard another sound.

What on earth is that? he thought.

From somewhere ahead he heard footsteps rhythmically treading over broken stone. The steps were light. Taku was making his way down the steep slope cautiously, choosing his footing over the slippery talc schist, but these other footsteps were rapidly disappearing ahead of him at an impressive pace. The thick mist made it impossible to see the figure itself.

What kind of person would be walking so lightly along here through this mist? he wondered.

He set off at breakneck speed to follow. He wasn't alone on Nijo after all; someone else was also walking the ridge. He concentrated all his nerves on the descent. Striding straight down over the twists in the path, his body slipped and slid as he went.

But even so, the footsteps stayed ahead of him. One moment he thought he was gaining on them, the next moment they were drawing away again.

I'll catch up with you if it kills me! he thought.

On went the regular footsteps, almost as if mocking him. There had been no break in their rhythm all this time.

So there are Sherpas here in Yamato, eh? Taku said to himself, and he laughed in the mist. Should he shout out loud? No, that would somehow be like an admission of defeat.

Right, then!

Reckless though he knew it was, Taku began to run. Suddenly the steep slope gave way to flat land. The saddleback ridge. At this moment, there was an unexpected break in the mist. The peak was still shrouded in thick grey vapor, but the view along the ridge path was straight and clear. Taku gazed intently.

The track up to the female peak rose straighter than the climb he'd just done. Along that track, he saw a figure. From behind he could make out that the figure wore leggings and a dark blue cotton kimono coat with the white printed symbol "Gods" enclosed in a circle on its back. The figure was making its way with marvelous speed up the path towards the female peak. It felt strange to Taku that, despite the mist that still swathed the mountainsides to left and right, the ridge path should be so clear of it. The man who climbed ahead of him seemed poised to be engulfed in the mist that hung about him.

Damn him!

Suddenly, Taku was overcome with the same fierce impulse that had caused him to knife the bar-owner who had hit his brother at the racetrack entrance that autumn back when he was still a high school student. He raced straight across the saddle and began to climb the path behind the figure.

Once on the slope, he found it in fact quite steep, climbing straight up as it did rather than winding. The ground beneath his shoes was crumbly. Unless he was careful, he could easily find himself slipping back down several meters at a step. The mist was beginning to close over the peak again.

The figure ahead in its dark blue coat was no longer visible.

Taku plunged recklessly on towards the peak. Glancing behind, he saw that the black shape of the male peak now rose above the clouds.

This mountain sure did have a lot of different faces.

The saddleback ridge was shrouded in thick vapor, making the male peak seem to float in the sky.

But where was the man…?

There was no sign of anyone on the narrow summit when he arrived. There could be no path down from it other than the one he'd just climbed. He searched around, and found among the bushes a narrow gap that ran through the rocks, apparently the remains of a drain that had been carved there. It didn't seem to be a path, but perhaps the man ahead of him had descended by this route.

Unhesitatingly, Taku plunged off down the track. For a moment he was thrown off balance and only just managed to pull up short of falling. Then, at top speed, he set off down the slope through the mist.

At length, he came upon the path that led towards Iwaya Pass. He hesitated a moment, wondering where to go, and as he turned to look back at the male peak, he saw an astonishing sight.

There, close to the summit of the male peak and climbing at amazing speed, was a human form. For a moment he assumed it wasn't the man he was following, but there could be no mistaking that particular light, rhythmic tread.

So while Taku had still been striding up the path to the female peak, this man had already descended, crossed the saddleback ridge and climbed more than half way back up the male peak again.

This guy isn't walking, he's flying, thought Taku as he stood rooted to the spot and gazed, finally beaten.

The mist continued to cling motionless to the mountainside. A heavy gloom had settled about the male peak. Walking disconsolately on along the path to Iwaya Pass, Taku was tortured by defeat.

From the pass, he took the path that led back towards the male peak again. At any rate, he decided, he must follow every route on the mountain. He planned to try the path down from the peak that the girls at the temple had climbed. This time, he climbed slowly, at a regular pace.

Some way along the path he happened to glance up, and suddenly he spied a group of fifteen or more people, dressed like the other man, climbing towards the male peak from the saddleback ridge ahead. A similar-sized group was gathered on the female peak opposite. Confused, Taku halted. A third group was moving between the two peaks.

These figures seemed sprung from the depths of the mist.

Would these be the same people those girls said they came across? He thought of the name "Wayfarers' League," and the image of a group of "pilgrims" moving through the moonlight down from the white stone heights of Dontsurubo Peak into Nijo Valley.

But no, that was the story the old man had told about a childhood memory, surely?

None of these shadowy figures were moving with the same speed as that lone man he'd followed. Each walked strongly, but they were very different from him. They seemed to be moving in independent groups, following various routes over the mountain.

Taku sat down on a rock a little back from the path and pulled out his notebook, to try to map out his sense of the topography around Nijo's double summit.

He had just begun to draw when suddenly he heard footsteps. The next moment, two groups had converged from left and right.

They moved past each other directly before his eyes. Their big sedge hats protected their faces from view, but he heard a woman speak.

"Midnight at the gate of Nintoku Tomb."

"Understood. Midnight at the gate of Nintoku Tomb," came a male voice in reply, and they were gone.

Taku slipped his notebook back in his pocket, stood up, and stepped out onto the path. Then suddenly, right in front of him and rapidly approaching, he saw a hatless woman. She passed him, walking at normal pace. She was tall, with a boyish haircut. Her skin was dark, and her eyebrows were strong. Her lips were tightly closed.

"Hello there," Taku said as she passed. The woman did not speak. She only cast him a quick glance with shining eyes. Five or so paces later he turned to look, but she had vanished. A thought occurred to him. Perhaps the person he'd followed up the path, who walked so swiftly, was not a man but this woman. But could this really be so?

Taku walked on through the mist up to the male peak. He planned to go down to Kasuga Shrine and back, then cross from the saddle-back ridge to Iwaya Pass, and descend from there to emerge along the Takenouchi Highway.

As he stood there, the mist suddenly cleared with astonishing speed, revealing the scene around him.

A single ray of sunlight fell like a knife through the clouds onto the side of the female peak, revealing a lone figure that was gliding rapidly up towards the summit.

It was she.

She moved with astonishing speed, and perfect equilibrium. It was clear that even from this distance she was aware of his gaze. Her back seemed somehow to be transmitting a greeting in his direction, and he felt his heart heave suddenly in response. Her walk was more vibrant and powerful than any he had ever seen. She wasn't rushing, there was no question that she walked, yet it seemed almost as if she flew. She was heedless of what was underfoot—her feet simply slid over the uneven rocky surface as if licking it softly. A beam of light lit the way ahead of her like a spotlight, and into that light she climbed like a beautiful golden bee.

What the hell…?

Taku found himself trembling with disbelief, as though he'd witnessed some miracle. There on the male peak, he stood stock still, astonished, as the light slowly intensified around him again. Then he heaved a sigh. *That was no walk*, he thought. She was flying. I'd be prepared to undergo any sort of training if only I could learn to walk like that.

God, it was like the amazing Walking Practice of those Thousand-Day Mountain Circuit monks. Just what kind of creature was this woman? And what on earth was this "Wayfarers' League"?

Ayashi ya tare ka / futakami no yama. The words suddenly flashed up into his consciousness with a new meaning. "Uncanny," the words seemed to be saying, "Who is it on Mount Futakami?" Then into his head came the name "Nintoku Tomb."

He recalled the brief exchange he had overheard between the two groups that had slipped past each other before his eyes. "Midnight at the gate of Nintoku Tomb," they had said. That's where they would gather. *Why?* Something had been written down the front of her *happi* coat, but he wasn't sure what. Drawn by her face, his eyes hadn't taken in those few words that he'd ordinarily have noticed.

Right, he decided, Let's go to the Nintoku Tomb.

She must belong to that group. If he went there at midnight, perhaps he'd manage to see her again.

Taku set off down the path of "Beauteous Futakami," now bathed once more in innocent sunlight and wrapped by tender mists, his feet carrying him along as if in a dream.

During the course of the afternoon, Taku traversed numerous paths, and by the end of the day had managed to cover all the routes on the mountain. As the sun set, he was lucky enough to see the mountain's silhouette against the setting sun from a fine vantage point in a village in its foothills.

No longer merely the friendly-looking camel's hump he'd seen from the train that morning, the mountain now emanated a profound bleakness, different again from the uncanny mist that had risen to assail him from the mountain depths. Perhaps the reddened eyes of the Chujo Maiden back there in Taima Temple were not the result of weeping. Surely it was precisely the color of the setting sun that was now dyeing the western sky.

He guessed Hanada back at headquarters would laugh in disbelief if he got a report including all this. "Hey Taku," he'd chuckle, "This isn't like you, my boy!"

But I've seen a lot today, he thought, as he strode along the Takenouchi Highway in the dusk toward Taishi.

All along the old road, road works were in progress. The freeway would soon be completed here too. How many times over more than a thousand years had this road been rebuilt?

Coming up to the pass, his vision was filled by the flicker of countless lights that pulsed everywhere below him against the still-purplish sky.

Nintoku Tomb would be over in that direction, he thought.

He began to stride a little faster. He must now get to the nearest station, catch a train to Kobe, complete the business of Shin'ichi's car, and manage to make it to the Nintoku Tomb in Sakai by midnight. Perhaps it was excitement that prevented him feeling tired. On he strode, down towards the Kawachi Plain with its net of lights below him.

This was the day when everything began.

4

"Tell me later."

Hanada held up a hand, to prevent Taku from embarking on the tale of his extraordinary experiences. They were sitting together in the coffee shop on the ground floor of Meteor Publications. "Your job's done with the report on Mount Nijo. You can tell me the personal stuff this evening if you like."

"But I really do want to just tell you this right now," Taku persisted. "The fact is," he went on, "I met someone extraordinary. Or maybe 'wonderful' is a better word."

A golf tournament was on the TV over the counter. The Japanese golfer had just missed a short six-centimeter birdie on the last long hole, giving the playoff match to his Australian opponent. Eyes on the screen, Hanada clicked his tongue in disappointment. "No, no, make it later. Let's meet this evening at eight."

"Where?"

"Anywhere will do. Quick, out!" Hanada leaned forward in his seat towards the screen. "The Rubicon!" he yelled over his shoulder. "And make that nine, not eight!"

"Right. I'll be there ahead of you." Why were middle-aged Japanese men so crazy about golf? Taku wondered as he left the coffee shop.

He still had quite a while till nine. Taku climbed the stairs to the third floor editing room, undecided whether he should call in on Kyoko Shimamura at the *Tramping* desk, or have a talk with Kozo Hayashi about his next piece for *Outroads*.

The two magazines weren't really business competitors, of course. They both belonged to different aspects of the outdoor sports genre. Both focused on a life of freedom out in the natural world, but in fact their attitude to nature was diametrically opposed.

While Kyoko was almost neurotically dedicated to low-impact living, Kozo was an advocate of the nomadic lifestyle. His editorial policy was to attract young people to the kind of freestyle traveling or wandering in which the motorbike took the place of the nomad's horse.

The editorial room was oddly quiet. Not a soul was in sight at the editorial desks of Meteor Publication's flagship magazine, *Life and Nature*, the publication with the longest history and the most stable subscription base, and the one that carried the most advertising.

Kyoko too was nowhere to be seen. Maybe she was over at the printer. Feeling a little disappointed, Taku went in search of Kozo Hayashi instead.

The *Outroads* editing desk was located between *Monthly Hikers' Guide* and *SW Journal*. As expected, Kozo wasn't there. He was seldom known to be at his own desk; he was far more easily found by looking around among the rest of the staff. Sure enough, he'd settled down beside Tamihiko Takeda at the *Traveling the Seasons* desk, where he sat puffing cigarette smoke into the surrounding air.

"Hayashi?"

Kozo turned a warm smile on Taku when he heard his name, and gestured him to come and sit down.

"Hey there. You been off somewhere? I haven't seen you round lately."

Editor of a bikers' magazine though he was, Kozo had an oddly middle-aged taste in clothes. Today he was wearing a grey tweed suit with conservative black shoes, a white shirt, and neat black knitted tie.

Taku went over and stood there waving away the fug of cigarette smoke. "I've been walking in Yamato, on a job for Hanada."

"Yamato? You?"

"You mean Yamato's not my kind of place?"

"Well, if it was in Bhutan or somewhere, maybe."

The long-haired Tamihiko, sitting beside Kozo, gave a laugh. "Kozo wants to sell you as some rootless adventure hero who wanders in foreign parts."

"Sure," rejoined Kozo. "Come on, our mag's popular with the readers, so we want our writers to have the right image, you know."

"There's no holding this hotshot editor."

The roaming international backpacker column that Taku wrote for *Outroads* had been Kozo's idea. As an editor he was as autocratic as Hanada, but there was a clear generational difference between them. He'd chosen the title with obsessive care, and readers responded astonishingly well. Taku, who believed he had no literary talent, was firmly convinced that this was all Kozo's doing.

"Was that story about the ghost bus really based on your own experience?" Tamihiko asked him.

"Yes."

"I thought it was probably a made-up tale that Kozo had gingered up with some additions of his own."

Kozo looked wry. "Real stories can often sound amazingly like lies, you know." he said. "But in my opinion it's precisely those bits that earn the special points with our readers."

"I don't write lies."

"I know you don't." Kozo blew smoke. "By the way, you're not forgetting the deadline for your follow-up piece on 'Farewell to the Dear Old Ghost Bus,' are you, Professor Hayami?"

"That's what I've come to discuss."

"So what kind of story have you got for us this time?"

"It's the story of taking the bus into the Black Sea resort area in Bulgaria and making a huge win in the casinos."

"I thought Bulgaria was a communist country," remarked Tamihiko, running a coy finger through his long locks. "Are there really such things as casinos there?"

"The government tourist bureau runs them. Mind you, most of the dealers come from around Beirut."

"How're the girls?"

"Nothing much."

"That's a shame."

Kozo crushed his cigarette butt. "There's something you must remember. Taku was probably still pretty young back then."

"I was twenty-six or twenty-seven."

Yes, I was young all right, he thought. He'd set off from Haneda airport when he was eighteen, and he was nineteen when he reached Europe. He'd roamed about, staying in youth hostels or YMCAs, then spent two years working six months of the year in northern Europe and spending the rest of the year living in Spain. It was around that time he went up to Lapland to see the midnight sun.

Eventually northern Europe became a difficult place for a Japanese to find work, so he'd headed south and got a job on a small Greek island, helping out in a certain tourist trade business that he preferred not to name. It was a time when several jets a day flew in a vast cargo of tourists to the tiny resort island.

A Japanese businessman he got to know there offered him a job in Cairo, and he'd made an honest living there for a while, working as a chauffeur and general odd-jobs man in a company office. This was when he first saw the Pyramids. He quit after a year, and went to India. This was before Goa went to pieces. He'd been given a job on the ghost bus by the boss of a car repairs factory in Nepal.

"Could I somehow twist your arm for some reference to a woman in this next piece?"

"I'll see what I can recall."

"You'd have to have a few stories, at twenty-six or seven."

"I was once threatened by a gypsy guy with a knife."

"Wanting to sleep with you?" Kozo loosened his tie a little. "It's something about a woman that I'm after."

"This story's just about putting a gypsy dancer on the bus."

"Are there gypsies in Bulgaria?" Tamihiko chimed in. He was becoming a bit of a pest, so Taku fobbed him off with the answer that there were indeed a few in the modern communist state. Then something occurred to him.

"Have you ever heard of something called the Wayfarers' League?" he asked them both.

"Huh?"

"Hmm."

Both scratched their heads. Yet as they did so, Taku thought he caught them exchanging a quick glance.

Somehow, he got the feeling they knew something. But how could they have heard of this group, when the memory was faint even for the old man at the temple?

"Hey Taku, your girlfriend's back." Kozo jerked his chin towards the far corner of the room, where Kyoko Shimamura had now appeared. "Maybe she's mad at you for writing for her rival *Outroads*."

"She had kind words to say about it, actually."

"Well, well." Kozo shrugged. Then, as Taku rose to leave, he added, "Right then, I'll work on a deadline for the fifth of next month, okay?"

"Fine."

From behind came Tamihiko's light and lilting voice. "Could you bring along something you've written to show *Traveling the Seasons* sometime too?"

"Sure. Thanks."

With a parting wave, Taku headed for the *Tramping* desk to find Kyoko.

They had so much to talk about that Taku ended by asking her to dinner to continue the conversation. He hesitated a moment, wondering where to take her.

"I really don't mind where we go," she said, guessing his difficulty. "But what about that place you mentioned once, Chinese was it?"

"Oh, you mean the Lotus?"

"Yes, that was it I think. The one run by the eccentric guy who knows everything."

"Yes, that's the one. But it's pretty scruffy."

"The food's no good?"

"The food's great."

"Well then, let's go."

He needed to say more to her. He hadn't told her anything of his mission in advance except that he was going to climb Mount Nijo. Now, with Hanada refusing to hear his story, he simply had to get it off his chest to someone. He was desperate to talk about the flying woman, and all he'd witnessed at the Nintoku Tomb.

"Wait for me downstairs," said Kyoko. "I'll be down right away."

A little later she appeared in the lobby, dressed in rather girlish fashion with a white hat and a little red pochette slung diagonally from her shoulder. Taku was planning to take a cab, but she declared they should walk.

"How far is it to the Lotus?"

"Well, at your pace it would probably take about thirty minutes."

"What about at your pace?"

"Maybe around twenty."

"Right then, let's walk. The food'll taste all the better if we work up an appetite."

She set off down the street, wafting along like a dandelion seed in a breeze. She was small, but she had quite a stride. Taku was particularly struck by how smoothly she transferred her weight through each leg in turn. As the weight came down on one foot, the knee straightened out beautifully, which meant the other leg naturally swung forward. She wore low-heeled shoes that were good for walking on city pavements, but even so her head sailed along remarkably smoothly, and her center of gravity held steady as she moved. It was a beautiful walk.

"I can see why you're in charge of a mag about walking," Taku remarked admiringly, falling into step beside her. "Where did you learn to walk like that, Kyoko?"

"I did some basic training, actually."

"I always assumed you were just an endurance walker."

"I'm not bad at that either. I like to do long distance stuff."

"I can see that. After all, you hold the record for walking the length of the Japanese archipelago and back, twice, don't you?"

Taku went on to ask where she'd been recently. He found they'd naturally begun to fall into a more friendly informality together.

"I did a walk along the outer rim of the caldera on Mount Aso down in Kyushu," she replied. "I wanted to walk through the town of Itsuki too, before it goes under water. The government's set to build the Kawabe Dam there."

Kyoko paused for a red light at the intersection, and continued. "While I was down there I also hiked from Mami Plain to Soyo Ravine."

"I've done a walk from Shiiba to Morotsuka down that way. There was a lot of volcanic tuff around those parts, I remember."

"Where did you go in Yamato?"

The lights changed and they set off together to cross.

"Mount Nijo and the old Takenouchi Highway. But I didn't get to the Chopsticks Grave you told me about."

"You were on the other side of the plain, I guess."

"Right. I went to Taima Temple."

"Have you ever read Shinobu Origuchi?" Kyoko asked suddenly.

"No."

"So you've never come across Yojuro Yasuda either then?"

"Never."

"Yasuda's also written about Prince Otsu, but he's the bright and cheerful type. That's why Origuchi's the one to read on Mount Nijo. He's fascinating."

Taku didn't reply. I think I'd better start reading a few things, he thought. Someone who walks a lot could also be someone who reads a lot, after all. And it was true, Kyoko always had her nose buried in some book.

"Yasuda is the morning sun on Nijo while Origuchi is the setting sun, you might say. At least that's how they strike me."

"Careful," Taku warned her as they stepped off the curb. "It's dangerous to get so absorbed while you walk, you know," he added.

"Really?" Kyoko looked dubious. "It's the opposite, in my opinion."

"How do you mean?"

"Well, I was brought up in a village up in the mountains of Kyushu. And I mean deep in the mountains. The round trip to elementary school took five hours."

"Five hours? That's incredible."

"Naturally we had no electricity or running water. Things are different now, of course."

She scarcely glanced down as she strode along. They were almost at the Lotus by now, and it would have taken just a little over twenty minutes.

"That's it, that's Cho's restaurant."

"It's tiny."

"Just a counter with seats."

It was around dinner time, so there were two or three other guests already seated. Seeing Taku arrive with Kyoko, Cho asked the others to move up and make space for them at one end of the counter.

"Hey there, found any sapphire?" he greeted Taku with a chuckle. "Who's the bride you wanna give it to, eh Taku?"

"I did buy some Kongo sand."

When he'd gone round to Dontsurubo after leaving the mountain, he'd suddenly remembered the request and found a shop that dealt in stone polishing materials, where he'd got them to put some in a plastic bag for him.

"Right. I'll tell you something interesting later. Anyhow, what you wanna eat?"

Taku ordered the fried beef and garlic shoots, while Kyoko chose tofu, and together they asked for abalone in oyster sauce and pickled mustard stalk soup.

"When did you get back from Yamato, Taku?" Cho asked.

"I drove through the night, and got in around ten yesterday morning."

"It's tiring to drive, eh?"

"Uh huh."

"Anyhow, as I was saying…" Kyoko looked firmly at Taku. Her upper eyelids were faintly flushed with red. Her lips, nose and ears, indeed all her features were fittingly small for her slight build. Even the white teeth that flashed when she smiled were small and neat.

"Right through elementary and middle school I used to walk about five hours a day. And it was up and down some pretty steep mountain paths, too. Rocky paths right on the edge of cliffs. I'd come across tangles of snakes, and when it rained the river crabs would come scuttling out of the streams."

"River crabs? Nice pickled," Cho cut in as he piled the food onto a plate. "You put hundreds of 'em live into light soy with heaps of chili. Called *ganzuke* in Kyushu."

"You know that? I'm impressed," Kyoko said delightedly. "I can see Taku was right when he said you know everything about everything."

"If you don't know everything you can't live in a foreign country." Cho narrowed his eyes in a smile as he replied, but his tone was serious.

Kyoko nodded. "True," she murmured. Then she went back to the story of her childhood. "I always carried a book when I was on my way to and from school. Mind you, I read anything and everything—manga, magazines, novels." She gave a humorous shrug.

"I pulled something out to read as soon as I left the house, and from then on my eyes were glued to the page, right? And the same coming home. It's hard to explain, looking back now. How could I have managed to walk along that steep, winding path without once glancing at where I was putting my feet? My eyes simply followed the words, and my mind was concentrated on wanting to know what came next. But I never fell over a cliff, or stumbled on a rock, or trod on a snake, though I walked incredibly fast. It seems amazing to me now, but it's true."

"Uh-huh."

"If a child can walk like that, without looking, that must mean that humans have that skill buried somewhere inside them, no?"

"Yes." Taku nodded. "I call it 'foot radar.' Once you reach a certain state—I can't explain just what that state is—your feet grow eyes."

"Yeah, we call them corns," Cho cut in cheerfully. "'Fish eyes' in Japanese, yeah?" But Taku went on without smiling.

"No, foot eyes. In other words, once the radar starts to work, your feet can read the lie of the land, avoid things that would get in the way, and carry your body faithfully to its destination. The sole of the foot becomes more than simply a practical thing that sustains your weight and becomes a kind of friend with its own will and senses."

"But wouldn't the feet become separate from yourself and be inclined to go walking off on their own accord?" asked Kyoko, half joking.

"That's why I said 'friend.' In that state you're no longer alone, there are two beings. Your soul and your body separate. And if all goes well, you're a soul with legs and legs with a soul, and each helps the other, and we can do twice or three times what a single person can do. I really believe we can gain this ability. My own experience has taught me that amazing things can happen to us, things the rational mind can't fathom. Walking itself is one of these. An old man in Hokkaido once told me that Ainu hunters used to walk two hundred fifty kilometers a day. No one else seems to believe this, but I do."

"I can believe that story," Kyoko said, nodding seriously. "When I was a kid the only thing in my head was the written word. I once lost my book and had to walk empty-handed. The walk took much longer than usual, and I was a lot more tired. Yes, I believe you can grow eyes in your feet."

I'm so happy I can talk to this woman, Taku thought. She at least wouldn't laugh when he told her of what he'd seen in the mist on Mount Nijo.

"Nijo was a weird place," he said.

"There's a strange poet by the name of Yoshimasu Gozo, you know." Kyoko spoke in a kind of singing murmur. "He described Nijo in a poem as 'the beautiful mountain, with double folded eyelid.'"

"The beautiful mountain with double folded eyelid, eh? Yes, it's true. Up close, it was a lovely, gentle mountain. But it just took a sudden change of weather and it became a very different place. I saw its other face, uncanny and brimming with malice. Then suddenly the sun broke through again, and it became a majestic mountain rising in the west against the setting sun. It was a weird, immensely changeable place. Though it's really just a little double mountain to look at."

"You've asked me to dinner to tell me about it, haven't you?"

Taku nodded. There was no deceiving Kyoko. She seemed able to understand things before she'd heard them. "That's right. Let me tell you about the flying woman I met on the mountain," he said.

"Please."

The other customers had left, and they were alone at the counter. Cho settled himself on a chair and listened in as Taku told his tale.

"Nijo's only about five hundred meters high, and I guess for a real climber it's just a knob on the plain, not even a real mountain, but it's a strangely alluring place. Or rather, there's a weird atmosphere there, a kind of sense that things are somehow not normal."

Kyoko nodded. Cho was listening silently. Taku lifted his hands and held them beside each other, one a little higher than the other. "The male and female peaks stand side by side like this," he went on. "There's a saddle between them, from which you can look out over Kawachi on one side and Yamato on the other. The day I climbed it, the weather started fine, but while I was taking a brief rest on the summit of the male peak, a mist suddenly came surging up from the valley."

He went on to explain that this wasn't like the usual extreme weather shifts you often encounter on mountains. "I was pretty intrigued, so I set off to cross to the female peak, but then ahead of me I heard footsteps. The path was just broken stones."

"You couldn't see who it was because of the mist?"

"That's right. And clearly this was no ordinary way of walking."

"I don't like scary stories," remarked Cho.

"No, it's not scary. Now I have a certain confidence in my walking abilities, so I decided I'd follow this person and find out just who it was…"

"Playing tag in the mist?"

"Yes, and I was all the more intrigued because I couldn't see the other person. So I went faster and faster, but for some reason I just couldn't gain on him. It seemed like the faster I went the more I fell behind. Then finally, at the saddle, there was a break in the mist. And there I saw, heading up the narrow track to the female peak at incredible speed, this figure that really seemed to be, yes, flying rather than walking. It was a real shock I can tell you. I've seen a lot of astonishing walkers around the world—Indians, the Masai tribes of the savannahs, the Bedouins of the desert…"

"Nepalese Sherpas, the Shan of Thailand." Kyoko picked up the litany. She was naming others that Taku had written about in pieces for other magazines.

"There were wonderful walkers in China too, you know," Cho chimed in.

"And there are those Tibetan monks too, the Lung-gom-pa runners," added Kyoko. "And the Katsuragi Ranges right next to Nijo were the home ground of the ancient walking saint, En no Ozunu, weren't they? He was a 'flying man.'"

"There's a translation by Jun'ichi Ono of Miguel Serrano's *Indian Pilgrimage* where he describes meeting Shivaists who come rushing up a cliffside path high in the mountains so fast they seem to fly," Taku continued. "He writes about quite incredible walkers. I haven't just read about them, I've seen people like that with my own eyes. But the person I saw on Nijo wasn't special like that. It was someone just like us, living as we do in modern Japan."

"Right." Cho poured them some tea. "And is that the end?"

"No, there's more. I passed this person in the mist. A woman. She was young, wearing an indigo *happi* coat and leggings, with a sedge hat strung on her back."

"A woman, eh? That must have been a shock."

"And then dozens of others, dressed the same, came out of the mist. It seemed like they were criss-crossing between the male and female peaks along various different paths. But not one of these others had achieved the amazing walking power of the woman I first saw. Then finally I saw her once again, flying up the mountainside, lit by a ray of light from the heavens. It looked almost as if she was emitting her own aura. I tell you, I forgot all about my mission on Mount Nijo and just stood there gaping in astonishment."

"I see." Kyoko's voice was oddly expressionless. Taku had been assuming she'd show much more curiosity about all he'd seen. He felt oddly deflated and betrayed. Hanada hadn't shown the slightest interest in hearing what he had to say, while Kozo and Tamihiko had become strangely distant when he mentioned the name "Wayfarers' League." He'd been foolishly relying on Kyoko to react with interest, indeed with visible amazement, to his story.

Shall I tell her about what happened in front of Nintoku Tomb? he wondered. For some reason, he found himself reluctant to speak of it. He changed strategies.

"I'm guessing they were members of the Wayfarers' League," he said. "They'd have been performing some kind of religious austerity up on the mountain."

He'd thrown the name Wayfarers' League straight in her face, but there was no reaction. She only sat there sipping her oolong tea. Yet he felt there was a certain self-consciousness in this silence of hers.

Cho was the one who reacted. "What's that? What did you say about the Wayfarers?" he said, leaning forward.

"Nothing," Taku muttered vaguely. "Thanks for the meal."

Kyoko rose with a smile. "It was really delicious, thanks. I'll be back to hear more of your interesting talk, Cho."

"You're leaving?"

"You had a date with Hanada after this, didn't you Taku?" she reminded him.

"True. But…"

"Thanks so much for the meal. I'm just going to get a cab and drop in somewhere on the way home."

"I see." Taku watched as she stepped out and hailed a taxi just outside the door. He had the frustrated sense that she'd somehow given him the slip.

"Hey Taku, you don't know much about women, do you?" said Cho from behind the counter. "You shouldn't have talked so enthusiastic in front of her about the woman you saw in the mist, you know."

Really? Taku cocked his head in puzzlement. But it was because he liked Kyoko that he'd told her about the flying woman, he thought, confused.

"Bring along that Kongo sand later, hey? I'll tell you something interesting," Cho added, as if in an attempt to comfort him.

5

When Taku arrived at the place where he'd arranged to meet Hanada, he was disconcerted to discover that Shimafune, the managing director, was there as well. Shimafune! He was the head of business management, a man seen by those outside as the number one power broker of Meteor Publications. Above a slight frame, he had an oddly large face, deeply carved like that of some samurai movie star. His commanding presence made him seem larger than Hanada as they sat there together.

"So you're the famous 'walkman' Taku Hayami, eh?" he said, drawing in his chin.

"Actually, Mr. Shimafune, I used the term 'walking man,' not 'walkman,'" Hanada corrected him. He refilled Hanada's glass from the personal bottle of whiskey he kept on the shelf behind the bar.

Taku bowed his head politely. "Pleased to meet you," he said.

"I had some business to discuss with Hanada, that's why I'm here. You won't mind, I hope? I'll be off directly."

"Shall I wait over there until you finish?" offered Taku.

"No, we're done now. Sit down and have a drink."

The Rubicon was a men-only bar in Iikura Katamachi. Hanada came here often. It was an unfriendly place, but the bartenders and waiters were at any rate well trained. One pleasant thing was the lack of background music.

"Professor Nishihaga is pleased with that report of yours," Hanada said.

"Is he? I was anticipating he might not like it much, actually."

"Oh, no. He's a very obliging fellow. He gave me a bottle of scotch to give you, but of course you don't drink, do you, so I'll look after it for you."

"I don't need it, thanks."

"You're a teetotaler?" asked Shimafune in disbelief. "Seems like there's a lot of this recently, guys in the publishing and magazine trade who don't drink."

"Young fellows these days are very slack," remarked Hanada.

"Hey, come on," said Shimafune teasingly. "Wasn't it Taku here who came to your rescue that time when you were left naked and close to tears in some foreign land? A famous story."

Hanada gave a pained grin, and tipped some more whiskey noisily into his glass. Swiftly changing the subject, he said, "So, Taku, you say you met someone interesting on your fact-finding climb up Nijo. Tell us about it. Don't be shy. You don't mind, do you Mr. Shimafune?"

"No, no, go ahead."

Despite his promise of being about to leave, Shimafune seemed prepared to settle down and listen.

"Well, I'll briefly give you the story," said Taku, and he proceeded to tell them what he'd just told Kyoko. He talked about the flying woman of Mount Nijo, but chose to keep the events at the Nintoku Tomb to himself for the moment. Sure enough, however, neither Hanada nor Shimafune seemed particularly interested in what he had to relate.

"That's the story, eh?" Hanada folded his arms and nodded. "Well then, Taku, what's the plan, eh? Tell me that."

Shimafune too was gazing at him intently, an acute look in his eye.

"Well, I…" Taku mumbled. "This may sound childish, but I want to somehow get to see that woman again. I want to meet her, and talk to her. Or rather, I want to beg her to instruct me."

"And?"

"That's all."

Hanada stole a glance at Shimafune, a glance that seemed to seek for instructions. Shimafune's expression remained immobile.

"Mr. Hayami," Shimafune said after a moment. His voice was calm and mild. "What is your final objective?"

"Objective?"

"Your objective in meeting this woman."

"It's not enough simply to explain that my sole objective is to meet her?"

"I don't think your average person would be satisfied with just that."

"I see."

So what really is my final objective? he asked himself. The answer came—walking is the only thing that makes life worthwhile for me right now.

It wasn't always so, he thought. On the other hand, he'd always somehow liked it, ever since he was a kid. He remembered that time after he'd left high school, helping his father with the business and getting to know how to handle the little engines of fishing boats. He'd had a go at diesel engines when he was subcontracting for the Komatsu tractor company too.

His mechanical skills with engines and cars had stood him in good stead when he was bumming around Europe and the Middle East. He got a job with a Japanese TV crew over there to make a program, doubling as land cruiser driver and mechanic as well as assistant camera man, and on another occasion he'd been one of the personal mechanics for a Japanese car that was in a safari rally.

He had always liked motorbikes as well as four wheelers. Indeed he still liked them. But he liked walking still more.

When did this begin? he wondered. The walking. Yes, putting one foot after another and moving endlessly over the earth—when was it that this had begun to seem to him something meaningful in itself?

He recalled how he'd been dismissed by the team owner just before the safari rally began. There'd been a bit of trouble that led to his being expelled from the team. At that point, he'd exchanged four wheels for two legs and a pair of walking boots, and gone walking through the towns and villages and over the plains of Kenya and Tanzania. The people he'd met there had been his first teachers in the lessons of the amazing nature of walking.

The piece he'd sent to Hanada at Meteor Publications before he came back to Japan had been about that experience. His essay,

"The Stone Throwers," was written from the point of view of the black people who stood along the rally route throwing stones at the cars. He thought the piece was terrible, but it was accepted by *Life and Nature*, and the money helped pay for his ticket home. Of course it must have taken Hanada's support to get the piece printed, he realized.

Finally he spoke, as if to himself, eyes lowered. "I feel as if by walking I can become someone different. Or maybe it's that I can become my real self. What I mean is, I have the sense that I can become part of the earth, water, fire, wind, air, sea—all the nature that's given me life. Just occasionally, for a moment or two, I can achieve that feeling. And if I can go further yet, learn to walk more beautifully, perhaps those moments will become more frequent, till all my experiences moment to moment will be filled with that sensation. I'd be prepared to undergo any hardship if only I could get to that place. Actually, I've seriously thought of undertaking the Thousand-Day Walking Practice that the Hiei monks do."

The two men exchanged glances again. The whiskey in their glasses remained virtually untouched.

"So you're saying that's why you want to meet this woman again," said Shimafune.

"That's right."

"You don't care what it takes, right?"

"No."

"That's how important walking is, eh?" Hanada shook his head in wonderment. "Well, it takes all sorts. But young people these days have these abstract ideas about their purpose in life, quite unrealistic—maybe it's the lack of hardship in the way they're brought up. That woman on the *Tramping Quarterly* desk talks the same way."

Shimafune cut him off. Turning to Taku, he spoke earnestly. "You say 'Whatever it takes.' You wouldn't go back on that, would you?"

Taku thought for a moment. What if he was asked to kill someone, for instance?

"No, I wouldn't," he answered. He'd deal with whatever happened when it came time. He could always break his promise and say farewell to Japan if need be. There were lots of others who'd done this, scattered about the globe.

"Good. Next Friday I'll bring you two together in a hotel in Shiba. Okay with you, Hanada?"

"Well, now…" Hanada seemed to be hesitating about what to answer. He shot a slightly worried glance at Taku. "What do you think, Taku?"

"You really will arrange for me to meet her?"

"Just so long as you do as I ask without questions, that is."

"This is some kind of deal?"

"You might call it that." Shimafune gazed levelly at him.

Taku made his decision. "Yes, please," he said, and bowed. Well, he thought, I guess this is my fate when it comes down to it. The way I've lived, I could well have ended up seized at the Nepalese border and spent twenty years in one of those infamous Indian jails, after all. How many times over the years have I been prepared to throw it all away in the last resort?

"Just be sure you really take on board what it means that our managing director is lending you his support," Hanada said with unaccustomed sternness. "Once you agree to this, there's no backing out, you understand."

"I have no problem with that."

"Right." Hanada shut his mouth firmly.

Beside him, Shimafune spoke. "I'll take you there myself next week. Hanada, you'll make sure that business we spoke of is all set in motion by then, okay?"

"I'll start the preparations right away." Hanada nodded. "He'll be introduced to her at the Ikarino 60th anniversary party, right?"

Shimafune stood up. "Well then, I'll be off," he said. "I must say you're an unusual fellow, Mr Hayami. But I'm not surprised. Not surprised at all."

After Shimafune's departure, Taku and Hanada stayed and talked at the Rubicon a while longer. It seemed to Taku he hadn't had the chance for a real chat like this with Hanada in quite a while.

"So what's the Wayfarers' League?" Taku dropped the question out of the blue, during a lull in their conversation. "You know, don't you?"

"Mm."

"I understand it's been around a long time, but just what sort of group is it?"

"It's not that old, actually."

"But…"

"I think it was formed in the early nineteenth century," Hanada explained offhandedly. "It was named after a man who went by the name of Henro, or 'Wayfarer,' Katsuragi. Not his real name, of course. A pseudonym. In the early days various groups formed around him, it seems. He was a charismatic character, with a lot of followers in various quarters. The group was a kind of fan club centered around him, you might say. It presented itself to the world as the Wayfarers' Spiritual Improvement League. But who told you about it?"

"An old fellow I happened to run into at Taima Temple. He said he'd heard the name from his father when he was a kid."

"I see."

"Can I ask you something else?"

"Don't go asking too many searching questions please. This is a bar, remember."

"Sorry." But Taku went on. "What's the Tenmu Jinshin Fraternity?"

"Hmm. That's for you to find out. Just go along to the party at the hotel next week and you'll have one foot in the door for the answers to all your questions. Your skill will determine whether the door's opened for you or shut in your face." Hanada looked a little downcast. "Hey Taku, you're officially an orphan, aren't you?"

"How did you know that?"

"Well, I'm your guarantor, after all."

Taku nodded. It wasn't something he needed to keep secret, after all.

"Your real parents…" Hanada began, then he came to a halt. "No," he continued, "I'll keep that for another time. But anyway, we'll have to make clear arrangements about all this."

"You and Mr. Shimafune certainly seem to be amazingly well coordinated," Taku remarked.

"Sometimes we aren't, you know. I have to say I'm not in favor of what's happening on this occasion."

"What do you think he's going to ask of me in return for putting me in touch with that woman?"

"Hey now, are you starting to worry already?"

"No, just interested."

"Too late. You're on board now. All you can do is start rowing out to sea. Don't look back. 'Go for broke!' as the saying goes. That's my advice."

"Got it."

Hanada raised his glass. "Here's to it," he said. Taku lifted his glass of ginger ale in response.

6

S aera Maki's manager, Sosuke Seta, was a young man of
twenty-seven, a graduate from Tokyo University. It was rare
for someone to come out of Japan's top university and enter
the world of professional show business, and at some point he'd
been featured in a running newspaper column called "Close-up on
Today's Youth."

Not so long back, people would have looked rather askance at a
manager like him as belonging to the risqué world of nightlife, but
these days such people were respected for their important role in
promotion and planning.

On the day Seta had arranged to meet him, Taku arrived a little
early in front of the Porsche showroom in Iikura, and hung around
looking at the cars. Exactly five minutes before the agreed time,
Seta approached in the crosswalk.

"Sorry to keep you waiting." Unlike the casually dressed Taku,
he wore a carefully knotted necktie and polished shoes, and carried
a large-ish bag. "Do you like Porsches?" he asked as they walked
along together, headed for a nearby coffee shop where they could
talk.

"Well, I guess I find them interesting. They're pretty
different from the Benzes, even though they both come out
of Germany."

The two settled themselves at a table at the far end of the coffee
shop, which was fitted out in the Art Deco style that had recently
overrun the fashion world.

"I'll have this one please," Seta said to the waiter, pointing to
an item on the menu that said "Appletiser" with the carefully

appended explanation "from South Africa." "And make sure to chill the glass, please," he added.

Taku nodded. "Same for me, please."

"So anyway, back to cars," Seta began, avoiding a direct approach to the matter they were there to discuss. Taku guessed what he had to say wasn't very pleasant. "Just what would you say is the difference between the Benz and Porsche?"

"Oh, nothing very significant. But even when a new model Porsche comes out, the old ones still look just as good. In terms of design, I mean."

"And Benz?"

"Well, everyone thinks the older ones are better when a new one comes on the market, but give it six months or a year and the earlier models start to look strangely unsophisticated. So Benz people always end up wanting the latest."

"Personally, I don't go for German cars. Give me Italian cars any day. I'd love to have the chance to take a real Ferrari down the freeway at full throttle." The color rose in Seta's cheeks, and his eyes shone like an enthusiastic youth.

"Well, there's Shin's 400i you could try," said Taku.

"No, not that one. Sure, it's a Ferrari of course…"

Taku grinned to himself. It must be tough to be a Tokyo U. boy, he thought—smart, good at your job and engaging to boot. Where does that leave a high school drop-out like me? Still, the fact that this high achiever had gone into the small world of show business rather than fast-tracked in the usual way to the Finance Ministry or the National Police Agency suggested there was something a bit perverse about him. Call it the music industry or whatever, when it came down to it, it was just showbiz, after all. It was no place for a respectable young fellow like him.

"So anyway, what was the urgent business you wanted to talk about?" he asked as they sipped the liquid that had traveled all the way from South Africa to their table in Roppongi.

"Well, it's about Shin's Maserati."

"Something's wrong with it again, eh? For god's sake."

"Yes, when I took it out of the studio parking lot last night, the catch on the bonnet was snapped and it wouldn't stay closed properly.

The afternoon before, it had a flat rear tire, and I think the week before that, both indicators were broken."

"That's weird. An Italian car like that. It's not just your average car, after all."

"I just wonder if someone isn't sending some kind of subtle warning. Saying, I could cause a really elaborate accident if I wanted to, you know."

"Hmm." Taku thought for a moment, impressed by Seta's powers of perception. First the warnings. Professionals will always try to reach a compromise at the initial talking stage, after all. If what Seta said was true, things didn't look good.

"Any wrangles over business rights or mastering stuff or anything?"

"Not exactly, but there's another dispute."

"Really? I hadn't heard."

"It's a problem that's been going on for the last two or three years, actually."

"I wouldn't understand even if you explained it to me, you know."

"So who do you think might be doing this?"

"How on earth would I know?"

"My own feeling is, it's probably someone close."

"Close?"

"In other words, someone who's been backing Saera in some way till now."

"What way?"

"I can't say. But…" Seta smiled. "It's a scary thing to betray someone you're close to. But I'm her manager…"

Taku let him talk without interrupting.

"Your brother Shin has come right out and said she should quit a place that forces her into work she doesn't want to do."

"Has the studio been having financial problems recently?"

"No, not particularly. I guess it's profit margin stuff. I have a strong feeling there's pressure on the whole Ikarino Corporation."

"Hey there, hang on a minute." Taku held up a hand. "Isn't this whatsitsname group the one that's having an anniversary party next Friday?"

"That would be the Ikarino Corporation anniversary party. Saera's a special performer there. Why do you ask?"

"I'm supposed to go along to it too. The managing director of Meteor Publications is taking me."

"Right, Meteor Publications is part of the Ikarino Corporation too. Well, you're a hit with your *Outroads* pieces, Taku, and you've published some great work, so you can go along with your head held high. It's a different matter with us at Mu Music. It's only Saera who's keeping us going at the moment. The boss can't come on strong with Saera, and if we don't watch out we could be taken over by SALA Music. I get a feeling the guys at the head office actually want that to happen."

"What can I do to help?" Taku asked. He wasn't much good at the inner workings of the business world. But if it was a question of helping Saera and Shin'ichi, he'd do whatever he could.

"I don't want this problem out in the open for now," said Seta. "So could you say something to Shin'ichi yourself? Just ask him to hold off for a while on being so picky over what work Saera does. If it comes from Shin'ichi, she'll do as she's told."

"Hey, what this amounts to is that you're on the company's side, doesn't it?"

"No." Seta shook his head firmly. "I respect her as a true artist. Ideally, I'd like her to get away from being bound to the company treadmill, branch out on her own, and sing the songs that only she can sing, even if it means dropping to minor status. The latest stuff she's put out is a real problem. She's not just refusing to appear on TV—she won't have anything to do with publicity at all. I'm at my wit's end. My boss is giving me the evil eye too. But trust me. If she makes trouble now, we'll lose everything. I need her to be a bit more cooperative with them, just for a while. If you could get Shin'ichi to tell her this…"

"Well, if it's really in her best interests," Taku replied.

Seta nodded. "It is. And what's more, a whole new path is going to open for her any time now. I'm working on it behind the scenes. Mind you, it could be dangerous."

Then he revealed there was something else on his mind. "I really don't want Shinichi buying her any more foreign cars," he said.

"That's a matter for the two of them to decide between themselves, surely. It's not for me to voice an opinion."

"But I'm the one who has to drive them," Seta came back. "By the way, sorry for the trouble over that 4WD. I do apologize. I hope it wasn't too hard to repair."

"Not at all." Taku had an impulse to tell him how he'd managed to shift the transfer case control lever from where it was stuck in low range, but he resisted. He'd simply braced himself against the rear seat and given the thing a good hard kick with his right foot. The way to handle cars like that was with a bit of rough treatment, but in this country, the more expensive the car, the more everyone treated it with kid gloves.

"Thanks for going out of your way to meet me like this," Seta said with an engaging smile. "I'll see you again at Ikarino's party on Friday."

"Oh yeah, there was something I wanted to ask," Taku cut in as Seta was rising from the table, bill in hand. "Have you ever heard the name 'Wayfarers' League'?"

"Yes, I believe Saera's a Friend of the League, in fact."

"A friend?"

"Yes, stars like her get their names on the list of all manner of organizations you know, from the Communist Party to professional baseball clubs. She apparently pays the fees as a friendly gesture."

"Is it a recognized religious organization?"

"Well, I guess you could say so. It's not one of the big ones like Rotary or anything, but it's got a lot of prominent figures on its Friends list, so yes, you could think of it that way, though it's not quite the same thing."

Seta said nothing further. They parted with Taku's reminder to him to use only hired limousines for now. As he walked away, Taku found himself wondering just how much ambition was packed away inside that slight frame.

7

The next day, Taku went back to the Lotus, dangling from one hand a plastic bag containing some of the Kongo sand he'd bought at the foot of Mount Nijo. It was mid-afternoon, when the place was pretty sure to be empty of customers.

"Here you are, use this to sharpen your knives," he said as he handed it to Cho and settled down at the counter. "A plate of fried mustard greens and some tea please," he added.

"That all?"

"It's not really meal time."

"You Japanese are poor, you know. Poor in enjoyment of life." Cho began to fry the greens, swishing them lavishly about in the wok. "Lots of ways you can enjoy Kongo sand too."

"Like how?"

"Here you are. You can help yourself to the tea."

While Taku set in to eat, Cho placed the bag of Kongo sand on a space on the counter and sat down. Then he picked up a spoon, scooped out a spoonful of the sand, and put it on a plate. His deft hand spread the coppery sand neatly over the white ceramic.

"Kongo sand, right?" he said. "Used to be called Osaka sand in the old days. Comes from eroded and dissolved biotite andesite? If you breathe on it it'll fly into the air, so be careful."

From a cupboard he took out a big magnifying glass, like the ones palm-readers use, and set about a painstaking examination of the sand on the plate.

"Playing around with sand was a sophisticated pursuit in Japan back in the old days of Edo Period, you know. Take a fine lacquer tray and place a piece of paper on it, then carry it out to a sunny spot on the veranda with a toothpick and magnifying glass, and settle down on a cushion. Chase away the cats and the grandkids, then take a good long look at the sand in the sunlight. Cup of fine tea by your side. Then with the toothpick you go searching. Needs a leisurely attitude and a happy life. Take half a day to look in detail, and you finally think you see something shining blue there. Use the toothpick to draw a circle round it about the size of a *go* piece, and push the surrounding sand back from it. Then take your time and push one grain of red sand at a time out of the circle. Take your time, take your time. Important to do that. Keep it up all day, you'll find a shiny blue hexagonal bit of sand, less than half the size of a poppy seed. Wonderful, right? Give yourself a good stretch, and yell. 'Ah, I had such a good time today!' Yell, 'Hey, I got a sapphire!' That was how the high class big guys enjoyed themselves back then."

Cho put the plate under the fluorescent light, and slowly examined the sand.

"Can you see any sapphires?" asked Taku.

"No good. I don't have happiness in my heart right now, so can't do it."

"Stones must be pretty interesting."

"Here, I'll lend you. A really good book." From beneath the counter Cho drew out and placed in front of Taku a book titled *Field Guide to Mineral Exploration* by Hideaki Kusaka, published by Soshi Press. It seemed that the area under the counter was Cho's private library.

"Cho, when you said you don't have happiness right now, do you mean something's happened?"

"Yeah. For certain reasons, I've lived away from my country for a long time. You're lucky, Taku."

"I sometimes think I'm not happy either, actually."

"Yeah, I'll bet it's not always easy. You're a bit different from most people, after all. But just show me your face a moment."

Cho picked up his big loupe and examined Taku's face thoroughly.

"You finding any bits of sapphire there?" joked Taku.

"No sapphire, but it's interesting." Cho shook his head. "In your face right now there are two signs right next to each other, one a really happy one and one a really dangerous one. But your fate is heading straight for it, and there's no turning back now. Can't get out of it."

"Uh huh." Taku nodded. He didn't think Cho was any great shakes as a fortune teller, but what he said might not be far wrong.

It could well be that the appearance of that dark horse Shimafune heralded a big change in fate for him. It was undreamed-of good fortune to be able to meet the flying woman—but what could be lying in wait for him as a consequence?

Suddenly he heard again in his head the strange voice that had spoken as he lay in a half-dreaming daze with his back to Prince Otsu's grave on Nijo's male peak. It seemed to him that it was the voice from the mandala sermon he'd heard in Taima Temple, telling a different tale.

The words in his half dream had flowed through him like water, and almost nothing of them remained in his consciousness. But the fact that he had heard *something* then was still branded deep in him.

Reading about Taima Temple later in his guidebook, he'd learned that this mandala didn't belong to esoteric Buddhism, as is normally the case. It depicted the vision of Amida's Pure Land found in the *Kangyô Sutra*, a key text of the Pure Land sect. Taku was particularly struck by a quotation from the final words of the sutra—"The Buddha then returned to Vulture Peak, his holy feet treading the emptiness."

"His holy feet treading the emptiness." Taku had repeated the words to himself to memorize them.

If I could see with my own eyes the 'feet that tread the emptiness,' he thought, I'd consider my life more than worth having lived.

The flying woman's feet had indeed seemed to slide over the mist, and as she climbed away, straight up the shaft of light on the mountainside, music had almost seemed to play about her. No, he thought, I won't regret my decision no matter what work Shimafune produces for me. I don't mind staking my life for the sake of seeing a miracle. After all, think of all those people out there willing to stake their lives for the sake of much more boring things such as money and fame.

At this moment, a couple of young student-types strode into the restaurant. They were in the midst of a loud conversation as they entered.

"Hey there, give us two fried rice," the little fellow with curled hair said curtly. Then he returned to the conversation, his tone persistent. "But wouldn't you say it's a bit much to go bombing art museums? I mean, what's the point? Blowing up paintings and sculptures and stuff. They don't mean a thing to most people."

"But look…" began the other, a tall young man with a trendy squared-off haircut. "They may not mean anything to us, but the media's going to make a great fuss, right? That's what they were after, and it's pretty clever."

"But it's weird to just plant a bomb without making any demands. There must be lotsa guys in America that are crazy about bombs or something."

"Okay, but why did they go for the Asian section?"

"How the hell would I know?"

"What museum are you talking about?" Cho asked casually, tossing the fried rice around in his wok.

"The Museum of Fine Arts in Boston, it's called. Boston's in America, right?"

"I think so," said the other.

There was a short silence.

"Hey there," one of them suddenly cried to Cho. "Watch out!"

"Our fried rice is gonna burn!" yelled the other.

Cho stood motionless in front of the gas cooker, staring at the wok, deep in thought. Beads of sweat stood on his brow. There was something unnerving in his fixed gaze.

Taku eased his way out behind the two young men and left.

A chill wind was blowing, but the sky was clear. The Nintoku Tomb at midnight, Mount Nijo in the mist, the flying woman, and now the art museum in Boston. All seemed somehow like hallucinations.

From somewhere came the sound of a child's laughter. Rays of spring sunlight fell in stripes beyond the edge of the awnings along the shop-lined street. Taku set off, taking his first steps towards the wilderness that lay hidden within this deceptively peaceful world.

PART II

8

The hotel chosen for the Ikarino Corporation's 60th year celebration party had three famous large reception areas— the Azure Room main hall, the reception hall known as the Orchid Garden, and the Pearl Room entrance hall. It was claimed that together they could hold more than five thousand people.

When Taku Hayami first stepped into the Azure Room he faltered a moment with a slight dizziness.

It wasn't that he was dazzled by the splendor of the room, the work of famous architect and Academy of Arts member Ryunosuke Miyagishi. No matter how much money humans pour into the creation of magnificent spaces, they are only ever an imitation of nature, when it comes down to it. As someone once wrote, out in the desert at night every star in the sky, even down to the tiniest, shines with such power that it seems to shout aloud. Compared to such an overwhelming sight, the Azure Room was downright modest.

Nor was it the vast number of people crowded into the room that made Taku falter. Compared to the feverish throngs of Muslims he had once seen massing at Mecca, the heaving crowd in this room seemed no more than a peaceful scene at an amusement park.

No, what brought him to a halt now was the blatant energy of the business world that this crowd gave off. For a moment, deep in some recess of his mind, he saw an image of countless snakes tangled together to form links in a vast and writhing chain.

"You look like this isn't your sort of place, Hayami." Shimafune was beside him. Coming to himself, Taku turned and discovered that Hanada was there as well. Both wore double-breasted striped suits with glossy ties. Hanada kept running his finger under the collar round his thick neck, evidently horribly uncomfortable.

"I really don't think I needed to come, you know," he said to Shimafune dejectedly. "It's impossible to even greet people in such a crowd."

"Let's go further in." Making his way through the guests, Shimafune moved in towards the front of the hall, Hanada and Taku following.

The meal was buffet style, and everyone was standing about rubbing shoulders, talking and laughing loudly. Young women in kimono or western dress were threading through the crowd, offering drinks. Light poured down from the vast chandeliers that hung from the high ceiling. The raised stage at the front of the hall was crammed with congratulatory wreaths bearing large inscriptions of the donors' names. Some were the names of individuals, others were famous company names. Taku was astonished at their number.

A large sign proclaimed that this was a party in celebration of the sixty years of Ikarino Corporation Ltd. Below it stood three rows of signs bearing the names of the various subsidiary organizations that came under its umbrella. Some Taku recognized, but there were many he didn't. First were listed engineering and construction companies, followed by transport and communications, trading companies and department stores, real estate and leisure industry groups, hotels and food service industry names, and even banks and securities companies. Taku's eyes also took in the names of movie theaters, companies in the performance industry, golf clubs and sports plazas, hospitals and private schools. He tried counting. It came to precisely fifty. Every one of them bore the name "Ikarino," variously written.

"I don't see Meteor Publications anywhere," he murmured, surprised.

Shimafune grimaced briefly. "Media companies don't advertise the fact that they belong to the Ikarino Corporation," he explained. "So what you're seeing there is just the tip of the iceberg. I could list lots of broadcasting companies and regional newspapers whose shares are owned by Ikarino. And the overseas joint ventures and survey organizations, they keep their association hidden from the public as well."

"What sort of companies are those?"

"Private agencies, think tanks, human resources banks, security guard companies, that sort of thing."

"It's a whole empire, isn't it?"

"Yes, but the age of empires has passed," Hanada joked quietly. Shimafune gave a small smile.

What manner of man was Meido Ikarino, to have constructed such a vast business conglomerate in a single generation? Taku wondered. He must be like an armored war tank, with a huge surplus energy stored in his tremendous frame. But there also seemed something enigmatic about him. Yes, come to think of it, it was strange how rarely a photograph of this man Ikarino appeared in the media.

In the packed hall, only the area to the left of the stage was empty of people. Rows of chairs were set before a splendid golden screen. Taku saw numerous faces he recognized from media photographs. Evidently this was the throne room of the gods of the modern world.

Installing himself by a table to the right of the stage, Shimafune began to toss back whiskey. "So do you recognize any of the faces of those famous folk gathered over there?" he asked Taku, jerking his chin in their direction.

Then he set about explaining. "The fat guy on the left edge is Jisuke Nomi, the one next to him is Ryoji Mishima, then there's Sogoro Yako, Gen Aoe, Bunzo Sakurai, Yoshitaka Tanabe, Shun Maihara, Sakonji Miyagishi—they're all big players in the finance world. Then there's the ex-prime minister Toshige Murata, and round him are guys from politics and the bureaucracy. I can see some congressmen scampering about too. But it's just occurred to me, Hanada—there doesn't seem to be any sign of Secretary General Hariya."

"I think that's him over there talking to Gojo, the head of Tokeiren." Hanada, with nothing stronger than a glass of juice in his hand for once, was gazing around the room with an alert and observant eye.

"The pianist Lucia Mizumori's here too. And the Russian ambassador. Then there're all the cultural folks, and the journalists. There'd be some faces you'd recognize too, Hayami, no?"

"I recognize almost no one."

"This fellow's Rip van Winkle," Hanada cut in from beside them.

"But at least you must know the beautiful actress over there being charming to the bunch of old fogeys. Surely."

"Mm." He did recognize the movie star who had run away with all the film prizes last year. He remembered seeing a photo of her in the magazine with the picture of the Nintoku Tomb, arriving at the Cannes Film Festival dressed in kimono.

"Well, well, so we're graced with the presence of the Great Master Sekimori," Hanada broke in, a certain irony in his tone. A little old pink-faced man was making his smiling way through the midst of the throng towards the gold screen, left hand thrust in his coat pocket. The crowd automatically parted before him, and all eyes turned to him with a mixture of reverence and curiosity. This was Juken Sekimori, the elder statesman of the political world and subject of much recent rumor. He was unobtrusively surrounded by a number of well-built men who had the air of security police.

"You know who he is, don't you?" said Hanada, nudging Taku's side with an elbow. "Some of the papers were writing him off as a ghost from the past, but he's far from that. That old fellow probably plans to manipulate the political world till he's reached a hundred."

"So where is the emperor of Ikarino?" Taku asked. He'd been wondering this for some time.

"The boss will show himself any moment now. He's not fond of big noisy gatherings. My guess is he's holed up in the special guest room in the hotel listening to classical music right now."

"Classical music?"

"That's right. He particularly likes Bartok, Poulenc, that sort of thing. I must admit when I first heard it myself I thought that this story was a bit over the top, even given the campaign to raise his image as head of Ikarino. But no…"

"It's true, he's a music lover," Shimafune chimed in. "It's a well-known fact in Europe's social circles that the secret patron of the Varna Music Festival is Monsieur Ikarino. Our own company's set to start producing a classical music magazine very soon. The boss's idea, you understand."

"Well, well."

"It's not just music either. He's taking a great interest in art recently too. Apparently he's devoted to the conservation and study of historical items of artistic cultural heritage. He was a fan of Heinrich Schliemann in his youth, you see."

Something registered briefly deep in Taku's brain, like a faint passing comet.

Schliemann? he thought. This despot who rules an industrial empire was a fan of his?

"You're surprised?" said Shimafune, noticing his expression.

"No." Taku shook his head. "Well, I guess I was a bit surprised to hear that he has a taste for classical music, but I can kind of understand the Schliemann connection. When I was working in Greece I heard a story about him from a friend. He told me that after Schliemann had made his money in the business world, he changed tack and set out to excavate ancient Greek ruins."

A caviar-loaded cracker poised in his hand, Hanada nodded, intrigued.

"Well, apparently," Taku went on, "There was another dark side to the tale of how Schliemann had amassed his fortunes, besides the one he talked about himself. My Greek friend told me this Schliemann had been in cahoots with a politician in what was then the Czarist Russian government, and had made a killing on black market trading in the Middle East. And there were lots of other suspicious rumors about how he made his money, too."

"Here's the boss," Hanada said suddenly, breaking in on Taku's tale.

Taku watched across the wall of people in front of him as an old man with beautiful silver hair approached, smiling.

He'd heard that Meido Ikarino was well over seventy, but his gait was still remarkably firm. The body encased in the silver silk suit was taut as a sportsman's, the tanned skin seemed to glow. He would be close to six feet tall, taller than anyone around him, and his features were refined. All that might give away his age was the row of overly white teeth, surely false. He was an eminently stylish older gentleman with an intellectual air.

Yet though his expression was mild, an unmistakably fierce willpower was manifest in the deep double cleft of the chin.

He moved through the crowd, acknowledging this person and that, flanked by two steely-eyed men. Even from where he stood Taku could sense the tingle of tension that emanated from their bodies.

"That's the boss of the Ikarino Corporation. Take a good look, and remember what you see," said Shimafune. "Right, so it looks like all the players are assembled for the evening."

"But one person still doesn't seem to be here," remarked Hanada dubiously, craning to peer about him. "The person who's the real point, the one Taku has been on tenterhooks to see all this time."

"Someone is bound to come along from the Fraternity—a representative at least, even if not the leader. Actually, the interest really lies in who'll turn up as acting leader, I'd say."

Listening to their conversation with half an ear, Taku was carefully scanning the hall. Shimafune had promised to introduce him to the flying woman at this party, but no one resembling her could be seen. Would she even come, in fact?

At length, the commemoration ceremony began. The MC was Akira Tagoto, a television newscaster who had a big following among married women.

First came a small documentary film presenting the various companies affiliated with the Ikarino Corporation. This was followed by the usual formal toasts to guests. As Sekimori finally took the stage, Shimafune gave Taku a light tap on the shoulder.

His eyes indicated the door to his right. Taku turned, and saw there a tall woman in a long black dress. Her hair was cropped short. Her mouth was a line carved deep as if by a knife. Beneath thick brows, the eyes brimmed like dark lakes. It was the flying woman he'd brushed past that day on the ridge of Mount Nijo.

"It's her," he said. His voice was husky. When he first saw her on the mountain, he'd mistaken her for a man, and later, under the street lights at the Nintoku Tomb, she seemed a youth. Now, however, standing there unadorned, with only a black cloth wrapped about her like a sari, the flying woman was unmistakably a beautiful lady.

The soft, glistening dress revealed the contours of her body more clearly than if she had been naked.

"So Tenro isn't coming, it seems," murmured Hanada.

"In which case, she's…"

"That's what it must mean, yes."

Shimafune put his glass down on a side table, folded his arms and sighed. Taku was suddenly aware of men here and there in the crowd turning penetrating gazes in her direction.

Over one arm she held what looked like a tightly folded shawl. Her gaze emanated a coolness that seemed to reject the happy energy of the crowd before her. One of the guests went over and greeted her. She smiled wordlessly, and bowed her head in response.

Sekitori's long and rather inaudible speech ended, to a burst of applause. Waving a hand in response to the MC's extravagant words of thanks, the old man descended from the stage. This was followed by a reading of congratulatory messages sent by various kingpins of the finance world, top-level politicians, American senators, a German conductor, and others. To round things off the MC, in a voice strangely charged with mystery, called on the final speaker.

"We were hoping to hear now from Tenro Katsuragi, dear friend of the head of our Ikarino Corporation, who has been its warmest, though at times quite critical, supporter through the corporation's sixty years of existence. However, I regret to say that Mr. Katsuragi is indisposed and couldn't come today."

As the MC paused to draw breath, there was a small but unmistakable voiceless stirring in the assembled crowd. Hanada and Shimafune looked at each other, and seemed to exchange a subtle nod. The MC raised his voice and continued.

"We sincerely hope that Mr. Katsuragi, who has now reached a venerable age, will recover as soon as possible, but we are delighted to welcome in his stead his daughter, Ai Katsuragi, who has just arrived. Ms. Katsuragi, we would be deeply grateful if you could grace this celebratory occasion with a few words. Ms. Katsuragi is a beauty reputed to be the absolute apple of her father's doting eye. Please give her a big hand, everyone!"

Spontaneous applause erupted from the guests, by now thoroughly tired of the formulaic speeches of the old and famous.

Shimafune and Hanada both clapped enthusiastically. Taku ducked around the back of the foreigner standing in front of him and positioned himself so he had a clear view of the stage.

With a small bow to the head of the Ikarino Corporation seated before his gold screen, she stepped to the microphone. The soft cloth of her skirt swayed as she walked, revealing the rich swell of her thighs beneath. Taku found it suddenly difficult to breathe. Even in high heels, her walk had the silky grace of a wild animal's. Dazed, he stood gazing up at her before the microphone.

There she stood on the stage, bathed in the strong light of the Azure Room. The assembled crowd grew momentarily hushed. Slowly, she unfolded the cloth that was draped over one shoulder, and with an elegant gesture put it on, while the audience watched raptly.

That coat of theirs!

Taku recalled the traditional *happi* the whole group had been wearing at the gathering before the Nintoku Tomb, which bore the words "Company of Fifty-Five" and "Tenmu Jinshin Group." The rather short dark indigo coat worked peculiarly well with her long black dress, and didn't look at all odd. Indeed the combination was far more compellingly lovely than the magnificent kimonos worn by some of the women in the audience.

"What's she up to?" muttered Shimafune. "This won't just be the usual speech."

Now in her *happi*, she drew herself up and faced the audience, placed her hands politely on her thighs and gave a deep bow. Then, in a calm voice, she began to speak.

"I am here today not as the daughter of Katsuragi Tenro but as representative of the head of the religious organization known as the Tenmu Jinshin Group. I would ask you please to keep this in mind as I speak."

The vibrant contralto voice came flooding out from the numerous speakers placed about the hall. It had a purity suggestive of a voice from the distant heavens.

"Before I go on, I would like just to correct a few things that the MC said. First, our head Mr. Katsuragi is not indisposed. He chose for his own reasons not to be present today but to send me in his place. Nor does my father dote on me as described. In fact, he has raised me with far more strictness than he treats others in the Fraternity, and without regard for the fact that I happen to be a woman. Having set these matters straight, I will now read the message sent by him."

The MC, a popular man, stood at the edge of the stage with eyes fixed on the ceiling, making no attempt to hide his discomfort. Ai closed her eyes for a moment and was silent, then began to speak without a text, apparently reciting by heart.

"I wish to offer my warm congratulations to Mr. Meido Ikarino, member in perpetuity of our Wayfarers' Spiritual Improvement League, on the occasion of his group's sixtieth anniversary, and to wish it prosperity for the future. Our Wayfarers' League was established to honor the philosophy and the person of its first leader, Henro Katsuragi. Mr. Ikarino was a direct disciple of Henro Katsuragi, who placed great faith in him as a man of exceptional ability. Through his financial activities, Mr. Ikarino has for the past sixty years enacted in the business world the beliefs and philosophy of his teacher Henro, thereby achieving his present greatness."

Taku was aware that Meido Ikarino, sitting with eyes closed before his gold screen listening to the speech, was fiercely clenching and unclenching his hands on his knees.

The voice went on. She was reciting every word perfectly, without notes of any kind. Noticing Taku's puzzled look, Hanada quickly whispered in his ear, "Communications in the Fraternity are pretty much done by word of mouth only. They have quite terrifying powers of recall. It's one of the things they learn."

Taku nodded, then turned his full attention back to the voice coming over the loud speaker.

"I believe I am right to claim that the Ikarino Corporation owes its success and prosperity to the manner in which Mr. Ikarino has applied the beliefs of our Wayfarers' League founder Henro Katsuragi to the realm of business. Furthermore, it is my belief that we must all pay due regard to Henro's ideas and practice, place them firmly in our hearts, and live in accord with them. These beliefs are: One, helping one another, and Two, living in harmony with nature. The spirit of mutual aid and sharing he called

Isshin Mushi, which translates as 'Single Heart No Self.' His concept *Issho Fuju*, meaning 'Living in No Fixed Place,' refers to the ideal of calling the natural world one's true home. Indeed our teacher lived his more than eighty years of life helping suffering friends, loving the natural world, and wandering homeless among the mountains.

"The Ikarino Corporation began its life with recycling in the inner city, and it is thanks to the secret help of Henro that it has evolved down the years, overcoming numerous challenges to attain its present prosperity. This is affirmed by the due reverence with which Mr. Ikarino has always treated his teacher and mentor."

Meido Ikarino's hands were rapidly clasping and unclasping each other by now. He nodded as if deeply moved by what he heard, but Taku could see the blood vessels standing out on his forehead below the elegantly coiffed silver hair.

"I wish to take the opportunity of this occasion to urge everyone to consider anew the founding philosophy of the Wayfarers' League. Those who forget the teaching of mutual help and aid for our weaker fellow humans in their suffering lose the right to be counted among the members of the Wayfarers' League. To no longer love the natural world and live as a friend to nature is to forego the status of Henro's disciple.

"I will speak clearly. It seems to me that among the Wayfarers' League members today there are those who have left the path and turned their back on the teaching of our master. I believe there are companies that, under the banner of mutual aid, form associations whose primary aim is profit, and which in the name of development of the natural world involve themselves in projects that destroy our irreplaceable natural environment. I will refrain from giving concrete examples here. But I would ask you, those gathered here in the audience today and the representatives of those companies under the umbrella of the Ikarino Corporation which boasts of sixty glorious years of business, to recall the fact that our teacher Henro did not speak of mutual aid simply as a means to achieve commercial greatness. At the heart of this concept is individual autonomy, not the desire for aid from the nation or the government.

"Henro explicitly condemned associations that sought to profit from the political world and the bureaucracy. His founding principle was, rather, the spirit of mutual aid for friends and comrades. The Wayfarers' League could not exist without continued belief in the principles of harmony with nature and mutual help. In conclusion, let me reiterate. Projects such as the Lake Biwa Comprehensive Development Scheme, the Kiso Mount Ontake Tourist Development, the Amazonas Reclamation and Development Project, the Philippine Laguna de Bay Infill Reclamation Scheme, the Mount Nijo Foothills New Town Project..."

The MC was approaching, mike in hand, his face tense.

"I'm sorry to interrupt you, but I'm afraid our program timing means that..."

"Get back!" The low but penetrating words came from in front of the gold screen. Meido Ikarino waved a defiant hand at the MC. Still seated, he went on in a clear voice, "It's most impolite to interrupt her in the middle of this important speech. Let's hear her through."

Everyone in the hushed Azure Room heard what he said. He smiled and bowed to Ai. "Please, mademoiselle, do continue."

Taku saw a sudden flush rise in her dark skin. Closing her eyes again, she went on.

"The life-giving mountains, the streams that bless us with their water, the forests, the lakes, the very seas and sky—all this is in dire danger of destruction in our country. What would he say if our teacher Henro were here today? At the very least, one who calls himself a member of the Wayfarers' League should cease from involving himself in development projects that destroy our precious natural environment. My earnest hope is that the Ikarino Corporation will use this occasion of its sixtieth anniversary to return to its early principles, and will commit its future development to the spirit of the Wayfarers' League.

"I am well aware of my disrespect in speaking like this. However, it is out of a deep regard for the talents and character of Mr. Ikarino, the man whom Henro Sensei so loved and trusted, that I have dared to speak harsh words today. These words must stand in the stead of a celebratory speech.

"Signed Tenro Katsuragi, Second Head of the Tenmu Jinshin Group. Spoken on his behalf by Ai Katsuragi."

She raised her eyes and calmly surveyed the room, then bowed and stepped from the stage. As she passed the gold screen, Ikarino put out a hand to shake hers, but she studiously ignored him and continued walking. A momentary rage shadowed his calm profile, but he instantly resumed his smile.

The MC made a few shrill and desperate jokes, and a popular sumo wrestler who had just become grand champion took the stage. Released from its tension, the audience suddenly broke into chatter. In the midst of the stir, Taku noticed clusters of men whispering urgently together, their faces so close they almost touched.

"Wow, that Tenro doesn't pull any punches," muttered Shimafune, standing there with arms folded. "This amounts to a clear declaration of war on the Ikarino Corporation, I'd say."

"So it's full-scale warfare?" Hanada asked softly. "In that case, I wonder if this is the right moment to bring Taku and Ai together. She was looking pretty tense…"

"Hmm. I wasn't anticipating this would happen today, I must admit."

"If there's a problem, that's okay," said Taku. "I'll take myself off to this Tenmu Jinshin Fraternity or whatever it's called and ask to join. I imagine if I become a member I'll be able to meet the woman who's acting head."

"Well, well, it seems Mr. Hayami here has been deeply struck by Ms. Ai's speech," said Shimafune, slapping Hanada's shoulder with a delighted laugh. "Here you are, Hanada, a perfect example of the saying, 'Action trumps planning.'"

"Her name is Ai Katsuragi, right?" Taku asked earnestly.

"That's right. It's written with the character for 'sorrow' or 'pity.' Though as you can see, steel is a more appropriate word than sorrow, in her case."

Hanada lit a cigarette. "One of the Fraternity's retreats is down in the south of the Izu Peninsula, near Basara Pass in the Kamo district. It's called a retreat, but actually it's an old farm house of sorts. Mind you, they have about five study camps around the country, from Shibetsu up in Hokkaido down to Mount Hiko in

Kyushu, but I don't know much about them. Your father may be able to tell you more."

"Why do you think my father would know? He's a motor mechanic in backroads Fukui."

Hanada tapped his ash onto the side of a plate of hors d'oeuvres, while Shimafune sent him an accusing glare.

"Your father has long had a *connection* with the Fraternity, Taku. Of course he's only a Friend, so he's not much aware of recent developments on the inside."

Taku was silent. He was feeling suddenly angry at just how much he didn't know. He realized now that he'd never bothered to find out about anything around him. He knew even less about himself than he knew about foreign countries, people, and the desert. In fact, he suspected, he'd gone out of his way not to know. It may well be that something inside him was secretly reluctant to approach the question of his real family and all that had happened from his birth up until he was adopted by the Hayamis. He was suddenly assailed by an oppressive sensation, a feeling similar to the sad melancholy that had occasionally come over him in childhood.

"Mr. Hayami," came a voice from behind him. He turned to find a slim young man in a white suit standing there, smiling genially. It was Sosuke Seta, Saera's manager. He made an affable bow to Shimafune and Hanada. "I've been looking for you," he said to Taku.

"She's singing tonight, right?"

"Yes. Actually, I just wanted to have a word with you on the subject." Seta took his sleeve and drew him aside, then whispered urgently in his ear, "Sorry, but would you mind coming up to her room?"

"Shin'ichi's not answering the phone again, eh?" Taku asked, but Seta shook his head.

"No, it's not that. I'd appreciate it if you could talk to her for me. She seems to be pretty open to what you say. She won't listen to a word from me."

"That's not true, you know. If she won't listen to her own manager, she certainly wouldn't listen to anything I had to say."

"Well, please just come along and try." Seta's expression was grim. There was obviously some trouble brewing.

"Right. Where's the room?"

"I'll take you."

Explaining to Hanada that he was just going off for a moment to talk to a friend, Taku made his way out of the hall with Seta.

9

Taku followed Seta round to a separate part of the hotel reserved for the use of paying guests. They made their way through deserted corridors and at length arrived at the door of the special fifth floor room set aside for Saera Maki. Seta rang the bell. There was the sound of the chain being released, and the door opened to reveal a pleasant and spacious suite, with a splendid bunch of colored lilies arrayed in a vase before the mirror.

"So you've brought in Taku for support," said Saera coldly, addressing Seta. She was dressed in a white stage dress, and long shimmering earrings dangled from her ears. Her face was caked in thick makeup and her hair was piled on her head in a striking arrangement. The effect was impressively beautiful, though it was a beauty unlike that of the everyday relaxed Saera he saw at home. "Taku, for all I respect you, I'd ask you not to go sticking your nose into matters of business," she went on. Her trembling hand attempted to put a match to a cigarette.

"Right then, I'll be off. I'll look forward to hearing you sing out there."

Taku had his hand on the door when Saera said quickly behind him, "I'm sorry, Taku. I think I'm a bit crazy right now. I really don't know what to do."

"What's happened?" Taku asked, turning to sit down. Saera had finally managed to light her cigarette, but she now stubbed it out forcefully and continued to thrust it fiercely into the ash tray till it stood on end.

"Let me explain, okay, Miss Maki?" said Seta in a conciliatory tone. Standing by the window with her back to them, Saera nodded.

"Saera is on the program to sing three numbers at the gathering today, but there's been a last-minute request from Mr. Kozushima to sing a duet with her."

Taku knew the name of Gosuke Kozushima. He was what could be called a "media babe" politician, a-man-of-the-people type who always grabbed all the attention in television debates with his abrasive swagger. He was a conservative party congressman, the leader of a political faction of around ten members, who had been a minister in his time and was rumored to have strong connections with the Ikarino Corporation.

"If it's part of the post-party entertainment, surely he can sing by himself," Saera intervened.

Taku privately agreed. But he could see that for Seta this was a situation in which he simply couldn't refuse the request. "The congressman wants to sing a duet, eh?" he said. "With Saera?"

"Yes. And the thing is, he's a passionate longtime fan of hers."

"So what does he want to sing?"

"The 'Geisha Waltz,' he says."

"The 'Geisha Waltz'?" Taku burst into laughter. "Come on, that's gotta be a joke. If it was the 'Tennessee Waltz' it might make sense."

"No, he means it, that's the problem." Seta spread his hands and stood there hunched.

"Well I'm not singing it." Saera's tone was firm. "It's not that I'm objecting because I don't like the 'Geisha Waltz.' I'm not putting on airs just because I'm a more modern kind of singer, you know. After all, I sing traditional pop. But I'm just not the kind who can do a skillful job of that kind of entertainment stuff on stage, post-party show or not. I don't have it in me. You know that, Seta."

"So you can't turn him down, Seta?" Taku asked.

"It's just that that mobster Ryuzaki from the Konryu gang is involved in this. He's the one who came up with it."

"You mean those guys have got their fingers in this pie as well?"

Before Seta could reply, there was a knock on the door. He rose and went to open it. Then he seemed to choke. "Ah, Mr. Ryuzaki…"

"Sorry to bother you like this. I apologize for the unreasonable request. I've come to pay my respects to the lady in question."

The visitor spoke with disconcerting politeness. His voice was unpleasant.

"Ah, thank you, yes."

"May I come in?"

"Please," said Seta. Saera sent Taku an urgent look signaling that he should leave, and Taku slid swiftly into the adjoining bedroom as the man entered. Fearing he would make a noise if he closed the door, he left it open and instead hid in the shadows behind the far wall closet.

"Miss Maki, is it?" Ryuzaki's voice was gentle, but something in it betrayed the fact that he wasn't the usual type of man.

"Yes, I'm Saera Maki."

"My name is Ryuzaki. I do apologize for the unreasonable request I've made. It's the earnest desire of Mr. Kozushima, you see. I'm sure you have your position as a professional to consider, but please do us the honor of joining us…"

"Actually, Mr. Ryuzaki…" Seta began, but Ryuzaki's laugh cut him off.

"No, no, don't say a word. I stood there in front of Mr. Kozushima and boldly undertook to organize this, so you must simply accept the offer with good grace or I'll be in a real fix. It's a question of the gang not losing face, see."

A moment later, Taku heard something being placed on the table. "Here," came Ryuzaki's voice. "A small token. No pesky income tax forms involved, you understand. Please tuck it away in your wallet."

"Your name is Mr. Ryuzaki, you say?" Saera's voice trembled slightly. "This is most impertinent of me, but please excuse me. I'm no good at this sort of thing. The arrangement is that I am to sing three songs at this event, of my own choosing. In return, I've agreed to do it without a commercial fee. So please excuse me from performing a duet with Mr Kozushima."

"We have a problem here." Ryuzaki's voice was low. "Actually, there's just been a very strange guest at the gathering down there who spoiled the splendid celebrations by making a quite absurd speech. Everyone's feeling most put out. So Mr. Kozushima has come up with the wonderfully considerate plan to get things swinging again by performing a really cool, relaxed-style duet with this fabulously beautiful singer, see? Now, look, I'm bowing my head and begging you, aren't I?"

Saera didn't answer. Seta too was silent. The air twanged with a tense silence. The hum of the air conditioner was suddenly disturbingly loud.

"I'm sorry!" Saera cried. Taku leant forward and peered into the other room. A large man in a well-made black suit stood there. There was no visible scar on his cheek, nor any sign of the missing tip of the little finger characteristic of a Japanese yakuza. His hair was nicely combed, his shoes were glossy polished black, and a white silk tie was knotted tight at his neck. At a glance, he seemed to belong to a world somewhere between the solid citizen's and the entertainment underworld, perhaps that of the restaurant owner or proprietor of a downtown rental building. His eyes were narrow, and a huge gold ring glinted on his finger.

On the table lay a white envelope, thick enough to be holding perhaps 100 ten-thousand-yen notes. As payment for indulging the exhibitionism of Congressman Kozushima and livening up the Ikarino Corporation party, this was cheap money. The cash must have come from the coffers of this Konryu gang or whatever its name was.

"Do forgive me, Mr. Ryuzaki." He could see Saera now. She had knelt formally at the big man's feet in her long dress. Her hands were placed before her on the blue carpet, and she was gazing up at him with eyes that seemed about to overflow with tears. Her voice was hoarse. "I humbly beg you on bended knees," she said, "Please overlook my wilfullness this once. I implore you."

Her shimmering earrings swayed. Kneeling there, she looked like a swan brought to earth. Taku felt something tighten in his breast at the sight. Averting his eyes, he swallowed down the surge of emotion.

"You're making things very difficult." Something had changed in Ryuzaki's tone. Flinging back the ends of his coat, he thrust his hands into his trouser pockets and stood there gazing down at Saera. His narrow eyes narrowed further till they became slits a knife could have carved in his face. He clicked his tongue softly.

His hitherto calm demeanor was now replaced by gestures that clearly spoke of his role as professional yakuza in the world of criminal violence.

"Listen, I ain't some kid messenger you can push around." He lifted a glossily shod foot, pushed the pointy tip of his shoe under Saera's chin as she knelt before him with bowed head, and slowly raised her face. "And such a classy mug here, eh? I don't know if you're pullin' the wool over everyone's eyes out there or not, but I can tell you, lady, it don't work with us. So you think you're in a position to call the shots, do you? Talkin' big about how you don't wanna sing the 'Geisha Waltz' with the congressman who's always so kind to us. Eh?"

"Mr. Ryuzaki…" Seta cut in. No sooner had he begun than Ryuzaki's hand shot out and slapped his face in a swift gesture that bent his wrist back with the impact. There was a dull thwack, and blood began to flow from Seta's cut lip.

"Stay out of this! Who said you could speak? Or are you telling me you're prepared to settle this business?"

Seta drew out his handkerchief and applied it to his mouth. "Yes," he replied in an unexpectedly calm voice. "I would indeed like to 'settle this business,' if I may. In exchange for putting this idea of the duet with Mr. Kozushima behind us."

He sounded strangely impassive. Taku was impressed to witness another side to this elite young Tokyo University graduate.

Apparently intrigued, Ryuzaki poked a finger into his forehead. "Well, well. So what kind of settlement are you proposing, hey? I'll tell you right now, money won't do the trick."

"I will sever my little finger," replied Seta. "I understand that this is an accepted way of settling problems in your world, Mr. Ryuzaki."

"You'll sever your little finger?" Ryuzaki shook his head in amazement. "You mean to tell me you still see us in that old-fashioned way, huh? This isn't the sort of thing you can get out of with a dirty little finger or two, you know. We've got a situation here we can only solve by her singin' a duet. You're ten years too young to go acting the cool guy like this, pup. Get it? Now pull yer neck in."

As he spoke, Ryuzaki placed the glossy toe of his shoe over Saera's white fingers on the carpet. "How's this? Does it hurt, eh?" he asked, bringing his weight slowly down on them.

"Yes!"

"If you can still answer it's not bad enough." He thrust his weight into the foot. Saera grimaced in pain, and tears slid down her cheeks. Watching, Taku felt his blood vessels swell close to bursting point. "Let me tell you somethin'. You're in no position to go turning down the offer to sing the 'Geisha Waltz' when the Konryu gang comes politely requesting like this. Just remember what you were doin' back in Sapporo twenty years ago, lady. And if you've forgotten, I'll remind you. Who was it took you up and put you in a position to go struttin' about the world in your fancy gear actin' the celebrity singer, hey? Who? Think of those porno videos and erotic tapes. No, you're in no position to turn down an offer from the Konryu gang, my girl. You know what I'm talkin' about well enough, don't you, eh?"

Saera didn't reply. Ryuzaki pressed a little more heavily with the toe of his shoe, now pushing against Saera's white fingers until they bent far back. She gave a cry. "That hurts!"

"How about it, eh?"

"I won't!" Saera forced the words from between clenched teeth. "I'd rather die!"

"So. You won't, eh?" Ryuzaki's tone sounded almost exultant. "Right. I get it. Fine, fine. You can do as you like." He removed his shoe from Saera's fingers. "Now that it's clear you're lacking in all gratitude and sense of duty, I have other ideas. You don't wanna sing a duet with Mr. Kozushima? Okay, you don't have to. Instead I'll make that pimp of yours—what his name? Ah yes, Shin'ichi Hayami—I'll make him suffer so he won't be answering your calls any more. That okay by you?"

"What are you going to do to Shin?!" cried Saera.

Ryuzaki gave a dry chuckle. "Hmm. Maybe pour a bit of acid into those ears of his so he can't hear the telephone ring. I understand it's hard to damage only the ear drum, but we have a guy who specializes in this. Right this minute a young one of ours has grabbed him and he's all set to go, I'd say."

"It's a lie. You can't change my mind with threats."

"So you don't believe it, eh?" Ryuzaki picked up the telephone from the side table, and placed it before Saera. "Your house is in Yokohama, right?"

He dialed 0, then the 045 of Yokohama, then pulled a piece of paper out of his pocket and dialed Shin'ichi's private number.

"Hey there, that you, Yuji? Ryuzaki here," he said in an insolent tone. "You lookin' after the feller there okay? You be kind to him, now. No smashin' his teeth or anything. The name's Shin'ichi. Put him on a second, will ya?"

"You terrible people!" It was a voice Taku had never heard from Saera before. She flung herself at the telephone Ryuzaki held out to her, and shrieked, "Shin!"

"Dear, oh dear." Ryuzaki grinned wryly and settled back onto the sofa by the wall. Then he lifted his foot and began to meticulously polish the shoe that had been crushing Saera's fingers.

"Don't resist them, Shin!" sobbed Saera. "Please, just wait calmly. I'll sort it out at this end right now. Okay? Got it?"

Well, thought Taku, This looks like the closing scene of a successful plan. This fuss over the duet is just a bit of distracting mischief-making. I'd say there's a bigger trap lurking behind all this. That much is pretty clear from the fact that these guys were already waiting round at Shin'ichi's place. There's obviously some reason why they plan to intimidate Saera and Seta and Shin'ichi. Which means that if she'd given in, she'd certainly have been dragged deeper into difficulties. And not just her, but Shin too.

Taku unclenched his fists, and breathed deeply to relax his tense muscles.

He found himself recalling the summer night back when he was in high school, when Shin'ichi had come home with a ripped ear dangling like a dog's after being beaten up by the bar owner in Awara. This image was followed by that of his own face, swollen to the size of a watermelon after being roughed up in Tehran by the secret police for causing trouble, and the time he'd fled through Kalashnikov strafing on a gravel plain in Afghanistan.

He crept to the door and gazed at the well-dressed man who sat there on the sofa in the elegant suite, thoughtfully polishing his already mirror-bright shoe, the shoe that had recently crushed Saera's fingers. A sudden rage, cold and sharp as a blade, seethed up in him.

I'll get this guy!

Silently, he moved to the bathroom. He took the cloth bathmat from the floor, rolled it tightly, and wet it. Then he twisted the big hotel bath towel tightly around it, and doused it all thoroughly in water.

He ripped the drier cord from its socket, and set to work to tie it swiftly around the sodden rod he'd made. Finally, he dunked it all in water once more, and experimentally flicked it about. It was so powerful and heavy that he had difficulty wielding it with one hand.

Right, this'll do! he thought.

A single roll of wet towel packs a weight of several kilograms, and Taku had learned how to make such a weapon from a drug dealer he got to know in Kabul, who'd recommended it as the best way to kill a man if you have to. He'd maintained it was a better weapon for the job than a rubber hose filled with lead or a tied-off shirt sleeve packed with sand. You wet the bath towel, twist it tight, double it up and push it into a sturdy knee-length sock.

"It doesn't leave a mark when you hit someone," he'd said. " A single blow to the base of the neck, then you keep hitting his head till it goes floppy. After that you wipe the corpse's face with the towel, put on the sock and go home. You've got a nice cold sock," he'd added with a laugh. After that, whenever Taku was staying in cheap lodgings where he was likely to be robbed, or in a hotel room where the lock was broken, he'd twisted up a wet towel and put it under his pillow. It served nicely to wipe down his sweat if he was staying somewhere hot, too.

Taku wrung the towel one more time, then went to the door, the weapon hanging from his hand, and checked how things were going.

Ryuzaki was still deeply engaged in his obsessive shoe-polishing. Saera was sobbing hysterically, the receiver clutched to her breast. Seta stood frozen against the wall, bloody handkerchief pressed to his mouth, his face deathly pale.

It was now or never.

Taku slipped quickly into the room. When he came within Ryuzaki's field of vision the mobster was caught off-balance, one leg still propped across the other knee. Given his disadvantage, Ryuzaki's reaction was remarkably swift, but Taku moved faster. The deadly weight of the wet towel caught Ryuzaki perfectly on the side of the head. With a dull fleshy thud, he tumbled from the sofa onto the floor.

Ryuzaki was as tough as he looked. He seemed lightly concussed. He spread his legs wide on the carpet and attempted to sit up, but failed. He shook his head a couple of times, then put a hand up to check the side of his head. When he discovered there was no blood, his expression suddenly grew grim, and he turned a fearsome look on Taku.

"Don't move!" Taku ordered. Out of the corner of his eye, he saw Seta silently slip out the door.

"Who…the hell…are you?" Ryuzaki ground the question out between clenched teeth. Taku said nothing. Ryuzaki groaned and glared at him.

"You…I'll kill you!" He propped up his right knee in an attempt to rise. His hand slid towards his breast.

Without a word, Taku swung the towel sideways and struck him under the raised knee.

The moment he had seen the creases on those polished shoes and the particular way the heels had worn, Taku had realized that this man's legs were surprisingly weak given his stout frame. Marathon runners will sometimes develop a problem called "runner's knee," and mountaineers can have something similar, called Osgood-Schlatter disease. In Ryuzaki's case, however, his body type clearly showed that he'd done a lot of judo as a young man. No doubt the excessive training had damaged his knees. He'd then retired from active practice, and now his legs were extremely weak.

Taku had aimed his blow with scientific precision at the inside point in that weak knee known as the collateral ligament. A thick supporting muscle runs down the outside of the knee, but the inside lacks this, so the ligament can easily be snapped by the application of force from the side.

Taku had put his weight solidly behind the blow, and it looked as though he'd managed to effectively damage Ryuzaki's right knee. He had collapsed sideways onto the carpet again, and when he tried to rise this time he toppled awkwardly over again.

"How…dare…you!" Ryuzaki gritted his teeth and managed to sit up. Silently, expressionlessly, Taku stepped in, raised his towel, and brought it down on Ryuzaki's face. Ryuzaki threw out an arm and attempted to grab him by the leg. Again Taku's heavy towel struck his head, with an audible snap. Then he brought his foot down hard on Ryuzaki's damaged right knee.

Ryuzaki's body bent backwards and shuddered. But he didn't cry out. The whites of his narrow eyes rolled up like a frog's belly, and his expression grew ferocious.

"I'll…kill…you!" he gasped.

Taku applied greater pressure to his knee. Beads of sweat were suddenly standing out on Ryuzaki's neck.

"Who…sent you?"

"You can still speak, eh?" Taku stamped harder on the knee. Ryuzaki groaned, and spewed a little vomit onto the carpet. The frothy white liquid stank.

"Taku…" cried Saera in a trembling voice. "No more! He'll die!"

"That's the plan." Once more, Taku raised his towel and struck Ryuzaki on the neck, throwing his weight behind the blow.

For the first time, fear showed on Ryuzaki's face. He seemed to have finally understood that Taku was not a man to hold back on a beating.

"Stop!" he pleaded, covering his mangled face with his hands. Blood from his nose trickled down his chin. "I'll talk to…the guys in Yokohama."

"Please! Help Shin!" Saera pressed her hands together in supplication to Taku. He nodded and stepped back.

The receiver was still dangling on its cord. Saera pushed it towards Ryuzaki, and he drew it over and began to speak in a hoarse voice, breathing heavily.

"It's me… No, nothing's up… Just do as I say, okay?"

Ryuzaki looked up at Taku, and made a gesture asking him to remove his foot from the knee. Taku did as asked. Shoulders heaving as he breathed, Ryuzaki shifted the receiver to his left hand. His right hand rubbed his stomach as he gave a series of brief orders. Once finished, he weakly held the receiver out to Taku.

"Okay…your turn to talk. They'll do…whatever you say." He tossed the receiver to Taku. As Taku instinctively put out a hand to catch it, one side of Ryuzaki's jacket flipped back to reveal a silver metal object clutched in his right hand, and in a moment a shining muzzle was pointed at Taku's stomach.

"I don't enjoy this sort of thing," Ryuzaki said. "But I have no option with a madman like you."

Taku didn't panic. He'd anticipated that something of the sort could happen. Coolly, he inspected the revolver in Ryuzaki's hand.

It gleamed with a richer polish even that his shoes, and its chrome finish was shiny enough to reflect a face. A Smith & Wesson .38 Chief's Special, maybe model 36. No, the hammer was quite invisible, so maybe a model 40 Centennial. It'd be about ten years since it dropped out of the catalogs, but it was a perfectly good gun. Not bad taste for a middle-ranking yakuza. They generally went for the top brands.

"Right. Check if the guy on the other end is a feller called Yuji." After giving his order, he managed to sit himself back on the sofa, lifting the damaged knee with his left hand.

"Hullo there. You a guy called Yuji?" Taku said into the receiver.

There was a moment's silence, before the answer. The voice was tense. "I'm Yuji. What's happened there?"

"Fellow called Ryuzaki wants a word with you."

"Put the receiver slowly on the table," Ryuzaki ordered. "And put that dangerous thing down too while you're at it."

Taku put the wadded towel down as instructed. Ryuzaki picked up the phone. "Call the hotel here right away and get the gang. Tell 'em to come up to Saera Maki's room. And to send round a car to the exit. I'll be taking something out to it. That's right. I'll need a big bag to put it in. Yep, man-size. Got that? Right. You stay there and keep watch. I'll call again later."

Ryuzaki put down the receiver and addressed Saera. "Appearance time coming up. Fix your makeup and get down there. You'll sing the first song, then the MC'll get Mr. Kozushima up. Then just make sure it all goes to plan. Give it your sexy best, okay? Real erotic. You're not up to much in that department, I gotta say."

The gun was still firmly pointed at Taku's stomach. It meant business. If this was merely a threat, he'd probably be pointing it at his face. The grip was textbook perfect, and the large hand would be quite able to control the recoil of the short muzzle.

He addressed Saera again. "If you pull it off well down there, I'll call off the guys in Yokohama. Got it?"

"Yes," she answered tremulously. "I'll do what you want, I promise. So please let this man go too."

"Get down there. Don't worry," said Ryuzaki happily. "I just have a few things I wanna ask him. I'll let him go after that."

"That's a lie," said Saera. She gazed at Taku. "You're going to die, Taku."

"Please don't worry."

Large tears suddenly overflowed from Saera's eyes. "Forgive me. It's Shin I care about."

"Sing well." Taku nodded to her. She's an honest person, he thought. He could kind of understand why Shin'ichi would choose to give up his life to live with her. Standing there in the doorway gazing at him, she was truly lovely. No doubt Shin'ichi was well aware of all the past things Ryuzaki had accused her of, and accepted them.

Still, he thought, it would be unforgivable to let these two become the pawns of this gang. Whatever happened, that would be terrible.

I mustn't die.

How many bullets would Ryuzaki fire before he could bring him down with a tackle? This .38 caliber held a round of five.

"Funny the things you find yourself thinking, eh?" Ryuzaki seemed to be reading his thoughts. "Take a step back."

Just then, he heard the unexpected sound of the door opening, and Seta appeared. Behind him stood a tall woman in a black dress, holding a posy of little violets.

It was the flying woman!

Taku's breath stopped.

"Here's a guest for you." Seta's voice was calm. "The titular head of the Fraternity, Ai Katsuragi, says she'd like to meet Miss Maki."

Ryuzaki tutted in vexation. He thought for a second, brow wrinkled, then gave an expressionless nod. "Things are a little busy here right now, but do feel free."

Saera's sigh was audible. She fell dizzily against Seta's chest.

Bouquet in hand, the flying woman entered. She took in Ryuzaki and Taku with an ironic glance.

"Mr. Ryuzaki," she said in her low, silky voice. "I don't think what you're holding there is very suitable for this auspicious occasion. Please put it away."

"You don't have any role to play in this scene, Miss Katsuragi."

"I think you know my position at this gathering." Handing her bouquet to Saera, she smiled and dropped a light kiss on her cheek. "Well, it's time to be up on stage, I think," she said. "You'd better hurry. Please don't worry about the rest."

Saera nodded, and gave the kind of bow a lady might make before a queen. With that, she and Seta swiftly disappeared down the corridor.

"Put that dangerous thing away," the flying woman said firmly, walking over to Ryuzaki. "And will you hand this man over to me, please?"

"No, that I won't hear of."

"I speak as the acting head of the Fraternity."

"And I refuse as Ryuzaki of the Konryu gang."

A short silence followed, as the two stood face to face and stared each other down. At length, the flying woman slowly put out her hand and pushed the small gleaming gun aside. Ryuzaki's nostrils flared and he breathed heavily. The muscles of his cheeks flexed a little. But he made no further attempt to withstand her, and tucked the gun wordlessly back under his jacket.

"I was gonna kill this man, you know," he said.

She only smiled silently in response. "Right then," she said to Taku. "Please leave the room ahead of me. You'll be wanting to hear Saera sing, won't you?"

"Most certainly," said Taku. Then he went on, pointing to Ryuzaki, "Thanks to this man, someone dear is being held captive at Saera's house in Yokohama."

"You've no need to worry." As she spoke, she glanced at Ryuzaki with a smile. "Ryuzaki's a man of influence in those circles. Our Fraternity has some dealings with them, and I'm sure they'll be careful. Isn't that true, Mr. Ryuzaki?"

"Yes, that's so." Ryuzaki, head down, was nursing his wounded knee. He turned his eyes up to the flying woman. "I assure you I'll see to the business properly. I won't forget."

"Good." Her eyes signaled to Taku to leave. He stepped across the room ahead of her, and opened the door. As he went out into the corridor, he turned for a final glimpse of Ryuzaki standing on one leg, fists clenched as he watched him go.

10

They walked together towards the reception hall. The flying woman was silent, apparently deep in thought.

As they approached the Azure Room, singing could be heard. It was the beginning of "Set Me Free, Darling," a big hit from Saera's twenties. The song was an in-tempo Latin-style piece, but she was singing it sentimentally, with the embellishments of old-style Japanese popular songs. All the security guards hired to stand about the hall were gathered with the hotel staff at the door, listening intently. The lobby held none of the usual figures standing about conversing or smoking. The Azure Room was crammed to capacity.

Taku stood beside the flying woman by a door to the right of the stage and watched Saera singing, through a small gap in the wall of people. The woman standing there so vibrantly in the spotlight seemed a different person from the Saera who had so recently wept as Ryuzaki crushed her fingers with his shoe. As her gaze moved over the crowd like a laser beam, the people it brushed fell into a momentary paralyzed stillness.

She was thin, but her body's movement beneath her dress was extraordinarily provocative and alluring. Taku was conscious of the sigh that unconsciously escaped the woman beside him as she watched.

"I've been a fan of Saera Maki's ever since I was little," she whispered, addressing her first words to him since they had left the room. "She's older than me, but I love her so much I could hug her."

"Me too," Taku found himself responding. Then he wondered just what it was he'd said.

"I'll bet," replied the flying woman quietly. "It would take love for a man to put his life on the line for her like that."

When Saera's song ended, there was a burst of applause and whistling. Then the MC stepped hastily forward and informed the audience that they'd come up with a special idea. In a rich voice, he went on to propose theatrically that Congressman Kozushima, known so well to all from his media appearances, should sing a duet with Miss Maki.

"What do you think, everyone?" he asked. The question was greeted with encouraging cries and applause. Waving his hand in a great show of embarrassment, Kozushima was pushed onto the stage. With a practiced hand he took the mike that the MC held out for him, and, bashfully scratching his chin, he bowed to the seated guests.

His husky voice echoed through the hall. "Well then, for a duet between Beauty and the Beast, ha ha, I'd like to sing the 'Geisha Waltz'. Thank you, Miss Maki, and thank you to the band."

There was laughter. The orchestra turned the pages of the score that had just appeared before them, and began reluctantly to play.

"I instructed the manager that this duet wouldn't be necessary," muttered the flying woman, biting her lip. Up on stage, Saera had linked arms with the congressman as the introduction was played, and was smiling for all she was worth. It was a forlorn smile.

With the line, "*And oh! That sensuous cheek-to-cheek*," Kozushima seized Saera's fragile waist, pulled her against him, and pressed his cheek to hers. An audible sigh rose everywhere in the room. "*The shame, the joy, of her disheveled skirts*," sang Kozushima, and on impulse he even dared to reach down and lift the hem of Saera's slit dress with his finger.

"How disgusting!" The flying woman spat out the words quite audibly. Nearby guests turned in surprise.

"Let's go." She turned on her heels and walked out into the corridor, with Taku behind her. Her stride was fierce. As he followed her meekly up the stairs, Taku was thinking that for tonight's encore Saera would surely choose that old favorite of hers.

"*Pass on by, try not to look. There goes another fellow-man.*" He began to whistle the refrain. At this, the flying woman turned. "That's 'Don't Judge and Turn Your Eyes Away,' isn't it?"

"That's right."

"I like that song too." And she softly sang the lines in her low contralto voice.

"What will you do now?" Taku asked.

"I'm taking you away," she replied, as if this was perfectly natural. Our leader is waiting for you down in the Mount Izu headquarters."

"For me? Who did you say's waiting?"

The flying woman paused, and turned her dark eyes earnestly on his face. "The head of the Futakami Fraternity, Katsuragi Tenro. My father, in other words. He's waiting to greet Taku Hayami, formerly Taku Ishiuchi, the son of one of our Friends."

"I have no idea what you're talking about."

"You'll know everything once you arrive." The flying woman smiled. Taku stared at her, confused.

"I haven't really introduced myself, have I?" she continued. "But let's make a proper *connection* once we've arrived there safely."

I wonder just what "arrive there safely" implies, thought Taku.

The flying woman seemed to guess his thoughts, for she added, "What I mean is, once you've managed to follow me to Mount Izu."

"And how are we going to get there?"

She laughed, showing the tips of her sharp amber teeth. Then she said, almost challengingly, "Walk, of course."

"To Mount Izu? Now?" asked Taku in astonishment. Then he was ashamed to have revealed his consternation.

"We'll set off at nine tonight. Let's meet near here, at the stone marker for the old Okido post station by Sengakuji Temple in Takanawa 2-chome. Our objective is the Inner Temple of Izuyama Gongen at Mount Izu. Estimated time of arrival is five tomorrow evening. Please prepare yourself however you like."

Taku stared at her wordlessly.

"You can call it off if you don't think you can make it," she went on, her tone ironic. "We'll be covering 120 kilometers in less than twenty hours, you understand."

Taku's heart began to beat strong and fast. She's testing me! he thought. He felt his blood grow warm under her challenging gaze.

"I'll take it on, don't worry," he responded with a nod. "Tonight at the Okido marker by Sengakuji, right?"

"Correct."

"Thank you for asking me along. I'm a bit of a walking man, so no need to worry."

"Yes, you showed that on Mount Nijo." With these words, the flying woman set off up the stairs ahead of him. She swung upward with impressive style, her gluteal muscles tensing strongly at each step, like the hard revving of an overpowered engine.

11

His watch showed six-thirty. Taku took a taxi from the door of the hotel. He seldom used taxis in the city, but now time was of the essence.

Alighting on the one-way Azabu Juban, he dropped in on the Lotus. It was dinner time, and the counter was crammed with customers.

"Hey, Cho," Taku called over their backs.

"Hey, there Taku. Sorry, we're full."

"No, it's not that. I wanted you to tell me how the weather's going to be from this evening into tomorrow."

"No worry about rain."

"You're sure?"

"I guarantee. No rain. Don't worry."

"Thanks." Taku waved and left the restaurant.

Cho's weather forecasts were almost always spot on. He explained it by saying that he knew rain was on the way when smoke from the cooking oil and the smell of garlic chives tended to hang heavy in the air as he cooked. If a warm front or a low-pressure system was coming in, he said, it always affected the shop's ventilation. It was a dead giveaway. Apparently it had to do with the relation between the air inside and the outside atmosphere, but Taku had never learned the details.

At any rate, Cho's instincts told him there'd be no rain. The weather forecast he'd overheard on the taxi's radio had said the same.

As he was rattling the key in the lock, the door across the passageway opened to reveal Kaoru, the "girl" who worked in the gay bar in

Roppongi. No doubt she was on her way to work. A pleasant smile hovered on her prettily made-up face. "Hi, it's been a while," she said, waving a lovely manicured hand.

"Hey, Kaoru. How's tomorrow's weather looking?"

"Well, the makeup goes on well, so the next two days will be fine, I'd say. Thank heavens for that."

"Thanks. Good luck with the work."

"Leave it to me. I'll slay 'em."

Kaoru was a chronic sufferer of a condition called cervicobrachial syndrome. When a weather system with a pressure of less than 1010 millibars was approaching she inevitably came down with a migraine that lasted half a day. She said it was an occupational illness, but it wasn't clear just what he meant. She carried a pack of Cafergot, a blood pressure medication, wherever she went, and when she was full of bounce it was evidence that there was a high-pressure system over Japan just then.

Taku decided that he could definitely rule out rain.

As usual, his room was comfortably chaotic. Yet there was something disturbing about it. He had a feeling someone had been in there in his absence. Deciding not to worry about it, he hastily picked up the telephone and dialed the Yokohama house. The phone was picked up immediately.

"Shin? It's me."

"Ah. Taku. God, I've had a horrible time."

"You hurt?"

"A bit."

"We'll talk about it all properly once I'm back. I'm heading straight off to Mount Izu right now. Listen, I don't think you should let anyone else use the car at your place for a while. Something's bothering me about it."

"Got it. Listen, I had a call from Saera a while ago giving me most of the story. She said you had a real gun pointed at you. What type was it?"

This was the old Shin'ichi. Taku chuckled into the phone, relieved. "Do you think I had time to check up on a thing like that? It was a hand gun, a dazzlingly shiny one. You could almost see your face in it."

"Polished nickel, I'd say. Maybe a Smith & Wesson Chief's Special. How was the hammer on it?"

"Look, I'm in a rush. I'll give you a full report once I'm back. I'm setting off this evening for a long nonstop walk, and right now I'm in preparation mode."

"Right. Take care, then."

"Will do." Taku felt like adding, "And be sure you're especially good to her this evening," but he just hung up. Shin'ichi knew this better than he did, after all.

Next he tried putting in a direct call to the *Tramping* desk at work. Just as he thought, Kyoko Shimamura was still there.

"It's Taku."

"Hullo there." Kyoko's voice was as relaxed as always.

Taku began rapidly to talk. "I'm setting off to walk to Mount Izu tonight at nine. The plan is to start from the Okido marker in Takanawa. If something happens to me, please call Hanada. Tell him I've gone with the acting Fraternity head to meet a man called Katsuragi Tenro. I'll leave the key to my room behind the gas meter by the door."

"Wait!" said Kyoko sharply. "I'll be right round. I think I might be able to help."

"I'll be here at home."

The phone clicked off at the other end. Taku glanced at the weather report in the evening paper, just to double check. He was relieved to see that a 1022-millibar migratory high-pressure system was currently over Honshu, and the satellite picture confirmed what he'd heard from Cho and Kaoru. Flipping idly through the pages, he noticed a headline, "Boston Art Museum Incident Puzzle." The subheading read, "Bomb scare the work of terrorists?" Ignoring the article, he turned to his preparations. Just now, his main preoccupation was the thought of walking to Mount Izu with the flying woman.

Kyoko arrived at his door astonishingly quickly. She seemed to flutter into his room like a little butterfly.

"Right, let's start with the boots," she said, opening her notebook. "If you're walking straight to Mount Izu, I imagine you'll be on sealed roads all the way."

"I'd say so. We won't be playing soldiers, will we."

"Rain?"

"I've decided not to factor it in."

"If you'll be doing it at a single stretch, let's just go for light. Not carrying a thing. If you're with her, that's your only option. Just think in terms of speed."

"So you know her?" Taku stared at Kyoko, who nodded.

"You said on the phone just now it was the acting head of the Fraternity, right? That's got to be Ai. She does a superb *nori*. I once went on a long *nori* with her myself."

There were things Taku wanted to ask Kyoko, but he had too many questions in his head, and time was short.

Just concentrate on the walk right now, he told himself. You'll find out everything sooner or later.

He stood before his shelves of boots, arms folded, examining the rows. There were three shelves. On the lowest were tough mountain boots, designed to carry a backpack of twenty kilos or more over rough terrain for long distances. There was an old pair of Galibiers whose soles had been repaired, and a pair of boots of unknown provenance that he'd found by the entrance to a pawn shop in Kyoto. The original owner must have been a highly experimental fellow, to judge from the bold inventiveness of their construction. Supports had been inserted into the insteps, and the metal shoelace loops at the ankles had been carefully removed. They were good for walking, but definitely showed wear and tear by now. The Galibiers he had received on the cheap from Shin'ichi.

The second shelf held stream-walking shoes in a drawstring bag and a pair of cloth caravan shoes, plus two pairs of rough country hikers. Nothing there was relevant just now. He guessed he'd be walking exclusively on asphalt and concrete for this walk. He could be wrong, of course, but his only option was to assume this at least. Since he'd be carrying nothing, he should choose the freest form of footwear he could. Dismissing the possibility of getting wet meant he could ignore the rag-soled boots. All he should really go for was lightness—something even fractionally lighter than the others—and good soft soles to absorb the impact of the hard road surface.

"Right, these will do." Unhesitatingly, Kyoko pointed to one pair among the seven light shoes on the highest shelf. They were precisely the ones Taku had been thinking of himself, nylon training shoes with sponge soles, a thoroughly average pair with an open-weave line. Taku used them for the jogging he occasionally indulged in. "Just thinking in terms of speed alone, right?"

"I'm with you."

"Where's the underwear?"

"The lowest drawer there."

Kyoko swiftly drew out a short-sleeved knitted undershirt. The shoulders were of cloth, useful for carrying a backpack, but it was ragged with wear. He'd kept it just because he couldn't quite bring himself to throw it out.

"And these are the shorts to take. What about a shirt?"

"The dungaree one there."

"And socks?"

"These."

He assembled hat, bandana, watch, sunglasses, and knife, then put the sunglasses and knife back in the drawer. He wouldn't take either compass or map, he decided.

"And this is a gift from me." Kyoko tucked a little plastic bag into his shorts pocket. "Coins for vending machines and public telephones. And some emergency tape. Six aspirin-less codeine tablets. I imagine you'll be walking along roads from one town to the next, so this should be enough, wouldn't you say?"

"Thanks." Taku drew two ten-thousand-yen notes from a drawer and put them in his pocket.

"You really will be empty-handed."

"I want to be able to keep up with her."

"Right. You don't need to worry, Taku."

Taku felt his spirits rise a little at this encouragement from a woman who had twice walked the length of Japan. It's not only the right gear that you need for a long walk like that. Information and experience are also important, but even more crucial is determination, fight. An exultant spirit that sets the heart racing. Without this, your powers are limited to your natural ability.

"Is there anything else you need?"

"Can I kiss you?" Taku asked suddenly.

Kyoko nodded and closed her eyes. Holding her delicate body, so slender he could enclose it in a single arm, he placed a kiss on her small lips. They tasted of Muji lipstick.

"Don't let her intimidate you," she said, pressing her cheek against his chest.

He nodded. "I'll leave the key to the apartment with you, Kyoko."

"Ring me when you get there. I'll be waiting right here from five o'clock onwards."

So this was what Kyoko meant when she said she could be of use, thought Taku as he closed the door behind him.

He planned on warming up by walking to Sengakuji Temple. His right-hand pocket held Kyoko's plastic bag, while in the left was a paper packet of dried sweet potato. His heart swelled with anticipation at the thought that he would soon be walking with the flying woman, and he had to rein in the urge to skip as he walked along.

As he approached the temple, his pace gradually quickened.

12

Back in the Edo Period, the old Okido station at Takanawa had been a strategic point on the western boundary between two government regions. It had also played an important role in the history of measurement in Japan, for the great eighteenth-century surveyor and cartographer Tadataka Ino chose this spot as the point from which all national measurements were made. Now, the only record of its existence was a stone marker bearing its name.

The flying woman arrived five minutes before the appointed hour. She had changed from her earlier formal wear, and was now dressed for walking.

She wore traditional clothing—dark blue, close-fitting trousers with leggings, plus a T-shirt over which she wore the short traditional *happi* coat he'd seen earlier. On her feet were traditional two-toed cloth shoes with thick stitched soles, beneath a pair of straw sandals. The straw seemed somehow different from the usual straw used for weaving such sandals. The cords were plaited in the Shinshu Omachi style, but not tied as high up the ankle as is usual. This would be because they would be trekking over level ground almost all the way, as Kyoko had guessed. The Shinshu style was a looser tie over the foot joints and points of flexion, for ease of walking through streams and over rocks.

She stood before Taku and made a formal bow, both hands placed on her knees. The hint of irony he'd seen in her expression at the hotel was now gone. Taku felt himself somehow wrong-footed.

"You're being very humble, considering you're about to put me to the test," he said.

"I'm not testing you," she replied quietly. Then she went on, "We call it *walking practice*. It's one of the important practices for us *brothers and sisters*. It's not like the old days, you see, when transport was hard to come by. We no longer walk for practical reasons."

"For me, walking is for pleasure. I walk because it feels good. I hope you don't mind?"

"No, of course not." She nodded easily. "But right now, as far as I'm concerned, you're an important *fellow traveler*. So I hereby formally beg you to keep me company till our destination."

Somewhat bewildered, Taku asked half-jokingly, "What should I call you?"

"Ah, yes. Please just use my name, Ai. You're Taku Hayami, aren't you?"

"That's right."

"Well then, I'll walk ahead if you don't mind. Please understand, when we perform what we call *nori*, two people walk as one."

"Don't make any allowances for me please. If I can't handle it, I won't be embarrassed to just give up."

"This is an ascetic practice, not a competition." Ai Katsuragi's look was grave. "There's no meaning to the idea of the *fellow traveler* unless we can attain twice or three times the level of a single person's strength in our *nori*. If I'm testing you in any way, it's only to discover whether you can walk cooperatively, helping the other, whether you can fit your step to nature's own pace, can find in yourself that breadth and generosity of heart. If I learn that you possess nothing more than physical strength and willpower, I'll cease to be your *fellow traveler* forthwith. If that happens, you and I *part ways*, never to meet again."

Ai's words carried a mother's emotional warmth. Taku accepted them at face value. He nodded silently. "I understand. Please accompany me, then."

"Very well. Now for our *nori*," she responded. As she spoke, the lights of a large passing truck suddenly lit up her face, and Taku saw that around her mouth, incised into her face like the clean cut of a Damascus knife, there hovered a little smile. It was the same enigmatic smile that hovered on the lips of the Chujo Princess in the Mandala Hall of Taima Temple.

On he walked, matching his stride to that of Ai Katsuragi two meters ahead of him.

Taku didn't concern himself with the question of what route she would choose. He had had enough experience and confidence in his walking to feel that he had attained a certain personal walking style, but right now he wasn't inclined to quibble about such things. It wasn't that he was altogether convinced by Ai's idea of walking as a kind of ascetic exercise. He did understand, however, that she and her group understood it as more than a simple matter of technique, but rather as a kind of spiritual act. And he certainly was aware of the powerful sense of caring concern as "fellow traveler" that emanated towards him from the woman who strode before him.

It flowed out in invisible waves from her back, the motion of her muscles, the rhythmic movement of her limbs. The nuances of her bearing altered subtly according to time and place. There were times when her rear leg kicked back a little as she walked, with a kind of esprit; at others, her heel planted itself on the earth almost tenderly. Her pelvis might sway with something like a warm eroticism at one point, while at other times her movements evinced a subtle roguishness that Taku found quite startling.

To all these shifts and messages, Taku answered through the rhythm of his own footsteps on the paved road. He was beginning to feel increasingly at ease, as he walked on through the night city, with this wordless walking conversation.

Most adults walk at a speed of around fifty to seventy meters a minute, and consume around three to six hundred milliliters of oxygen. It's said that in the old imperial Japanese army, a platoon was required to cover eighty meters while maintaining a rhythm of 114 paces a minute. They would do this for ten to twelve hours at a stretch, in ill-fitting army boots and carrying guns, ammunition, and regulation knapsack, and under all manner of adverse conditions.

Ai had for some time been walking 120 paces a minute, with a stride of a little under eighty centimeters' length. This was impressive—the usual stride length of a young man is seventy-five centimeters. From the start she had set an unwavering speed of something under six kilometers per hour, perhaps with the idea of getting beyond the city limits before dawn.

As she walked, she sometimes branched off from the main road to take odd detours. She went warily through red lights, though there was no car nearby that presented any danger. The lateness of the hour meant the streets were virtually deserted. Occasionally, a racing taxi would pass, bathing their walking figures in light.

The wind was from the north. It was a clear night, and in the northern sky the Big Dipper blazed, vivid as a tangle of new barbed wire.

They emerged onto a wide road, that ran along a river embankment. Ai signaled to him with her hand, a gesture that seemed to say they should walk side by side. Taku stepped up and walked shoulder to shoulder with her.

"We'll soon cross the Tama River," she said.

"At Maruko Bridge?"

"No. Have you heard of the Yaguchi Crossing?"

"But that's in the opposite direction, surely."

"That's Yagiri Crossing. We're going through the Yaguchi area right now. Very soon we'll go over the gas bridge. The plan is to go on through Musashi and Sagami."

Her pace quickened slightly. Taku's step followed hers, as synchronized as a musician responding to the conductor's baton.

"I want to get to the point where we can see the sea by seven this morning," she explained. "I plan to spend the daylight hours walking beside Sagami Bay."

Slowly her pace had begun to increase.

It was a strange route that Ai chose to follow. It tracked along highways and old roads, to be sure, but with occasional startling twists and turns. She was still walking normally—there was no sign of what Taku had secretly longed to see, that extraordinary phenomenon of the "wind-walker." She was quite different now from the "flying woman" she had been on Mount Nijo.

Back in the Edo Period, the samurai used to prime their strength and willpower by performing the feat of a walking the sixty-odd kilometer road from Kamakura to the capital and back again in a single day. The total distance of that route was roughly equivalent to the walk to Mount Izu that he and Ai were undertaking now. But the hard paved roads of today were less suited to walking than the soft earth of earlier days, and there were many more obstacles on their path besides.

Ai was now walking ahead of him at somewhere between one hundred ten and one hundred twenty meters a minute—still well within the range of normal human ability. Professional racewalkers moved at over twice this speed. Considering the winding city terrain and the one-hundred-twenty-kilometer distance, however, this was an impressive pace.

Viewed from behind, her walking style could hardly have been called scientifically correct. Indeed from Taku's point of view it seemed that, given her symmetrical body, the hips were too low-slung and the slipstream effect that he felt walking behind her was somehow jerky and unrhythmical. He detected a certain unnecessary, lurching motion to her step. What could it be? he wondered as he walked.

Not long before dawn, she paused before a small park, and indicated that they would take a short rest. Taku went to the toilet in a corner of the park, and when he returned he found Ai sitting on the stone steps, in the process of changing her straw sandals, left for right.

"Would you mind if I asked you something rather personal?" he said hesitantly.

"Please do."

"I'd like to take a look at the soles of your feet, if I may."

"The soles of my feet?" A faint blush tinged her dark-complexioned face. "I know why you've asked that," she went on. "You suspect I may be flatfooted."

"Yes, I did wonder."

"Here, take a look."

Unhesitatingly, Ai removed her straw sandals and padded toe socks, and stretched a foot out before him. His heart beating faster, he examined it from a tactful distance. Ai smiled.

"Don't be embarrassed. Take it in your hands and have a thorough look."

She lifted her right foot high in front of her. He knelt on one knee before her, took the foot in the palm of his hand, and pored over it at close range.

The foot was not so much beautiful as sturdy. The firm ankle looked strong, and both the big and little toe were astonishingly well developed, but there seemed to be something wrong with the arch under the foot. As he'd thought, the area was thick and fleshy, with no sign of the high arch that indicates a healthy foot.

"What do you think?" she asked, watching him mischievously. Her eyes were like a child's.

"I'm not sure," Taku said, puzzled. "Do forgive me."

Ai nodded and withdrew her foot. "Did it look flatfooted?"

"Well, yes, but still, you're a marvelous walker... It's weird."

Ai laughed happily, showing her teeth. Far from having buck teeth, they were turned slightly inward, and when she laughed she looked like a charming boy.

"Have you ever read anything by the renowned Shotaro Mizuno?" she asked.

"No. I don't go much for the printed word."

"He has a fascinating book called *The Human Foot*, put out by Sogensha, in which he says that it was the early modern writer Rintaro Mori, alias Ogai, who first propounded the idea that the Japanese flat foot is bad. Apparently Ogai, who was an army physician with great respect for German learning, applied the standards of German medicine and condemned out of hand all young men with flat feet like these as unsuitable for the army. Someone pointed out, however, that this literary man was considerably excusing hard-working farming lads from the necessity of military duty."

"Well. Well, I've never heard that before."

"Human motility is a very complex and extraordinary thing, after all. Apparently the great runner of the past Takanori Yoshioka, who had the nickname 'The Dawn Super Express,' and the Giants' pitcher Egawa and Hankyu's Fukumoto in the baseball world, all had soles like mine. And there's a theory that a lot of wonderful football players also have flat feet."

Taku found himself recalling the fleshy soles of the Sherpa guide he'd walked with in Nepal and the Egyptian student from Cairo who had walked the desert with him.

Ai finished putting her toed socks back on, and swiftly set about tying the cords of her straw sandals, now worn on opposite feet, while she went on. "So I don't think my feet are an example of a physical fault. They come from overdeveloped planta muscles due to rigorous training. We Fraternity members have always been proud of such feet, actually. We call them 'straw-sandal feet.'"

She stood up, and stamped the ground lightly a few times. Then she said dryly, "Apparently there used to be a belief that a lot of people with flat feet were criminals. There was a scholar who applied this to the fact that we have a lot of 'straw-sandal foot' people, and came up with a theory that members of the Fraternity are criminals. Isn't that just terrible?"

Taku was about to reply, but Ai was already walking off through the early morning light, at an astonishing speed—his first glimpse of her in her flying woman incarnation again. Alarmed, Taku hurried off behind her.

On she went, cutting like a knife through the hard, cold air of dawn. Though her legs rolled along effortlessly, her head slid smoothly through the air, while a kind of halo seemed to emanate from her body in syncopated waves.

"I can see the sea!" she cried. But for Taku, almost running behind her, no sea was yet visible.

A haze hung over the ocean. Transparent sun rays poured from the sky, but clouds hung on the horizon. The roughly surging waves seemed fraught with malice.

They had followed the bicycle and pedestrian path that ran beside Highway 135, and were now walking along the sandy beach.

Taku's eyes scarcely registered the sun, the sea, the surrounding scenery, or the sand. He was entirely focused on synchronizing his body with the subtle waves that came flowing back to him from Ai's body moving ahead. His muscles had passed the limits of pain, and reached a condition of almost total lack of sensation. Inside the nylon shoes, as unsteady as they were light, his toenails and soles burned with sweat and friction. A tiny pebble had found its way into his left shoe, forming a blister on his sole that had burst, and the pebble had now moved on to begin its work on another spot. The way things were going, another hour would see the sole of his foot pulverized to mincemeat.

Colin Fletcher wrote that there are only two ways to walk long distance carrying a heavy weight for days on end—slow, and slower still. In other words, take your time, then take some more.

Take your time to breathe, sending a good draught of oxygen down to the bottom of the lungs, slowing the blood circulation, relaxing the muscles so that they don't slacken from fatigue, and control your pace. Just keep walking at a set rhythm, imagining the flowing marks of wind ripples over endless sand dunes or the monotonous rhythm of waves on the beach, and sometimes you'll find yourself slipping into a kind of stupor. You are no longer conscious of walking; the external world recedes like something viewed down the wrong end of a telescope, and your feet move effortlessly forward, on and on. Some people have called this unconscious state a "walking trip," or a "walker's high." It's inside you that you are walking. You see nothing—not the sun, not the scenery, not the woods you move through. And yet your feet choose their way perfectly.

Taku had tasted this experience many times. And that unconscious immersion in the world of stories that Kyoko had experienced as she walked to and from school would surely be the same sort of state.

But what Taku was now experiencing was a kind of ascetic mortification of the flesh, very different from these other states of being. It would only take the simple request to be allowed to rest, and the woman walking ahead would no doubt stop for him. But come what may he did not want to ask. He had walked through harsh deserts, the rough gravel plains of Shiraz, the safari rally route where rally cars hurtled towards him at 150 kilometers an hour, and the source of the Ganges—how could he give up here, on the beach of this little playground of an island country?

But the speed he was moving at now was different from those other walks. They had paused only once, before dawn at the edge of the park. The rest of the time had been continuous walking, and she must now be moving at more than 160 meters a minute, about twice the speed of those pre-war army marches. The lower half of her body moved along in a strange kind of dance, while her head slid through the air as poised and serene as that of a Noh actor as he glides over the stage. Taku had long since given up walking, and was now running. His heartbeat trembled near its limit.

Yet Ai was far from ignoring him as she walked. Soundless encouragement was endlessly streaming out to him from her back: "Okay, keep it up. On we go together, on and on, holding hands…"

Taku could hear her quite clearly. He closed his eyes. I'll fall, he thought. But he didn't stumble. He was intent on walking, on and on, until his heart burst. His middle ear had lost its sense of balance, and he held himself upright by spreading his arms like a bird in flight. He staggered. *I'm going to fall*, he thought again. Then, suddenly, under his eyelids he saw a golden road shining in the distance. It moved towards him, and now, strangely, he no longer felt any pain in his feet or lungs. Something like a band of light began to flow along on either side of him.

He had the sensation of standing in a wind tunnel. The landscape, distorted as if viewed through a fisheye lens, sped towards him with increasing speed, then at the last moment before impact it split in two and flew past him.

A force like strong magnetism was constantly pulling at him, and a loud percussion thudded rapidly above his head. His body swam on the waves of the offbeat rhythm—and he was not alone. Through the swirling mists, Ai's arms supported him. Peppermint-scented bubbles pulsed in his veins, and deep in his chest a cold wind blew.

"Ai!" he cried silently.

"Taku!" came back the voice, like an echo to his. The voice wove about itself like a fugue, streaming away through the atmosphere.

"Am I flying?" As this thought flashed through his mind, he saw himself curving down through black space like a stone. The band of light disappeared, and he lost consciousness.

13

All around was dark. His eyes could see nothing, his body burned as if aflame. His muscles trembled and twitched. There was no feeling in his knees, and his feet from the ankles down throbbed with a pain that seemed beyond his own.

Where am I?

He sat up. Consciousness was slowly returning.

"Ai?" he called. He seemed still half hallucinating.

"So you're awake." The deep contralto voice came from behind him. In the dark, he turned over.

"Don't move." It was her voice again.

"Where am I?" he asked.

Her voice was close to him now. "You're in a room in the annex of an inn called Ryukien at Mount Izu."

"You mean…"

"Yes. We arrived at the inner Mount Izu Gongen Temple at three yesterday afternoon. You lost consciousness there, and were carried here."

From somewhere came the sound of running water. Otherwise, it was almost frighteningly quiet, and the room was flooded with utter darkness. Her voice came from right beside his face. She seemed to be lying beside him as she spoke.

"So I didn't collapse en route?"

"That's right. You were a wonderful companion. You managed the *walking practice* with me for one hundred twenty kilometers, without a word of complaint."

"I can't believe it," he said, stretching out his hand towards where her voice came from. "I still feel as though I'm dreaming in the darkness. Could you give me your hand?"

Cool, damp fingers touched his. Their cold touch felt good.

"Do your feet hurt?" she asked.

"They don't feel like my own feet. They feel absolutely barbequed."

"Your left sole was as pulpy as tartar steak."

The air seemed to sway. The sheet that covered him was lifted back, and something cold and damp touched his foot—a strange, soft sensation.

"I hope this might make it feel a little better." Ai's muffled voice came from his feet. Then the sensation of something like an invisible feather moved hesitantly over his foot from the burning sole to the toes and on to the heel. He felt again as if he was in a dream. The flying woman was soothing the pain with her own lips.

"Thank you," he said huskily. "That's fine. Please stop."

"Why?"

"I'm a healthy adult male, that's why."

Through the throbbing of his lower body, he was aware of a surprising awakening taking place, and he shifted his body. Pain and desire were sweeping through him together.

"And I'm a healthy adult female."

Her cool lips touched the underside of his knee. And then Taku felt her lips moving on up, at first tentatively and then with increasing conviction, tracing a sure path to his center.

I'm dreaming, he told himself. This can't be happening. This is a hallucination.

"Hold still, *brother*," whispered the flying woman, shifting her position. Her lips were cool and moist, but her breath was hot. He caught the faint scent of woodland trees.

He sank into sleep once more. In his dream, he witnessed a naked Saera Maki being raped by Ryuzaki, while she responded to him with all the smile she could muster. Then Ryuzaki became Shin'ichi, hanging from a rope, his body swaying in the breeze. Saera, still naked, was running along the ridge path of

Mount Nijo. Beside Prince Otsu's grave she took out a knife, slashed herself below the breasts, and fell to the ground. A long mourning procession moved slowly through the mist. Meido Ikarino's car drew up in front of the Nintoku tomb, a large wooden box in its trunk. A Greek detective handcuffed his companions and led them off. He escaped through the skylight and made off over the roofs, cradling a polyester bag full of black hashish. That dangerous job with the tourists who poured in from Europe and America was clearly over now. The bearded face of an Afghani border guard. Run for it! Some idiot's attached a machine gun under the bonnet. You'd have to thank your lucky stars if you only got ten years for it. He yelled aloud—*Help!*

"You're awake?" came a man's voice. Taku abruptly switched off his dream. The room was faintly lit. He sat up. A young man with thick eyebrows, wearing a *happi* coat, sat at his pillow. He was light-skinned, with high cheekbones. A strong body. Shaven head.

Taku got to his feet, gritting his teeth with the pain. "Are you...?"

"I do apologize about the painful muscles. How is your foot now?" the young man asked with a smile.

It was the young monk beside whom he had sat on the train from Kyoto, the day he went to Mount Nijo. The man who had haunted him by telling him about the Thousand-Day Circuit of Mount Hiei and the strange poem monument on Mount Nijo, but had left without revealing his name.

By why was he...?

"You must still be tired, but the *parent*, the *uncles* and the *aunts* are all waiting to see you nearby. Your feet will be hurting you, I know, but while you're taking a bath I'll bring you a meal. I'll take you there in half an hour."

"How long have I slept?"

"It's now one in the morning."

So how many hours would that make? He recalled the events that had taken place in the dark.

Had that been a dream? He shook his head.

"Ai is waiting over there as well," the young monk went on. "She was full of praise for your walking."

"Please tell them I'll wash my face and be right there. I don't need to eat just yet."

Perhaps he was too tired, but he had no appetite. More important to him now was to learn as soon as possible what kind of people were waiting for him, and what would happen there.

Ai had told him he'd learn everything once he was here. There was no question that those words had set a fuse deep in his consciousness and become one of his motivations for coming to Mount Izu.

"Over there you'll find some clothes for you to wear, if you don't mind," said the monk. Then, with a bow, he left the room.

Taku wiped away his sweat, washed his face, and donned the underclothes left waiting for him. Then he turned to face the bathroom mirror, and, for the first time in ages, surveyed his own image. He normally never made a habit of looking in the mirror.

So this was Taku Hayami, he thought. Thirty-two years of age… He examined the image in the mirror objectively, like a stranger. What he saw there was a rather undistinguished man, no longer young but not yet old enough to carry the authority of middle age.

This is me, he thought.

He'd weighed himself just now, and discovered he was down to sixty kilos. Since coming back to Japan he'd been slightly on the heavy side, at sixty-three or sixty-four. Now, though still the same one hundred sixty-eight centimeters tall, his weight had dropped overnight to something like its ideal level. His brother Shin was five centimeters taller but two kilos lighter, a fact he took great pride in.

Both feet were bandaged, making him look ridiculously like something out of a zombie movie, but there wasn't much he could do about that. Someone must have bandaged him while he was asleep. Had it been her? Recalling the sensation of her cool lips that still lingered between his toes, his body suddenly grew hot again.

You fool! Look at your flabby face, he told himself accusingly, noting the loose flesh of his bronzed face in the mirror. The stubble on his cheeks had grown considerably since he last shaved. Normally, he only bothered to shave once a week, so that he was beardless every Monday and bearded again by Saturday. On his travels abroad he had cultivated a beard to avoid looking childish, but since coming back to Japan he'd shaved it off on Hanada's advice.

No, it was without doubt an undistinguished face. His eyes had deep-set double-folded lids. Eyes and lips both typified a Mongolian lineage. If pressed to name one attractive feature, he thought it was probably his smile.

A charming smile was the single most important tool for a hitchhiker in an unknown country. He had learned this from a wonderful young Japanese man, K., whom he'd gotten to know by chance in Oslo, who did indeed have a fresh and entrancing smile himself. He wasn't particularly handsome as men go, but when he smiled even the Norwegians, normally a thoroughly curt and grim-faced people, immediately responded with human warmth.

"I didn't have much of a smile originally," he'd said, "In fact I was really very shy. But when you travel in some unknown place, especially someplace fraught with hidden dangers, you may not have a pistol on you but you must never forget a great big smile. That smile has to be the best you can produce, and it should reveal all. Japanese are bad at smiling. Get yourself a good smile—it's good training, and besides, it's good for the heart."

K. had already done one solo walking trip in Africa, and he was in Oslo making a bit of money for a second. He was two years younger than Taku, but Taku felt he'd learned a great deal from this baby-faced young fellow. From that day on, Taku put in a lot of practice baring his teeth to himself in the mirror to cultivate a convincing smile.

Good training, and good for the heart. Those words, from one so young, still stayed with him. K. had gone on to attempt a record-breaking solo crossing of the Sahara, dying of thirst in the desert somewhere in the vicinity of Menaka in the attempt. He was only twenty-two. Taku had heard the news from someone in the Japanese embassy while he was employed as a driver by the Japanese company in Cairo. He had only spent that one night with him, talking through the white night in Oslo, but the news of his death had had a profound influence on the way Taku lived, he thought now. The two travel journals K. left behind had an important place in his tiny book collection.

This is all you've got going for you, he said to himself, smiling his best into the bathroom mirror. He took in the sun-darkened face and the strong white teeth.

A smile like a horse's. He pulled a face at himself, then climbed into the Japanese robe that had been left for him. It wasn't the normal men's kimono but something quite odd. It was of strong cotton, and the coat was something like the Zen monk's working *samue* coat, but not quite the same. Nor was it the usual *happi*. If anything, it was like a simpler version of a monk's gauze over-robe, while the pants section was the wide-skirted *hakama* that horse riders would wear. When the strings of the front and rear panels were tied tight, the body's gravity became centered just below the navel, drawing the body's posture naturally upright.

"Pardon me." The voice came from the doorway. It was the young monk who had been there earlier. "I've come to fetch you."

Taku ran his fingers through his hair, gave up worrying about his stubbly beard, and turned from the mirror.

Following the young monk out into the large garden towards the annex, he looked up through the trees at the blaze of the Milky Way overhead. For a moment, he forgot the pain in his feet, as he drew in a great draught of the sea-scented night air.

"This is the southern slope of Mount Izu," the monk told him, stepping from rock to rock along the path across the garden. "The sea's over that way, and in the daytime you get a clear view of Hatsushima Island. A famous New Religions art museum has recently been built just down from here."

"Does this inn have connections with the Fraternity?"

"Yes. It was set up by one of our founder's *brothers*. The building's old and rotting now, but the setting is beautiful, and there's a lot of pressure from various developers to sell. Ikarino Tourism is desperate to pull the place down and build a big hotel here."

In a far corner of the garden stood a dark and unlit building, a black, earth-walled storehouse of the sort seldom seen now. It looked well on in years, with parts of the rendering come away from the walls, and the roof tiles near the eaves perilously close to falling.

"Wait a moment, please." The monk knocked on the heavy door, and after a few moments it opened with a creak. Taku followed him into the dimly lit interior.

Great wooden rafters supported a high ceiling, and a staircase led to an upper story. A faint whiff of incense hung in the air. Taku followed the monk up the stairs. At the top was another door, with iron rivets.

"I've brought Mr. Taku Hayami," the monk announced.

The door opened to reveal a dark room larger than the one below, about twenty tatami mats in size. By the faint light of the paper lanterns that stood here and there, Taku could make out about ten figures. At the front, like a Buddhist statue, sat a tiny old man. A white cloth, rather like a faded banner, hung on the wall behind him. On it, written in dynamic brush strokes, were four lines of writing:

> *Plough no furrow   Live in no place*
> *Belong to no nation Have no self*

"Welcome." It was the old man speaking. His voice was the voice of the old man Taku had heard that night at the Nintoku tomb, who had prostrated himself before it and howled like an animal—AU AU AU. Taku knelt formally on the straw matting spread before him at the entrance, and gazed at him.

"Your feet must be very sore. Please sit comfortably, as we do," said a man sitting cross-legged in the middle of the left-hand row of figures.

"Well then, if I may." Taku followed the suggestion and crossed his legs. He had a sudden memory of the time he was invited to visit the tent of nomadic herdsmen in the plains south of Shiraz. He was accustomed to being vetted by folk he didn't know in the course of his wanderings. The important thing was to be calm and focused, and behave resolutely. The others will let you know by their demeanor if you make the mistake of being too forthright.

A different person now spoke, in a gentle tone. "We're pleased to see you here. We like to dispense with the usual show of greetings and formalities. But you've been *parted*, so we should give you a *connection*, just to make things easy. Yugaku, could you give us all a simple introduction?"

"Certainly." Yugaku was apparently the name of the young monk who had led him here. He gave a small bow, and began to speak to Taku.

"Everyone gathered here this evening is from the Eight Houses *lineage*. In front is Tenro Katsuragi, the second generation *parent* of the Futakami Fraternity. On the right, starting at the near end, the *proxy parent* Ai Katsuragi, the *uncle* from the First House, the *uncle* from the Third House, the *aunt* from the Fifth House, the *uncle* from the Seventh House, and the *uncle* from the Eighth House."

Yugaku went on to name those on the left. "Here we have Dr. Rokotsu Sarashino, our teacher of *Scholarly Practice*; the teacher of *Wandering Practice*, Dr. Hokuyo Hachimai; next to him, Dr. Shirabe Yusurido, the teacher of *Walking Practice*; then the Wayfarers' League manager, Shuso Kariya; and finally the Konryu gang's..."

"Don't worry about the name," said this last man curtly. The rest of the Fraternity nodded.

The young monk, Yugaku, now turned encouragingly to Taku, who acknowledged this, and in a clear voice said, "How do you do, everyone. My name is Taku Hayami, and I write for a publishing company. Pleased to meet you all." He bowed, and in the dim room everyone made a slight bow in response.

The old man in the center, Tenro Katsuragi, was a small, white-haired gentleman with large ears. His gentle eyes gazed steadily at Taku. It suddenly occurred to Taku that he looked like the samurai movie actor Komon Mizuta.

Aside from Ai, the only women present in the room were the Aunt, and the Walking Practice specialist, Shirabe Yusurido—in all, there were three women, and ten men including Taku. Yugaku had disappeared without his noticing.

"Well then, Mr. Hayami," said Tenro. His tone was a mixture of gentleness and firmness. "Shimafune from Meteor Publications informs me that you wish to join our Fraternity."

"That's correct."

"Would you mind telling me your reason?"

"I don't really know myself. It's just that, somehow, I've developed an overwhelming desire to do so."

"Hmm." A faint smile played on Tenro's lips. "I see. I'm glad you're honest. No doubt you've given me one of the reasons, certainly."

"Also..." Taku continued boldly. He knew he shouldn't say too much, but he felt he simply had to add a little more. "I'm probably speaking out of turn, but the things that Miss Katsuragi said in her speech at the Ikarino Corporation party yesterday really rang true for me. I was deeply moved."

"I see," said Tenro, nodding. Then, with a smile, he added, "By the way, I hear that you came across some of our *children* on Mount Futakami the other day when they were engaged in a practice."

"You mean Mount Nijo?"

"That is its present name, yes. We're touched that you were impressed with Ai's walking there on the mountain and took the trouble to wait to see us at the Nintoku Tomb later."

"So you knew I was there."

Tenro gazed levelly at Taku. "It could be said you have a very strong karmic connection to us, young man. It was a most unlikely coincidence that we should come across you on the Futakami Pilgrimage, which is performed only once a year." Tenro sighed deeply. "But unlike the Wayfarers' League, our Fraternity is not something that just anyone can join, you know. The official religious organization known as the Tenmu Jinshin Group, or Futakami Fraternity, is an organization of a single clan whose members all have a *connection* with the Eight Family clan, you see. So you must have that particular qualification in order to join the Fraternity."

Taku listened silently to Tenro Katsuragi's low, gravelly voice. He'd vaguely felt that this would be the case. He also felt a premonition that somewhere in Ai's riddling statements lurked the fact that he may turn out to have such a connection.

"Could you please explain, Uncle of the Seventh House?" asked Tenro.

The man he called on was so thin he could scarcely be any thinner, a man of indeterminate age who looked like a withered tree. The yogis of India were often of this physical type—sunken eye sockets, with an untended beard that reached to the chest. His lamplit profile was extraordinary. When he opened his mouth it gaped like a dark hole, revealing that he was completely toothless.

The Uncle of the Seventh House made a slight bow in response to Tenro's request, then addressed Taku in a startlingly strong voice. "I want you to answer honestly the questions I will now put to you. Do you understand?"

Taku nodded.

The Uncle of the Seventh House opened his cavernous mouth once more. "Inform us of the date and place of your birth."

Taku replied that he was born on the first of October 1951, adding that he did not know the precise place.

"Hmm. Well then, I'll tell you. Your father's name was Gen Ishiuchi, your mother was Sayo. You were born beneath a cliff in the Ochi River valley, in a village called Otaki in the mountains of the Chichibu region. Your birth was registered in October of the following year. These are your true origins. Commit them to your memory. Written records are almost never kept in the Fraternity. Our way is to preserve the facts through oral transmission down the centuries."

Taku felt a little dizzy.

"Could you perhaps tell us a little of your early memories?" broke in the woman who had been introduced as the Aunt of the Fifth House, in an apparent attempt to soothe his evident agitation. Her tone was like a tender hug.

She was a woman around her mid-fifties, with the suntanned skin and red cheeks of a farmer. Her gentle face spoke of a heart that would open to even the most sullen and difficult person. She had ankles as thick as an elephant's, and her bosom was round and full, like well-wrapped melons.

Taku began. "I don't have any really clear memories. I think my family had already moved to Izu by the time I was old enough to be aware of things. My father always wore traditional workmen's split-toed boots and a towel around his head in the workman's style. I have a feeling my mom was often in traditional working clothing too. She had a small build, and never spoke much."

Although he was addressing the woman known as the Aunt of the Fifth House, it was Ai Katsuragi to whom he was really talking. She hadn't uttered a word, but kept her eyes steadily on him. Recalling the cool lips and warm breath of last night, he felt his chest grow tight. To suppress this sensation, he forced himself to focus in an attempt to immerse himself in the faint memories of his childhood.

His first recollections of what must have been his home started from the age of around four. He recalled a single room, in which his parents slept with his newborn baby sister between them, while he lay alone on a piece of matting spread by the door, huddled under a heavily patched blanket.

Unaware that he'd woken, his parents lay tangled together and moaning. He had scarcely any memory of the event. The hut was tucked in right under a cliff, and the sound of the river filled the air all night, mingled with the soughing of wind in the trees.

Wanting to urinate, he had got up and stepped outside, rubbing his eyes at the glitter of light from the river below as he stood there. The steep black mountainside across the ravine loomed over him, blocking the night sky almost completely. Needless to say, the hut had neither running water nor electricity, and there was no other house nearby.

From his earliest memories, he had gone barefooted. His father wasn't a real employee of the mine, just an assistant to the geological survey workers. With his cotton work gloves and the hammer and chisel slung at his waist, he had been an object of worship for the little boy. He would often be scolded for secretly playing with a little hammer of his own, in imitation of his dad. On holidays, his father would take him on walks through the mountains and valleys of Izu, and sometimes out to the coast. He also frequently scrambled about on the slag heaps left at abandoned mines, searching for unusual rocks.

Sometimes, when you strike your hammer on an innocuous-looking lump, it will break open to reveal a hidden wealth of blue, pink or yellow crystals. His father had what might be termed a nose for finding such rocks. He would break open some black, shapeless thing and there would be a rose crystal center, or a hidden band of pale green. After every holiday collecting expedition, his dad would take these rocks to sell to a collector in town, and come back with various presents.

Sometimes he'd get drunk at a bar in the town, staggering back home at dawn. Taku had a faint memory of the way he would sit stroking his beloved hammer, cheerful after a drink of rough spirits, saying, "I'm gonna find me a great big piece of spiroffite any day now, and make big bucks."

Taku was astonished that these fragments of memory were still with him all these years later. He'd spoken to no one of his early childhood in Izu, and had even ceased to bother recalling them himself.

"Looking back on it, I think now what a poverty-stricken existence it was," he continued. "But there was no one else around to compare my life to, so it didn't bother me in the slightest. Sure, we didn't pound rice for New Year cakes like everyone else. I seem to remember all we ate all year round was egg-rice gruel, thick noodles, and sweet potatoes."

Everyone listened in silence to Taku's halting description.

Yes, and then came the flood, that autumn the year he turned six. He didn't much want to talk about that.

"Your father, young feller, he went by the name of 'Stone-break Gen.' He *moved through* from Kyushu right up to Hokkaido when he was a youngster, after the rare mineral rocks. Good-natured feller, he was. The silent type."

It was the man on the right identified as the Uncle of the First House who spoke. His voice was subdued. An elderly man, he had the appearance of an old-fashioned craftsman, though there was something rather dapper about him. He went on in a murmur, his thin shoulders slumped, "But no matter how poor, he'd always devotedly show up to *connect* with us, and he never once asked us for a thing. If he had no money, he'd hand over to his *connection* for safekeeping the minerals he'd carefully tucked in his pocket. I remember a professor from Tokyo University was amazed at how rare and precious some of his rocks were."

"You were a friend of my father's?" asked Taku.

The Uncle of the First House nodded. "I was. I knew Gen when he got caught by the draft as a young feller and sent to work in the mines at Nogata, so that would have been, let's see, 1943 or '44, towards the end of the war. He was placid as an ox, Gen was, but there was a time he and I had a go together at doing for the labor superintendent at the mine. He had this scary way of going all quiet when he got seriously mad. But he was never mean to weaker folk, never showed off. He liked his own company. It would've been around that time he got himself officially registered. Up until then he wasn't on any family register, he just wandered the country from one mountain to another."

"So my father was a member of the Fraternity?"

The Uncle of the Seventh House took up the story. "Gen was what we call a Friend, someone who's not actually a member but who fulfills its requirements. After he was arrested in 1947 on suspicion of vagrancy, he got himself officially registered, and it was then that he would have come up with the name Gen Ishiuchi—a common name, of course, but the literal meaning is 'Stone Hitter,' so it was a kind of play on the nickname 'Stone-break.' This talk of vagrancy was actually a pretext, you know. It was how the military manufacturing sector colluded with the Ministry of Home Affairs Police Department to round up unregistered drifters and set them to work, since all the other young men had gone off to war. They sent out local fire brigade members, police constables, even the military police, to go hunting the woods and make a huge roundup of wandering artisans and performers and such like. Gen was originally the son of Mondo, the Great Uncle of our Sixth House. He was apparently born in 1925 in a shed at the Horonai coalfields in Hokkaido. Various events led to him being handed over to the Fraternity at the age of fourteen. He did a splendid job of completing the Three Austerities, then of his own volition he chose to *part* from the Fraternity, get himself an official family register, and *blend* with the outside world, and became a Friend. You're his eldest son, which means your *lineage* would give you a claim to membership in the Fraternity."

Taku listened with increasing bewilderment. His brain could no longer cope with the amount of information that had poured into it in the time since he'd been summoned to this room. The only thing that was clear to him was that he had some strange familial connection to the head of the Fraternity, Tenro Katsuragi, which apparently gives him the right to claim membership.

"Mr. Hayami." Ai spoke at last. "I don't think it's possible for you to understand everything at once. In fact, we've called you here this evening primarily to hear things from you."

"I don't know of anything I might be able to talk to you about," said Taku.

"Fine. Then may I ask a few questions?"

"Please," Taku replied.

"When were you adopted into the Hayami family in Fukui?"

"I believe it was in 1959, the summer I turned seven."

"After elementary and middle school, you proceeded to the technical high school, right? And what happened the following year?"

"I got into a fight and wounded the proprietor of a bar in the hot springs town of Awara."

"And why was this settled by a suspended sentence?"

"I think it was because I had no previous record, and the other party kindly went out of his way to file a petition to have the charge dropped."

"That was lucky, wasn't it?" There was a touch of irony in her tone.

The Aunt of the Fifth House nodded and smiled, her eyes on Taku. "So then you dropped out of high school and got a temporary mechanic's job in a Komatsu tractor parts factory, correct?"

Taku agreed this was so. He was beginning to feel irritated at how these people seemed to know so much about his past, things that even he had forgotten.

"And was your employer kind to this problem kid he'd hired?" asked Ai.

It was an odd question. "Yes. He was very understanding."

"Then in August 1970, you set off on your world travels."

"Correct."

"What did you do for money?"

"I had the savings from when I worked, plus about two hundred thousand yen that my brother had asked our parents to give me."

"Did your employer help raise some funds as well?"

"Yes. I received fifty thousand in lieu of severance pay."

"Please tell us what happened next, simply and honestly."

"I've been answering honestly all along." Taku did his best to come up with a mental summary of the essential outline of his travels after the age of eighteen. "After departing from Haneda airport, I put my cheap airline ticket to good use by stopping off in Taiwan and Bangkok en route to New Delhi. From India I travelled by bus, hitchhiking, train, boat, and occasionally on foot, following a route through Lahore, Kabul, Tehran and Tabriz to Greece, Yugoslavia, and on to western Europe. From West Germany I went north. I worked in Scandinavia for a while, traveling north till I reached Finland in November, where I settled down for a while in a town called Turku. I was nineteen by then."

"So you worked in northern Europe."

"I took jobs as I traveled. I went up to Lapland to see the midnight sun, and dropped over to visit Soviet Karelia. Over winter I spent some time in Spain and Morocco, then the next summer I worked in the north again..."

"So when did you stop living like this?"

"I was working in Oslo until the end of 1973. But it was getting difficult to arrange a work visa, and anyway, I'd had enough of northern Europe by then, so I moved south. I was now twenty-two."

"And what about 1974?"

"I was doing business with tourists around the Greek resort areas."

"What business was that?"

"Trading marijuana cigarettes and hashish."

Someone cleared his throat. The Uncle of the First House sat there impassively, while the Aunt of the Fifth House continued to listen with a smile.

"And then?"

"There was a police crackdown which prevented me from going on with that, so I contacted a Japanese businessman who'd given me his card, and made my way to Cairo, where I worked as a chauffeur for a Japanese company. Whenever I got time off, I did walking trips in various parts of Africa. After a while, I quit the job."

"Please tell us about the incident that led to your dismissal after you'd joined the safari rally team."

"I was sacked before the race. I heard a white man boasting about how he'd run down a local black and settled the matter with money, and I hit him with a wrench."

"He's Gen's son all right," remarked the Uncle of the First House, shaking his head. "Just the same."

Ai continued her questioning. "What happened then?"

"I learned that a young Japanese by the name of K. whom I'd met in Oslo had died in the Sahara. He'd been attempting to cross from one side of the desert to the other. His camel had collapsed en route, and he'd died of thirst. He was an extraordinary young man, brave and intelligent. From then on, I gradually became more and more drawn to the idea of walking. That year I walked the route of the safari rally. It was a kind of act of mourning for K., really."

"I've made copies of that piece you wrote, *The Stone Throwers*, and circulated it to our leader and the other Fraternity teachers. I was very impressed at the sensibility it displayed."

"Yes, a fine piece," broke in the man on the left who had been introduced as Hokuyo Hachimai, the teacher of Wandering Practice. "I found it very moving. I've been following your name ever since you published it in Meteor Publications' *Life and Nature*."

"Thank you very much."

"I hear that this piece appeared there thanks to the publications manager, Mr. Hanada," Ai went on.

"Yes."

"How did you come to know him?"

"He'd run into trouble in a city in Morocco. He'd been robbed of all he had."

"Robbed? The version I heard was that he got tangled up in a sex blackmail scam," the Uncle of the Eighth House remarked loudly. It was the first time he'd spoken. His straightforward frankness caused general laughter.

"From then until around 1980 was a rather stormy period for you, is that right? I've seen your pieces in *Outroads*, by the way."

"Let's just close the books on this period. I'm sure you know the story already."

"You were arrested for running arms over the Iran-Afghan border."

"Yes, I did one run for someone connected with the Afghan guerrillas. The Iranian secret police nabbed me and took me to headquarters in Tehran. I could easily have gotten ten years."

"How did you avoid it?"

"I really don't know. I guess I was lucky."

"Mr. Hayami." Ai's voice was solemn. "You have been blessed with altogether too much luck in your life, have you not? Have you never paused to wonder why?"

"What do you mean?"

"A quick run through your life story reveals five times when good fortune has been with you." She counted them off on her fingers as she went on. "You were adopted from the orphanage by the Hayamis. Where you were pampered more than their own son, correct?"

"Yes, well, that was…"

"Next, you were let off without charges after that incident while you were a student. Despite the fact that your victim sustained considerable injuries."

Taku said nothing.

"Third, the immediate appearance of your kind factory employer. He took on a problem kid, and when you wanted to leave he went so far as to collect funds for your travels."

Taku gazed at her. Everyone present was listening to the exchange in silence. Tenro Katsuragi sat with eyes closed, a benign smile on his lips. There was a faint sound of snoring—the old man introduced as the teacher of Scholarly Practice had begun to drift off, his head lurching backwards and forwards. No one seemed worried by this, however.

"Fourth," came Ai's voice, "The kindly businessman in Cairo gave you all those opportunities to learn about different parts of Africa, not to mention paying you a very good salary."

"Well, I believe I was an able chauffeur, you know."

"You apparently totaled a company car in the desert, however."

Taku had had enough. "Right. Okay. What about the fifth?"

"The Iranian secret police simply released a machine gun smuggler without charges."

"And there's more, right?" Taku's voice was strong. "Once back in Japan, Meteor Publications took me on despite my lack of any real skill."

"No," said Ai firmly. "You got that job through your own talents. If you hadn't, it's quite possible you would have been approached by Ryuzaki's gangsters. Do you think they'd pass up the chance to employ an able man like yourself, with your knowledge of car mechanics and experience in drug handling and weaponry sales?"

Taku fell silent. He had by now realized what implication lay behind Ai's words. It was true, again and again he'd been lucky. He had the feeling he was seeing into the mechanism hidden in a black box that until now he'd never paused to consider.

But I can hardly believe…he said to himself. Yet he couldn't deny what she was suggesting. After all, there was that extraordinary incident in the hotel room. If she hadn't appeared then, Ryuzaki would probably have jammed him into the trunk of a car and either buried him somewhere or drowned him.

"Mr. Hayami," said the Uncle of the First House. "Ever since you were born as Gen's son there in the mountains of Chichibu, the Fraternity has been looking after you. Our leader here went especially to see you as a baby. He was the one who named you Taku. You are Gen's son, so we and the Fraternity have been quietly keeping an eye on you from afar. When and only when you were really in need of help, the Fraternity gave you support, though it was kept to a minimum. These are the facts."

Taku remained silent for a moment, staring down at his bandaged feet. He was suddenly acutely aware of the pain in his left sole. Then he raised his eyes to the words written on the banner behind Tenro Katsuragi. He had a feeling they were beginning to convey some special meaning to him.

Plough no furrow   *Live in no place*
Belong to no nation   *Have no self*

Taku arranged his legs to sit formally on the floor, enduring the pain in his feet. Squaring his chest, he gazed first at the old man in front of him, then his gaze traveled over everyone in the rows on either side.

"Could I ask you please to explain things to me clearly now. I have had enough of this enigmatic dialogue. I've answered everything truthfully."

The snores of Rokotsu Sarashino, the teacher of Scholarly Practice, suddenly ceased. Taku continued. "Tell me why, please. You say I'm the son of Gen Ishiuchi, a poor mine worker who was not directly involved with the Fraternity, so why have you all watched over me so carefully all these years? Why should the leader himself give me my name, and make a point of coming all the way to the mountains of Chichibu to see me as a baby? Why have you all gathered like this to wait for me, though I'm only a lowly descendant from one of the families? Who on earth am I?"

Still on his knees, he shuffled forward a little. "Tell me, I beg you." His hands gripped each other on his lap. His eyes were fixed on Tenro Katsuragi. He was determined that he would not budge until he had learned the answer.

"Let me be the one to tell him." The voice was a sleepy, drawn-out drawl. The strange old man named Rokotsu Sarashino thumped the back of his neck a few times as if to loosen the muscles, gave another large yawn, and looked around at the assembled gathering. "That okay, everyone?"

The leader was the first to nod. Then the others to the left and right added their agreement.

"Taku, you say the name is?" He spoke with unaffected warmth. Taku listened carefully. "I'm the sort who can only give you a simple answer to what you want to know, lad. Besides, I'm an old fogey. So I'll just say as much as I want to say, okay? Listen well."

Taku concentrated. The old man continued. "You're the only man alive who's a direct descendant of our first leader, Henro Katsuragi."

Taku repeated the old man's words silently to himself. The words were clear and straightforward enough, but there was too much he didn't understand. "Me? I'm a descendant of Henro? So you mean that Tenro and Ai…"

"We don't choose our leader by bloodline," Sarashino went on bluntly. "Henro was the founder of the Fraternity. The families who were members from the beginning are what we term The Eight Families. A total of fifty-five, counting the babies. A representative's chosen from each family, who devotes him- or herself to the running of the Fraternity. It's kind of like taking monastic vows. They're called Fraternity Comrades. They're the folks we call Uncle and Aunt. When our first Parent, Henro Katsuragi, died at eighty-eight, he left a will stating that the next leader should be chosen from among the eight Aunts and Uncles, and take the name Katsuragi. Tenro Katsuragi here is that man. When he passes away, we choose the next one in the same manner, see? So it's not a matter of bloodline. It's a matter of popular trust in someone who lives up to Henro's hopes. You got that?"

"Yes, I understand. So why is Henro's bloodline an issue? It doesn't make sense."

"Precisely. But listen, Taku, it's the weird things about humans that make them human, you know. Our leader Henro was a special person for us Fraternity members. That fact is, for those of us who had the good fortune to know him in life and to hear his words, it's inexplicably precious to be able to remember him through you, his direct descendant. You have his face, Taku. Just hearing your voice and watching how you move brings back to us the image of our beloved teacher as a young man. It's incredibly stirring. I'll admit there's no logic to the feelings that made us follow your career from afar, and lend you a little support from time to time—but you see, you're the only person alive who's Henro's direct descendant. It's out of a kind of nostalgia, a remembering, a yearning for his pure and unsullied spirit. We beg you to understand this, and to forgive our impertinence. Eventually, you'll learn about the life of Henro and those who came after him—an activity we call *Scholarly Practice*. I'll tell you all, the whole truth of the Family that's been hidden beneath the terms 'history' and 'scholarship.' This is the real reason you've been brought here, Taku."

All trace of the sleepy drawl had disappeared from the old man's voice. As he spoke, his tone became increasingly passionate, his withered, weirdly stonefish-like features grew crimson, and his tiny body seemed to swell and loom over Taku.

"Taku, I welcome you here with all my heart. You've been a long time wandering on the way, but it wasn't time ill spent. We're not planning to treat you in any special way or accord you special status on account of your lineage. It's simply a personal thing, you understand. But it seems, Taku, that for more than a decade you were unwittingly pursuing a study of the *wandering practice* and the *walking practice* outside the Fraternity. That was clear to me when I was shown your piece in *Life and Nature*. There's a new breadth of vision unknown to us in that essay of yours. It's convinced me that you can inject a new spirit into our degenerating Fraternity, indeed I believe you're the only one who can. Ai understood this, and that's why she brought you here. The Fraternity is preparing to put its very life on the line by undertaking this great test. It's also desperately seeking a way forward, a new *raison d'être* for its place in the modern world. Let me ask you, for instance—what do you think of that?"

The old man pointed to the writing on the banner behind Tenro, and sighed deeply. "*Plough no furrow*, it says. The problem is—is it right to continue to reject the farming life of rice cultivation and go on following the ancient way of planting, burning, and moving on? Is it still okay to do as people once did and cut the forests for fuel to smelt iron? What happens once the wild animals are all hunted out? I'm not speaking of five hundred or a thousand years ago—look at the present state of minority hill tribes in Southeast Asia such as the Kha, the Hmong, the Yao, etc. It's obvious what's happening to them. The anthropologist Lévi-Strauss divided human activity into collecting and making. The former is the nomadic consumer existence of gathering, using, discarding, and moving on, while the latter is its opposite, the settler-farmer existence. According to him, the settled life promotes more imaginative ability than the throwaway life of the nomad who lives in the moment. I disagree, though I do concede he has a point. But nature has its limits. The life of the mountain folk who take no thought for conserving and reusing is no longer possible. 'Live in no place'—Henro devoted his life to living this principle. But as for us today…"

"Excuse me, Mr. Sarashino," Tenro Katsuragi said in a gentle voice, holding out a hand. "I don't think your student here is going anywhere. Let's leave the lectures till later, shall we? The pleasures of teaching are the finer for a little anticipation."

"I do apologize. It's just that I don't have much time left. I've let myself rush on."

"Mr. Hayami." The leader turned to Taku. "Everyone has gathered here this evening out of a desire to see the man who is Henro's direct descendant. Not only my daughter but I too want to ask you to lend your support to the Fraternity if possible. I'm delighted to hear that you've asked of your own volition to join us. I've no doubt you're still feeling completely in the dark about the Fraternity, the Wayfarers, and your own place in all this, but I'm sure all will be explained to you by Ai and our Scholarly Practice teacher, Mr. Sarashino. I hope you won't mind if we appoint Yugaku as your helper. He's the man responsible for the Fraternity's Youth Department. He's adept in the martial arts, from Chinese *kenpo* to ancient Korean jujutsu, Mongolian wrestling, as well as various Japanese martial arts. He's bound to be of use to you. He's also said he'd love to learn whatever he can from you about foreign countries. I'd be personally grateful if you two became friends. He's the brother of my daughter Ai here."

Here he broke off and turned to survey everyone.

"Uncles, Aunts, and everyone present, I'm sure you're feeling weary by now. Please have another rest before tomorrow morning. Thank you all very much for coming here this evening. I must say, though, it's been a good evening. Speaking for myself, I've seen before me for the first time in many decades the face of my teacher Henro, and it's made me…"

Tenro pressed the palms of his hands to his eyes. The Aunt of the Fifth House was sniffling. The Uncle of the Seventh House gave what sounded like a sob, and his thin shoulders shook.

What kind of person must this Henro have been, wondered Taku, to make them all so moved at the memory of him? And here he was, the direct inheritor of the bloodline.

"Thank you very much," he said, head bowed low. He tried to rise, and staggered. Then, gritting his teeth to produce a final, desperate smile, he backed out of the room.

14

While the strapping young monk was leading Taku back to the room where he'd slept, Taku introduced himself. "Your name is Yukaku, is that right? How do you do. I'm Taku Hayami. I look forward to knowing you better." His tone was carefully polite.

"It's pronounced Yugaku, not Yukaku, actually," the monk replied. "I'm Ai's elder brother. I look forward to learning much from you."

Taku decided now was the moment to ask about something he'd been wondering for some time. "Was it just sheer chance that we met the other day on that train from Kyoto? Or was it in fact…"

"It was just chance. I was setting off early to provide backup for the Youth Department's Futakami Pilgrimage—you know, making sure things go smoothly, picking up stragglers by car, and so on. So our happening to meet that day must really have been thanks to some karmic connection. Though to tell the truth, as soon as I got on I noticed you, and immediately decided I must sit beside you and talk to you. It so happened the seat next to you was free, so I sat myself down there."

"Why?"

"When I saw you I instantly thought, That fellow can walk. Sorry, it must sound rude to put it like that."

"I thought the same thing about you the moment I saw you, too."

"Really?" said Yugaku with a smile. "In that case, I still need further training."

"I'd say the same for myself."

The two looked at each other and laughed. I think I'm going to be friends with this guy, thought Taku.

"Truly great walkers don't look anything special under normal circumstances," Yugaku went on. "Those monks I told you about that day, who perform the Thousand-Day Mountain Circuit—they never have the air of being anything special."

"The Sherpas I met from the Himalayan foothills had skinny legs half the size of those warrior walkers you find in mountaineering clubs," responded Taku.

The two paused by a stone lantern in the little garden, and stood gazing out over the town's lights to the dark sea beyond.

"I spent ten years practicing austerities in the temple up on Mount Hiei," Yugaku remarked. "These days I'm working for the Group, but once this particular problem is resolved I have a firm plan to take myself off to do the ancient pilgrimage of the mountain monks in the Omine mountains, and make an attempt of the Thousand-Day Circuit. That's my life's dream. But I'm not sure if I will survive until I can return to the mountains…"

The words made Taku instantly alert. "Survive until you return to the mountains? What do you mean?"

"As our leader said earlier, our Group faces a crisis. We're pitting our very existence against a huge power right now. Do you know what it is?"

"It would be the Ikarino Corporation, right?"

Yugaku nodded silently. Then he went on, "It's not actually the Group's enemy, you know. It was originally an offspring created by our Wayfarers' League, and Meido Ikarino used to be a trusted brother and companion for us. But as the corporation grew huger and huger, it mutated into an abnormal monster. Meido's corporation is actually part of us. It's a kind of cancer bred inside our own body, and now it's suddenly threatening to overwhelm us. We may well have to take a laser beam and excise our own lungs, our gut, perhaps most of our body. If we fail, life will be lost. But if we leave the cancer cells to spread, they can only lead to destruction. We must go on living, even if it means we have to sever our own limbs and cut out our own innards. But who knows if this will prove possible?" He paused abruptly, then continued in a low murmur, "If only our founder Henro were here right now…"

The lights of the little fishing boats were moving over the dark sea. The salty tang of the sea seemed suddenly more intense. Taku's eyes followed the black outline of cape and mountain ridge that rose from the water. Beyond those mountains was the deep valley where he had lived his short infancy with his original family.

Gen Ishiuchi.

In his youth, his father had walked alone through the mountains of this nation in search of precious stone, a wanderer with only his hammer and chisel for a friend. A "stone breaker."

So this was Taku's grandfather. All his life he'd been a homeless wandering miner. Taku tried to imagine the scene of him cradling his little son in the hut in Hokkaido's Horonai coalfields.

From somewhere deep within him rose a mysterious emotion. The extraordinary feeling broke surface in his heart like the fin of some huge shark. He shuddered, gripped by a sudden urge to raise his voice and cry out to those far mountains from where he stood deep in the mountains of Izu.

15

Taku woke at seven the next morning. Out on the glassed veranda facing onto the garden, a bright strip of slanting sunlight shone in through a gap in the curtains.

His feet felt less painful than the night before, and he sensed his old energy coursing again through his body.

I'm not past it yet, he told himself.

He rose, washed his face, and shaved. The dark circles under his eyes had gone.

When he opened the curtains, through the garden trees he could see a view of the distant sea, cape, and mountains. Out in the garden, a strange shape was standing on the stones of the little path. It looked like a stone lantern, but was in fact the figure of Yugaku Katsuragi, clad in grey practice wear.

He was upside down on the stone. And not only that, his fists were clenched and his body supported only by his thumbs. After a moment or two, he lifted one hand from the stone, his legs tipping slightly right and left in the air for balance as he did so. His entire frame was now supported, perfectly steady, on only one thumb.

"Outstanding!" Taku called to him. Yugaku gently lowered his other hand to the ground again, then brought down his legs.

"You slept well?" he asked with a smile as he wiped his hands with a cloth. "A little while ago there was a phone call from someone named Goro Hanada from Meteor Publications. He wanted you to contact him when you woke up."

"Right."

Taku picked up the room telephone, and asked the front desk to call Hanada's home number.

Hanada answered without delay.

"I hear you called earlier," said Taku.

"Ah, Taku. What's happened? I've been really worried. Why haven't you contacted me?" Unlike his work voice, Hanada's home voice had the cautious tone of a family man aware of those around him.

"I walked from Tokyo to Mount Izu that evening. With Ai Katsuragi. It was quite a marathon."

He knew that, Hanada said. "Little Kyoko from *Tramping* told me," he went on. "The poor girl has been sitting in front of your apartment phone since yesterday, you know. What're you going to do, eh? Not that I'd mind particularly if you want to marry her."

"I'll call her right after this."

"That's a good idea." Hanada's tone became suddenly serious. "So when will you leave there?"

"I'll ask someone in the Group. But my plan is to go back, regardless. There are lots of things I need to deal with back there."

"By the way, there's just been a news flash on the television." Hanada's voice was suddenly barely audible. "Something about Saera Maki's manager being hurt in an accident."

"What?"

"That's the young fellow you were talking to at the party, right?"

"Sorry. I'll call you right back." Taku hung up, and immediately dialed Shin'ichi's Yokohama number.

When his brother came on the phone, Taku said, "Shin? It's me. I hear Seta's had some kind of accident?"

"Where are you calling from?" Shinichi sounded wary.

"From Mount Izu. Don't worry, we can talk. What on earth's happened?"

"He went over the guard rail at around four this morning somewhere near Hamagawa-saki on the Yokohane Line."

"How is he?"

"Apparently he'll survive, but…" Shin'ichi didn't finish. "Saera rushed straight to the hospital. Well, that was fine, but when she saw the state he was in, the shock was enough to put her into the same hospital."

"Didn't I tell you on the phone not to let anyone use the car for now?" Taku's tone was unaccustomedly fierce. He was berating his brother, he realized.

"Right, so I've been leaving the Quattroporte in the garage."

"It was the Ferrari then, was it?"

"He just kept insisting that one would be okay, you see."

Taku fell silent. He had the feeling he was responsible. He shouldn't have simply passed the warning over the phone, he should have gone there personally and pulled the batteries out of all the cars or something. That young lad looked clever enough, but in fact he was completely crazy about cars. It was only a standard four-seater, but it was still a Ferrari. Seta just had to get his hands on the steering wheel, apparently. Still, what an idiot!

"Can you get the car checked out?"

"It went straight off an overpass and burst into flames."

"What do the police say?"

"They think he probably fell asleep at the wheel. It was four in the morning, and apparently no other cars where in the vicinity. There are no witnesses."

"I'll head back there as soon as I can. You'll be leaving Saera in the hospital for now, right? Look Shin, if anything happens ring the Ryukien at Mount Izu."

Taku gave the number, reminded his brother once more to touch none of the other cars, and hung up.

"Is something the matter?" asked Yugaku from the cane chair on the veranda where he sat. He gazed intently at Taku.

"Saera Maki's manager has had a bad accident and is in the hospital."

"A car accident?"

"Someone from the Konryu gang was present last night, weren't they?"

Yugaku nodded silently.

"Could you let me talk to him?"

"He's gone home, I'm afraid."

"I see." Taku stared out at the brilliantly sunlit garden. Too bright, he said silently to himself. It's a sham. Somewhere behind this peaceful landscape lurks a black and desolate world.

"Sulphuric acid," he said aloud.

"What?" asked Yugaku in surprise.

Taku shook his head.

Yes, it was sulphuric acid that Ryuzaki had threatened to pour into Shin'ichi's ears. We've got someone who's a professional at it, he'd said. So that's it—instead of burning Shin's ear drums with the stuff, they'd used it to skillfully erode the break hose on the 400i! When the breaks were applied normally the effect wouldn't be apparent, but if you rammed them on hard in panic the fluid pressure would snap the hose. Even if the backup safety system was activated, pumping on the brake would have the same result. And Seta wouldn't have had the skill to know to shift down a gear and countersteer with the necessary fine coordination.

"I'll accompany you when you leave here,"Yugaku said."Actually, Sarashino Sensei has announced that after breakfast he'll hold a special *scholarly practice* for you. It's to be a twelve-hour lecture, from nine until nine this evening."

Taku nodded. He was very eager to hear what the old man Rokotsu Sarashino had to say. Once this first lesson was over, he could take the bullet train back to Tokyo, perhaps the following day.

With an apology to Yugaku, he asked the receptionist to put him through to his home phone number. As he waited, he wondered what excuse he was going to tell Kyoko.

The second floor room of the storehouse was as dark as it had been the night before. Five figures were dimly outlined in the faint light that penetrated the room from the small skylight.

The teacher, Sarashino Sensei, sat cross-legged on the floor at the front. Glasses as thick as the base of a bottle were perched on his nose, and he was wearing a dark blue *happi* coat that bore the words "Tenmu Jinshin Group" down one lapel, and down the other "Company of Fifty-Five." He was murmuring under his breath what sounded like a chanted sutra.

To his right Ai Katsuragi sat formally on her heels. Her back was straight, her chin tucked in, and she sat as still as a statue.

Beside her was the fat elderly woman who had been introduced the night before as the Aunt of the Fifth House. She was shifting constantly on her knees under the weight of what must have been over seventy kilos of flesh.

Taku was seated on his heels before Sarashino, hands placed neatly on his thighs before him. He was worried about how long he could sustain this traditional sitting position, but the tension of his first training session helped him to bear the discomfort. On his left, Yugaku held his formal seated pose with a perfect and unwavering focus. Taku guessed that it was his extensive training at the monastery of Mount Hiei that had instilled in him this poised ability to sit as if rooted to the earth.

"Right." Sarashino raised his face at last and began to speak.

"Let me begin by telling you that we have long valued the transmission of knowledge by word of mouth rather than in written form. However, our present age is a complex one, and the world has come to share a common fate. To adapt to the times, we can no longer afford to ignore the various others means of communication such as writing, use of symbols, screen images, diagrams, and the rest. We mustn't stint in our efforts to draw on all these as tools for our own culture and lives. Yet our hearts still lie primarily in the spoken word form of oral transmission. This will never alter, whatever new forms of communication are developed in the future. Indeed it is imperative that it remain. I'd like to just confirm this fact. Is this understood, Mr. Hayami?"

Sarashino fixed his gaze on Taku from behind his thick glasses.

"Yes, I understand."

The old man turned to gaze fondly at Ai. "Young Ai here has already engraved firmly in her memory all that I myself have memorized. Our ancient legends, the anecdotes about our life, the tales and songs, the family lineage, and most particularly, the words of our teacher Henro Katsuragi and the history of the *wandering practice*—all this has been marvelously stored away deep within her. From the age of three she displayed outstanding powers of memory compared to the other Group children, and she quickly acquired competence in her chosen field of training. My role has ended. Each passing year erodes my memory more, and my body is no longer reliable. Therefore, I've asked Ai to be here as my assistant for the occasion. I imagine you will be my final student, Mr. Hayami.

I've been told by the doctors that I have at most another six months to live."

"Sensei, I…" Ai began, but Sarashino held up a hand to silence her.

"There's no need to comfort me. I'm happy to have gained such a fine successor. I only ask that you feel free to correct me today whenever I make mistakes or my memory fails me."

Ai bowed her head in silent acquiescence. Drawing a cloth from his pocket, Sarashino held it to his mouth and gave a couple of coughs. Yugaku rose and stood behind him, rubbing his back.

Sarashino then turned to the Aunt. "When did you first hear me talk, do you remember, Aunt?" he asked hoarsely.

"I've heard you three times," the woman replied. "The first time was the spring when I was seventeen, then the autumn after my third son was born, and finally the year I turned fifty. Yes, three times I've heard you, Sensei, and I count myself a lucky woman for it, I do."

"Ah no, it's I who must do the thanking. Please take care of Ai here after I'm gone, won't you?"

"There's no need to…" The Aunt of the Fifth House shook her head and laughed gently. Wiping the phlegm that his coughing had dislodged, he nodded his thanks to Yugaku, who continued to rub his back.

"I'm fine now," he said. "Right then, where shall I begin?" He thought for a moment, then turned to Taku. "Whenever I need to use writing, Yugaku can put it on paper for me. Please look at that while you listen. Some other time Ai will be able to tell you the stories of the old days and the long history of the Kenshi clan. I'll skip the tales of long ago, and concentrate today on briefly informing you about how our teacher Henro established the Group. Please feel free to ask about anything you don't understand."

Yugaku spread a sheet of white paper beside Taku, took up a brush pen, and nodded to the old man.

Sarashino's low, powerful voice began to fill the dimly lit room. "The first person to appear on our stage is a provincial governor by the name of Atsushi Saisho."

Yugaku's pen moved swiftly over the paper, and he nodded to Taku to look where he had written the name. The vigorous characters stood out strongly even in the half light.

"The term used in those days was a more old-fashioned one than the present-day 'provincial governor,' of course. 'District commander,' it was back then, a term deriving originally from Chinese and introduced in the early days of the Meiji government here, in the late nineteenth century, for what we now call a prefectural governor. So this man Saisho was a district commander, in fact."

Yugaku wrote the term.

"We're speaking here of the moment when Japanese history had just turned the corner from the feudal isolation of the Edo period to the modernizing Meiji period. Though the sovereignty had shifted from the shogun to the Meiji emperor, of course there was still no change in the respective roles of the powerful and the powerless. Apparently those men from the old samurai factions who took control in the new government strutted their stuff even more proudly than the old feudal lords had. And all the more so, of course, once the government abolished the old feudal domains in 1871 and took centralized control of the nation."

"'Abolition of Domains,'" wrote Yugaku's dancing brush.

"So this moment was the beginning of true centralization of power for the new Meiji government," Sarashino went on. "The country was divided into seventy-five prefectures, and instead of the old local lords, these were now governed by completely unrelated government officials who were sent by special dispensation. By 'special dispensation' I mean the practice of the main faction in government, made up of samurai from the three victorious domains of the recent civil war, using its muscle to push through whoever it chose for the jobs."

"In the beginning the nation was divided into three hundred five prefectures, wasn't it, Sensei, and later they were amalgamated to the present seventy-five," Ai broke in gently.

Sarashino nodded. "Yes, yes, that's correct. So anyway, here we had the start of the modern national administrative policy, whereby, with a single proclamation, the government set about grasping central control of the nation. Then followed the steps of creating family registers for the entire population, and the implementation of conscription.

"Anyway, the advance scouts for this nationalized political system were the chosen appointees from those three domains who scrambled for their new positions as local governors. And one of them was Atsushi Saisho, the personage who from 1869 for many years reigned supreme, like some viceroy in the colonies, over the Kawachi and Yamato areas around Nara and Osaka. Ai, could you just speak a little more about Saisho now please?"

"Certainly," she answered readily. Her voice began to flow like water through the room, while Yugaku's brush whispered down the white page in response to her words.

"Saisho would have been among the most famous of the district commanders or prefectural governors put in place by the central government at the start of the Meiji era. By 'famous' I mean notorious for the various scandals he provoked. It was spoken of as common knowledge among the population that wherever he went in Kawachi, Sakai, and Yamato, strange dark rumors would always follow him."

"That's true," Sarashino said forcefully. "Make things clearer there if you would please, Ai. I mean about just what sort of man he was. No need to pull your punches."

"Certainly." Ai proceeded coolly. "We don't know a great deal about Atsushi Saisho. He was born in 1828 into an impoverished samurai family in the loyalist Satsuma domain in southern Kyushu, and from an early age he struggled to educate himself in the face of circumstance. He had close dealings with the loyalist Satsuma samurai who reinstated the emperor in the civil war and ushered in the Meiji era, and apparently he later went up to the capital and became a student of the great classics scholar Atsutane Hirata. He was both a hard worker and an able official, who had earned the trust of his feudal lord, but he also had a more mysterious side to him, and was rumored to have been the killer in the assassination of the exclusionist Kintomo Anegakoji at Gogatsudo Temple in 1863. When the Satsuma samurai later sent out their forces to overthrow the feudal shogunate, under the banner of restoring the emperor,

Saisho took over the position of treasurer in charge of finances and raised a vast sum from the financiers of the Osaka region. Businessmen in the region still quote tongue in cheek the words he spoke on that occasion to Okubo..."

"That's right." Sarashino took up the tale. "What he said was this: 'You must devote yourselves to your country, and leave to me the matter of money.' In other words, you go out and fight, boys, I'll raise the dough. You can probably imagine how he went about raising it. Then, when the battle of Toba Fushimi caused the opposing shogunate forces to besiege the Satsuma lord's residence, Saisho performed the feat of escaping with thirty thousand *ryo* of money. Those war funds were apparently a great resource when the Satsuma forces attacked the capital. So once the emperor was restored and the new Meiji government established by the Satsuma samurai and their allies, his distinguished service to the cause shot him up the ladder of success without a hitch."

Ai's voice picked up the story again.

"His first appointment was as provisional justice in Osaka. Then he became first governor of Kawachi, provisional governor of Hyogo, and after the domains became prefectures in 1871, he gained the position of district commander of Sakai. Now this area had long been a very important one, both historically and economically, and having control of the region was equivalent to being one of the great feudal lords of old. This period, up until he became governor of Nara prefecture in 1887, was his heyday. His interests didn't lie in the lives of the people he governed but were entirely concentrated on winning the favor of the top bureaucrats and statesmen who ruled the central government. His secret ambition was to turn around his fate as a poor samurai boy from an outer domain who had got caught up in the disturbances, and gain a place among the nobility, the aristocratic class of new Meiji lords."

It was Sarashino's turn again. "And now another dark rumor sprang up around him. Sakai's first district commander, the man appointed before Saisho, was one Kazutoshi Ogo. He was just the opposite of Saisho, a real eccentric. Let me tell you a bit about him.

"This fine personage hailed from Kyushu too, but he was the son of a samurai, Sojuro Ogo, from a small domain called Oka, in the

Oita region. Now the Oka clan had fought on the defeated shogun's side in the civil war, so that meant Ogo wasn't in the mainstream faction in the new government. It probably wasn't just the outsider defiance that made him place priority on creating policies to aid the sufferings of the poverty-stricken populace in his new role as Sakai district commander. He voluntarily reduced his own salary and got his subordinates to do the same, lowered local taxes, lent out money to strengthen the levies, and generally set himself up in opposition to the central government, which was ordering a stronger enforcement of taxation. For this reason, he was swiftly relieved of his duties as district commander, and forced out of Sakai. And…"

"And the man who replaced him," Yugaku suddenly said beside Taku, "was Atsushi Saisho, a man who'd do anything to please the central government. The people put up a stone in memory of Ogo, who had looked after them in their suffering and been sacked by the central government. It's still there today."

"That's so," said Sarashino. "Ogo had a very high reputation among the local people. But the Meiji government was strapped for funds, so he was a real bane for them. And what's more, the secret reports were pouring in that Ogo was being highly critical of the government. It was a plot, of course. And the man who was pulling the strings…"

"Was a man called Yosuke Nawagi," Ai broke in.

Yugaku wrote the name on his page.

"Just so." Sarashino's voice now grew more somber. "Now this fellow happened to be the head of a press gang recruiting workers for a coal mine up in Hokkaido. He ran a labor camp that functioned by deceiving poor folk from other parts of the country into come to Hokkaido for work, then compelling them into life-threatening hard labor in the mine. He killed a man, fled, and went to ground down in Osaka. Later, when he was involved in an engineering company that dealt with embankment reinforcement, he began to have private communications with Saisho, and became a key player in setting up the plot that removed Ogo. This feat led to his later nefarious role as personal spy for Saisho, and the dirty part he played in all kinds of stories. He'll come in again when we get to the Futakami Incident, so remember him."

"Yosuke Nawagi," Taku repeated. He was concentrating his whole attention on the old man's words, committing them to memory.

Sarashino continued. "So Saisho had made use of informers to get rid of Ogo, and he'd attained his desire of becoming district commander of Sakai. He went on to create for himself a special means of furthering his ambitions and climbing the ladder to power. And finally, he attained his dream of joining the ranks of the nobility and being given the title of viscount. In 1890 he was placed in charge of the imperial treasures, then he took on the task of organizing the important cultural treasures held in the Shosoin Treasure House in Nara. Well, it was like putting a wolf in the sheepfold, you might say." Sarashino chuckled.

"What were the special means he created for furthering his ambitions?" Taku asked.

Ai answered before the old man could open his mouth. "It seems that in those days district commanders held the kind of absolute power accorded to viceroys of a colony. So they could get away with all sorts of things unimaginable today. The first thing Saisho did to impress the central government with his prowess was to strengthen the local taxation system. Then he discovered another means to his ends—he did the rounds of all the treasures held in the region's shrines and temples, which were full of ancient cultural and historical objects, on the strength of making an inspection of them."

"It sounds as if he was unusually fond of cultural relics," Taku observed. "It reminds me of the rumor I heard that the boss of Ikarino Corporation is a great fan of classical music."

The Aunt of the Fifth House gave a laugh.

Ai continued. "There's certainly nothing wrong with touring around inspecting ancient art and artifacts, true. But Saisho wasn't really the same kind of guy. The idea he'd come up with made use of the fad among the central government elite at the time for collecting antique art."

"How would he do that?"

"Well, Saisho himself apparently made quite a study of art appreciation. On his official rounds of inspection, he would make a point of carrying off anything that looked particularly valuable, which he then presented as a gift to a senior official or passed along to powerful businessmen. This was actually publicized in the pre-war magazine I have here. Go on, take a look."

Ai drew over an old magazine and passed it to Taku. It was an old *Bungei Shunju*, the cover yellowed with age, dated 1927.

"Sorry, it's a bit dark. Can you read it?"

"Yes, fine." He opened it to the page marked with a little slip of paper, and found an article consisting of a four-person round-table discussion. He read the names, "The famous folklorist Kunio Yanagida, novelists Ryunosuke Akutagawa and Kan Kikuchi—I've heard of these three. Who's this other one, something Osatake?—I can't read his first name. Is he a novelist too?"

"Those characters are read Takeki Osatake," Sarashino explained. "He was a lawyer. He was a justice of the Supreme Court, and head of the committee that compiled the history of the constitutional government for the Lower House. He died just after the war ended, if I remember rightly."

"1927. That's quite a while ago," Taku remarked.

"Akutagawa, the famous novelist, committed suicide the summer of the year he was part of that discussion. The discussion actually begins with talk of the Japanese summer night ghost story tradition—a rather spooky coincidence, you might say."

Taku skipped the opening section and began to read. Beside him Yugaku pointed to a particular passage:

Yanagida: …But the worst was Viscount X, wasn't it?

Osatake: Yes, while he was district commander of Sakai he made off with most of the treasures of the Nara temples and shrines. He either seized them on the strength of his powers as district commander, or secretly switched them for others.

Akutagawa: And this never came before the courts?

Osatake: Well, back in the early days of Meiji, district commanders were a force to be reckoned with. They acted like the old feudal lords of their domains, and they had at their disposal the powers of the judiciary, the police, and part of the military. Besides which, the populace still had an almost slave mentality with regard to those in power.

Yanagida: Apparently Nara lost the greater part of its antique treasures during that time.

Otake: Yes, they were carried off on the grounds that the district commander wished to view them, and never returned. Or a sword in its scabbard, for example, would be returned with a different sword instead. And that wasn't the worst of it. One of his subordinates would go off with some traveling funds and dig up all the burial mounds of the ancient emperors, take up residence under orders in a local rich man's house, and its valuable objects would be pocketed by the district commander. Mind you, by the standards of the old feudal regime this was perfectly acceptable governance.

Akutagawa: Is that so? How disgusting.

Yanagida: Well, from that point of view at least, Japan today is a better place. If people were to do that sort of thing today they wouldn't get away with it.

Osatake: There's more besides, but it doesn't do to say too much about it.

Taku read the passage quickly, then closed the magazine and handed it back to Ai.

"This 'Viscount X' is the Saisho in question, is it?"

Sarashino nodded. "One novelist wrote that it was Viscount Kitahara, but that's wrong. Everyone was aware at the time that it was Saisho. But why do you think no one brought him to task while he was alive?"

"I'd guess it was because the treasures he made off with weren't in his possession but held in the collections of the Meiji high officials and statesmen."

"Correct. Prime Minister Ito and his ilk were all dedicated antique collectors. Later, when Ito was the first Resident General of Korea, he sent back to Japan all manner of treasure plundered from the burial mound excavations there."

Taku suddenly felt a little firework flash of odd associations light up in his mind.

"Recently, the Greek Culture Minister Marina Mercouri has put in a formal request to Great Britain to have the Elgin marbles that were part of the temple of the Parthenon returned, hasn't she?

And apparently the Indian President and the head of the national art gallery in Egypt are also asking for the return of part of the treasures that made their way to France and England in the colonial period."

"It's *said* that a precious zodiac mirror and a ring pommel sword were taken from the Nintoku Tomb and are held in the Boston Museum of Fine Arts," Sarashino said calmly.

"The Boston Museum?" Taku tensed slightly. Surely it was the same museum in Boston that all that fuss about an unexploded time bomb was about? He recalled how Cho had suddenly stiffened and looked thoughtful when he heard the two men talking about it in the Lotus that day.

"But let's move on a bit more quickly," the old man continued. "So you've probably more or less got the picture about what sort of man Saisho was. But he never soiled his own hands. No, he left the dirty work to his trusted friend Nawagi, the man who'd turned up in Osaka on the run, you'll recall. In fact Nawagi should by rights have been on our side, but he went the opposite way. We're aware that that sort of thing can happen quite a lot. Sadly . . ."

Ai took up the story. "In 1876, Sakai prefecture was having a prosperous period. It already had the Kawachi and Izumi regions under its umbrella, and that year Nara prefecture was abolished and amalgamated with Sakai as well."

Taku could sense a certain growing emotion in Ai's voice as she spoke. Yugaku now broke in.

"What this meant, you see, was that the Nintoku Tomb, Mount Nijo, the Takenouchi Highway, were all handed over to Saisho."

"Precisely. It started with the old highway. I believe you already know about the Takenouchi, correct?"

"Yes, I had a lecture about it from Professor Nishihaga. But I may have forgotten the details."

"I don't think you'll have forgotten a place you walked yourself," said Ai. This was true, Taku thought. He did indeed have a vivid memory of walking along the old highway in the dusk after his numerous climbs to the twin peaks of Nijo that day.

Ai began to speak again. "That road has been laid and laid again, countless times since the early days. It's a difficult road to make.

It was an important official route in the beginning, of course, but it's never been easy going—the gradients are steep, the mists can make you lose your way, and the rains can cause landslides.

"But maintenance of this highway was the visible proof of the authority of the area's rulers. Their power was gauged by how easy the passage was along this highway, how wide it was, and how good the gradients were during their reign. So it's perfectly comprehensible that Saisho, the district commander who had for so long caused all those suspicious rumors throughout the region, should decide to undertake a huge improvement project there at the hands of the new Meiji government, in other words, himself. His bosom buddy Nawagi had no doubt informed him of the fact that he had an unsavory reputation in the area.

"If Sakai prefecture was going to take over Nara prefecture's territory, that is to say, the Yamato area, the arterial road connecting them would obviously become very important. And besides, he wanted to leave a monument to himself as a great district commander. And to create something worth seeing to prove his worth to the central government. For a combination of all these reasons, he set his heart on undertaking a great renovation of the Takenouchi Highway. In fact, Nara prefecture had tried to do this itself the previous year, and failed. He must prove to the newly-acquired Yamato the power of his own great prefecture. And so the difficult work began on this huge undertaking. This was in 1877."

Ai paused for breath, and looked at Taku. He nodded to reassure her that he'd understood. There was a small pause, then she continued.

"The man on site who was responsible for overseeing the work was Yosuke Nawagi. He began by collecting laborers from the area, but the district commander was urging the project forward as fast as possible, and besides, Nawagi was there in the middle taking a rake-off from the laborer's wages, so it wasn't long before they all dug in their heels and refused to cooperate. The work involved cutting back through the hilltops, and widening and flattening the road, and there were continual accidents from the frequent landslides and falling rocks. And what's more, the laborers all hated the high-handed manner in which those recruiters from Hokkaido and Kyushu treated the workers. So very soon the work force was down by half.

"You can imagine the fix Nawagi found himself in, with the district commander urging the work to be completed on the one hand, and his laborers and stone-breakers running off on the other. So he came up with the solution of using convict chain gangs like those used in the coal mines of Kyushu. He took prisoners from the local prison and set them to work, but this didn't improve things. Besides which, of course, if he was using prisoners he couldn't skim anything from government-paid wages as he had before. He racked his brains. And then he came up with a wonderful idea for enlisting new laborers—"

"Which was a Kenshi roundup." Yugaku almost muttered the words.

The expression meant nothing to Taku, but he nevertheless shivered slightly at its sound. "What's that?" he asked. "Some kind of conscripted labor?"

"Yes, you could call it that. But that's not all it was." Sarashino hunched over in a spasm of dry, weak coughing. For some reason, Ai remained silent.

"You're familiar with the term 'gypsy,' I assume," Sarashino finally said.

Taku nodded. "Yes of course. They're the wandering folk who began to come out of India in the tenth and eleventh centuries and spread through most of the western world, aren't they? I met lots, not only in Spain and Bulgaria but in northern Europe as well."

"So there are Gypsies in northern Europe are there?" Yugaku said wonderingly. "I had the idea they were confined to the warmer countries."

"They're even in Siberia and Sakhalin. There are many living more or less permanently in Finland too."

"Could I ask you something?" Sarashino said. "We call these people 'Gypsies,' don't we. But how do they refer to themselves?"

"Er, I think they use the name 'Roma' for themselves."

"That's right. 'Roma.' They don't use the term 'Gypsy.' Because that's a made-up slang expression based on misconceptions and prejudices, one that outsiders use to refer to them."

"The name 'Roma' is said to come from the Sanskrit 'domba,'" Ai said, half chanting the words. "Which means 'human.' They're looked on as a different ethnic group by everyone else, but to themselves they're actually just 'humans.' They no doubt believe that their way of life is the truly human one."

Taku nodded. "Yes, it's true. Those around them give them different names—'Gitan,' for example, or 'Tsigane.' But they simply called themselves 'Romas,' that is to say, humans." He was remembering the young Gypsy boys and girls he'd come across in Helsinki. He'd picked them out right away, just from the way they walked. They didn't take long, slow strides like the Finns. They had a unique walk, a wonderful spring in their step.

They were black-haired, black-eyed, and brown-skinned. The girls wore a scarf with gold ornaments, the boys were in boots. And they had their own language, Romany. Even though they had become Finns and merged with the local populace, they were clearly different. They lived proudly despite the deeply rooted, hidden prejudice against them.

"'Roma,'" Sarashino repeated. "It's a good word. Has a fine ring, and a deep meaning. Not to mention a long history dating back to Sanskrit. But even today no one hesitates to call them 'Gypsies.' Apparently the term is based on the fallacy that they came out of Egypt. And *we* are the same. Since the Meiji era, we've been mistakenly referred to by the common name 'Sanka.' We are the Kenshi people."

Here Sarashino straightened his back, and looked Taku in the eye. Ai, Yugaku, and the Aunt of the Fifth House all silently exchanged glances, evidently in the grip of emotion. A rich silence filled the room, a silence dense and weighty.

I am about to set off on a long journey, Taku thought. He didn't know why, but he felt that, as a member of this group that called themselves 'Kenshi,' a long journey to a distant place awaited him, a place unlike anywhere he'd been before.

"'Kenshi,'" he murmured, trying the word on his tongue. "So I'm a member of the Kenshi people. And it was a distant member of my own family who was among those conscripted by Nawagi, Saisho's subordinate."

"Correct." Sarashino's voice rang strongly. "'Vagrant hunt' was the term they gave to the 1877 roundup and forced labor conscription of the itinerants with no formal family register who were based in the Kawachi, Izumi, and Yamato areas. Some referred to it as a 'Sanka hunt.' We unregistered folk, who had always lived by our own *Code* and took no part in the Meiji government's new family-register policy, were viewed as non-citizens and hounded like animals, hunted and cornered.

"At the southern foot of Mount Nijo, near where the Takenouchi Highway was being upgraded, there was a fenced-in hollow. This is where the unfortunate two hundred forty-odd Kenshi were captured and incarcerated.

"Over time I'll tell you just what our life had always been, how we'd worked and lived. Wanderers who embodied the philosophy of 'Live in no place,' we were labeled with the derogatory term 'Sanka' by those heartless people who saw us as some kind of wicked criminal gang, or people who lived a strange, wild life. Others, on the other hand, projected onto us their romantic illusions of some unrealistically free nomads, and sang songs that were full of fantasy and yearning. But neither of these views had anything to do with the real Kenshi and their philosophy, their lifestyle and traditions, their sufferings and joys. Why this happened is a question for you to answer through your own study and thinking, Mr. Hayami. This we call *scholarly practice*. Where did we come from? Who are we? And where do we go from here? These three questions are the focus of *scholarly practice*, the things you must study and ponder. *Scholarly practice*…"

At this point, the old man was overcome by another fit of coughing. When it was over he shook his head and sighed.

"Well, well, I'm a bit tired," he said. "I've probably talked too much. I'll just lie down and take a nap, if I may. While I'm asleep, Ai and Yugaku can explain all that happened on the Takenouchi Highway. I'd like you to help out too please, Aunt. Right." Sarashino flopped down on the mat, and soon a gentle snore rose from him.

"Isn't he a darling?" murmured the Aunt of the Fifth house, gazing at him as fondly as if he were a baby.

While Sarashino dozed, Ai and Yugaku answered Taku's flood of questions with untiring patience. There was altogether too much he didn't understand. He'd given up hope of a clear, compass-and-map path to knowledge. Like a man wandering lost in the wild, he felt his only means of comprehension lay in gathering all the fragments of information he could, and somehow piecing them together himself.

"Why is the Tenmu Jinshin Group also called the Futakami Fraternity?" he asked. This was something he'd long been puzzled by.

"Well, the name 'Futakami' is of course the old name for Mount Nijo," Ai explained. "Henro borrowed this ancient name for the group he founded, I imagine out of a strong desire that the mountain never be forgotten. We'll tell you about all this over the course of time."

Yugaku stepped in to help out. "Buddhist monks apparently had a secret code for counting, you see. It goes like this.

"The secret name for number one was *daimujin*, meaning 'the character *dai* minus person.' *Dai* is of course written with a horizontal stroke plus the character for person, so if you take the 'person' part away you're left with the single stroke, the character for 'one.' Now *ten*, meaning 'heaven,' is written in the same way but with two horizontal strokes, so *tenmujin*, their secret word for 'two,' means 'the character *ten* minus person'—two horizontal strokes, you see? Nowadays the group's name, Tenmujin, is written with different characters, using the name of the ancient emperor Tenmu, but its secret meaning is 'two.' The *shin* part of the group's name means 'god.' Are you with me? So, 'two gods.' And if you think about it, the name 'Futakami' actually means the same thing, 'two gods'—'futa' is another word for 'two,' right?

The name officially registered as a religious group is 'Tenmu Jinshin Group' because there were good reasons why the name 'Futakami' should be kept private. This kind of secret code language was the speciality of various artisan groups in the old days. Take the word for 'three,' which is written with three horizontal strokes. It was known as *omubo*, meaning "*o* minus stick"—as you know, the character *o*, or 'king,' is written with three horizontal strokes one above the other connected by a down stroke, the 'stick.' And four, five, six, seven, eight, and nine were all codified in the same clever way. Nine is particularly good—*kyu* minus bird. Think about it. *Kyu* is one way of pronouncing the character for 'pigeon,' which is written with the character for 'nine' beside 'bird' of course."

"In other words," said Taku, "when Group members speak among themselves they refer to it as the Futakami Fraternity, but to the outside world it's the Tenmu Jinshin Group, right?"

"That's right." Yugaku nodded. "You already know, I think, that our leader is called the *parent*, the key representatives are *uncles* and *aunts*, and general members are *brothers* and *sisters* or *family*."

"And the families of the *brothers* and *sisters* are *children*, yes?"

"Yes. If the *children* become independent and leave their parents, they're considered to have formed their own family and are included among the *brothers* and *sisters*. But if they apply to leave the Group entirely, they become *parted*, and officially the Group has nothing more to do with such *children*. But there are some people on the outside who don't participate in Group activities or have dealings with members but nevertheless secretly work to help the Group. These are known as *friends*. We have numerous *friends* out there among people who are quite famous."

"My adoptive father Yuzo Hayami is one…"

"Yes, he's a very good *friend*. But his son Shin'ichi has nothing at all to do with us. He doesn't even *communicate*, and I doubt if he has any idea that his father is a *friend*. He'll know nothing, unless of course you tell him."

"It would be completely taboo to talk to those on the outside about internal Group matters, wouldn't it?"

"That's just naturally something we don't do. If we did, the Group could no longer be sustained. We never speak of inside matters outside. Even when people who are close friends inside the Group meet in the outside world, they pass each other without a nod of recognition. Even if it's a *brother* or *sister* who's suffering and in need of help."

Pass on by, try not to look.
There goes another fellow-man.

The words of the song Saera loved came into his mind. Strange, thought Taku. Surely she'd told him she was just a nominal supporter of the Wanderers' League.

"Just to go back to what you were saying earlier," Taku said. "This fellow Nawagi who was such a good friend of the district commander's, and was having all the trouble with the Takenouchi Highway upgrade project. How did he go about that Kenshi roundup?"

"Well, the Kenshi always camped in out-of-the-way spots in their wandering life. Anyone who settled in one place, made an official register for their family, and started living permanently in one spot was no longer a real Kenshi, even though that was their origin. Those people were rapidly absorbed into the local populace, like water disappearing into sand in a desert. And of course that was fine. But those who never gave up the spirit of 'Live in no place,' they could be called the true original Kenshi. Nawagi put some money in the hands of an informant who'd infiltrated this Kenshi group, learned where they were and attacked the camps, captured well over two hundred of them, women and children included, and arrested them."

"There were quite a few different family groups, it seems," Ai cut in.

"Some were captured on the banks of the Yoshino River, others on the Yamato River and the Ishikawa, and other groups who were camping by other smaller streams," Yugaku went on. "There were some families who were beggars. Others went about mending farmers' winnowers. Itinerant performers, apprentice monks, the sick…the really unfortunate ones were the Kenshi caught in the Katsuragi Mountains. Their hands were tied and a stick passed between them, and apparently they were carried back like so many bears on poles, with great shouts of 'vagrants!'"

"They really did that?"

"Yes."

"But what was the reason given for their arrest?"

"People of no fixed address are a real headache for those in power. You can't conscript them for military service, you can't tax them, they won't submit to compulsory education. In other words, they reject the three duties of a citizen. It's not only the Meiji government that treated them as non-citizens—all governments right from the beginning have viewed these people in the same light. Before the war, the government and the police got together with the journalists to make a big thing out of this weird 'Sanka' image they'd created. All manner of bizarre crimes were laid at their door whenever such things happened. The writer Hiroshi Misumi wrote a long series of 'Sanka novels' in that mode, though in his last years he wrote a piece regretting it deeply."

As he listened, Taku was recalling a book he'd read long ago. "I remember hearing it said that the Japanese can be divided into the 'sea people' and the 'mountain people' in terms of origin," he said. "Which do the Kenshi belong to?"

"Well, I can't vouch for the very early days, when Japan was still joined to the continent, but humans crossed to Japan over the sea, almost without exception, early on. The sea connects with rivers, rivers with valleys, and valleys go up into mountains. Those who dwell in the mountains always have a hidden longing for the sea. You know the expression *yamanami* for a mountain range—it's literally 'mountain waves,' isn't it? The ancestors of the mountain folk were sea folk, in brief. That's why a child brought up in the remotest mountain fastness will always long to see the sea. People spend their lives in the mountains with a love of the sea deep inside them. The great folklorist Kunio Yanagida wrote with fascination of how the mountain gods love to eat a certain sea fish. Well of course they too long for the sea. Mountain gods also came from the sea long ago, after all."

"I see, so mountain people were originally sea people and then river people."

"That's right. Also, there were inlets here and there all round the coast—even the areas that are high mountain country today could once be accessed by boats, apparently."

"Where does the name 'Kenshi' come from?"

"This is something that will need a lot more study. There are many things we still don't know. But I'll tell you something you should always remember. In the words of Henro Sensei, 'Those who come down from the mountains yet do not dwell in villages, those who dwell in villages yet are of the mountains, those who flow through the membrane between mountain and village, their name is *Sekenshi*.' *Seken* people, in other words, people between worlds."

"So Kenshi is short for Sekenshi."

"We can't be sure of that. That common term Sanka, which means 'cave-dweller,' has created misconceptions, but in fact the Kenshi were never people who simply lived deep in the mountains. They were a tribe of people who chose to move between mountain and village, the natural and the human worlds, to live out their lives wandering in the realm between them, what's known as the liminal world.

"Our ancestors didn't leave the mountains and settle in the lowlands, and their dealings with others were always kept rather at arm's length. It's believed that more than half their number were localized itinerants who traveled seasonal routes from farmhouse to farmhouse, mending winnowers or making and selling them, but that wasn't all the Kenshi did. They made their living in many different ways. It seems to me we can be traced back to a nomadic people who chose to live a rootless life of wandering rather than submit to being governed by a centralized power. Today, in this regimented society of ours, we're attempting to see if life can still be lived according to Henro Sensei's words. This is the way I look at it, anyway."

Yugaku paused and looked at Ai, scratching his head. "I've talked too much," he said. "It's actually you who should be talking about this."

Ai gave him a smiling look in return. Little by little, quite chaotically but nevertheless surely, Taku was beginning to see the outlines of another world. He felt that he was poised now at the very entrance to a vast terrain, the deep world of *scholarly practice*.

I must go and see my adoptive father Yuzo and thank him, he thought. After all, he had freely given his services to the Group and their clan by taking Taku into his family and favoring him over his own son.

He didn't yet have any real idea about the Group's founder Henro Katsuragi. Nevertheless, he already felt that he was part of the Group. What, he wondered, would Shimafune and Hanada back at Meteor Publications want of him now? What exactly was their stance on the Group?

Taku watched as Sarashino awoke, yawning hugely. Taku's mind was filled with thoughts—that he was no longer alone, that he now stood like a single tree in a great dark forest, and that that forest itself was even now sunk in agony and threatened by engulfing flames.

"Ah, that was a good nap!" Sarashino muttered. "Well then, we must move the story forward from the Takenouchi Highway to the Nintoku Tomb Incident."

"Every time I hear this story it gives me the horrors." The Aunt of the Fifth House hunched forward as she spoke, and her great watermelon breasts swayed.

Seating himself formally again, Sarashino began to talk. From his mild and tranquil manner it was hard to imagine that this was a man who had only six months to live.

PART III

16

The seats on the Kodama bullet train from Atami to Tokyo were unusually empty. Taku sat in the middle of the carriage, next to Yugaku, who was clad in black monk's robes. There was no one around them, neither front and back nor across the aisle.

When the train set off from Atami Station, Yugaku's thick-browed, manly face took on the expression of a young boy, and he suddenly grew loquacious. "Well, Taku, you must be exhausted. I hear you had another long session with Sarashino last night," he said with a grin.

Taku shook his head. "No, oddly I don't feel tired at all. Though I didn't sleep last night, probably from all the excitement."

"I meant to buy a box of special Atami mackerel sushi." Yugaku clicked his tongue in vexation. "I love sitting in a train staring out the window while I eat."

"Ah yes, you were tucking into a box of sushi in salted persimmon leaves when I first met you on the train out of Kyoto, weren't you?"

"That's right." Yugaku nodded. Then he turned to gaze out the window, screwing up his eyes against the light. It was just after ten, a soft spring morning, and the sunlight poured down over the mandarin orchards that lined the shore.

"I feel as if I'm in some dream," murmured Taku. The events that had swept him along since that moment in the reception room of Meteor Publications when he'd first heard the name of Mount Nijo now came back to him as a kind of reverse image, like a photographic negative. It was similar to the shock he'd felt as a boy when Shin'ichi had told him of the existence of a mysterious, invisible mountain range deep under the sea.

"It's no dream," Yugaku replied. "Everyone reaches a point where they long to know just who they really are and where they came from. We all believe we know ourselves, but actually we only know the most superficial things. I mean, we may more or less know about our parents, but it's safe to say we'll generally know next to nothing about our grandparents, great-grandparents, or the generation or two before them. I really think if we could find out the real facts, almost everyone in the world would be struck dumb with disbelief. This must be some kind of bad dream! they'd think. Everyone has some hidden surprise in their family history. I think the Japanese don't bother to find out about their ancestors because unconsciously they all fear they might discover something unpleasant. But we in the Group don't turn our eyes away as others do. We try to live with clear vision, and you're now in the same position, Taku."

"So you think our present life is controlled by our past?" asked Taku.

Yugaku shook his head. "No, I think the opposite. Our present creates our past, it's not controlled by it. Our position is that we should strive to bravely face the past, and in that way free ourselves from it. Knowledge makes one free. Don't you agree?"

"I wonder." Taku thought for a moment, then said half to himself, "I now know what manner of people I'm *connected* to, and I feel this knowledge has somehow changed me. It's certainly true that I was overwhelmed by a strange sensation when I first saw myself as part of a great continuous life cycle that included my parents, their parents, and all who had given birth to them."

Outside the window, the sea had now been replaced by white metal factory roofs. Taku felt himself trembling lightly with the train's vibrations as he went on. "I can't really express it, but it felt somehow like a steel frame had been inserted into my backbone. Like I wasn't a fragment so much as part of an immensely long, vast organic body. A comforting sense of security. Yes. How can I put it? As if even if I were to die right now, the end of life wouldn't mean the end of everything; a leaf may fall from the tree but the trees keep living, the forest keeps living…"

"That forest is threatened with destruction," Yugaku cut in, his expression suddenly stern.

"You're speaking of the Ikarino Corporation, right?"

Yugaku nodded. "Like it or not, you're going to learn about the real face of Ikarino, Taku. I'm afraid I'm not good at explaining it."

"When you say it will be destroyed, this is some kind of metaphor, right?"

"It's no metaphor. Henro Katsuragi created the Wayfarers' League as an organization that would interpenetrate with our Group's autonomous way of living, and used it as a base from which to promote all sorts of politicial, economic, and cultural activities out in the world. It's the form the Kenshi took when they revived themselves in a difficult world, where only the strong survive. So it's natural that the whole of the Wayfarers' League would support and encourage the development of the Ikarino Corporation, you see. And it's certainly true that Ikarino Corporation, which after the war became the mainstay of the Wayfarers, has been a huge support for the Group until now. It introduced the children of Group members and those with *connections* into its companies, helped our talented young people into the worlds of culture, administration, and politics, and provided strong support for those of our family who were struggling to run their own companies, businesses, and households. And yet, now…"

Yugaku fell silent. Then he unwrapped a cloth-wrapped package, drew out a thin pamphlet, and handed it to Taku.

"Please read this later. I'll just explain it to you briefly. The red arrows on the map show the places where new developments are occurring with the aid of companies under the Ikarino umbrella. Twenty-eight coastal reclamation projects, fifty-two major excavations and mountains leveled, eighteen river infills, and that's just in Japan. There are many more large-scale projects happening in the Philippines, Thailand, Brazil, and elsewhere.

"You realize, don't you, that the removal of every hill changes the local climatic conditions. I'm not talking here about abstract concepts such as haphazard destruction of the ecosystem. My point is simple. No matter what claims can be made that this business activity is providing support for our family's autonomy, it's wrong to damage oceans, mountains, forests, and rivers like this.

"Henro taught this, and it's the Group's most important law. We originally came from the sea. We traveled up valleys, and lived among mountains. We moved through forests and made our home by rivers. Even after the Futakami Fraternity emerged from the mountains and chose to live a wandering life in the human world, we've always continued to think of the mountains and valleys as our true home. In every age our law has always been that we should strive to live at one with nature. When that law is broken, our clan will be no more. This is what I've been taught, and I do believe it. And this is why the Futakami Fraternity is putting its very existence on the line to try to convince Meido Ikarino to abide by that law."

Taku looked at the map. The Japanese archipelago was everywhere pierced with red arrows. He focused on one of them.

"This one's close to Mikuni Bay, isn't it."

"Where?" Yugaku leaned over to look more closely. Then he nodded. "That's a beautiful part of the Japan Sea coastline," he said. "That's right, I seem to remember you were brought up around there."

"Yes, I know this area well. It has truly beautiful sandy beaches."

"Not any more. That's where they're investing billions to construct a mammoth oil storage depot."

"You mean it?"

"I made this map myself and personally walked the areas. I walked almost five thousand kilometers in six months to do it."

Taku was silent. The dazzlingly bright scenery beyond the train window seemed oddly unreal. After a moment, he fixed a steady gaze on Yugaku. "How does the Group deal with someone who's clearly breaking their laws?"

"We kill him." Yugaku's answer was crisp. "The law is, if someone ignores continued warnings and goes on blithely breaking the law, he will be killed."

Taku closed the pamphlet, and stared at Yugaku. "And who will do this?"

"Me, or possibly…"

"Me?"

Yugaku didn't answer. Taku noticed a faint flush rise in his pale cheeks.

17

Taku had learned that Saera's manager Seta was in a hospital not far from Kawasaki Station. He arrived at his bedside at one that afternoon. With him was Yugaku, who apparently intended to accompany Taku wherever he went from now on.

Seta lay there bathed by the light of the western sun. He was bandaged from head to neck, only his eyes and mouth showing. He looked like an astronaut.

"Hi," said Taku, raising a hand in greeting. Seta blinked a reply. He seemed fully conscious.

"This is a friend of mine, Yugaku. He's a monk, but don't worry, he's not here to give you last rites or anything."

Seta's eyes smiled. He was apparently a much more resilient fellow than appearances suggested.

"I've just been talking to your doctor, and he tells me that it may take a while but your manhood's going to be just fine."

The eyes deep in their bandages were unresponsive.

"It wasn't a simple matter of something happening while you were driving along, was it?" Taku asked. The eyes acknowledged that this was so.

"Maybe a big semitrailer came up beside and nudged you?"

Yes, said Seta's eyes.

"I thought so. So you slammed on the emergency brake and it didn't work. Is that right?"

Seta closed his eyes. His breath whistled. The corners of his lips trembled slightly.

"Just tell me a little more. Was the Konryu gang somehow involved in this accident? What do you think?"

The white head managed a nod.

"Maybe I'd find out more if I talk to Saera?"

Seta didn't reply.

"Right then. Well, Seta, hang in there, and do what the doctor tells you. Don't worry about anything else. I'll make sure I see to it all."

Taku found his mind suddenly producing an image of the Ferrari driving swiftly along the freeway late at night. A huge semitrailer was right beside it in the right lane, refusing to make way. The 400i on its left changed back a gear and lunged suddenly forward to get ahead. He had the image of the front tires of the semitrailer moving in against the left lane. The long, tank-like steel body of the truck snaked left just ahead of the car, blocking its path. A squeal of brakes, which worked for a moment then suddenly failed to grip. The driver shifted down to reduce speed, but almost instantly the front of the car came in contact with the wall beside it.

Striving to escape to the right, the Ferrari found itself faced with the great metal body thirty times its weight bearing down on it as if to crush it, and with a rain of sparks and a stench of burning rubber the field of vision gradually tilted. The engine screamed. A sound of shattering glass. If the brakes hadn't been tampered with he could've pulled it off somehow. But pumping on the brakes only sent the brake fluid back down the brake hose, which had been skillfully eroded by sulphuric acid, and the car swiftly broke up. All done in such a way that it was almost impossible to find proof of the setup after the event.

"Bye. Get well as soon as you can."Taku raised a hand in farewell and left. If he'd stayed any longer, a mounting black rage would have almost lifted him from his seat.

"I'm off to see my brother in Yokohama," he said to Yugaku. "Can you come with me?"

"Yes, if I'm not in your way." Yugaku soothingly patted Taku's angrily tensed shoulder, and set off striding powerfully along beside him.

18

They walked together up the steep hill, their paces matched. The sky was clear, but the sea breeze was startlingly cold for April. It carried a faint scent of the sea.

Halfway up the slope, Yugaku paused. "This feels so good!" he murmured. Gazing out towards the port, he shaded his eyes against the dazzle. Then he went on. "Imagine a group of people, children and old folks included, who come hurrying out of a forest lit with the morning sun. They cross a valley, scramble up a steep cliff face, and there suddenly before their eyes is the blue sea. A cool breeze. Flashing waves. A horizon extending infinitely. What an indescribable feeling, eh?"

Taku wiped the sweat from his forehead and was silent. They had walked from Sakuragicho Station down the side of Yamashita Park and up to this hilly residential area at high speed, but Yugaku's breath was steady, and he wasn't even sweating.

"It could have been a moment like that that drew our clan more than a thousand years ago to take up a life of wandering," he continued. "But I'd say the debt they would've paid for this life of freedom was a heavy one."

"A debt of blood, you mean?" Taku asked. "In northern Europe and the socialist countries, the government extends all manner of protection to the Gypsies in an effort to get them to settle. But it's never really successful. If given a chance, they always revert to a roving life, and if they're forced to settle they slide into alcoholism and poverty, and end up at the bottom of the social heap. I've seen a lot of such people in my travels."

"No, that's not it." Yugaku shook his head. "I could stretch the point a bit and put it like this—the collective historical memory of the group is unconsciously handed down to individuals. The feelings experienced more than a thousand years ago, possibly many thousands, over all those generations as they moved around in the natural world, are always inherited by following generations. Quite likely the same goes for the unspoken prejudices that the settled tribes have always felt for the nomads and wanderers. What the Group is attempting through its *scholarly practice* and *wandering practice* is to bring this unconscious content into consciousness. We're striving to forge feelings into a philosophy, and discover the positive significance of the wandering life in the contemporary world. Our deceased leader Henro called this 'the soul of the nomads.'"

"The soul of the nomads," Taku repeated.

"Yes. And we nomads who go by the name of Kenshi are not just a group who've fled from the civic policies of the system. Still less are we merely a group of social dropouts and failures. There have always been quite a number of people who lived their lives in the mountains, but we are the remnants of a tribe that emerged from the mountains, yet didn't settle on the plain. In folklore religion's terms, the mountains are 'the other shore,' the death realm, while the plains and villages are 'this shore,' this world. And between them is *seken*, the in-between realm. Henro Sensei taught that the way of the *sekenshi*, that life lived between worlds, is the nomadic life."

Taku nodded, and began to walk. He had a general understanding of Yugaku's ideas, but he still didn't fully grasp them. Somewhat hesitantly, he asked, "But we're speaking of the past here, right?"

"No, it's a present problem I'm talking about."

"But 'Live in no place, Belong to no nation' is simply impossible today. The law requires that everyone's name be on a family register, and resident registration is a legal requirement, after all. Everyone in the Group is part of society now, and you all live like normal citizens, surely. How could you set about putting the 'nomad's soul' teaching into practice in this day and age, when every corner of Japan is bureaucratically controlled?"

"I understand what you're saying," Yugaku replied. "Henro Sensei's first aim was that we in the Group wouldn't destroy ourselves by becoming mere dropouts from the modern nation. Our greatest tool in this is mutual aid. And it does seem to have proved successful. We've somehow managed to retain our 'nomad's soul' and stay independent. And when my father Tenro took over Henro's position, he set his sights on a spiritual awareness and understanding of this clan of ours that had overcome such struggles to survive and grow, on a revival of the 'nomad's soul.' This is why he perfected the *Three Practices*, and why he's poured his energy into the education of the members and their offspring. This is all steadily bearing fruit. At some stage you'll be shown our 'practice ground,' Taku."

"What I'd really like to know…"

"Yes, I know. How do we live as 'nomads' in this age of bureaucratic control? This is the task of those such as myself who'll inherit the Group from Tenro. In recent years there's been a thorough debate about this in the Group, to which my sister Ai has been central, and we've only just determined on a way forward. You should take it that the recent criticism of the Ikarino Corporation is part of this new push."

"I see." Taku had arrived at the entrance to a white house. In the midday light, grimy patches showed here and there on the walls, and the place had a faint air of decay.

"This is Saera Maki's house," he said. "My brother lives with her."

He pressed the bell. "Who is it?" came Shin'ichi's voice through the speaker.

"It's me, Shin."

"Taku. Right, I'm just opening up for you."

The steel gates slid back to left and right. They were usually left open, but he was probably keeping them closed on account of recent events.

The front door opened and Shin'ichi emerged, wearing a striking lumberjack coat. "I've been waiting for you," he said, as his curious gaze turned to Yugaku's black-clad monkish figure.

"My brother Shin'ichi," Taku said. "Shin, this is Yugaku Katsuragi. A man I respect."

"How do you do." Shin'ichi bowed his head in greeting. "Come on in. We're a bit busy just now so you'll find it rather a mess, I'm afraid."

Shin'ichi led them in to the dining room, where Saera, evidently now back from hospital, was lying on the couch. She was wearing a pale pink house dress, and her hair was plaited and wound around her head. She looked like a sick little Indian girl.

"Taku…" She sat up, looking as if she were about to cry.

"Saera," said Shin'ichi, tidying a magazine from the table as he spoke. "Don't worry about being polite, just stay lying down. I'll get coffee."

"Sorry, Shin."

"This is a friend of Taku's," Shin'ichi went on.

Saera smiled wanly, a pale little hand pressed against her breast. "How do you do. I'm Saera Maki. I do apologize for appearing like this."

"My name is Yugaku Katsuragi, and I've been a great fan of yours for a long time." The sturdy-framed young monk spoke in a voice that trembled slightly. A blush unexpectedly suffused his cheeks. He seemed suddenly as nervous as a boy.

"I'll go grind the beans. What kind of coffee do you like, Mr. Katsuragi?"

"Any way is fine, thank you."

"I've got some good beans from Guatemala. I'll make you a really good strong brew, okay?"

The sound of a coffee grinder came from the kitchen. From the sideboard Taku picked up the magazine that Shin'ichi had evidently been reading. His eyes had caught a large heading with the word "Ikarino." While Yugaku and Saera exchanged awkward conversation, he ran his eyes quickly over the piece.

Scandal in the Finance World—Anonymous Discussion
Discussion moderator: Finance editor of a certain newspaper
K.: Young manager of a corporate racketeer group
S.: Reporter for a weekly

Ikarino President Expelled from Religious Group

Moderator: This isn't something you saw much about in the media, but there are rumors that Meido Ikarino, the general head of

Ikarino Corporation, has received his marching orders from the head of the religious group he reveres as his teacher. K., could you quickly fill us in on what this is about?

K.: I've no idea. I gather your weekly was aiming to run a special edition on the subject but the piece got suppressed, is that right, S.?

S.: It wasn't taken out as a result of any particular pressure, that is.

K.: So why didn't it run?

S.: Well, how about you then? You proclaimed you were planning to disrupt the general meeting of Ikarino Tourism the other day, but when it came to the point you were quiet as a mouse, weren't you?

K.: Hey, wait a minute there! You guys may not know it, but our job is actually to make general meetings end smoothly. While you weeklies, on the other hand, are all about stirring things up.

S.: Okay, there's no point in infighting here, let me just quickly give readers a summary. The situation is that things went wrong for our great Ikarino Corporation at its sixtieth anniversary party the other day. There are some fifty companies officially under the umbrella of this corporation, and it calls the shots behind the scenes for countless others. The sole head of this new multinational syndicate that's seen such a rapid rise is Meido Ikarino, 78. This powerful financier is a one-generation wonder who has garnered a variety of reputations since he first began a recycling business in Tokyo's Taito Ward at the age of 19. But he also has a surprisingly strong religious side, and all through the postwar era he's been a passionate believer in the teachings of a certain small religious group.

Moderator: You're referring to the Tenmu Jinshin Group, right?

K.: Correct. He was apparently quite reckless in his youth, till the founder of this group took him under his wing. So even once he'd achieved success in the business world, whenever he had a problem he would always go cap in hand to sit at the feet of this man. I guess it's a bit like that story about the prime minister and that old fellow off in the country whom he worships as his teacher.

S.:   You know perfectly well about Ikarino and his wonderful sensei, K., so why bother pretending. Surely this admirable little tale is common knowledge. There's no point in trying to make some kind of heartwarming revelation out of it. For one thing, Ikarino has a relationship with the Wayfarers' League.

Moderator: So how does the Wayfarers' League fit in to this?

K.:   I've no idea. But I guess the Wayfarers is some kind of training group made up of famous people from various walks of life.

S.:   Come on, what's this "training group" idea? The Wayfarers is an invisible syndicate, a kind of underground cooperative organization. It makes decisions about all manner of things. You might call it the Japan chapter of the Freemasons.

Moderator: All that's pretty interesting, isn't it. I've heard stories about how the Tenmu Jinshin Group is actually a kind of fraternity that was secretly formed back before the turn of the century by a band of mountain religious practitioners who'd been refused recognition as a religious group in the Meiji government crackdowns.

K.:   That's quite wrong.

S.:   Come on, let's hear a bit more.

Moderator: Well, I haven't really gone into it thoroughly, but I gather one of these people was a famed practitioner by the name of Henro Katsuragi, who set up a kind of mutual association for members of this outcast group to aid each other. They set to work collecting funds for the mountain priests and their families and kids who'd been chased out of the mountains by the government, and proceeded to help them out in secret and get them an astonishing amount of social power in fact. I heard, for instance, that the Q. Mutual Bank developed out of this mutual funds association.

K.:   Seems to me someone's been reading too many popular novels.

S.:   This founder of the Tenmu Jinshin Group sounds like one of those flawless characters. He was so popular that his followers got together and formed the Wayfarers' League in his honor. And Meido Ikarino was one of the members back then. While Henro was alive the Wayfarers did indeed have a strong religious side to them. The members dressed as white-robed pilgrims, climbed mountains, and held study sessions on how to live in the natural world. Then, the year the war ended, the great Henro died at the age of 88, and the group soon began to change. The second head is a man called Tenro, apparently. He ought by rights to have taken charge of the Wayfarers, but for some reason he's only listed there as a sponsor. In fact, it seems it's Meido Ikarino, Henro's beloved disciple, who pulls the strings in the Wayfarers. So the group is actually no longer strictly a religious group. It's more like a kind of underground rigging organization for the bureaucracy and the political and financial worlds. There are cultural types and journalists involved too, and it's turned into a secret industrial cooperative of the Ikarino Corporation. And the present leader, Tenro, is out gunning for Ikarino over this, see. So this is what lies behind that explosive incident we witnessed at the sixtieth anniversary party the other day.

Moderator: But from Ikarino's point of view, of course, his old teacher Henro has died, and he's the one in firm control of the Wayfarers. So what's it to him if he's cast out of a group that's nothing but one of those new religious organizations? It wouldn't matter a damn, surely.

S.:   But in fact I think it does.

Moderator: Why?

S.:   The Tenmu Jinshin Group may be small, but it's a bit like the Catholic Vatican. It's a kind of spiritual pillar and parent. Seems like it still maintains a shadowy influence over the main members of the Wayfarers' League even now. So it may well be that the first thing to happen will be an internal split among the Wayfarers. This is like withdrawing the official seal of approval or the imperial standard, you see.

Moderator: So perhaps you could compare it to a standoff between the government and the Communist Party in Russia, say?

K.:   That's a pretty neat comparison. But of course the question is, which side is the army on?

Moderator: The army? What do you mean?

K.:   Nothing really. Just that we were talking about Russia.

S.:   The government has control of the army. It's not the party that makes the budget.

K.:   You think so?

S.:   You don't?

K.:   Soldiers don't necessarily always act out of pure self-interest, you know. There's a question of human justice as well.

S.:   Well the K. gang were the frontline for defense of the Group back in the old days, so naturally they were absolutely loyal, but that's not the case today. I think they'd be susceptible to a different sponsor.

Moderator: I don't quite see what you're getting at.

K.:   We're talking about Russia, right? (*laughter*)

S.:   What do you think the party can do once it's got the government and the army as enemies?

K.:   There are two possibilities. One is, to get the general populace on side and call a general strike. The other—

S.:   Is a suicide attack.

K.:   Let's forget that. Isn't there something more cheerful we can talk about?

Moderator: I know I keep coming back to this, but just one further thing. Essentially, this present business of expulsion from the Group has been caused by a leadership struggle in the Wayfarers, right?

S.:   No, that's wrong. What it's about is that Tenro has taken exception to the fact that Ikarino Corporation has hijacked the Wayfarers into taking part in its ongoing destruction of the natural world. The worship of nature is their key teaching, see. And the Ikarino Corporation is actually busy causing havoc in the natural world in many countries. Wasn't it Ikarino Tourism, for instance, that came up with the plan to build an enormous new suburb in the Mount Nijo area down near Nara?

K.:   I haven't heard that one.

S.:   Oh, come on now.

K.:   Let's change the subject. What about that business about NTT selling off public land?

S.:   And here again Ikarino Corporation's involved.

K.:   Moving right along, then. (*laughter*)
Moderator: Right, so let's say we've wound this topic up for now.
    Next…

Taku had reached this point when Shin'ichi arrived carrying the coffee. He replaced the magazine on the sideboard. The strong aroma filled the room.

"Apparently there's a National Coffee Institute in Guatemala," said Shin'ichi, handing a cup to Saera. "Hey, don't spill it. It's hot."

"Thank you. You're a darling, Shin."

"Come off it," Shin'ichi said with an embarrassed grimace. He sat down at the table. "Right then, where do we begin?"

"We've just come from visiting Seta at the hospital in Kawasaki," said Taku.

"Have you?" Shin'ichi put his coffee cup down on the white saucer and heaved a sigh. "It was my fault. You told me over the phone not to let anyone use the car."

"Tell me who came here that night."

"They said they were from the Konryu gang, I think it was. Three of them."

"The man called Yuji?"

"Ah, yes, he seemed to be the leader. A man with an awful burn scar on his face. He knew an amazing amount about cars."

"Would he have tampered with the Ferrari?"

"I was bound hand and foot with packing tape and dumped in the bathroom, so I've no idea."

"That fellow called Yuji used to be a car stuntsman for movies and television," Yugaku broke in. "Then five years ago there was an accident during a shoot and he was badly burned. He retired, and the Konryu gang apparently scooped him up. They say that even now once he's behind the wheel he'll leave any racecar driver in the shade. I've heard he does some very hazardous work with cars."

"That's him all right," said Taku. "He'll be the one who pushed the Ferrari over the edge with his semitrailer."

"How did he do that?"

"Okay, here's how it would've gone. There's a car waiting near the toll-gate entrance to the expressway, and when the Ferrari goes past he trails him, while he communicates by radio to a semitrailer that's waiting up at the next interchange and tells him to get on the road. It's around four a.m., so there are almost no cars about. He tailgates the Ferrari and picks up speed, and there blocking the way up ahead is the semi. Unless he's very cautious, the driver will step on the accelerator and try to slip past him. And particularly if he's in a 400i that you can push up to two-forty KPH, even if it's only a 310-horsepower domestic four-seater. All you need to do is have one tailgating while the other edges over into the lane and pushes it up against the barrier. Easy."

"He should've been sent home in a taxi."

"There aren't many drivers who know just how scary those big semitrailers can be. They're over ten meters long, and pack more than fifty tons when fully loaded. Say the Ferrari's 1.8 tons, that's still about thirty times its weight. There are cases where a truck like that has crushed a sedan with the steel tubes along its side without the driver even being aware of it. Those model 74 army tanks are only thirty tons, so a front-on collision would send even them flying."

Taku had made his point, and everyone was silent for a while. Saera hiccuped softly.

"Don't start crying," Shin'ichi said to her.

"But tell me," said Taku. "Why did he set off at four in the morning?"

"After all that had happened that night, he settled down to stay the night with us," Shin'ichi explained. "But around three-thirty he had a phone call from someone and he took off in a great hurry, saying he had urgent business in Tokyo."

"Those guys set him up," said Saera. "The message was that his pregnant wife was miscarrying and she was on her way to the emergency hospital in Shinagawa. I took the call for him."

"Saera, why didn't you tell me?" said Shin'ichi, putting down his cup.

"Seta insisted he didn't want to worry you after all you'd just been through."

"Who was it who rang?"

"The first person was a woman from the exchange. She said she was calling from the Minato Ward fire station and she was putting me through to the ambulance brigade. Then there was a middle-aged man's voice…"

"He was usually such a cautious guy, too," said Shin'ichi. "Fancy him falling for such an obvious ploy."

"I shook him awake, and I guess I looked pretty scared. I said his wife was in trouble. I must have given him a real fright. It was my fault."

Saera pressed her face into the back of the couch and sobbed. Taku watched her shoulder blades heave in and out like wings. He felt terrible for her. If Shin'ichi hadn't been there he'd be inclined to sit beside her and hold her, he thought.

Saera raised her face and wailed, "I'm the cause of everything! Everything! …Taku, you must be wondering why all this happened."

"All I want to know is what kind of trouble you're in, Saera."

"I'll have to tell you everything about myself in order to explain that." Saera sat herself up on the couch. Her eyes were hollow, and a dark fire smoldered in their depths.

"Shin, I want to confess everything to Taku now. Straight. Okay?"

She gazed at Shin'ichi. He took a sip of his coffee, and after a moment he replied, "Yes, in fact I've been wanting to tell Taku everything about us for some time, too."

"I should leave you in privacy." Yugaku slowly rose to his feet.

Saera shook her head, and held him back. "No, please stay here. It's better that way."

Then she placed her hands formally on her knees, and gave a small smile. "It could take some time to tell everything…"

"Don't worry."

"Hold on a moment." Shin'ichi got up and pulled the lace curtains over the windows. The room grew somewhat darker. From somewhere nearby came the sound of a motorbike. The white lilies in a vase by the wall swayed lightly, although the air was still. Saera took up the story, her gentle voice like flowing water.

I wasn't brought up like the media says I was, but in Otaru up in Hokkaido. My dad says I was born in Tokyo, but my first memories are of Otaru.

Dad was a tailor of western clothing. He eked out a living from our dark little two-story house down a side alley near the canal. "Nishimoto Tailoring," his wooden sign said. I still have a vivid memory of him sitting there all day hunched over, sewing at the machine. He didn't have any young apprentices or anything.

His one boast was that for a short time when he was young he'd learned his trade in Tokyo, at T. Tailor in the Ginza.

He was good at his trade, I think, but he had occasional epileptic fits. I believe this could be the reason he left Tokyo.

My mum was a light-skinned woman with a squint, who went to pieces whenever she got on the booze. I remember she was forever abusing my father horribly.

I hated our dark, dank house, and when I was little I always used to play by myself over on the other side of the canal. The only time I felt really at peace was there among the old factory buildings, the wharves, the switchyards, and brick warehouses, all the boats that came and went, and the sea.

I hated school. On days when I was given lunch money or any other money to take, I always headed across the canal and hung out there for the day, doing nothing much. Dad never made much from his work, and he never managed to pay off the debt from buying an electric sewing machine when they came out.

Round about the time I graduated from elementary school, Dad had a really bad fit, and he never really recovered. He was bedridden from then on and couldn't work. He just lay there all day in his dark second-floor room, staring at the ceiling. When I went up to bring him his food or help him with his toilet, that was the only time he'd manage a wan smile.

"When you grow up you'll marry into a good family, Toshiko," he once said. "And your husband will buy you a Chanel dress. Chanel makes particularly well-made women's clothes, you know."

"What's Chanel?" I asked.

"A French seamstress," he told me. "She's a wonderful woman who's rumored to have Gypsy blood in her. When I was in the shop in the Ginza, the wife of the boss who was so kind to me always wore Chanel. The sewing was a bit rough, but it always kept its shape beautifully. It used to amaze me."

When I was clearing away the bedpan I'd stare out the window at the glimpse of factories, warehouses, and the canal I could see between the roofs. There were icicles as long as a man hanging from that window in winter.

I didn't want to know how our household managed to survive in that period. Once or twice a week my mother gave me a bit of money, and on those nights I was told not to come back to the house till after ten.

I wasn't the kind of kid who was happy to go off on my own and see movies or sit around in coffee shops, so I used to take myself off to the bridge over the canal, where I'd lean on the railing for hours on end, watching the little boats and the dirty water, and staring at the brick warehouses. When the lights of the city over on the foothills began to blink off, I'd ring home. Mum was always drunk. Sometimes I could hear a man's voice in the background.

"Can I come home now?"

"Give it another half hour."

When I thought of my dad up there in the second-floor room staring at the ceiling, it was hard to bear. And when I thought of the optometrist and the guys from the shipping company who came to visit Mum, I just wanted to die. I was contemplating suicide even back in elementary school. I'd decided when I did it I'd throw myself into the canal.

Dad died when I was in middle school. He somehow got out of the house one night and fell into the canal and drowned. They found him floating there dressed in a black suit he'd made himself.

After that, the guys who visited my mother took to coming quite openly. One cold night when I called from the public phone booth, she asked me to call again an hour later. Snow began to fall as I stood there on the bridge. Looking at the flakes slowly disappearing into the dark water, I wanted to cry. I phoned again after midnight, and this time a man answered. It was the optometrist.

'Your mum's in a drunken stupor,' he said. 'I can't wake her. I'll stay here tonight, but come on home, don't worry about me.'

I said nothing and put the receiver down. I missed Dad like crazy. I wanted to kill myself. But instead of dying, I rang the guy who ran a nearby restaurant, who'd been eyeing me for some time.

He came right away, and he took me down to Sapporo. He fed me sushi, and gave me a bit of beer, then he took me to a hotel. Before I went in, I phoned home again from the phone booth there. I was planning to drop the guy and run back home if she came on the phone. But though I let it ring and ring, no one answered. I tried a number of times, in tears, but Mum never answered. So I went into the hotel. It was the autumn I was fifteen, I think.

After that, I stayed away from home for a while, and lived at a Sapporo cabaret where I worked.

In order to look as adult as I could, I piled on the makeup and tried to fatten up with food. If you saw photos of me from that time you'd laugh till you cried, I tell you. I had rolls of fat all over—arms, legs, body, face—and my chin wasn't just double but triple. And I was dark-tanned, with dyed-blond hair. I ate like I was avenging my father's death or something. I was just desperate not to look as young as I was. My bust would've been almost ninety centimeters.

I loved singing, and after work I'd drop into a snack bar and sing away to my heart's content. In those days I was completely sold on old sentimental Japanese songs. I knew I had a good voice. Sometimes I'd go off to spend the night at a hotel with the guy who'd rescued me.

Some time later I decided to leave the guy from Otaru, so I moved in with a hoodlum from Susukino. He got me onto marijuana and amphetamines, and it wasn't long before I was working in the massage parlor district.

About six months later, an old fellow with a white beard came into the massage parlor, and I looked after his needs. This strange man came again the following night, and asked me to go off to Tokyo with him. I was leading a pretty dissolute life at the time. I was only seventeen, but my skin had gone all dark, I'd lost my appetite, and my hair was beginning to fall out. I was starting to have bad reactions to the drugs.

Before I really knew what was happening, I found I'd left the young Susukino gangster and had been taken down to Tokyo by the old man. I imagine quite a bit of money changed hands, but I don't know.

I quickly discovered that he was the famous boss of the gangster mob called the Konryu gang.

I'm grateful to him even now. If I'd stayed on at that massage parlor I'd have become truly addicted to drugs and no doubt died a miserable death. Quite likely I was secretly hoping this was the way things would go.

But this boss didn't just treat me like some sort of pet. One night he asked me what I loved most.

"To sing," I said.

"To sing, eh? That's good," he said, and the next morning he told me he'd decided to make me into a singer.

The following month, I was put into the hands of a farmer named Q. from a tiny out-of-the-way village up in the mountains of Chugoku, who made his living collecting herbs for medicinal drinks. It was incredibly remote—there were only a couple of houses in the area.

This man and his family were all wonderful people. But the food was really rough, just local mountain vegetables and mixed grains, and I remember I had a very hard time getting used to it. I lived there, helping with the housework, and six months later I'd regained all my health. I'd slimmed down, and my skin was amazingly pale again. If I'd met any of the girls from where I worked back in Sapporo, they'd never have picked me for that fat, blonde, dark-skinned girl they'd known.

Then at last the boss sent someone up to fetch me. As soon as I was back in Tokyo, I had my eyelids lifted and my teeth straightened. It didn't take much to make me look completely different from the way I'd looked as a young girl.

From then on events just rolled smoothly along. I took singing lessons, had some dance training, learned some French and English conversation. First off I spent a year learning the ropes as a singer in a club, then I was employed as the exclusive singer for a Shibuya salon run by one of the boss's grandkids. I cut my first record just before I turned twenty. My debut song was a great hit, but I have a feeling the boss and his friends played a pretty large part in that.

After my first hit, the recording company took me to France for the first time. And no sooner had the plane arrived than I was wheedling my driver to take me to the Chanel boutique. It was the memory of my poverty-stricken tailor father that drove me.

Some years later, the young gangster I used to live with back in Sapporo came back around. He was killed in a car crash very soon after. Then, a few years later, there was a phone call from my mother. I told her straight that she'd killed my father. That was the last I ever heard from her.

Finally the old boss went into hospital, and he didn't come out. I became the oldest star in the Mu Music Company stable. Once the boss had died I felt free at last, but at the same time I was really lost and depressed.

I seem to have spent the years from then until after I turned thirty simply devoting my life to singing and buying clothes. I was thirty-two when I heard my mother had killed herself. It was about then that I started drowning myself in drink again. I was soon drinking more and more, and I was even drunk on stage. I realized I was slowly gaining weight. I started thinking maybe I'd dye my hair, and have more surgery to return my eyelids to the way they used to be. Maybe I was finding it hard to live as a different person, or maybe something deep down inside me wanted to punish myself.

It was round about then that I skipped work and headed back to Otaru on my own. The place where Nishimoto Tailoring had been no longer existed, but the area around the canal was still as it had been. I spent half a day standing on that bridge staring at the water, then I went back to Tokyo, without throwing myself in.

Then I began to drink more. This was when Shin first arrived in my life. He was a skilled mixer at K. Studio, and he always helped out with my recordings.

I had real trouble recording "Do Not Point the Finger"—we tried take after take. At one stage, I ran off out the back of the studio, feeling like all I wanted to do was die. It was nighttime. I went and stood on a pedestrian overpass, leaning over the railing, wondering whether to throw myself down into the passing traffic beneath.

Then someone tapped me on the shoulder. It was Shin. "Don't worry, it's going to go fine," he said to me, and he handed me a mini bottle of whiskey.

"My song's terrible, isn't it," I said.

"Yes," he said, "but I like it. I think it's going to be a great song."

"Truly?"

"No lie."

The whiskey brought back a little confidence. "I feel ashamed to be alive," I said to him.

"Seems like it, yes."

"Once I've done this recording properly, would you listen to my story?"

"Sure."

"Okay then, I'll do it," I said.

I returned the whiskey bottle to him, and went back to the studio. Then, strengthened by the sense of his eyes on me through the window, I managed to do the song—and once the recording was over I asked Shin to my house and talked on and on unstoppably till morning.

"How are you going to be able to stop drinking?" he asked me

"It would just take someone always being by my side," I answered.

"I'll give it some thought."

Then a week later he turned up at my house again. One look at his face and I knew he'd made the decision to stop his work at the studio and give up his future career. He'd thrown it all away and come to be with me.

With his encouragement, I went into rehab, and after that I gave up alcohol completely. But you know, I became unable to live without Shin there. While I'm at work, I'm always terrified by the thought that he might have left me. I can't sing unless I'm constantly phoning to check whether he's still there.

Shin is the mainstay of my life. The thought makes me miserable—but what can I do?

I used to constantly weep and apologize to him. I also felt guilty over his parents. And over you too, Taku. If I could set Shin free by leaving the world, I'd do it in a flash. But I know he doesn't just not want me to die, he's actually happy to live with me, and the thought of that always stops me.

I don't care what happens to me as a singer, all I care about is somehow living with Shin as long as possible.

I've recently begun slowly cutting back on work. I'm turning down more and more promos and television appearances when I release a new song. I'd be happy just to occasionally sing in some small club with a tiny audience.

No, actually, if I could stop singing, just become Shin's wife, run a little coffee shop in some country town…

Seta wanted to convince me not to give in, he had plans for work in a new area. He was against the company's goal of just putting on cabaret shows, he was planning to start a new company making music videos with me as the main performer. He was always telling me I had to cut my ties with the Konryu gang so we could do this. Whenever he got drunk he'd say he'd thrown himself into the entertainment world for the sake of modernizing and internationalizing the music industry. Recently it seems he's been enlisting the help of an American show business investment company called QCR that's a rival of Ikarino, to try to transfer me over. QCR pretty much has control of the West Coast, so if the Konryu gang gets too presumptuous there'd apparently be pressure brought down on the Ikarino hotel chain in Hawaii and Las Vegas. This move of Seta's has been provoking all sorts of harassment recently.

But I'm tired. These days I'm more and more nostalgic for Otaru. I don't care about singing any more. Shin says I mustn't feel this way, of course.

You may not believe me when I say this, but Shin and I aren't lovers in the usual way. I haven't once gone in for any of that sort of thing since I stopped working in the massage parlor. The boss too, he just slept with his arms around me, that's all. I'm happy just to be sharing my life with Shin like this. Back when I was just a kid, standing on the bridge staring at the canal, I used to long for someone who'd just stand beside me. But now I'm not alone. I feel like now I'm standing there on that bridge gazing at the distant lights with Shin beside me.

I'm sorry, I've talked a long time. But I wanted you to hear the story, Taku. I really apologize for all this talk about myself.

Shin'ichi had sat quite still while she spoke, saying nothing and staring into his coffee cup. Yugaku too was silent. To Taku, the woman sitting there on the sofa seemed like a little girl who couldn't go home.

"You've told them everything," Shin'ichi said at last.

"Have I surprised you?" Saera asked Yugaku.

"Yes."

"I'll make some fresh coffee." Shin'ichi made to rise, but Yugaku held him back with a gesture.

"I'd like to ask Saera something, if I may."

"Go ahead."

Yugaku hesitated a moment, then said, "Do you remember the name of that Konryu gang boss who died?"

Saera looked at Yugaku, her eyes shining softly. She nodded. "Yes. I do. He had an unusual name—Gen'ichiro Mushiro, it was."

"He was my uncle."

Saera and Shin'ichi barely reacted. It was only Taku who was surprised, and their lack of amazement surprised him further.

"I knew you were from the Group the moment I heard the name 'Katsuragi,'" Shin'ichi said with a smile.

"So Shin, you…" Taku faltered, his eyes boring into Shin'ichi's face. "You've known about the Group before now?"

"Yes, in a general sort of way."

"Why didn't you tell me anything about them before, then?"

"The Hayamis *departed* the Group and *blended*. The family were *friends* till the old man's generation, but I'm an outsider unless I voluntarily *return*. So, being a Hayami, you never had anything to do with the Group, you see. That's why the old man never told you anything."

Shin'ichi turned to Saera, and went on. "There's just one thing she left out in that story. Can I tell them, Saera?"

"Go ahead." Saera nodded.

In a quiet voice, Shin'ichi went on, "It seems Saera's dad the tailor was also one of the *parted* who'd *blended* with society. He never told her anything about it, mind you."

"Why do you think so?" Taku asked Saera.

"At the end of every month, Dad sent me off to the post office to send a money order. It was a secret from Mum, but no matter how poor we were he'd always give me a few thousand yen notes to send. The addressee was 'Tenmu Jinshin Group Religious Organization'—quite a mouthful, so I've never forgotten it. I asked him once why he did it, and he gave me the odd answer that it was the task of a *friend* to stay *connected*. There's been no further relationship since he died, mind you."

"I gather you're a member of the Wayfarers' League, though."

"Yes, I became a member when I first made my debut. I was told it would be useful for my career."

"So how has it actually been useful?"

"Well, I don't really know, but Seta said it was thanks to this that my first song was a hit. But since I've made my name I've had to repay the debt in all sorts of ways—when there's an election, for instance, or someone famous has a party."

"Pardon me," Yugaku broke in. "What was your father's name?"

"Heigo Nishimoto. It's a funny name, isn't it."

"The Group has always been sustained by people such as your father." Yugaku closed his eyes and hung his head briefly, as though sunk in silent prayer. Then he spoke again, and his voice was strong. "I will henceforth undertake the responsibility of helping both of you. It has indeed been a happy thing to have met you today."

Saera heaved a deep sigh, and sank back onto the sofa again. Shin'ichi replaced his coffee cup in its saucer and stood up. Picking up the magazine from the sideboard, Taku set it down before Yugaku.

19

All afternoon, Yugaku and Shin'ichi talked quietly together. Yugaku seemed deeply fascinated by Shin'ichi's collection of gear, and for his part Shin'ichi was clearly delighted to have someone to talk to besides Taku.

When evening came, the two went out to the backyard to take a look at the framework of the log hut Shin'ichi was building, and Taku was left alone with Saera in the dining room.

"Taku," she called from where she was lying on the sofa.

"What is it?"

"Come over here."

He did so, and Saera indicated that he should sit on a cushion on the floor below the sofa.

He settled himself down cross-legged, close by her.

"Taku, you love me, don't you," she said.

"I do."

"I'm so happy." She put out a thin white hand and gently stroked the nape of his neck with her fingers.

"I love you too, Taku."

"Thank you."

"If I ever die…" Saera began, peering into his face as she spoke, "Dress me in that suit I've got in the armoire. Please, okay?"

"Why are you saying this?"

"I'm just saying if. I have this feeling I'm not going to live a long time. I don't know why."

"I'd be sad if you were gone, Saera."

"You know, don't you—you know Shin and I love each other even though we don't have a physical relationship?"

"Yes."

"Kiss me. Like a real brother would…"

Taku looked at her. Her eyes were shut and her faintly flushed lips were softly closed. Taku brushed his lips lightly over hers, barely touching them.

"Thank you, brother," Saera murmured. Then she fell asleep, apparently content, her breath soft as a child's.

Shin'ichi and Yugaku stayed outside inspecting the log hut for a long time. Shin'ichi must have lured him on to check out his proud collection in the tool shed, Taku guessed.

Stealthily, so as not to awaken the sleeping Saera, he went into the corridor and dialled a number. When he got the exchange at Meteor Publications, he asked to speak to Hanada.

"Taku? Where are you calling from?" Hanada's voice lacked its usual offhand tone. Taku sensed he was wary of who might be listening.

"I'm at my brother's home in Yokohama."

"Can you spare some time this evening?"

"Yes, depending."

"Apparently the boss wants to meet at nine. I've been looking for you."

"The boss?" Taku's voice rose slightly. "You mean Meido Ikarino, the man himself? He wants to meet me?"

"That's right."

"Where?"

"Keiro Lodge. You come off the Tomei Express at Numazu. It's in the Ikarino One Hundred Club. Follow the private drive up to the golf course and it's right there."

"Nine, you say."

"Come a bit early."

"Got it." Taku was just putting down the receiver when he thought to ask, "You're coming too?"

"Yes, I'll be there with Shimafune."

"I should come alone, right?"

"You're not trying to tell me you can't come without the damn whole Group in tow, are you?"

"Okay, okay. I'll go by car, alone. What time should I aim to come off at Numazu so I can get there fifteen minutes early?"

"It's fifteen minutes from the off ramp to the start of the golf club drive. Then I'd say give it twenty minutes up the winding road to the lodge."

"Right then, see you tonight."

Taku replaced the receiver. He thought of Meido Ikarino's imposing presence at the hotel party, and shivered slightly.

20

Early that evening, Taku set off from Shin'ichi's house. He was tempted to take either the Maserati or the Porsche from the garage, but he decided against it. If the brakes had been interfered with it would just lead to more trouble. Before he left he decided to remove both batteries and hide them in a corner of the garage, to prevent anyone using the cars before they'd been professionally checked over at the repair shop.

There was a third car as well, the Mercedes Geländewagen that he'd brought back from Kobe. Apparently this was usually kept in the Motomachi parking lot.

Taku walked down the slope and cut through the graveyard to the building with the garage in its basement. He paid the exorbitant parking fee and left, then went round to the nearby gasoline stand where he topped up the gas, and checked the water, oil, and tires. He was planning to take the expressway, so he added a little pressure to the tires. After all, it was a lump of metal weighing almost two tons. Given its vulgar boxiness, the metallic radius rods and so on, it made sense that it had been developed in collaboration with a weapons manufacturer.

Still, the fact was he was really quite taken with this heavy diesel engine car. The OM617 engine produced an incredibly modest degree of power—a mere 88 hp—for the weight of the car, but it ran as beautifully as a top-end brand. The hard metallic sound it produced at high RPM was also pretty nice. And the weight of the power steering had a pleasantly crisp resistance to it.

Once he'd got the gas, it suddenly occurred to him to ring the *Tramping* desk at work.

"Hullo. This is *Tramping*." It was Kyoko's voice. The sound filled him with a sudden fond nostalgia. Why should he feel like this, he wondered, though it was only a few days since he'd last seen her?

Still, he decided, this wasn't really boy-girl stuff.

He remained silent for a few moments, and Kyoko did likewise.

"Taku?" she finally asked a little hesitantly. Her voice was low.

"Yes, it's me."

"I've been worrying about you."

"I know."

"Hanada told me about you just now."

"Oh?"

"That you're meeting him—the boss, I mean."

"So you've heard already, eh?"

"I thought that would happen. But tell me, how was it to walk with Ai?"

"I learned a lot."

At the other end, Kyoko gave a faint chuckle. "Anything you learn has got to be good."

Taku seemed to see Kyoko's expression before his eyes.

"Take care, won't you. I know I always say that."

"Sure thing."

"Cho's restaurant has been shut since yesterday. Maybe something's happened."

"That's odd." Cradling the receiver, Taku scratched his head in puzzlement. Cho almost never closed up shop, even if he wasn't there himself.

I wonder if something's up, he thought.

"I put the key to your apartment back behind the gas meter," Kyoko said casually. "I won't be going back there."

"Why not?"

"You're going to be with the Group from now on, Taku. Ai really needs someone like you."

Taku was silent.

"So long then," came Kyoko's voice. She hung up.

He continued to stand there motionless. He had the feeling that something very precious had just slipped through his grasp.

21

It was night. The white steel tables and chairs placed on the lawn were damp and chill to the touch. The spacious garden, with its magnificent view over distant Suruga Bay to the south, contrasted with the fortress-like and almost windowless concrete building that was Keiryo Lodge.

Below Taku spread the gentle undulations of the one-hundred-member exclusive Ikarino One Hundred Club Golf Course. The lights trembling on the horizon off to the left would be Port Heda in West Izu.

The whole garden was dimly lit by a bluish light that spilled from the tasteless fountain modeled on Rome's Trevi Fountain. Behind it loomed a vast mountain. All was quiet. No one seemed to be about.

Three men were sitting across the pear-shaped table from Taku. He watched their tense profiles, idly appreciating the feel of the beautifully cut lawn with the toe of his shoe. To the left sat Professor Nishihaga, a pair of metal-frame glasses on his nose. For some time now he had been nervously running his fingertips over the lapels of his dark blue suit in an attempt to smooth them. The careful choice of matching pocket square and tie in different shades of burgundy, and mocassin-style slip-on shoes, tan rather than the usual black, produced a strong impression of a celebrity intellectual striving to appear youthful.

By contrast, Goro Haneda was the very picture of an old-fashioned journalist, in tweed coat and with fountain pen clipped in his breast pocket. He betrayed the tension beneath his cool exterior by lighting and then stubbing out one cigarette after another.

Taku was tense too. For some time now he'd felt horribly self-conscious about the casual mustard-yellow Viyella shirt, suede jacket, and brown corduroy pants that he'd borrowed from Shin'ichi. He really should have at least put on a tie, he thought, running his fingers through his tousled hair. After all, the invitation had come from the famous Meido Ikarino himself.

"So you meet with the boss from time to time, do you, Professor?" he asked.

"Oh, once or twice a year at most, you know. And only at crowded gatherings. He may know my name, but I don't imagine he'd recognize my face," Nishihaga replied carefully. "Still, I must say it's a surprise to find that it was the boss himself who came up with the idea to name the first volume in the *Japan—Its Lights and Shadows* series '*Yamato.*' I'd simply assumed it was the idea of Shimafune."

Shimafune, his large face looking even more villainous than usual thanks to the light's angle, simply continued to face the sea. He gave a low chuckle. "Well, our boss is what you might call something of a genius. He can bring together all the companies he owns and combine them in quite startling ways to great effect, you see. That publication has linked up in his mind with some other enterprise and produced a different, quite unforeseen plan, one that will increase the publication's sales and add to the profits of the other business as well. That's how it will go, for sure."

"I see." Professor Nishihaga folded his arms and groaned softly. "Well, all I can say is, he's a quite astonishing person. Not only an excellent businessman, a man of real culture as well. I've heard that he's planning to create a new foundation for the study of ancient history."

"There are rumors of it, yes."

"Who's handling it in the academic world? Surely it wouldn't be Tokyo University's Kitamori would it?"

"I'm afraid I've no idea."

"It's all very well to set up a foundation, but listen here, the problem is who he gets for the job. He's got to appoint someone who's free from all the factions, so it doesn't become a hot potato for the academics to fight over. I plan to bring this up with him myself this evening. What do you think?"

"Hmm." Shimafune averted his face, evidently annoyed. Beside him, Hanada stubbed his cigarette upright into the ashtray and said bluntly, "I really don't think that would be wise, you know."

"But listen here…"

"I think he's arrived." Shimafune raised a hand to his eyes and gazed up at the eastern sky.

The chop of a light engine sounded overhead, and an aircraft's red lights could be seen slowly approaching. A powerful light shone from the building's roof onto the deserted parking lot beside it, and the silver belly of a small helicopter gently descended directly onto a white mark painted on the tarmac. Then the explosive pounding sank to a different rhythm, the door opened, and three men emerged. They made their way under a rose arbor in the garden and headed straight for where Taku and the others were seated.

"Well, my friends, I apologize for the delay." It was the voice Taku had heard the other night in the hall at the sixtieth anniversary party, a strong baritone delivered from a thickset chest.

The tall, stylish gentleman nodded to everyone as he stood there, the black shape of the mountain towering behind him. His splendid silver hair glowed in the faint light. He gave an elegant little bow. "Thank you all for coming. Ah, you're Taku Hayami, eh? I'm Ikarino. Nice to meet you."

"How do you do?" Hesitantly, Taku shook the outstretched hand. The grip was astonishingly strong for a man of seventy-eight, but the skin was dry, and horribly cold.

Two men stood behind him. One wore a black suit, and walked with an awkward limp. Taku didn't need to look twice to recognize that frame. It was the Konryu gang's Ryuzaki. He narrowed his eyes as he gazed at Taku but didn't speak.

The other was dressed in traditional Japanese style, and had a splendid black beard. Taku felt he'd met him somewhere before, but couldn't recall where.

"Sit down," Ikarino said in a resonant voice. He seated himself at the head of the table, the mountain behind him. A smile hovered on his lips, and like a crown over his head hung the Big Dipper. Backlit as it was, his face had the stateliness of a bronze warrior.

Shimafune greeted him with nervous politeness, and introduced Hanada. Ikarino simply nodded silently. "And who is this gentleman?" he asked, indicating Nishihaga with his chin.

Nishihaga sprang to his feet. "You were so good as to lend me your support when I published my book *The Road to Yamato—Its Lights and Shadows*. Meiryo University's..." he began hoarsely.

"Ah, Professor Nishihaga," Ikarino cut in. "I apologize. Yes, thank you for the work."

"I'm honored that you remember."

"But of course. I also recommended you for the Japan Art Essay Prize, and it was I who asked you to deliver the keynote address at the Asian Culture Conference. I was also the one who asked Shimafune here to employ you to supervise the new series when I heard that Meteor Publications was planning it."

The elderly white-clad waiter brought over a splendid cut-glass decanter and some glasses. A brown liquid swayed in the decanter. Ryuzaki stood up, and placed a glass before Ikarino.

"How about the rest of you?" inquired the boss. "Viper tea. Highly efficacious."

"I, er, won't thank you," said Nishihaga tremulously, drawing back.

"I must get you to be the leader in the new cultural movement the Ikarino Corporation is planning, Professor. Could you just answer something for me?"

"Anything that might be within my powers..."

Ikarino gulped down the brown liquid that Ryuzaki had poured for him, without losing his smile.

Taku had only seen him from some distance away at the party, but now that Ikarino was before his eyes, he was struck still more by his impressive posture and features. The wavy silver hair, the strong-willed jaw, the taut cheeks, the strikingly neat ears and nose. Still, there was something over-perfect about him, that sense of looking at a bronze sculpture rather than a human being.

"So." Meido Ikarino turned to face Taku. "Mr. Hayami, you're the guest here tonight. I've been wanting to meet you for a long time. I'm sure you'll know why. You'll have had it all explained to you by the Group members at Ryukien on Mount Izu. Tenro was longing to meet you, and I too have wanted to see you, to hear you voice. You're the sole young fellow who inherits the blood of my master, Henro Katsuragi, after all. I was a beloved disciple of Henro's, you know, more so even than Tenro, the present leader. Not just beloved, in fact. No one knows this, but he was planning to leave the entire future of the Group in my hands. If the truth be known, it was I and not Tenro who should have taken over the Group after Henro's death…"

A flood of emotion suddenly thickened Ikarino's controlled voice. He broke off and was silent for a moment, in an apparent effort to calm himself. No one spoke. At length, Ikarino resumed. "Well, never mind. I'll tell you about this later. But I also wanted you to hear it, Nishihaga. If the time ever comes when you write up our history, you must put all this down, you know."

"I understand."

Ikarino tossed back another glass of the liquid. Then he leaned forward and stared at Taku. "By the way, Hayami, just what orders did you receive from the assembled folks at the Group?"

"I wasn't actually given any orders. They just explained to me in detail about all sorts of things I never knew."

"I see." Ikarino nodded. "And?"

"I learned that I'm someone who has a deep connection with the Group." Taku chose his words carefully, to sound neither servile nor rude. "And I'm now hoping to rejoin the Group as a member of the Wayfarers' League. That's all."

"That's pleasing news. It's entirely natural that the descendant of Henro Sensei should want to *return*." Ikarino nodded in apparent satisfaction. Then he pursued his questioning. "How much do you know?"

"About what?"

"About Henro Sensei."

"A teacher by the name of Rokotsu Sarashino gave me a careful explanation. I think I understand the general story now."

"Good. Well, then…" Ikarino signaled something to Ryuzaki, who nodded and disappeared into the main building. Ikarino continued, "There used to be a ceremony called 'The Opening of the Lectern' in country temples back in the old days—do you know of it, Professor Nishihaga?"

"'The Opening of the Lectern'...well, I'm not so well-versed in matters of religion, I'm afraid..."

Ikarino nodded and went on. "No, no, I'm not talking of academic matters here. Traditional country temples often used to send the son of the incumbent to study at a sect university as part of his training to take over the reins. The parishioners would sponsor the lad. A few years later, he'd graduate and come back to the temple, and on his return the more fervent believers among the parishioners, men who were deeply versed in the Buddhist texts and sutras, would get together and hold a meeting to hear the son preach. This event was called 'The Opening of the Lectern.' Every parish would have its pernickety old timers who set themselves up to rival the priest in knowledge, you see, and if the young fellow did a bad job of the sermon there'd be a stream of difficult questions intended to show him up. A lad who'd spent his student days getting funds from home just to sit around playing mah-jong would really have to face the music. What it really amounted to was a rather malicious test of his caliber. 'The Opening of the Lectern' was a way of finding out what stuff the future incumbent of the temple was made of."

Ikarino gave a dry laugh. "Anyway, I'd like to follow this precedent by just putting a few questions to you, Mr. Hayami."

"So this is to be my 'Opening of the Lectern,' is it?" Taku asked. "I'm sorry, but I have no memory of having been sponsored by the Ikarino Corporation."

"That doesn't really matter though, surely?" Shimafune broke in, waving a soothing hand. "Mr. Ikarino simply brought up the 'Opening of the Lectern' by way of illustration. What he's saying is, he'd like to learn just what the Group has been telling you."

"I understand." Taku rearranged himself on the chair. Then he turned to Nishihaga and addressed him politely. "The report on Mount Nijo that I gave Mr. Hanada the other day was a very rough one, sir. Since then, I've learned quite a lot more, which I'd like you to hear about now. Matters concerning the 'shadow' side of the 'light and shadow' that you intend to treat in your book. It may take some time, but I'd appreciate it if you could correct me on any matter I've mistaken or misremembered."

Nishihaga drew his brows together and gave a slight nod, though he seemed somewhat reluctant.

Ignoring this, Taku continued. "With your permission, then, I will now give a brief summary of what I learned from Sarashino Sensei concerning the life of Henro Katsuragi and the founding of the Wayfarers' League. I'm not confident of doing a good job, I'm afraid…"

At this point, Ryuzaki reappeared carrying a camel robe and a small tape recorder. Ikarino slipped the robe around his shoulders, folded his arms, and nodded to Taku to proceed.

A soft breeze blew. The lights went out, and the garden was wrapped in thick darkness. Only the softly glowing tip of Hanada's cigarette was visible. Taku drew a breath, then softly began to speak.

We'll go back to the beginning of the Meiji period, back around the 1870s.

In those days, there was a young mountain monk who lived in the Katsuragi Mountains that rise above the Yamato Plain to the west. This was an area with ancient connections to the founder of the mountain ascetic sect, a man by the name of En no Ozune, and mountain *yamabushi* monks as well as the more formal *shugenja* sect practitioners from around the nation would frequently gather there to engage in their arduous ascetic practices.

No one really knew where this monk came from, or what his origins were. He was a small-framed, thin young man, with sunken eyes and a face that was somehow reminiscent of a wild monkey.

It was rumored that he moved about among the Katsuragi Mountains pursuing his practice, and was making an attempt to perform the Thousand-Day Mountain Circuit of the peaks of Kongo, Katsuragi, and Ikoma. But his real practice centered on Mount Nijo, the mountain that connects to the Takenouchi Highway. It was his goal to circle the male and female peaks of Nijo thirty thousand times, and it was said that there was never a day, be it misty morning or snowy evening, that his swift figure was not seen, moving as if on wings over Mount Nijo.

This young mountain monk didn't look like the usual rough *yamabushi* monks, or the elaborately dressed *shugenja* monks.

He was as poorly clad as a beggar, and the old folk of the local villages remarked to each other that he seemed like the holy hermit monks of old that used to be known as *hijiri*.

He never went near the villagers. The only human contact he seemed to have was in secret with the group of itinerant folk known as the Kenshi, people outside the registered social world who followed a seasonal, wandering nomadic life along the mountain waterways of the area from Yoshino to Yamato.

These people were later commonly referred to by the dismissive term *Sanka*, a name applied to them by the media and the authorities. They were the people known as *mitsukuri* or "winnowers," a class that had long been the butt of misconceptions and prejudice.

The name "winnower" derived from the fact that they used to specialize in the making and repairing of winnows, tools that were an essential part of agricultural life. They also fished in the mountain streams and gathered wild food as the need arose. These people, nomads of no fixed address who traveled in family groups who called themselves *Sekenshi*, or Kenshi for short, had for well over a thousand years maintained their own unique lifestyle and customs.

At this point, Taku paused. He was a little annoyed with himself for not being able to tell the tale of the clan as vividly and engagingly as Sarashino Sensei had done that day in the dark storehouse.

"Professor Nishihaga," he said. "I'm afraid I don't quite know what a winnow is. Could you explain it to me?"

"Well, a winnow…" Nishihaga began rather reluctantly. "A winnow is a tool that used to be found in every country home before agriculture was mechanized. It was woven out of natural fiber. The winnow was an essential everyday implement, whose foremost use was to sort grain and seeds, but some were also shaped like a basket or colander and used as containers or for transport. There was a time when they were also used in areas such as the Chikuho region of northern Kyushu to carry coal from the coal pits, and in the gold-mining central mountains of Izu, the winnow was used to pan for gold dust.

"Just as a quick aside here, in Izu you'll find the place name Mitsukuri, just down from Basara Pass. It was a center for winnow making, and an important spot along the old Izu route. The interesting thing is, way back in 686 when Prince Otsu was condemned to death, the man by the name of Toki no Michitsukuri was said to have been exiled to this very place for his role as accomplice. *Michitsukuri* means 'roadmaker,' and the implication is that the word *mitsukuri*, 'winnower,' may have been conflated with this word. Then there's the fact that the great mountain ascetic En no Ozunu was also exiled to Izu. I won't go into the connection between Yamato and Izu here. Anyway, a winnower could be variously used to sort or winnow grain, tea, flour, dirt, or other objects. It could be woven from cherry bark, wisteria vine, dwarf bamboo, cedar bark, and so on. In Kyushu they used the akebia vine, in Koshu they used straw. I assume there's no need for me to go into the process here."

"Well, well, Professor. Very impressive," said Ikarino. "You obviously have a fine grasp of matters outside your field as well as within it." There was a certain irony in his tone.

"Back in the country area I come from, we had dialect names for a sieve—*mego*, or *shoké* we called it," Hanada murmured. "When they used akebia vine to make them they had to do it as soon as the vine was cut, or it would harden too much."

"Let's get back to your story, Hayami." Ikarino folded his arms, closed his eyes, and resumed the pose of a listener. Taku nodded and began again.

Anyway, these "winnowers," the Kenshi, used to set up their camps in out-of-the-way places in the mountains and river valleys, make their winnows, and hawk them around the villages in a twenty- or thirty-kilometer radius. In exchange they received grains and vegetables, and later money, but this wasn't so much payment for services as a form of alms such as pilgrims or monks might receive, what the Indians refer to as *baksheesh*. The Kenshi never really had a tradition of gratitude for things they received from the villagers, pretty much like the Gypsies and some Hindu followers. Essentially, they seem to have believed that it was only natural that humans and nature should live in mutual cooperation and extend help to each other as need be. Begging was once a respectable way of life, you see.

So the Kenshi in their turn would go out of their way to care for lepers and the like, people who were spurned by society. It was their custom to take in these people, whose limbs were half eaten away, and make them part of the family. It's not hard to imagine how this would only have reinforced the world's fears and prejudices towards them.

Well, this traditional Kenshi way of life grew increasingly difficult as time passed. Back when sovereignty was first established over the Yamato Plain, the foundation of the country's unification rested on the bureaucratic registering of households and fixed addresses. Household registration has been the basis for a ruler's power ever since the promulgation of the laws related to it in 670. But for all that, there's no denying the fact that there have been many who continued to resist the demand to register, even with increasing pressure from modern unification in the last hundred or so years—a whole underground stream quietly flowing throughout Japan consisting of people who continued to ignore the three great obligations of the modern citizen: military service, payment of taxes, and compulsory education.

It's been claimed that even after the 1890s mobilization for the Sino-Japanese War, there were still more than two hundred thousand unregistered "winnower" Kenshi wandering loose in the land, and in 1949, after the Pacific War, there were still about fourteen thousand. And if you include the unregistered wandering Kenshi who had taken up other trades, this figure would rise to some eight hundred thousand. What finally forced all these "non-citizens" to take up fixed and registered abodes was the Citizens' Registration Act of 1952 that was promulgated nationwide during the Korean War as part of a fundamental reorganization of the nation.

Everyone in Japan was required by law to register his place of residence, as well as being obliged to register for a rice-ration book, national pension, national health insurance, and the electoral roll. This law, which later became enshrined as the Basic Residents' Register, sprang from a fierce determination to prevent every last registration-resister from living in Japan. It was the final blow for the unregistered.

This marked the apparent end of the history of the "drifters," a history that went back thousands of years.

"Well, I knew all that," came Ikarino's voice in the darkness. "That's all absolutely common knowledge," he said again, and now a fierce anger trembled in his voice.

"After that event happened back in 1877, at the hour of his death Henro Sensei already clearly foresaw the end of the drifter folk a hundred years hence. That's precisely why he founded the Fraternity. It was he who created the plan whereby people would chose to *blend* with society and live for all appearances as normal citizens while pursuing a life that preserved the self-respect of the clan's proud independence. He revealed to the Fraternity that to *blend* was not to vanish, it was the establishment of a kingdom that would be reborn underground. I have never for a single day forgotten this teaching in my life. And now…"

Ikarino sighed heavily. He seemed to be struggling to suppress the emotion that rose in him. "But never mind that. Go on please, Mr. Hayami. Let's get back to the young mountain monk in the Katsuragi Mountains."

In Taku's mind rose the idea of a spindly young man, like a wild monkey dressed in a ragged cloak. His imagination took flight at the image of this man speeding like an animal in and out of gaps in the mist of Mount Nijo. He began to speak, this time with a little more feeling.

From the very early days, the Katsuragi Mountains had strong connections with these drifters who "ploughed no furrow." The mountain ascetic En no Ozunu, commonly referred to as En no Gyoja and famous as an outstanding member of the ancient mountain ascetic community, is said to have meditated and performed ascetic mountain circuits in the Katsuragi Mountains. He was also, as Professor Nishihaga just mentioned, exiled to Izu by the court for creating a disturbance with his superhuman powers. There's still a little statue of him crouching quietly in a corner off the Gold Hall at Taima Temple behind the Indian-style images.

Also, according to documents in the Todaiji Temple, apparently an annual tribute was "several times plundered by monks named Kawachi and Kusunoki" en route to the court from the provinces via the Takenouchi Highway. The monk Kusunoki, leader of a guerilla group of bandits who had infiltrated the Katsuragi Mountains, was long associated in local legend with the famous fourteenth-century warrior Masashige Kusunoki.

But back to the saintly young mountain monk. He was secretly in touch with the Kenshi, and in the midst of his arduous thirty-thousand day mountain circuit of Nijo, the 1877 incident occurred.

Atsushi Saisho, the District Commander of Sakai, was a man who flaunted the powers of the central government official to the distress of citizens by such acts as arbitrarily cutting down all the pines along the shoreline of Hamadera. In 1876, on top of having swallowed the Kawachi and Izumi areas, Sakai grew still larger with the amalgamation of Nara Prefecture, with the result that Saisho now wielded supreme power among the major prefectures of the area. And in order to display this power and authority to the people, he undertook a major rebuilding of the Takenouchi Highway.

He was probably following the example of Takatoshi Shijo, the popular and famous former Nara prefectural governor, who'd won the approval of his people by successfully building a road over Kamenose Pass. Aside from flood control works, you see, it was a long-standing condition of power in the region to put in work on the Takenouchi Highway.

The man on site who orchestrated this major and difficult undertaking was Yosuke Nawagi, the governor's much-feared henchman.

Well, it hardly needs saying that the work had its problems. On top of this, Nawagi was taking his cut from the laborers' miserable daily wages, provoking continual incidents of sabotage and desertion. He came up with the idea of using prison labor, but that didn't work either.

And so we come to his final round-up of laborers—the so-called *Sanka-gari* or Roundup of the Homeless of 1877, a great mustering of the homeless drifters in the Yamato, Izumi, and Kawachi areas.

To do this according to the law, the prefecture must go through the process of registering all those arrested, extend them citizens' rights, and provide employment. But Nawagi's methods were a blatant display of the bureaucracy's violence and prejudice towards the drifters.

The two hundred forty-odd who were arrested, of both sexes and all ages, were all herded together and locked into a stone quarry at the foot of Nijo, a fenced-in, sunless hollow below a cliff where there were a mere three huts, more like animal sheds really.

The homeless who'd been rounded up in the mountains belonged to various groups. Besides the "winnower" Kenshi, who numbered around one hundred forty, there were the ill and poverty-stricken, vagrants, beggars, prostitutes, ruffians, criminals on the run, wandering entertainers and so on. And among them was the young Katsuragi mountain monk, arrested for failing to provide an address and family name. As luck would have it, on the day of the roundup he'd called on the Kenshi encampment near Mount Nijo, so he was rounded up along with the sick to whom he'd been ministering with herbs.

He made no attempt to explain himself to the authorities. "Everyone without a fixed address is a 'vagrant,'" he told them. As he came from the Katsuragi Mountains, he was given the surname of "Katsuragi," along with the other Kenshi. Later, his scrawniness and general appearance earned him the name "The Katsuragi Monkey."

The Nijo roadwork began soon after the roundup. Everyone was forced into hard labor—even women, the elderly, children, and invalids.

June came, and with it the humid rainy season. It's easy to imagine the terrible problems those workers faced in the wet weather, working in a place renowned for its mists, and particularly since they were all quite unused to such engineering work. The sick dropped like flies, and there were many deaths from falling rocks and landslides as well. There were also reports of rough fellows being beaten to death when they dared to stand up to the boss, and prostitutes who'd attempted escape who were captured, tied up naked, and left in the quarry to die.

Amidst all this, the Katsuragi Monkey took on a kind of caretaker role for the others, and found himself looked up to as their leader. He was indeed a man who embodied the Buddhist ideal of "single-minded selflessness." He was also a man of great ingenuity and drive, whose fine survival skills had been honed by his long years in the mountains. So it came about that the Katsuragi Monkey gradually found himself elevated to a secret leadership role among the workers of the Nijo camp.

When someone died, the Monkey would carry the body, often of someone bigger than himself, up to a secluded place on Mount Nijo and bury it. This gave him the opportunity to escape on his own, but he never did. It was said that he would share his food with starving children while eating roots and leaves gathered in the mountains himself, and feed the ill with rice gruel. "We all have to help each other," he was fond of saying.

As July gave way to August and the worst of the summer heat set in, their numbers had dwindled by about seventy. No doubt there were some who had successfully escaped.

In mid-August, on a night of fierce thunder and rain, the man in charge of operations, Yosuke Nawagi, showed up at the camp with a few underlings in tow.

"Choose eight strong-looking men," he ordered, without any explanation of why or where they'd be going. The Monkey wasn't among the eight originally chosen, but he stepped forward and offered himself in the place of one.

Nawagi promised he'd have them back in a few days, and he told them he was aware of the need for medicine for the sick, and better food.

"You'll only get it if the eight of you do the work well and don't go trying to escape or anything," he added.

His underlings led the eight off down the Takenouchi Highway towards Kawachi. All eight were Kenshi.

Taku broke off the story here. The seven men who sat listening were all silent, apparently sunk in their own thoughts. There was no sign of the usual lit cigarette in Hanada's hand. Black bands of cloud were appearing in the sky above, and there was a faint scent of moisture in the air.

There'll be rain tomorrow, thought Taku. He took a breath, and plunged on with his story.

They were marched through the night, these eight with the Monkey among them. At some point along the way they crossed the Ishi River and were led on towards Sakai. They finally arrived at the beach of Hamadera, to a ruined house.

There they had the unusual experience of being fed to the full and allowed to sleep on straw matting.

"What will they make us do?" they whispered to the Monkey.

"I've no idea."

"I have a feeling something horrible is in the works."

"Just take good care, okay?"

"If anything happens, please look after the group, won't you. Everyone will protect you."

"Well, we must just do as we're told, that's all we can do."

A wind howled outside. The men lay there consumed with indefinable anxiety, each thinking of the family and friends he'd left behind in the Nijo camp.

At one point, one of the men thrust something hard and heavy into the Monkey's hands. "Here, I'm giving you this," he said. "Hide it so they don't find it."

Inside the cloth wrapping was a double-edged workman's knife. The Monkey bound it carefully to his inner thigh.

It was late at night when the guards came to lead them away. Dark clouds filled the sky, a fierce wind blew, and the town was empty of figures.

They walked for a while along the seafront, then turned east, and finally found themselves being led northward through the darkness.

"Where are we going?" someone whispered, but no one answered.

At length, the eight men arrived at the edge of a great, dark wood surrounded by a double moat. An extraordinary aura of solemnity seemed to emanate from deep within the dense forest growth.

"Get in the boat," the guards ordered. The men stepped into the little boat and crossed both moats, the first a narrow one and the second considerably wider. Then they scrambled to the edge of the large mounded hill that rose before them. Their bodies were stiff and their limbs uncooperative. Then, at further orders, they proceeded to crawl up the rough uneven slope. Twice on the way up they came upon flattened areas like galleries, which they crossed, then proceeded on up.

Finally they emerged at the top onto level ground. The lights of Sakai were visible through the trees. From the west the breeze carried the faint scent of the sea.

"So you're here."

The silhouetted shape of Nawagi emerged suddenly from the darkness. He gazed at each of the eight in turn, examining them carefully. Then he ordered them to follow him, and led them over to a corner of the flattened summit.

Looking carefully, they could make out to their immediate right the vague black shape of bushes surrounded by a meter-high stone fence. It was somehow similar to the familiar grave of Prince Otsu on the summit of Mount Nijo's male peak.

"We've no business here," Nawagi muttered to himself. Then he said aloud, "Right, then. That scoundrel Hideyoshi carried off the stone lid back in the sixteenth century, but I think this is probably the place."

He stood a little away from the fence, and stamped hard on the earth. "Yes, this is it," came his voice. "Dig here."

Trembling with incomprehensible terror and apprehension, the eight men were handed shovels and mattocks, and under Nawagi's directions began carefully to dig.

The woods around them roared with each fresh gust of wind. The men dug on as instructed, their minds blank. They felt that if they dared to wonder just what this place was or what they were doing, they would be flung with a bellow down the hillside into the black moat below. On they dug, mindlessly.

At length their spades struck something hard like stone. It was a huge, thick slab of stone, like a vast rectangular board. Removing this covering, they dug on, and after some time a wall of round river stones began to emerge. They dug this away in turn, and within it they found buried a strange object, something they had never before seen.

In the moonless night and without a light, it was impossible to make out the details, but as they peered in they could see an oddly-shaped lump of stone like the vast shell of a huge turtle, with projections coming off it on both sides. Both the surface and the angles were beautifully made, and it seemed the work of a fine craftsman.

Stroking the thick cylindrical protuberance, larger than a man's head, that resembled the mouth of a great cannon, one of the men murmured, "What marvelous workmanship! I'd say this rock could be Mount Nijo tuff."

"Well look at this," came Nawagi's voice from above them. "This one's bigger than the one we got from the base five years ago, but it's exactly the same shape. Come on, out of my way there."

Nawagi lowered himself into the dark hole. "No sign of anyone having touched it. Good," he murmured happily.

The men were given hammers and chisels and ordered to set about opening a hole in the stone surface.

It must have taken hours, but at last they had chipped open a hole big enough for a man to put his head in. Finally, Nawagi ordered the men to leave the site.

"Take them away," he said to the guards, "and do as we agreed. Right?"

Nawagi and one of his men stayed behind, and the eight were taken by the others some way down the hillside. It was a steep and thickly wooded part of the slope, with the water of the leaden moat glinting blackly below.

"This is the place."

Below the tall grass they could make out a kind of deep cleft in the earth, a hole about twice a man's height in depth. It must have been around six meters across. Along the upper edge stood a kind of fence made of river stones, the sort that surrounds imperial tombs. The pit seemed to have been dug some time ago, and water lay puddled at the bottom.

"Dig here," said the fat one. "Everyone get in and dig for all you're worth. If you dig down three feet and still find nothing, that's the end of tonight's work. We'll give you your wages plus food and medicine for your families and send you home."

The eight men lowered themselves into the pit and began to dig as hard as they could. Three feet down, they received further orders and dug another two feet. By the time it was clear there was nothing there, the sky overhead had begun to soften with dawn light.

"Nothing there?"

"No."

"Right, just one more foot then. You can take a short break first."

The eight men flopped down. Sensing something odd in the voices of the guards above, the Katsuragi Monkey glanced up.

"Something strange is going on. Watch out," whispered the man who'd given him the knife, leaning forward protectively from behind him. As he spoke, there came the sudden rushing sound of a rockfall from above. The pile of river stones at the edge of the pit was suddenly hurtling downwards. Stones flew, blood flew, cries filled the air. From above came the sound of laughter. Those who tried to scramble out tumbled back again, their heads split open. The Katsuragi Monkey found himself at the bottom of the pit, covered and protected by the crush of body upon body of his companions. There in the slippery mud and blood, he lost consciousness.

A sudden chill ran over his skin, and Taku shivered. He signed to the white-clothed waiter who was hovering a little distance away, still as a tree.

"I'd like something warm to drink, please," he said. Then he went back to his story.

Late the following night, a fierce storm struck Mount Nijo. A heavy pall of anxiety hung over the camp as everyone waited for the eight men—their husbands and brothers—who had not yet returned.

There was a knock at the door, and a man almost fell through the doorway out of the darkness beyond. It was the Katsuragi Monkey.

"You've got to run…" he gasped hoarsely. He looked scarcely human. "They're all dead. So I killed Nawagi."

Everyone gathered around him fell silent, waiting for his next words. The Katsuragi Monkey paused to draw breath, then after a moment he proceeded to tell them the details of all that had happened to the eight men. Buried there in the pit, he had miraculously regained consciousness, he told them. With the knife he had cut his way through the earth wall, and with a superhuman effort of will had managed to escape to the surface.

His companions had protected him. There beneath their corpses, he alone had escaped death. He had crawled out onto the surface, made his way down and swum the moats, and then spent the day hiding in the thick woods. At nightfall, he had made his way back to the town. He'd scared the night watchman into revealing where Nawagi's house was, then run through the darkness to where he lay, slain him with a single knife thrust, and returned to Mount Nijo.

"So from today…" The Katsuragi Monkey ended softly, his palms together before him as if in solemn pledge, "From today I will devote my life to you, my brethren."

Then, at last, everyone began to talk. The Katsuragi Monkey was urging that they must all leave Mount Nijo right away. As soon as Nawagi's henchmen learned of his death, they would come for their revenge. And all the more if they discovered that one of the eight buried men had escaped. The dark work done that night was a dangerous matter that must be kept dark and secret for ever—if it ever came to light, it would implicate the prefectural governor himself.

"That's surely the reason why they plotted to obliterate us all," he concluded.

A fierce debate ensued. Finally, as day was dawning, a decision was reached. Almost all the Kenshi agreed with the Katsuragi Monkey, and chose to flee Mount Nijo. Eight families with a total of fifty-five people, including women, children, and the elderly, were to set out with him. The remaining people decided that it was more sensible to remain passively at the camp. "If we escape," they said, "they'd be sure to track us down. It would be wiser to wait here and see what move they make. After all, there's no guaranteeing that we'd actually be killed."

The fifty-five of the eight fleeing families made hasty preparations to leave, and, choosing their moment, quietly broke a way out through the enclosure. Then they set off on an undertaking none had attempted before—a long, rapid walk that they later came to refer to as the "*Great Nori.*"

The *Great Nori* would take them through the mountains of Kawachi, Yamato, and Yoshino, places full of memories for them, and on a long journey into distant and unknown territory. But they left behind them their fellow-Kenshi who had chosen to part with them and remain, unable to face the thought of leaving the Yamato area where their ancestors had lived and wandered all these years.

Dawn was approaching. The rain had ceased, but a still fiercer wind now blew, and both the peaks of Mount Nijo were smothered in thick grey mist.

The camp now behind them, the group of fifty-five walked on into the mountains until suddenly the Katsuragi Monkey at their head came to a halt. He gathered them around him and, in a voice thick with emotion, began to speak.

"My friends, we are now about to leave this land. Ahead of us is distant Kanto. I have a 'brother' there, and that's where I plan to take us. We have no way of living in this land any longer. In fifty, one hundred years from now, the last of the Kenshi will have disappeared from this country. But we must not perish. No, we must blend with the rest of the world, strengthen ourselves, and continue to keep the spirit of the Kenshi secretly safe within us. We must never forget mist-shrouded Mount Futakami. Whatever our trials and privations, we fifty-five of the eight families must help each other as brethren, and continue our line into future generations as the clan from Futakami. This is the first time we Kenshi of Yamato and Kawachi have gone to the East, to the Kanto region. This *Great Nori* will be hard, but we must make it through. Once we've achieved it, life will open before us. I've kept this from you all, but my real name is Henro Basara. I am from the Izu branch of the Kenshi, but living *apart*. You people cared for me while I was undertaking my austerities on Mount Katsuragi, and you continued to treat me well when we were all incarcerated together at Mount Nijo. Now it's my turn to help you all. Today, it's been decided that my grave will be here in Yamato on Mount Nijo, and henceforth my name is changed to Henro Katsuragi. I hereby vow to set myself at naught and devote myself to you, the fifty-five. Please place your trust in me, and follow me."

As he finished speaking, there came from the camp in the quarry below them great shouts and the screams of women, together with a sudden fierce noise.

"The camp's on fire!" someone yelled. Through breaks in the mist that swirled around them, they saw crimson flames and black smoke erupting. Everyone ran to the edge of the cliff and peered over to stare at the burning camp. Below, club-wielding men were beating down the women and old people who were frantically trying to escape the flames. There was the sound of gunshots. Young mothers clutching their children leapt, hair flying, into the gushing flames of the camp. These were their Kenshi brethren who had stayed behind at Nijo. The witnesses could make out Yosuke Nawagi's henchmen apparently dipping ladles into buckets and tossing oil into the camp. They watched as young people rushed from the camp only to fall to the sound of gunshots.

"Don't speak," the Monkey who was now renamed Henro Katsuragi said in an agonized voice. "Don't look away. Watch carefully. What you're seeing is the real face of our brave new age. Burn it onto your retina, and tell it to future generations. Nijo, Futakami, will henceforth be the place of origin of our Eight Families, and the grave we must return to again and again. Look well, everyone. What you see will be our own fate if we ever for one moment cease to help each other. You must not cry. Just look, and remember."

All—children and adults alike—stood trembling as they gazed silently at the scene below. A few of the girls, unable to stand the sight, vomited. Some of the old people put their hands together in prayer and chanted the name of the Buddha.

"Right, we must go," cried Henro Katsuragi in a firm voice. "We must leave this place before they find us. Now begins our long *nori* of one hundred fifty, no, two hundred miles, along secret mountain paths to Izu."

And so the journey of the fifty-five of the Eight Families began, a journey that was also the beginning for their leader, the man who would henceforth be known as Henro Katsuragi.

There was a sound like the groan of an animal. A burgundy handkerchief clutched to his mouth, Professor Nishihaga rose from his chair, crouched in the shade of the shrubbery, and vomited.

"A man of strong sensibility," said Meido Ikarino with a low chuckle. "Rare in a scholar."

"I understand he's distantly related to one of those left behind in the camp and murdered," Hanada cut in. "Whenever the talk turns to Mount Nijo it affects him strongly."

"Poor fellow." Ikarino's tone was ironic. "Still, you could say that this is precisely why his *Yamato's Lights and Shadows* was imbued with that special sense of realism another scholar wouldn't have brought to the job."

"*The Road to Yamato—Its Lights and Shadows*," Nishihaga corrected him as he staggered back to his seat. "I do apologize for the unseemly sight," he went on.

Ikarino waved a hand in light dismissal, and nodded. "No, no, it's just proof that you're a Kenshi descendent," he replied. "Well, now, Mr. Hayami," he went on, "I'd like you to turn to brighter matters now please. Please take up the tale from the point where the young mountain ascetic transformed himself into the leader of the group that made its way east to Izu."

"So what do you think of my 'Opening of the Lectern'?"

"Not bad so far. Mind you, your explanation of the Kenshi glossed over things a touch too much."

Taku nodded. He'd been aware of that. But his reuniting with the clan was still so fresh and powerful for him that it was a kind of vivid dream he craved, rather than dry scholarly evidence.

"Professor Nishihaga," he began. "I'd like you to provide some supplementary explanation. This strange word *Sanka* or 'cave-dweller'—just where does it come from?"

"Might I just say a little here?" Nishihaga asked Ikarino. He seemed to be somewhat recovered.

"Make it brief," muttered Hanada. Nishihaga ignored this, and began to talk.

"Let me begin by answering Mr. Hayami's question. *Sanka* is written with unusual characters, as you know. There are various theories on this, as also on the origin of the word itself, but I'll leave discussion of that aside here, and just relate the ways in which the term has been used in national policy since the Meiji era.

"In fact, the characters used to write the word *sanka* were arbitrarily applied to the original word. *San* is written with 'mountain,' and *ka* is one way of writing 'cave.' Now in the old days of the Silk Road in China, many of the robbers and bandits who lurked along the road lived in rock caves in the mountains, and from this the idea of the cave or *ka* came to additionally refer to a place where stolen goods were hidden, and also by extension to a nest or group of robbers. This came across to our country and, added to the character for 'mountain,' was used to mean 'brigand' by an official of Izumo's Matsue domain who was a Chinese scholar.

"Now, the area of Izumo backs onto the mountain ridge of the Chukoku mountains, and the road from its main town of Matsue to the capital at Edo was a difficult mountain path. After the famous famine of 1732, bandits were prevalent in the area, many of them hiding in mountain caves and causing constant problems for the citizens. It was apparently the idea of an official of the ruling Matsudairas, a man well-versed in Chinese studies, to name these mountain brigands *Sanka*.

"It seems that this word was already widely used around Izumo in the time of Lord Fumai Matsudaira. Kanji Naruse in his *Tea Jar Essays* writes that in a document of the period, *The Record of Lord Fumai of the Land of Izumo*, it's recorded that, roughly quoting, 'Around the beginning of the Meiwa era, in the Sakai mountains of Uki in Izumo there dwelt *Sanka*, who frequently entered the villages and stole money and provisions, targeting houses that had goods in their storehouses. In appearance, they wore animal skins and hats of woven vine, carried knives, and formed gangs of twenty or thirty who forced their way in and stole many things. Oddly, they never entered the houses of the poor or harmed them...'

"So it's no surprise to find reference in Misumi Hiroshi's book *The Sanka Society* to a February 1876 police report made under the Shimane Prefectural Governor Moritome Izeki, which mentions the presence of '*Sanka* and other vagrants,' and reports that the *Sanka* had 'occupied the deep mountain fastnesses around the Unhakuseki Mikuni area.'

"At all events, this official term '*Sanka*' was later used throughout the Meiji and subsequent Taisho and Showa eras as a catch-all term to designate vagrants of no fixed address in the drive to extirpate this class and force them to become registered citizens. The pre-war Home Ministry's Police Department in particular used the term to great effect. In a word, there was a major campaign to create the image of the *Sanka* as deviants living a primitive existence, a collection of anti-social criminals.

"A series of bestsellers with titles like *Tales of Real Crimes* and *Weird Tales of the Sanka* hit the market, inspired by material proffered by the police, while magazines serialized floods of novels detailing similar bizarre stories. All this sprang from the desire of the authorities to eradicate all vagrants and wanderers who resisted the constitution's requirements to register a fixed address.

"The worst were the popular novels that held such sway over the general public—with the aid of materials provided by assimilationist groups under the Home Ministry's control, they inundated the populace with an endless stream of sensationalist crime fiction.

"Why were the Kenshi particularly singled out among this multifarious group of drifters and homeless? We can guess it was because they believed that the consumption of rice 'rots the guts,' as they put it, and they were quietly pursuing a lifestyle that was directly contrary to the settled rice cultivator's existence that had been seen as the essence of everyday life since the long-ago formation of the Yamato court. But there was also a very interesting reaction to this scare campaign.

"While on the one hand readers of these blood-curdling *Sanka* crime novels felt terror at the image of the outlandish folk who roamed free of the heavy yoke imposed by the ultra-nationalist society, defied the will of the statesmen, and ran amok in the wilderness, on the other hand the image awakened in many a fierce longing.

"Think, for instance, of the works of Hatoju Muku—romantic 'mountain folk tales' such as *Song of the Sanka* and *Hawksong*. Surely their appeal derives from this longing for freedom that people felt. Takeshi Kimura, a newspaper commentator of the time, wrote this sort of thing: 'What first attracts us in this writer's work is his fresh and natural touch. The extravagant passions of these roaming folk, these as it were Japanese Gypsies, strikes a lingering chord within us. When a Gypsy boards a train in London he arouses certain feelings in the breasts of the other passengers, feelings derived from the fact that he symbolizes a yearning for a world free of constraints. Muku's writing is of precisely this nature. It is surely only natural in our present Japan, beset as we are on every side by a hundred pressures visible and invisible, that we should feel drawn to depictions of a way of life in which mountains are the waystations through which one's companions move.' Muku's fiction collection was forthwith banned within a week of publication—not, as the authorities claimed, because they were works depicting unpatriotic scoundrels, but because they imparted a beguiling glow to the freedoms of the wandering life. At the same time, the authorities made no complaints about works that showed the *Sanka* as deviant criminals.

"On the other hand, the meticulous and painstakingly detailed *Sanka* research of Hiroshi Misumi quite fails to move the reader to empathy, despite its inclusion of overwhelming numbers of reports from the time. Why? Surely because his entire research was carried out with the protection and help of the police and associated assimilationist bodies. I cannot read these detailings of surveys on statistics of sexual congress among the *sanka*, or the 'physical examinations' that noted details of their sexual organs, without rage. I, I…" Professor Nishihaga drew his handkerchief from his pocket again and pressed it to his face.

What a disgusting display! murmured Hanada under his breath.

But Taku had suddenly begun to feel a strange liking for this stylish scholar. Though he found Nishihaga's blatant emotional excesses rather hard to take, he found himself oddly drawn to him as well.

"Well, leaving aside any further complex discussion of all this…" Ikarino broke in in a low voice, "Let me just take up the story for a moment.

"The fifty-five of the Eight Families who had set off from Mount Nijo, hiding among the mountains and slipping along the ridges as they went, and helped along the way by the local Kenshi, arrived that autumn in the Izu Peninsula and crossed the Amagi Range. Mind you, they'd lost eight people along the way, so only forty-seven arrived in fact. The clan to which the Katsuragi Monkey, later Henro Sensei, belonged lived in the mountains of southern Izu, and it was here that the group finally ended their *Great Nori*.

"It makes me weep just to think of Henro's selfless service from this time on. He began by setting up the Futakami Fraternity, what's known to the world as the Tenmu Jinshin Group. This bonded the Eight Families together. I'm sure you'll learn in due course, Mr. Hayami, just how fervently Sensei set about the task of establishing the life of his companions.

"He fought tooth and nail to ensure that our forebears should henceforth be able to hide their true identity as Kenshi and *blend* with the rest of society. He had to start from nothing. These people had no schooling, no blood relations to rely on, no funds, no experience. But we *blended* into the many cracks in society. There were girls who sold themselves on the streets of hot spring resorts. Others went out as children's nannies. People took up trades as fishermen's assistants, miners, gangsters' underlings, fortunetellers, itinerant actors. There were also those who took to crime. This is a fact, Mr. Hayami."

"I hadn't heard that."

"That's why I say that the Group's *Scholarly Practice* glosses things over." Ikarino chuckled softly.

"There was one Group member who managed to *connect* back a tiny pittance back to the Group every month while serving a fifteen-year prison sentence, you know. The forebear of the Aunt of the Fifth House, that was."

"So what did the Group do about this?" Taku asked.

"The Group?" replied Ikarino. "For its part, the Group planned a united *thrust* into society under the leadership of Henro Sensei.

A push forward that would knock aside all resistance, that's what a *thrust* is.

"The Ikarino Corporation's sixty years of progress is part of the history of this Great *Thrust*. We had to begin by becoming strong. If an opponent defeats one, then two will *thrust* together. If two isn't enough, then three. And every month, no matter what the hardship, you *connect* back whatever money you can to the Group. Henro Sensei invested this income by setting up a mutual funds company. Slowly all the clan members *blended* into society and set up their own official family registers. *Making bits of paper*, we called it. They could be tossed away any time we wanted. For the moment, the important thing was to find some way for the members of the eight families to make their way in the world of Meiji Japan. To do this, they had to formally register as citizens. They hid their origins, and *blended*.

"We constantly exchanged information, aiding each other and working hard and selflessly. And Sensei walked between the Group members who were spread here and there around Izu and the wider Kanto area, maintaining the *connections*. He worked himself to the bone, looking for work for the offspring, raising funds to help start businesses, giving aid to families down on their luck. In time, some Group members signed up to fight in the Sino-Japanese War. If they could succeed in being decorated for their feats, after all, it would prove useful in the future. This was really another form of *making bits of paper*, you see. And the Group gave all the help it could towards the education of the children. Japanese society is all about academic achievement, Sensei said. Everyone's dream was to produce children who would go on to enter the prestigious Tokyo Imperial University.

"After some time, Henro Sensei married and settled down with a young widow from the clan. But his lifestyle didn't change. He continued to wear the same poor clothes he had when he was practicing his austerities up on Katsuragi, and he sacrificed sleep for the sake of his endless activities, or so his wife said. She bore him a daughter, then died of an illness, and some say her death was hastened by the excessive privations. The daughter was given into the care of the Uncle of the Fifth House, and Henro Sensei proceeded to devote himself body and soul to even greater extremes.

"It was around this time that a few of the clan at last began to achieve success. Other young men, meanwhile, had become heavily involved in labor unions and the anti-government activities of the socialist Shusui Kotoku and others. A number of clan members also went off to Korea, Manchuria, and China after Korea was annexed to Japan after the Russo-Japanese War in 1910. A few immigrated to Maui Island in Hawaii to work in the sugar cane plantations and *connect* money back. Some girls went to the Philippines and Borneo, or sold themselves to foreigners up in Vladivostok and sent huge amounts home.

"The Group's funds grew, partly thanks to Henro Sensei's clever dealings. When a borrower was successful, a one-hundred-yen loan would be repaid as a thousand. There was also a custom for the Group to receive half the estate of any member who died. It gave meaning to people's lives to work so that they could give as much as possible to the Group.

"Slowly the Group took shape, with the Parent, the Intimates (the Uncles and Aunts), the Group members and children, and those who had quietly *parted*, the descendants who had *blended* with society at large. But for them too, the rule was that while they lived they continued to be *friends* and to *connect*.

"Inside and outside the Group, an organization called the Wayfarers' (or "Henro") League was formed, with Sensei at its center—a club whose aim was to give still more practical aid to those in need. It grew large, with those who had achieved success in the business and cultural worlds and so on coming together once a month to hear Henro speak, and once a year performing a pilgrimage to Mount Nijo.

"All traces of the work place and the camp had by now disappeared. But the first Group members to revisit the place with Henro Sensei clung together and wept.

"Time moved on. By the time our present Showa era dawned in 1926, the Group's mutual funds company had achieved independent status, and its funds began to be utilized for a fresh *thrust* into the world. Members who had achieved success overseas were sending back information that proved helpful with this.

"The number of offspring grew—it was believed that the more children one bore, the more one was supporting the future of the clan. Large families of over ten children were not uncommon, and in time some of these entered Tokyo University and moved on into the bureaucratic and finance worlds. Both the Group and the Wayfarers' League gave them all the backup they could, and for their part the offspring threw themselves into their studies in order to participate in the *thrust* into the police, the miliary, the judiciary, and the legal professions. The secret transmission of their clan's history and philosophy that Sensei imparted imbued them with a sense of their importance for the future of the clan, and galvanized them to intense efforts.

"To turn to myself, at nineteen I founded the Ikarino business. I'd decided, you see, that I could demonstrate my skills better by jumping straight into the business world rather than going on to higher education. Needless to say, the Group's mutual funds company helped me financially, and a steel foundry run by a member of the League also lent aid.

"I was in my twenties and had become director of the registered company Ikarino Corporation Ltd when I became an official member of the Wayfarers' League. There I got to know a young man of around the same age, a teacher—that young elementary school teacher has now become the second Parent, Tenro."

Ikarino suddenly paused at this point, and heaved a great sigh. Taku gazed into the dark, cavernous eyes of this old man who sat bathed in light before him.

"You've got to be strong. You've got to fight. You've got to *thrust* through with all your strength. Hold fast to the *brothers* and *friends*. If you don't, you'll very quickly be crushed by the world and the nation. That's what I've believed these last sixty years. Tell yourself everything is for the Group, for the clan.

"Tenro says Ikarino Corporation has gotten too big. But there are only two ways—*thrusting* forward or *retreating*. There's no such thing as a 'comfortable' position to take. Remember, young man, Mao Zedong said, 'Act to excess, and stop where it's right to stop.' Fine words, are they not? Eh?"

Ikarino leaned forward and pointed a finger at Taku.

"What do you think? Eh?"

"I don't know. The original philosophy of Henro Katsuragi Sensei…"

"The first principle is autonomy and independence. That's what mutual help is aimed at. Don't let the world crush you, don't let the nation destroy you—that's the first teaching. Those who condemn violence will have violence done to them. That's the age we live in. The Konryu gang was born from the need to protect us from unjust violence. Henro Sensei used to say with a laugh that those who could only study should go to university and those whose only talent was for quarrelling should join the Konryu gang. There was room in the Group for both gangsters and attorneys. That's what he said."

"If it weren't for the Konryu gang the Group would have gone long ago, that's my belief."

For the first time the man in Japanese clothes spoke. Taku had the feeling he'd heard the voice somewhere before. That's right, he thought, it was that night in the storehouse room at Ryukien in Izu, where the leading figures of the Group had gathered to greet him.

He recalled that when Yugaku had introduced everyone in the room there'd been one man who said brusquely, "Don't worry about the name."

Now at last Ikarino introduced him. "This is Kenyo Mushiro, third head of the Konryu gang," he said. "I understand there's no necessity for anyone to get too close."

"I've met you once before," Taku said, gazing at his splendidly kempt beard. "My friend Seta is much obliged to Mr. Ryuzaki here and another member of yours, Yuji I believe the name is."

Ryuzaki turned away expressionlessly. The boss was also silent.

"Well then, back to Henro Sensei…" Ikarino continued. "I was about to say that Sensei especially doted on two young men—the teacher Tenro, and myself, who had immersed himself in the business world. Tenro went on to resign from teaching and instead took up the post of leader of the Group's youth organization. He went on to create the system of Practices that passed down to later generations the history of the Kenshi and of the Eight Families. It was also his idea for the Group's children to spend time living as a group twice a year, summer and winter from infancy onwards, at the Basara Training Ground. And his wise suggestion was behind the plan during the difficult war years to assure the Group's existence by volunteering troops for the front and bands of patriotic frontier settlers.

"Then, when Henro Sensei died at 88 in the autumn of 1945, the year the war ended, Tenro bowed to pressure from the Intimates to become his successor and take the family name of Katsuragi.

"I was in Manchuria at the time, where we were engaged in difficult negotiations with the Russian army to protect the Japanese during withdrawal. My job was to find a way to secure us against the Russians' plans to remove all industrial equipment, materials, and labor to Siberia. At the time, the greater part of Ikarino Industrial Corporation's new factories were located in North Korea and on the Chinese continent."

"Then two years later," Shimafune interjected, "when you came back to Japan, Ikarino Corporation's miraculous *Great Thrust* occurred, I believe."

"That's right. In the chaos after the war both the Group and the clan were brought to their knees. The *connections* dried up, and people lost sight of Henro Sensei's vision. For those next ten years, both myself and the Konryu gang gave ourselves over to the struggle of living. We also devoted ourselves day and night to the task of providing food and work for the clan descendants. It was literally a life of 'selfless dedication.' Each day was a fresh battle. And thirty years on I find we've come to this…"

Ikarino fell silent. He sat, mouth clamped shut, gazing at the distant night sea. The shadow of two deep hollows lay below his chin.

"You know, Taku," Shimafune said, "the boss doesn't touch alcohol, even now. He doesn't smoke. He eats only twice a day, a meager meal with mixed grains or potatoes instead of rice. All that impressive appearance is really just for show. Ikarino Corporation's fifty subsidiary companies, as well as all the other businesses and organizations that are privately affiliated, they all exist for the sake of the clan's children, their children in turn, and the descendants of other wandering folks beyond the Eight Families. His support of the annual Varna Music Festival has the aim of helping talented young pianists and conductors from the clan to go out into the world. It was for the Group that he established Meiryo University. That golf course, this building, that helicopter over there—all support the Group's members. Those development projects that Tenro is so critical of, they're all in places that would be developed far more disastrously by the big established conglomerates in financial cahoots with the government, if Ikarino Corporation hadn't taken action. And that's not all. We're under constant pressure from the big businesses that have affiliations with outside multinationals. It's barking up the wrong tree to accuse Ikarino Corporation of collusion with bureaucracy, too. I've come to feel that Tenro and his idealism are threatening the Group's foundations with possible ruin. You agree don't you, Hanada?"

"Yes, well." Hanada nodded noncommittally. "I'm not sure it's all that dangerous really, though. Whatever criticisms Tenro might make, he has no real influence over Ikarino Corporation. You could just call it a kind of spiritual reining in, perhaps."

"That's so." Shimafune nodded and looked at Ikarino, who merely cocked his head as if listening to some far-off sound and didn't speak.

Finally he said, "No, I don't think that's true. I know Tenro's character well. He's a brave man. What he said at the party was no idle threat. I think he plans to act. But I can't guess just how."

"But what is he in a position to do?" asked Mushiro, the Konryu gang leader. "We've got final plans in place here."

"Things aren't the way they used to be in the old days, you know," said Ikarino.

The gang boss shook his head. "No, those Group guys haven't changed. They'd never blab to the authorities about their private goings on. There'd be no reports to the police if we rubbed someone out. No, they'll act as they always have. We won't be able to appeal to the law when that happens. You've got to remember that…"

"What do you mean?"

"I'm convinced there's a bullet coming your way, sir. That's what I believe."

Ryuzaki gave a soft laugh. There was something odd in it.

"Well, if that's the case, then that's that." Ikarino rose, and stood gazing out towards the golf course. "Sixty years later, and we've come to this. I've upheld the teachings of autonomy and selflessness all these years for the sake of the Group, of the clan that fled from Mount Nijo, and now I turn around and find that it's come to this."

He turned to Taku. "So, Mr. Hayami. I'm finally going to die. Just as Henro Sensei did. And Tenro too will die. And everyone here. In the face of this, Ikarino Corporation loses all meaning. But I'm not about to leave the world with the reputation of having been mistaken. No, I'm not about to do that. So I'm not retreating from my *Great Thrust*. Not until I've made Tenro say to me on behalf of the Group, 'It's thanks to you that the Group has survived until now.'"

"We should be getting back to Tokyo," Ryuzaki said.

"Right." Ikarino placed his camel robe on the chair and beckoned to Taku, who rose and stood before him.

Old man that he was, Ikarino gazed down at him. "I asked you here this evening with a request. I've been contemplating this for a long time…"

"Please name it."

"I want to hand over to you the position of Manager of the Wanderers' League." Ikarino laid a firm hand on his shoulder, in such a way as to suggest that he was seizing Taku by the scruff of the neck and wouldn't let go. "I'm going to bow humbly to the Group's criticisms, and relinquish my role with the League. This is a way of clearing the matter up. It won't hurt the Group members or harm Tenro's position. And I trust it will convince the clan that Ikarino Corporation wishes to devote itself to them in every situation."

"So I…"

"That's right. It would be dangerous if Tenro moved sideways to become League Manager, as some of the Group are plotting. He'd be in a position to hold power in both the Group and the League. It would satisfy everyone if you, with your direct bloodline connection to Henro Sensei, become the manager of the new

League. This is the only solution that will satisfy everyone, Group and League both."

Taku didn't reply. He slowly pushed away the heavy hand that lay on his shoulder.

"Let me hear your answer," came the daunting voice.

"I must refuse," said Taku.

A light of rage came into Ikarino's eyes for the first time, while his lips smiled. "Is that so?"

"I have no wish to be a robot controlled by Ikarino Corporation."

"You're being forced to make a momentous decision here, you know," said the old man. "Your mustn't act from your own ideas. Your task is to consider the whole Group."

"What do you mean?"

"The Tenmu Jinshin Group and Ikarino Corporation are on the verge of a fierce struggle over the fate of the Wanderers' League. Terrible things could happen if both don't step back. How many people do you think would be delighted if we both went on to *thrust* against each other until our mutual wounds destroyed us both? All the spiritual and economic foundations of the clan that Henro Sensei labored so hard to create after he left Mount Nijo would be destroyed overnight. It might be possible step by step to achieve a turnaround of this situation, if you had a mind to do it. Ikarino Corporation is prepared to be conciliatory. Things could be made to change course, not immediately of course, but slowly over time. But something will happen if I were to stay with the League and ignore all the criticism, no question about that. And when it does, it will be the trigger for the ruination of the clan. Are you telling me you can't see the hidden forces that are moving with that aim? Already these forces that hate our existence are busy setting their loathsome traps here and there to catch me. I'll give you one example…"

"What?"

"Take the Boston Museum of Fine Arts 'incident.' That was a disgustingly cowardly challenge to Ikarino Corporation and the Group. We're now confronted with an international counter-*thrust*, see. That's what Tenro doesn't get. If the Group and our conglomerate give way here…"

The light went out of Ikarino's eyes. He turned away and gave a couple of coughs. Then he shook his head, and continued in a low voice, "I turn around and this is what it's come to. I can only go on to where I have to go now. Ah, if only Henro Sensei could have been here now..."

Taku bowed his head. "Thank you," he said. "I'm grateful that you've told me so much I didn't know today."

"Mm." Meido Ikarino gazed steadily at Taku, who found himself flinching a little at the wash of real nostalgia that flooded those eyes.

Perhaps my answer wasn't a mistake, he thought.

"Remember—mutual aid, selfless dedication." Ikarino gripped his hand. This time the hand was warm. "Right then, I'll be off." He said with a nod.

"I'll stay, with your permission," said Ryuzaki.

Shimafune, Hanada, and Nishihaga all rose. From the car park came the sound of the helicopter starting up. Heavy clouds had gathered in the sky, and the first raindrops were plopping down. The wind had risen.

"A shame he wouldn't take it on," Ikarino said to himself as he turned and walked off. "A real shame."

Taku picked up a quick signal that flashed between Mushiro and Ryuzaki.

22

Brushing the low clouds, Meido Ikarino's silver helicopter skimmed away eastward and disappeared. Professor Nishihaga and the others moved off towards the main building, where they were evidently being put up overnight. As he was leaving, Hanada turned as if on the point of saying something, but when he saw Taku face to face with Ryuzaki he changed his mind and walked on, shaking his head.

"It's been a while, Mr. Hayami." Taku was heading towards the car park when Ryuzaki spoke. His leg dragged, and he seemed to find walking difficult.

"I wouldn't call it that long ago," replied Taku. "You have some business with me?"

"What an unfriendly gentleman!" Ryuzaki didn't seem angry. He took out a cigarette, lit it, and took a pleasurable puff.

"The boss's presence makes me awkward, dammit," he went on. "By the way, Hayami, you said something back there about Saera Maki's manager. Well, forget it. Remember the leg? So we're even."

"No way."

"Well, well."

"His body's covered in terrible burns—so young! He could've died!"

"Weren't you after my life when you were beating me in the hotel room, eh?"

Taku stopped and turned around. "You'd hurt Saera, that's why. Just what does the Konryu gang want with her, eh? She's just a singer."

"We're trying to tell her to stay clear of QCR."

"QCR?"

"That's right. It's an entertainment industry company over on the West Coast of the US. One of America's biggest syndicates is behind it. We're just trying to make it clear to her we won't stand for her leaving the Konryu gang by trying to set herself up with their Japan branch."

"So why don't you complain to QCR about it?"

"You kiddin' me?" Ryuzaki's voice was hard. "Surely you know Ikarino Group has a hotel chain in Hawaii, Los Angeles, and Vegas? We can't be seen locking horns with QCR."

"Well then, just leave things be. You've earned plenty from Saera already, surely."

"We won't stand for her smoochin' up to QCR, that's all."

"Why?"

"There are reasons."

"What reasons?"

"They're trying to push Ikarino Corporation out of the States, that's why. They're doing lots of underhand research, sending out information, using dirty tricks…"

"So Ikarino's got a vulnerable spot, eh? I get it. Right, I'll advise her to stick with 'the present course.'"

"Are you cocking your nose at us?"

"Not especially, no."

"Now that you've turned down Mr. Ikarino's offer you're no longer necessary to us, you know. You get what that means, don't you?"

"Thanks. That's finally clear to me."

Ryuzaki opened his mouth and stood staring at Taku. He ran the tip of his tongue over his lips a few times, then lifted his hand to his pocket. Taku didn't move. He was pretty sure he wouldn't be shot then and there.

Ryuzaki's fingers slid smoothly to grasp a small white stick. "My lips are so dry they bleed," he remarked, raising the stick and running it over his lips.

Taku felt a wave of relief, but he didn't show it. "I'm not asking on my own behalf, but at least leave Saera Maki and my brother alone, okay?" he said.

"And what if I said I wouldn't?"

"This is what I'd do." Taku's hand shot out and he landed a sudden slap on Ryuzaki's mouth. The lip salve flew through the air. But Ryuzaki didn't fall, he only staggered momentarily. Blood fell from the split lip onto his striped shirt. Something flared momentarily in his dark eyes.

"I'm a dumb guy, you know," Taku said. "I can't tell the difference between what's good for me and what's not. If you go meddling with Saera again, I'm going after your boss Mushiro. I'm not just trying to be impressive. I mean it."

Ryuzaki was silent. Taku was aware of the beloved .38-caliber nickle-plated Centennial that hung invisibly under his left arm. But for some reason, Ryuzaki made no move to use it.

When he got back to the 300GD in the car park, Taku gave the car a quick once-over before clambering up into the driver's seat. It was like climbing up onto a second story. He turned the key. The diesel engine gave a shudder and leapt into life. Taku was beginning to grow fonder and fonder of this old-style diesel that lacked the turbo engine now all the rage. He particularly liked the way the engine shuddered to a sudden stop the instant he turned off the ignition, a bit like a camel falling to its knees. The car felt like a living creature.

Passing out the front gate of the golf club, the car moved onto the gentle winding descent of the private drive below. Rain was beginning to wet the asphalt. Perhaps a roadworks truck had recently gone through—the paved surface was covered with a slick of red mud. The falling rain was mingling with the mud to create a very slippery surface. He put on his seat belt, and shifted the transfer lever to the SA position. He felt a light thump as the front wheels engaged, and he could tell that there was torque in all four wheels. It wasn't usual to put the car into four wheel drive on a road like this, a series of tight curves requiring a slow speed, but he calculated that the wet mud would help the wheels to turn. After negotiating a few corners he turned on the fog lights. He needed to keep a close eye on the side of the road.

Five minutes into the drive, he braked. A showy silver metal car was blocking the way, stopped diagonally right across the lane.

It was an AMG-style Mercedes 500SEC with a showy spoiler and a slightly lowered body. In the driver's seat, he could see a man in dark glasses. There was a telephone antenna sticking out of the trunk top, incongruous on a coupe. Taku guessed that the guy inside was probably the fellow called Yuji. He'd have been waiting for a call from Ryuzaki.

Taku dropped back to 20 kph, locked the rear wheels, pulled the transfer lever down to the right and put it into GA. His hands registered a slight resistance. This 2.14-ratio slow-speed gear was fine when you turned it on, but it was sometimes tricky to release it again. Still, that couldn't be helped now.

As he approached the 500SEC he didn't draw to a halt, but instead put the 300GD bumper straight into the driver's door. He saw the driver shouting something behind the rolled up window. Ignoring him, Taku slowly stepped on the accelerator. With the driving power of its low gear doubled, the car easily pushed the 500SEC's P7 sideways on the mud. There was a crunch of car bodies grinding together. The 23-million-yen AMG slithered sideways off the road with absurd ease, its nose pointing the other way. As he went past, Taku unlocked the diff, and swiftly punched the GA lever forward. Then he drove off at normal speed. For some reason the AMG made no attempt to follow. Could be the driver was worrying about his repair bill.

23

I t was late at night by the time Taku pulled off the Tomei Expressway at Yokohama. He didn't feel he could just turn up back at Shin'ichi's place at this hour, so he found a telephone booth in Sakuragicho and called.

"Who is it?" came a hard woman's voice. At the sound, he felt a flash of heat run through him.

"Ai? Is that you? Why are you there?"

"I'll explain when you arrive. I've been waiting for you."

"I'll be there in fifteen minutes."

Taku put down the phone and leapt back into the car. Something must have happened. Ai's voice had sounded fraught with strong emotion.

He sped up the hill, ignoring several red lights. The diesel engine proved not to be the irritating drag it might have been at a time like this.

As he drew up in front of the house he saw Ai, clad in khaki pants. She stood lit by the street light, and her stern expression spoke of determination. Her fists were clenched like a baby's, her steely lips were clamped shut. When she saw Taku she wordlessly opened the gate for him.

"Has something happened?"

"My brother's been shot," she said quickly. Sweat glistened on her brow. "His life's not in danger. Our Group doctor is seeing to him right now. But…"

"What?"

"Saera's been taken."

"Saera?"

Kicking off his shoes at the door, Taku gazed into the drawing room. He saw Shin'ichi and an elderly man in a suit, with Yugaku stretched out on the sofa.

"I've been waiting." Shin'ichi seized Taku's arm and led him to the dining room. He began to talk urgently. "Around eight, it was. Five men from the Konryu gang turned up. When they saw Yugaku they fired immediately. I was taken into the bedroom, and while they were threatening me in there Saera was grabbed. That Yuji fellow who came the other day wasn't with them though."

"He was waiting for me somewhere else."

"Apparently Yugaku's wound isn't serious. Luckily the bullet just passed through his left arm."

"What kind of gun was it?"

"I was too beside myself to notice. I just lost it at the first sound of the gun." Shin'ichi lowered his head, shamefaced.

Taku turned to Ai.

"How did you come to be here, Ai?"

"I was meeting someone in Tokyo. The Group contacted me there, and I came flying over."

"I telephoned the Tenmu Jinshin Group in Izu, you see," Shin'ichi broke in.

"What were they saying to threaten you, Shin?" asked Taku.

Shin'ichi fell silent. Ai answered from beside him. "Apparently they told him that if his brother changed his mind and gave the okay, they'd send Saera back."

"Me?" cried Taku, suddenly incensed. "You mean they've kidnapped Saera to force me to accept Ikarino's proposal?"

"I understand you met Ikarino at Keiro Lodge," said Ai.

"That's right."

"And you were asked to take on the leadership of the Wayfarers' League?"

"How did you know that?"

Ai didn't reply, but bit her lip in thought. "Right then. I'll go," she said.

"Where?"

"To the Konryu gang headquarters. That's where Saera is."

"Take me too, then."

"Wait, Taku," said Shin'ichi.

"What is it?"

"I'm the one to go with Ai." He pushed Taku aside, and faced her. "I really should go on my own, but I don't know the place or what I'll find there. So please take me."

"I don't know what will happen, you know," she replied.

"Fine."

"Shin," said Taku, grabbing his arm. But Shin'ichi threw him off with unaccustomed roughness.

"Listen, Taku," he said forcefully. "I know you feel responsible for Saera. But..." His voice slowed, as if talking to himself now. "If I don't go, I think Saera may die. She'll be confined, you see, and unable to telephone me."

"Mm."

"If something were to happen to me, well, that's okay. Right? I'm a hopeless good-for-nothing, but at least this would give some point to my being here. And another thing, Taku. I just wanna do one thing for myself, see? Ever since we were kids I was the one who made the plans and you were the one who did things. Just this once, you could let me take the wheel, okay?"

"Okay, I get it." Taku fell silent. It was true. Shin had the right to want to do something for himself. He drew the car keys from his pocket and handed them to his brother. "Here are the keys. You know how to drive the 300GD, don't you? It's a tough car."

"I've memorized the entire manual. Of course this is the first time I've taken it past the gate, though."

"If the lever gets stuck, just give it a kick."

"Right."

Shin'ichi disappeared, saying to Ai he was just going to get ready. When he was gone, Taku said to her, "I really don't have to go, then?"

"If something were to happen to both of us it would cause real problems for the Group. Just in case anything goes wrong, please see to things for me."

"Take care, then. Where's the Konryu headquarters?"

"It's in the warehouse area of Katsushima. Near the race course." Ai sat down on the sofa, folded her arms and looked up at him. "Your face has changed somehow, Taku," she said.

"It could be because I'm really beginning to feel now that I'm a member of the Kenshi clan."

"Come along to the Basara Training Ground next time. You must see how the children get trained."

"I probably ought to enroll myself."

"No, your role's already decided. You're Assistant Teacher for the youth organization's *Wandering Practice* and *Walking Practice*. I've been Assistant Teacher for *Scholarly Practice* till now, you know." A happy light shone in Ai's dark eyes. "You're really going to become part of our Group," she added.

"You're talking about after the Ikarino problem's been resolved, I presume? He told me it was an affront to the pride of the clan to oppose Ikarino Corporation. He said the Group's criticisms are equivalent to saying we must revert to the old days, and give up all the social and economic gains that the clan has worked so hard to achieve."

"And do you agree, Taku?"

"I can see he has a point, but it's not quite like that. I don't see that the Group is idealistic while the business side is practical."

"Our clan began life with nothing. Our aim has been to live in harmony with nature, and with society. The actions of Ikarino Corporation aren't in harmony with nature, they're in competition with it. It's better to start again from nothing than to prosper at the expense of our ideals and goals, even if it means relinquishing all our social rights. The Wayfarers' League has gotten too big."

"Sorry I've kept you," came Shin'ichi's voice as he walked back in. For the first time he was wearing the gear he'd chosen himself, and he looked youthfully keyed up. "I've brought along my favorite deer-horn dagger," he announced, flashing the knife tucked in under his black leather jumper. "I don't imagine there's any point in taking my cross-bow, after all."

"I don't think that will be necessary," Ai remarked, cocking her head, but Shin'ichi smilingly informed her it was a good luck amulet.

"Our ancestors who lived long ago around Mount Nijo were the first people in the Japanese archipelago to make stone knives, you know. A man carries a knife for good luck. Just having it with him gives him confidence."

Yugaku had been sedated, and lay there asleep.

Ai and Shin'ichi left the house together. The tall pair made a fine-looking couple, Taku thought. Shin'ichi got into the driver's seat of the waiting 300GD, then with a tense expression he adjusted the mirrors, moved the seat back a touch, and started the engine.

The heavy door slammed. He gave a brief toot of the horn, sent Taku a sailor's salute, and off he drove.

Taku watched as the square-bodied car with its spare tire on the back disappeared into the night. From the window he could see mist flowing softly in over the town below. Suddenly he remembered the old song—"Saying farewell, the night mist around us..."

A fog horn gave a long blare from the harbor.

24

Night was coming on. Taku had been sitting for well over an hour at the top of the steps that led down to the road, waiting.

What if Ai and Shin'ichi didn't come back? he was thinking. Should he go to the Konryu gang's headquarters on his own and just march in? He could probably solve the problem perfectly simply then and there by announcing that he was willing to take on the leadership of the Wayfarers' League as Ikarino had asked. There'd be no need to go further and get Saera to promise to sever her ties with QCR.

But what about Ai and Shin'ichi?

As he sat gazing down over the city, where the mist was finally beginning to lift, Taku suddenly pricked up his ears. He thought he could hear the heavy sound of the diesel somewhere. Turning to look at the road uphill from him, he spied, paused at a red light, the black front grill of a Geländewagen, rather like a seal with sidelights attached. The light turned green, and it moved jerkily towards him.

Taku leapt down the staircase and rushed towards the approaching car. In the passenger seat he caught a glimpse of Ai's profile.

They're back safe! he told himself joyfully.

The diesel engine came to its usual thumping halt, and all was suddenly quiet.

"Shin!" Taku yelled. The driver's door opened and a man's face appeared. The sight of it made Taku take an unconscious step back.

"Ryuzaki…"

"Deeply obliged to you for taking the trouble to come out and greet me." Ryuzaki got painfully down from the driver's seat, one hand against his leg. Ai could be seen sitting behind him.

"Taku," she murmured. Her eyes were dark and her voice hoarse. She looked utterly exhausted.

"What's this about?" Taku demanded, turning to face Ryuzaki, poised at the ready. Ryuzaki raised both hands in the air and shook his head, apparently intending to show that he meant no harm.

"There are two people in the back," he said. "Get them out, will you?"

Taku climbed into the driver's seat. In the back he saw Saera, her face white as a sheet, and Shin'ichi, who lay on the floor with his eyes closed. There was a faint scent of blood. Saera wasn't crying—her face seemed frozen.

Shin'ichi lay on the double bed in the sun-filled bedroom, a sheet tucked up to his chin, asleep—a sleep from which he would never awaken.

Taku took his cold ankles and removed the boots that he had so carefully worn about the house to break in, laying them beside the bed. It was only when he saw that Shin'ichi was wearing five-toed Halison socks that he finally began to cry. Shin'ichi had probably only worn those socks for real this once in his life.

"No more, Saera."

Saera was intently scattering over the floor the square ice cubes she had carried from the ice box, her face fixed in an empty smile. She had been busying herself cramming all the ice she could find into plastic bags and packing them around the body. Her expression suggested that her mind was in the grip of this single idea.

"Yes. We must put the air conditioner on to cool the air in here," she responded. Swivelling the dial to Very Cold, she flipped on the switch. Her hair had been hacked short, giving her the look of an Auschwitz inmate.

Yugaku, his arm in a sling, sat formally on the carpet. "I wasn't prepared enough," he said. Then, eyes raised to the ceiling, he continued in a murmur, "*Meeting today but to part tomorrow.* And we really got on, too."

For the last half hour Ai had been on the phone, arguing fiercely with someone in the Group. Saera had now disappeared, no doubt gone off alone to cry, Taku thought. Better to leave her be for a while.

"Come here a moment," he said, addressing Ryuzaki, who sat on a chair by the wall, eyes closed. They left the room together, Ryuzaki limping as he walked.

Reaching a corner of the garden from which the headstones of the Foreigners' Cemetery were visible through the trees, Taku turned to Ryuzaki.

"What on earth happened?" he demanded. "Ai won't talk, and I can't ask Saera. Tell me the whole story."

"Fine," Ryuzaki nodded. "Well, after you knocked back the boss's offer and went off, our leader sent orders out to the gang to nab Saera."

"To get me to do as Meido wanted?"

"Yeah. And we needed to put the screws on her to get her to break contract with QCR too."

"There was a contract?"

"That's right. That Seta fellow's a smart worker."

"So?"

"No sooner was I back in the office than the Group's acting head lady and your brother turned up together. Well, they and the boss didn't see eye to eye about whether Saera should be returned. The lady started abusing the boss, claiming he was being disloyal to the Group, so he got mad. Right there in front of them he made Saera strip and got one of the youngsters to chop her hair off." Ryuzaki shrugged. "Actually, the boss has had a thing for her for a long time, see. He just doesn't see sense where she's concerned."

"So my brother lost it and flew at him?"

Ryuzaki nodded. "Yeah, he's quite a guy. He suddenly lunged at a couple of the nearby youngsters and stabbed them with his knife, then threw himself full force at the boss. That was a double-edged knife he had."

"It's called a dagger knife."

"Just as your brother pushed in the knife, the boss's henchman got him in the back. In the kidneys. With a sword."

Taku trembled slightly. Desperately trying to control it he asked, "So how did Ai and Saera get free?"

"I overcame the others, that's how."

"Why?"

Ryuzaki cocked his head thoughtfully. In a low murmur, he replied, "It gave me a strange feeling to hear the old stories about the clan there in the garden at the golf club. I hadn't heard them in quite a while, those stories about Mount Nijo and the early days of the Group. I'm descended from the Third House, and I went through the Group training back when I was a kid. I've been to Mount Nijo, and paid my respects at the Imperial burial mound where the seven are buried. The instant I saw your brother put his life on the line by throwing himself at the boss, I was just suddenly filled with disgust at the Konryu gang. And also…"

"Also?"

"I'm not like you, see, I can tell the difference between what's good for me and what's not. If the boss dies, the gang's going to be in big trouble. My leg's bad, my blood pressure's gone up recently, blood sugar's a worry… Reckon it's time to wash my hands of the gang and come back to the Group."

"You're a strange man."

"You think so? You're pretty strange yourself, you know."

At this point, Saera appeared at the back door. She was wearing the dark blue Chanel suit, and in her hand she held the key to the 300GD. She'd chosen shoes and a handbag to match the suit, but her hair was still hacked and jagged.

"Please don't try to stop me, Taku," she said.

"Where are you going?"

"I'm going to find Heigo Nishimoto at Nishimoto Tailoring," she replied in a sing-song voice. "And that unfaithful wife of his, Maki. Does this outfit suit me? I can finally wear it now. The suit I had made for me when I was nineteen. The suit I always heard about up there on the second floor, above the canal in Otaru while I was changing Daddy's bedpan." She gave a happy laugh. Her voice sounded quite different from normal.

"Let me drive you," said Taku, taking a step forward, but she shrank back and retreated from him.

"Don't stop me. You loved me, Taku, didn't you?"

"Yes."

"So don't stop me."

She slipped between them like the wind. Clambering at last into the driver's seat of the 300GD that was parked on the street, she searched around for the ignition, found it and turned it on. Then with both hands she released the hand brake and set off, swaying from side to side. Taku watched in silence. She had died when Shin'ichi did. It was only the living shell of her that was driving that car.

"You don't want to stop her?" Ryuzaki said worriedly.

"No."

"What's she going to do at the canal?"

"I'm guessing she'll drive straight into it."

"You're kidding."

"I loved her songs, you know," Taku said.

Ryuzaki scratched his head as he watched the white diesel driving off down the hill. It slowly turned a corner in the slanting morning light, and was seen no more.

25

Next day, Taku paid his first visit to the Wayfarers' League headquarters near Mount Basara on the Izu Peninsula. A microbus had been sent to bring him to the Group training ground, with Ai as his guide. Ryuzaki and Yugaku also came along, and with them came Shin'ichi's body, packed in dry ice.

The Group headquarters was an old wooden building somewhat like a little mountain schoolhouse.

Taku found a number of familiar faces there. There was the Aunt of the Fifth House with her elephantine legs, the Uncle of the Seventh House who looked like a yogi, and Rokotsu Sarashino, the teacher of *Scholarly Practice*, Shirabe Yusurido who taught *Walking Practice*, and others besides. He also saw Tenro Katsuragi, and another surprising face—sunburned, and creased like a rockface. A solid man with a slight stoop.

"Taku," the man said quietly. "Been a while. Your mother hurt her back last month. Still in bed, but she was cryin' and sayin' she wants to see you."

He'd just got in from Mikuni, he said. It was Yuzo Hayami, Taku's adoptive father.

Taku bowed his head wordlessly in greeting. "I'm really sorry I've caused you all this worry," he said.

"Come now. Both delighted to hear you'd finally *gone back* to the Group," his adoptive father responded warmly. His hair had grown noticeably whiter.

That evening, obsequies for the dead were held in the side building of the headquarters—a simple, heartfelt ceremony.

Late that night they climbed the mountain behind, and Shin'ichi was buried on the slope that faced west over the valley.

"Now, as ordained by Group *law*, I will speak the words of our founder, Henro Katsuragi," Tenro announced. All turned towards Mount Nijo and lowered their heads.

The sound of Tenro's voice flowed through the night like the purling rush of a mountain stream. "There is a people that dwell and die among mountains. They are the mountain people. There is a people that dwell and die among fields. They are the common people. There is a people that descend from the mountains yet do not live in villages, that spend their life in villages yet do not forget the mountains, that come and go between mountain and village, that is born in the journey and dies in the journey. *Live in no place, plough no furrow*—these are the wanderers.

"The mountain people are the bones; the common people are the flesh. And those who come and go between mountain and village—they are the lifeblood. A society without blood is one without life. The wanderers are the lifeblood of society. They vindicate existence. A society that does not recognize the wanderers will stagnate and wither. We who wander the world eternally are its very lifeblood and vital energy. Herein lies also the meaning of the wandering beggar. When begging pilgrims can find no place in society, we gain social acceptance by providing raw materials, stone or wood. Herein lie the origins of the *Sekenshi*. The mountains are death's farther shore; the village world is its hither realm. It is the way of the *Sekenshi* to pass through the membrane that divides these two. We are not, cannot be, under the sway of any rule. Our hearts' truth—it is this that we offer our companions. Yet among the realm of men, within the flow of history…"

Tenro's voice murmured on softly like a stream. A mist crept low and heavy, swathing the feet of those who stood, heads bowed, on the dark mountain.

26

The Group's mountain headquarters were located in the midst of an extensive forest. The area included bamboo groves, tea fields, slopes of conifers, and streams; there were also cliffs and valleys, threaded with numerous paths—paths that wound their way casually into the mountainous Izu uplands, down to rivers and out to the sea.

The streams were filled with fish. Small animals abounded—rabbits, weasels pheasants, river crabs. There were also quite a number of snakes, not to mention a constant buzz of mosquitoes, flies, horseflies, and bees, perhaps because so few chemical fertilizers and agricultural poisons were used in the fields. Birds too were abundant. Horses, cattle, goats, dogs, and cats all ran free.

The slopes held fields of millet of various kinds, and a plantation of sumac trees, while vivid clumps of flowers filled the gently undulating plateau that lay open to the rich sunlight of southern Izu.

This broad expanse, known as "Groupland," had only a scattering of real buildings—the headquarters, the hall, and a few storehouses. There were no electric lights, nor any television or newspapers. Important news, the real news that media reports never give, was carried by word of mouth, brought back each day when someone went down to the town over the mountain to deliver flowers and handicrafts, or by the endless flow of visitors who came and went.

"It won't be long before we'll be kept awake all night with the terrific frog chorus," Ai remarked with a young boy's grin, as she sat on the sunny slope, legs thrown out before her.

A week had already passed since Taku had been formally installed as assistant teacher at the headquarters training ground.

"On summer nights there are so many fireflies lighting up the stream down there it's almost scary," Ai went on.

A middle-aged man wearing a white shirt, blue cotton trousers, and a straw hat came panting up the hill towards them. He was barefoot, and limping badly.

"Mr. Hayami!" he cried as he approached. "Your things have arrived from Tokyo. I hope it's everything. There's very little there."

It was Ryuzaki, a small towel wrapped around his neck. He didn't look quite the part for a member of the animal husbandry personnel, but his expression was serene and untroubled.

"How's your knee, Mr. Ryuzaki?" Ai asked.

"The knee's not bad, it's the soles of my feet that're killing me. I mean, I haven't gone barefoot for twenty years or more."

"It won't take long to get used to it. Here, come and sit down," Ai went on in a friendly voice, moving to make room for him. A cool breeze toyed with her soft, short-cropped hair.

"It takes me back to when I was a kid in elementary school and we came out here to be taught camping skills," said Ryuzaki. "The lie of the land has hardly changed. It's like time's stood still."

"That's right." Ai smiled. "We don't think in terms of 'progress' in the Group, after all. In fact we're consciously yearning back to the past the whole time, moving back rather than forward. It's only natural that the landscape and the land haven't changed."

"Could you explain a bit more of how the *Practices* are set up?" Taku asked her.

"Well, my father used to be an elementary school teacher," Ai explained. "In those days he was a passionate young teacher who was set on dedicating his life to children's education."

"Yes, I've heard that."

"After the war, when he took over from Henro, he became convinced that lifelong education was essential for the Kenshi, and not just for the clan. He believed that education could provide the way forward for minority groups trying to live within nations everywhere."

A group of fifteen or so men and women moved briskly along the bank of the stream and was quickly lost to sight among the trees beyond.

"When a child is born to a Group member's household, our leader becomes the godfather, whose role is to choose a name. That name will always be written with a character that has some connection with the clan's origins. A child's name will go on influencing him right through his life, you see. His parents will provide careful training in walking from his infancy on. They'll train him for an hour a day to walk barefoot somewhere in the natural world. The primary characteristic of the clan is to be able to walk fast, long, and well, see. It's too late to start training as an adult. You have to start when someone's a toddler. If you do, you'll develop feet like mine. Look. Strange, aren't they?"

Ai stretched out a naked foot and wriggled her toes.

"That's interesting. The Sherpas in Nepal had feet like that too," Taku said, staring in surprise. She was moving her toes about with the precision of fingers. When she spread them, the five toes opened out like a palm leaf. The big toe swiveled sideways at almost ninety degrees.

"I could do that too once," Ryuzaki said regretfully. Ai gave a quizzical laugh.

"Another thing is, we do our best to prevent our kids eating anything sweet until they've grown up. I was brought up with no knowledge of sugar. Look at my teeth. Pretty good, eh?"

"Like an animal's."

"And then, the eyes. The right food plus certain exercises give us excellent night vision. The Group children generally don't wear glasses. My father's concept of the *Practices* was that everyone should do all this not just as children but right through their adult years as well. The basis of his philosophy is that the clan must preserve its physical characteristics. Our clan identity is contained above all in our bodies, he believes. That's why the *Walking Practice* is given precedence in our training here. The Group children come here twice a year, summer and winter, from elementary school onwards to do a two-week training course in *Walking Practice*. Our members send their kids as part of their clan obligation. Once the children have made a *connection* with each other here, they go up to the training camp in Shibetsu in Hokkaido in summer, and in winter they go down to Aso in Kyushu, where they divide off into groups ranging from five-year-olds to high school kids and walk. They walk for all they're worth. It's a kind of *Practice*, after all. They spend their days walking over mountains, through plains and forests, down valleys and over streams. They camp out by rivers, and by day they learn about vegetation, fish and animals, rocks and so on, while at night there are tales of the history of the clan, and they learn to use tools, to weave winnowing baskets, and study the stars. In the process, they all discover the thrill and fascination of walking and living in nature. And once they're home again, they eagerly count the days till the next *Practice* season comes around. I was the same," Ai added softly, a distant look in her eyes.

"It's only quite a bit later that we're taught the science of correct walking, beautiful walking. In the early days, you just walk. You learn with your body. You learn the joy of walking, and discover how good walking develops your physical senses and deepens your thinking. It changes people to realize that the feet carry you naturally, without your volition. Clan members who've done this since infancy will always recognize each other even in passing. There's something different about us. You just feel, *Ah, that's someone from the clan.*"

"You've reminded me that my dad often took me into the Izu mountains as a kid and walked with me."

"Your teeth, your eyes, and your gait all gave it away the first time I set eyes on you on Mount Nijo, Taku. Aha, I thought, this man's of our lineage."

"Is that so? Is that why you gave me such a powerful demonstration of your walking up there on Mount Nijo?"

"That's right. That was my heartfelt greeting to a young clan member who was being *re-met*."

"The word 'young' is a bit too flattering," Ryuzaki cut in. Ai gave a laugh.

"Professor Sarashino's *Scholarly Practice* is pretty unusual too, isn't it?" said Taku. "He really stumped me in the beginning, but it's kind of interesting."

"He always begins by teaching children the clan's form of discipline. Beginning with what we call '*menme-shinogi*.'"

"Doing whatever you can on your own," Ryuzaki said. "A man has to be disciplined and responsible."

"Women too!" Ai said, hitting him smartly on his bad knee. Ryuzaki winced.

"Children are taught from infancy to repeat the rule that people must maintain *menme-shinogi*," Ai went on calmly. Their parents and brothers and others around them are all constantly teaching them this, so by the time they come here they already know they should do things for themselves."

"Professor Sarashino used the word 'autonomy' to explain it to me," said Taku.

"And the *connection* between people is called 'mutual aid,'" Ai went on. "Everyone has this drilled into them before they reach the Elementary Youth Group. Then in the Youth Group at high school age there's more detail—things like the Origin and History of the clan, Nature and Environment, History of World Minorities and so on. It continues into adulthood too. Keep up the learning, Mr. Ryuzaki."

"Maybe I'll back out and head home after all," Ryuzaki said, flinching. "I joined the Konryu gang because I hated study, after all. Do I have to face the desk again now?"

"Come on Mr. Ryuzaki, you know Professor Sarashino's lessons don't involve a classroom. He teaches you with stories while you walk in the hills with him, or before bed, or while you're cooking up river fish on a camp fire or weaving winnowing baskets. And they're fascinating stories too. He's walked the world since he was young, like Taku."

"That professor of *Wandering Practice*, Hokuyo Hachimai, also seems to have had an unusual life."

"Yes, the *Wandering Practice* section consists of a course in skills and experience. The kids seem to enjoy it best of all. They learn how to camp, look at stars, catch fish and animals, identify plants, understand the weather, use knives, use flag signals and morse code, swim, do cross-country skiing, weave baskets and winnowers and other things from bamboo, make bamboo flutes and grass whistles, sing folk songs, and fight, as well as studying basic conversation in other minority group languages. They also do a week's journey on foot with backpacks. It takes nine years, starting from infancy, to complete the *Three Practices*, and when they graduate there's a celebratory overseas trip for them, where they spend six months going round to different places. So Group kids always go on to university or find employment a year later than most.

"What sort of places do they go?"

"Oh, Asia, Africa, Europe, America—all over the place. Wherever they go, they *connect* with other minority groups. It's been going on for ten years or so now, so the folks over there have learned to look forward to the next visit. They meet Burmese hill tribes, Kenyans, Inuit, Basques, American Indians, Haitian musicians. The trip takes them round the world learning first-hand about these people's history and present situation. They're young and impressionable, and they'll remember it for the rest of their lives. It'll all still be there when they're adults, deeply etched in the mind."

"It must cost quite a lot."

"It does. But Group people set aside money for this from the moment their child is born, and the Group Intimates and Friends do their very best to help. While the young people are abroad, they help out any Group member who's moved overseas for work. You'll be going with us next year as tour conductor, Taku."

At this point, Ai spread her arms and stretched luxuriously. "Well, I have to get ready for lunch. Would you give me a hand, Mr. Ryuzaki?"

Muttering under his breath, Ryuzaki struggled to his feet.

27

One afternoon, two weeks after Saera Maki had disappeared in her 300GD down the sloping road in the dawn, Taku went to visit Seta in the hospital in Kawasaki.

Seta was still encased in bandages like some astronaut, but he was feeling much more cheerful.

"Have you seen the papers?" His lips moved to produce a soft voice, while his eyes signaled the sports newspaper lying on the table.

"Saera Maki—Love Flight?" said the small headline. Taku ran his eyes over the story. The talented singer Saera Maki had disappeared with her lover, it reported, and went on to say that her popularity had been on the wane in recent times and she was rumored to have personal problems. Someone had speculated that she'd formerly been hospitalized for alcoholism and that this might be a relapse.

"The Konryu gang?" Seta asked.

Taku shook his head. "No, she and Shin are hanging out on Bora Bora."

"Okay, I'll choose to believe that."

"Get well soon. I've gone to help Ai with Group work. If there's anything you need, just let me know."

"Don't worry about me. I'll manage with some *menme-shinogi*," Seta replied, his eyes smiling.

From the hospital, Taku went round to his apartment in Azabu. He'd let the landlords know he was leaving, so he got a month's deposit back.

He was locking the door behind him on the way out, Boston bag over his shoulder, when Kaoru from across the way popped her head out and waved. For once she was without makeup, and looked quite masculine.

"I hear you're going, Taku?"

"Yep. All the best, Kaoru. Hope the work goes well."

"Sure. Though things are a bit slack at the shop lately." She handed Taku a piece of paper. "Cho from the Lotus came by to see you any number of times, I guess. He says to phone this number. It's just too bad that place of his closed down. Such a nice guy, too."

"Thanks for that. I'll give him a call."

Taku left the building and walked around to the Lotus. Its shutters were down. The old sign still hung there. Slipping into a nearby telephone booth, he dialed the number. A woman answered, speaking English, then was quickly replaced by Cho.

"I hear you've gone back to the Futakami Fraternity. That's a good thing." Cho spoke in perfect, fluent Japanese. Taku shifted the receiver in his hand, astonished. Was this really Cho? The voice was certainly his. But he no longer spoke in endearingly broken Japanese. Aside from the accent, his Japanese was impeccable.

"Who did you hear that from?"

"Remember that woman you brought along to the restaurant? I ran into her in front of your apartment one day, and we talked briefly. She's leaving the company and planning another walking circuit of Japan, she told me."

"Really? And why have you closed the shop, Cho?"

"I'm going back to Hong Kong. I'm going to start work all over again."

"When you say 'work,' you don't mean the restaurant, do you?"

"That was a camouflage. My real job was conducting a survey of the boss's collection."

"By 'the boss,' you don't mean Ikarino, by any chance?"

"That's right, him. During the war he based his activities in China, see. He colluded with the Japanese forces to illegally seize Chinese antiques, and sent it all back to hide in his storehouses in Shizuoka. There was an amazing amount of important Chinese cultural objects there. While we were looking into it all, we discovered that back around 1951 the Boston Museum of Fine Arts had bought a lot of it for its own collection, via one of the boss's sub-companies. So we set about looking into it, trying to get the museum to pay a just price for it all and convince the boss to return the remainder. The government doesn't want to go public because China's relations with Japan and the US are good right now, so we were given the job in Hong Kong and came over to Japan. There's a move all over the world to return stolen cultural objects to their rightful owners, of course. The Boston museum also holds a precious zodiac mirror and a ring pommel sword, which apparently left Japan back in the Meiji era."

"So I hear."

"The Futakami Fraternity's Professor Shirabe Yusurido looked into this—by what means these things had made their way to the US from Japan."

Taku was silent. Just what had been dug out from the tomb that night back in 1877 by Nawagi and the others, and where was it taken? And who had carried those objects from the tomb over to the museum in America?

"So why are you stopping your investigations and going back to Hong Kong, Cho?" he asked.

There was a sigh on the other end of the telephone.

"It's because of that Boston museum bomb incident. An Asian terrorist group calling themselves the Third World Cultural Revolution Army sent a threatening letter to the American government, demanding that Boston's cultural artifacts be returned to China and Japan, and stating that if they were successful they intended to move on to press for the return of cultural artifacts to Greece, India, Africa, and the Middle East from the British Museum and the Louvre."

"That hasn't been reported, has it? All I heard was that there'd been a bomb."

"That's right. The Americans suppressed all reports of the demands. I guess they decided that if it looked like they'd begun negotiations to return this stuff, the president would be condemned for being weak-kneed over the issue, and there'd be difficult repercussions for England and France as well. Then yesterday they made a secret decision to terminate all investigations, buy-backs and movement of Japanese cultural artifacts from the Boston museum. This means all the cautious work we've been doing has gone up in smoke. Now they've even put a stop to our hopes of doing things in an adult way, carrying out a thorough investigation of the wartime and postwar facts, and using our findings to buy things back at appropriate prices through a nongovernmental route. What a business, eh? And to think I spent ten years in Japan over this!"

Taku's head spun with bewildering thoughts of the ancient days, the Meiji era, and contemporary Japan. "Could you give me a bit more detail?" he asked Cho. "I'm feeling quite confused."

"I'm sorry, but there's no time. I'm due to fly out to Hong Kong this evening. My work may not have gone well, but I did enjoy life in Azabu running that restaurant. You look after yourself, Taku."

"Goodbye, Cho. Your fried mustard greens soup was delicious."

"The secret is to add dried prawns. Bye." With a final laugh, Cho was gone. Taku continued to stand there, the receiver still clutched in his hand.

28

O
nly the faintly lit alcove stood out clearly in the dark room. Its bamboo vase held a large red camellia that flamed in the dim light with the brilliance of blood. Above, on the alcove wall where a scroll would normally hang, was a sheet of cloth bearing the words:

> *Plough no furrow*   *Live in no place*
> *Belong to no nation*   *Have no self*

Taku Hayami had been placed at the far end of the seated row of teachers. Before them sat the leader, Tenro Katsuragi, and in another row were seated the Aunts and Uncles.

When Ai had informed him that there was a Group meeting at Ryukien, deep in the Izu mountains, Taku felt the moment had come at last. It seemed the Group was about to make its first real move since the day of Ikarino's party, when it had publicly announced its position.

"Shall we commence," said Yugaku from the entrance, and he closed the wooden door with a resounding thud. His arm was still in a sling, but he had recovered remarkably quickly, and was by now walking about freely beyond the Groupland.

"I have gathered you all here this evening at such short notice," Tenro began, his voice little more than a murmur, "to convey to you a decision. As you know, it was only after thorough consultation with the Aunts and Uncles and with the teachers that the Group recently made public its disapproval of the Ikarino Corporation. Meido Ikarino has been attempting to use our very own Wayfarers' League, sacred to the memory of our founder Henro, to back his own interests. Since his youth Ikarino has been a man of exceptional talents, intelligent and passionate, and with his finger on the pulse of the age. Henro Sensei himself apparently once considered calling him back from the business world to take charge of the Futakami Fraternity, an idea he abandoned during the Second World War when Ikarino used the Fraternity's connections with the army in China to hugely expand his enterprise.

"I remember it well," broke in the Seventh Uncle, the man whose beard hung to his chest like a yogi. "When Sensei came back from that trip to Manchuria, where he'd gone at Meido's invitation, he told me how he felt. He said then that he feared Ikarino could transform into a monster, and if that happened the Group must be very careful not to be sucked into its maw."

Tenro nodded and continued. "I acknowledge that the Wayfarers and Ikarino Corporation have been enormously helpful in the clan's financial and social *thrust*. There's no question about that. However, a boundary has been crossed. The time has come when the clan must return to first principles, even though it means crawling on all fours again. This is why we expressed ourselves so strongly on the occasion of the party. It was our hope that Meido would accept this with humility, and make the important gesture of stepping down from the Wayfarers' League.

"Aye, but he didn't," the Uncle of the First House interposed. "On the contrary, he's gone and severed the Wayfarers' League from the Group, has he not, and used the Konryu gang to try to undermine the Group."

"This was not unforeseeable. And this is why we planned to pass on to the Boston Museum of Fine Arts the material we'd secretly gathered with Professor Yusurido's help, and request that the reinvestigation and report be made public. Professor Yusurido, could you please explain briefly?"

"Certainly." Shirabe Yusurido, the teacher of *Walking Practice*, was a well-built woman in late middle age. In a strong, clear voice, she took up the story. "Top-ranking army officers gave Meido Ikarino charge of the cultural artifacts requisitioned by the army in China. These he concealed in his warehouse back in Shizuoka. There was a huge number of these objects. During the Forties and Fifties, Ikarino took it upon himself to sell a portion of them to the Boston Museum of

Fine Arts. Besides these, he also sold off many of the precious stones and metals he brought back with him from China, and these too were transformed into vast amounts of cash. His spectacular postwar success was achieved with the support of the numerous politicians he bought off with covert political donations. But the only real clues to this information were in the hands of the Boston museum. Our plan was to use this material to breach his defences, confront the Wayfarers' League with the facts about him, and force him to resign."

"Aye, and it didn't work," cut in the Uncle of the First House.

"True. As you know, he got wind of it, and played a card of astonishing self-sacrifice in response. He got a so-called terrorist group to set a bomb and demand total return of all Oriental cultural artifacts from the Boston museum."

"Ikarino did?" Taku said aloud before he could stop himself. "You mean he himself...?"

"That's right. He must've guessed how the American government would react. It's even possible that he'd actually arranged things with them beforehand. Be that as it may, the moment the threat was made the president put a stop to all surveys, sales, and movement of everything in the Boston museum's Oriental collection. This means that it's now impossible to use the public survey of the Boston museum's holdings to provide evidence for the private material we've gathered. If we report our findings independently, Ikarino will use his hold over the media to have it treated as false. It could even be construed as harassment on our part."

"A last-ditch plan to save himself," muttered Hokuyo Hachimai, the teacher of *Wandering Practice* admiringly. "Trust him to have a bold idea like that."

"It may be daring," Tenro said reprovingly, "but unfortunately for us, this freezing of all surveys and movement of the museum's collection doesn't just prevent us from playing our decisive trump card against Ikarino. Professor Yusurido had helped our investigations another step along, and this next matter has also now been effectively paralyzed."

"You're speaking of that business, aren't you," Sarashino broke in. "Those ancient objects said to come from the Nintoku Tomb, that someone passed on to the Boston museum."

"I am. Prof.Yusurido was on the verge of being able to establish the involvement of Saisho, the early Meiji provincial governor of Sakai. He could trace a line from Yosuke Nawagi through the provincial governor and the top Meiji statesmen through to the Boston museum. Now the American president has effectively put an end to all this painstaking investigation. In my view, that bomb scare was a very skillful piece of theatre on Ikarino's part, involving the American, English, and French governments, which were all beginning to show signs of caving in to the demands for return of the world's cultural treasures, along with our own politicians, who want to prevent the public learning about the Nintoku Tomb scandal. Still…"

"'Tis a dangerous game we played," said Sarashino with a sigh. "And for a while there, Meido looked like he was thoroughly cornered."

Tenro nodded heavily. "So now the Group is faced with the difficult question of how we should make our next decisive move against him. Just repeating our criticisms won't sway the Wayfarers' League."

The Uncle of the First House gave a groan. "Now if we were back in the old days of the League," he said, "everyone would have fallen into line unconditionally behind the Group's position at a single word from Henro Sensei."

"It's my own fault." Tenro hung his head. "As Henro's successor to the leadership, I must accept the shame of this." Taku saw a wave of distress shadow the heavily-lined profile.

"Well then, I guess our only remaining tactic is the one Yugaku has suggested," muttered the Uncle of the First House, folding his arms. "Our laws say that one who feels no shame in breaking the clan's laws must be done away with."

The room seemed to darken suddenly. Taku looked at Ai's face to judge her reaction, but he found nothing there. He heard someone sigh deeply.

"But I doubt it can be done," said the Uncle of the Seventh House.

"Why so?"

"It wouldn't be so hard to do away with Meido. But if he were to die, we'd have the entire vast Ikarino Corporation organization as our enemies. And then…"

"Then what?" Sarashino asked.

The Uncle of the Seventh House went on haltingly, "Well, we certainly have a clear idea of the pros and cons of Ikarino Corporation today… They're an interest group that has turned its back on Henro Sensei's legacy. But we cannot overlook the fact that the Kenshi clan, which rose from nothing a mere hundred years ago, only exists on a par with the rest of Japan's citizens thanks to the financial, political, and cultural support of the Wayfarers' League."

"Come on, Uncle, just what are you saying?" demanded the Uncle of the First House shortly. "The way you're talking, it sounds like you think the Group's existence would be threatened if Ikarino Corporation was destroyed!"

"I only wish to point out that Ikarino Corporation lent us a great deal of support in rebuilding the Group after the war when we were left powerless."

"That was then. This is now."

"I understand what the Uncle of the Seventh House is saying," Tenro interposed. "This is a real problem, it's true. And it wasn't just after the war. It continues today. We may have legitimized ourselves by creating family registers and blending with society, but fundamentally we remain outsiders at heart, and I do believe that we owe a great debt to the Wayfarers' League and Ikarino for our ability to maintain our autonomy as we do. Ikarino has always looked after the clan. He was at the head of the great *thrust*, and he's continued to quietly provide backup for the Group and its descendants. This is still true today. The position we've worked so hard to attain in society ever since the Meiji era would crumble in no time if we lost any power. I mean, the very existence of the Wayfarers' League is a thorn in the flesh for the present government and the old plutocracy alliances. They're just licking their lips waiting for the League to have an internal breakup. We have to consider this in our plans."

"It's quite true," Yusurido broke in quietly. "The plutocracy have been only too happy to help our investigations with a constant stream of helpful information and material about Ikarino's activities in Manchuria and after the war. It's clear they're eagerly anticipating a split in the Wayfarers' League."

"I don't want to give them the pleasure of breaking the League up. It's a precious organization set up by our founder. And I don't want Meido's life to be taken. He's been one of our number all this time. In which case, the best solution is that he should see the error of his ways, step down from his leadership of the League, rediscover his original impulse, and live in harmony with the Group again. So…"

"So how do we achieve that?" Sarashino asked, arms folded. "How do we get this fellow to take his hands off the Wayfarers' League, eh?"

"I think we should send out a call to the Futakami Fraternity and everyone in the Wayfarers' League to demand with one voice that Ikarino step down."

"Remove him from office, in other words," Yusurido muttered.

"That's right." Tenro nodded.

Yusurido scratched his head. "Everyone in the Group here would respond, but I'm not so sure about all the Wayfarers members. They have complicated loyalties."

"That's where I have an idea," said Tenro. "The Group and the Wayfarers' League were both originally born from a strong spiritual connection among the clan members. That was the original impulse. So we must now find a way to *reconnect* everyone in the clan. It may seem a faint hope, but I believe our only recourse is to take a stand, return to first principles, and appeal to the clan's fundamental sense of spiritual connection."

"Spiritual connection, you say?" The Aunt of the Fifth House looked quizzical. "Yes, I see what you mean. But it wouldn't be easy."

"No, and so…" Tenro paused, and sat in silent thought for a moment with downcast eyes. Then he looked up, and spoke in a voice that was quiet yet struck deep into the hearts of all his listeners. "I have decided to *go down*."

Everyone in the room drew an audible breath. Ai gave a little cry, and pressed her hand to her mouth.

Taku could see that Tenro had made some grave decision, but its meaning escaped him.

In the alcove, the bloom of the blood-red camellia fell suddenly with a soft thud.

29

Three days after the late-night meeting in Ryukien, fifty-five people set out on the annual Futakami Pilgrimage to Mount Nijo.

As this *Great Nori* would coincide with the ceremonial *going down* of the present leader, Tenro, and the inauguration of the new Group Parent, there was a rush to apply to be among the pilgrims, requiring three separate meetings before a final choice of participants was made.

The fifty-five pilgrims, with Tenro as their titular head, consisted of five from among the Intimates, four teachers and three external volunteers from the Wayfarers' League, with the rest chosen from among the wider Group membership around the country. Besides these, Ai Katsuragi came as Acting Head, and Yugaku as *nori* leader.

Though Taku was still only a new member and assistant teacher, he was given special permission to take part at the particular request of Tenro himself.

The pilgrims gathered late at night before the inner temple of Izuyama Gongen, and set off in silence. Clad in dark blue *happi* coat and leggings, with sedge hats hung on their backs, the fifty-five made their way down the mountain following ancient pathways, walking at first slowly and then gradually quickening pace. On the back of each coat was the white-dyed symbol "Gods," while down the lapels at the front were written in white "Company of Fifty-Five" and "Tenmu Jinshin Group."

The young man at their head carried a banner announcing "Religious Organization: Tenmu Jinshin Group," and from its pole fluttered a ribbon bearing the words "Pilgrimage to Nintoku

Tomb." This was no mere camouflage to reassure the general public and the authorities—it was the rule that they should end their pilgrimage to the mountain with a visit to the tomb.

In times past, their forebears had fled the tragedy of the Takenouchi Highway work camp under Mount Nijo, and walked their *Great Nori* to distant Izu. Now their descendants were setting out to travel once more the mountain paths these forebears had traveled over, this time in reverse.

As Taku walked, he turned his eyes towards the dark sea that could be glimpsed beyond the black shapes of the mountains. His mind was a tangle of thoughts. He was pondering his blood relative Henro Katsuragi and the clan, yet for some reason these thoughts prompted no warm feelings of love or nostalgia in him. He guessed it was because he had never actually had any personal contact with Henro. The strong affection that Tenro and the Aunts and Uncles still evinced towards Henro undoubtedly sprang from their experience of having directly mingled and had dealings with him in life. Even Meido Ikarino's expression softened when he spoke of Henro.

My family connection with Henro Katsuragi is actually pretty meaningless, he thought. The others—those on this difficult *Great Nori* with him such as Ai—who was devoting herself to strengthening the hidden bonds of the Group and testing the clan's means of survival in the modern world—or Yugaku, Tenro, Hokuyo Hachimai, or Shirabe Yusurido, not to mention those left behind, such as Ryuzaki—felt far more like family to him.

Taku smiled to himself, aware of a sense of oneness with these fifty-five companions as he walked with them through the night, with soft footfall and quiet breath.

"*Is-se-fu-ko, is-sho-fu-ju,*" came the hoarse, rhythmic chant of Tenro at their head. Everyone softly joined in the chorus. "*Is-sho-mu-seki, is-shin-mu-shi.*"

Puzzled at first by the obscure chanting, Taku at last realized that they were pronouncing one by one the characters written on the wall in the alcove—*Plough no furrow, live in no place, belong to no nation, have no self.*

"*Is-se-fu-ko,*" he joined in.

"*Is-sho-fu-ju*." Tenro's voice wafted back through the darkness again. The weird, endless chant seemed to be crawling on through the mountains ahead of him. Quickening his step, Taku walked through the darkness, sunk deep inside the chanting.

Silently the group of pilgrims made its way towards Mount Nijo, walking day and night with only a few hours of rest and sleep to break the journey. In towns and villages all along the way, they were met with warm *connections* from the local brotherhood and friends.

It seemed these houses had some secret way of signaling their affiliation, for Ai and Yugaku recognized them at a glance. The folks who welcomed this little band on its way to Mount Nijo treated them with unobtrusive yet evident emotion. An outside observer would have seen it simply as a devout family giving alms to a group of pilgrims. But Taku was astonished at this evidence of how many people living so far afield maintained some form of *connection* with the Group.

"These Friends don't actually have a direct *connection* with us," Ai explained to him. "But they're descendants of the Kenshi, and ever since the Meiji era, any of the big wars could have compelled the family to *blend* and join the outside world. Such families live all over Japan, and these days there's nothing to distinguish them from the original Japanese nationals. But they still secretly maintain their pride in being Kenshi. For instance, there are households that won't follow the national custom of eating rice cakes during the first three days of New Year. Other ones, that maintain separate customs more strongly, never pound rice at any time of year, or keep the substance in their homes. Strict followers of the Pure Land Buddhist sect apparently reject the custom of putting a pine branch by the door for New Year. Well, in the same way a lot of us won't use New Year rice straw decorations. 'Rice rots the guts,' the old Kenshi used to say. Households that belonged to the Futakami Fraternity never ate rice until the early 1900s, I've heard."

"So what was their staple food?" Taku wondered.

"They ate a variety of wild grains. All kinds of millet, plus horse chestnuts, buckwheat, beans such as soy and adzuki, wild vegetables, and taro, sweet potato, yam, and other root vegetables. They made dishes such as noodles, buckwheat mash, hot pot stews and soups, and boiled or dried vegetables. Even today, Group families eat only non-rice grains for the first three days of the year, and every fifth day of each month."

I see, Taku thought to himself. So that's why they'd eaten nothing but bread or noodles while he was at the Group headquarters.

But why? he wondered. Why should the Kenshi have been so extreme in their pronouncements about rice rotting the gut?

Turning to ask her, he discovered that Ai had drifted off to sleep where they lay resting in a hollow by a cliff, her head cradled against a rock. Her face bore the marks of weariness; through the trees filtered the afternoon sunlight, striping her cheek with gold.

It was night. A wind blew through the valley, setting the trees roaring like the sea as it passed. The spirit of the mountains filled the air. Beyond the black spine of the ridge, village lights twinkled faintly.

The fifty-five from the Futakami Fraternity had now completed about two thirds of their journey, and were spending a rare night of quiet rest. They were lodged in one of the places they referred to as "mountain dens," huts in the forest that were used by the mountain monk sects for their austerities. This place, called Ryuzetsuin or Dragon Tongue Villa, was only visited during the summer and winter austerities. It was badly dilapidated, but was at least somewhere they could sleep in peace after their long hardships.

People were moving freely about, some washing under the nearby waterfall, others busy hoisting an awning in the garden or clearing up after the meal, or applying moxa to their tired legs, examining the map to determine tomorrow's route, and so on. All looked relieved and happy; for all the problems they had had along the way, there was a sense of relief that everyone without exception was now approaching their goal as planned, and the tension of the *Great Nori* was clearly relaxing.

It was after nine that night, when the bonfire in the garden had died down to a flicker and the soft breathing of sleepers had already begun to be heard from within, that the leader Yugaku returned from his reconnaissance of the next day's route and came over to Taku.

"How's it going?" he asked. "I guess you're feeling tired."

"You can walk twice as fast as me, Yugaku."

"Ah well, this is my only real talent, you see." Yugaku jokingly stamped the ground as he spoke. "The teachers are in there talking with Tenro right now," he went on. "Would you care to join us?"

"Sure, I'd be only too happy as long as I'm not in the way."

"Okay, let's go then."

Taku followed him in, and was welcomed by Tenro's warm smile in the softly lit hut.

"I'm glad you've come, Mr. Hayami. Please make yourself at home."

Taku was placed between Hokuyo Hachimai and Shirabe Yusurido. Seated across from him was Ai, and beside her a slender-faced, elegant man with silver hair—Shuso Kariya, the leader of the Wayfarers' League, whom he'd met that first day at Ryukien.

"So how are you liking your first *Great Nori*? You look as though you're enjoying it to me," said Hachimai beside him. He was a middle-aged, approachable fellow, tanned dark from the sun, who close-cropped head was rapidly balding. This was the teacher of *Wandering Practice*, who had praised Taku's article so warmly.

"Well, I'm managing to keep up somehow," Taku replied. "A lot of the others are older than I am, after all, so I'm in no position to complain."

"Ai spoke highly of your walking abilities, and sure enough she was right. We're all impressed as well. You haven't inherited Henro Sensei's genes for nothing, it seems."

Taku could only accept Hachimai's words with a humble shrug. Meanwhile, Yugaku was coming around with tea for everyone. This was no normal tea, but seemed to be a brew of some kind of grass.

The casual talk went on for a while. Tenro and everyone around him was in high spirits, no doubt thanks to the delight of being back on a *Great Nori* again after so long. At first, Taku simply sat quietly listening to the talk. Then, at their request, he set in to recount the life he'd led on his travels in other countries.

At a pause in the conversation, Yusurido, the strong-bodied woman teacher with clear-cut features, spoke. "I'd just like to ask your honest opinion about something," she said. Then, after a

moment's hesitation, she continued. "Do you really think that in the
final analysis the Gypsies, the American Indians, the Eskimos, and
others like them will find it difficult to maintain their independence
and unique lifestyle into the future?"

"I feel it's going to be a hard road for them," Taku answered.
"But I'm not saying it's impossible."

Yusurido nodded "Yes, I realize that," she murmured. Then she
went on, "It seems to me that the twentieth century has been one
of 'nations' and their citizens. Everywhere, be it capitalist or socialist,
third world or first, has followed this same path of nationhood. And
it's certainly true that this new information society of ours will
go on pushing us more and more strongly in the same direction.
The central bureaucracy's computerized access to every part of the
nation means that information about the private lives of everyone
in all regions gets collected, and at the press of a button it will be
immediately accessible.

"Remember back in the eighth century when 'Japan' first became
constituted as a nation through a set of controlling laws? Well, I
think we're at a similar point again in modern history. Back then,
wandering folk were settled as serfs under the name of 'goodmen,'
but there was still room to choose to escape as a non-goodman and
drop out of the national framework. That's no longer the case today.
But we Kenshi resist the thought of simply allowing ourselves to be
submerged into 'society' and slowly assimilated away to nothing. On
the other hand, we're also against the idea of setting up a separate
nation of some sort. A nation is founded on the premise of fixing
and defining territory and citizens, and citizens are people who are
bound by law to remain within the boundaries of their own nation,
after all. But where does this leave us, then? We need to find a clear
way forward, no matter how hard it may be…"

Yusurido spoke in a clear, firm contralto, and her words were
crisp, but deep lines of suffering furrowed her brow. Taku listened
in silence as she spoke.

"Wouldn't you say that Meido Ikarino is someone who's put
forward one dangerous answer to your question?" Shuso Kariya
quietly interposed. "After all, in his own way he's been serious in
his attempt to come to grips with the problem. The conclusion he

reached is the belief that financial power transcends nations. And it's true, the realm of economics and finance exists beyond national boundaries. Think of those monstrosities, the multinationals. This is clearly Meido's idea—goods, capital, the means of production, technology, are all things in natural flux, that resist pinning down. Meido came to believe that the future of the Kenshi lay in this, and to that end he even went so far as attempting to use the power of the nation and its bureaucracy. I think this is why those state capitalists, the heads of the old traditional conglomerates, have been secretly out to get him—they're good at sniffing out the anti-nationalism hidden at the heart of his ambitions. His private dream for the Wayfarers' League is essentially to form an economic federation that transcends national power."

"He's a true member of the Kenshi, that man," Tenro broke in, having sat listening in silence to this point. "I believe he's genuinely tried to follow our path of '*no self*.' But the road he's chosen is clearly the wrong one. My hope is to place the Group clan in a position where we won't be trampled by the world at large, but I certainly have no wish for us to be able to trample others instead. Most people in the world think in terms of winning or losing, but I hate both these things."

At this point Taku hesitantly put a question to him. "But when you're faced with the situation of having no way around a choice between winning and losing...?"

Tenro looked at Taku and smiled. "There's always a way around," he said. "You'll have learned from this *Great Nori* that there are a great many other paths open to this country, extraordinary paths unknown to most people."

"Yes." Taku nodded. It was true. There's always a hidden way. It's just that we can't see it. But surely there are also situations where one is forced to choose between two options.

Tenro seemed to have guessed his thoughts, for he went on, "If the time comes when we have to choose..." he paused, and looked at Ai. "What will you do, Ai?"

Ai didn't hesitate. "Choose to lose," she replied.

"Well spoken. This means you really are the third Group leader." A flush rose in Tenro's cheeks, and his eyes shone with joy. "If you really find yourself up against a choice of winning or losing, it's better to lose. It's better to lose everything, return to nothing, and wander in the shadows of society again. That is the Kenshi Way. We don't want to lose, we don't want to win, and that's why we can't live in society. That's why we withdraw and choose to 'Live in no place.' I've understood that we Kenshi are people who lose, who relinquish, who part.

"Yes, Ai, you spoke well. All things in this world will come to an end in their time—even mountains, oceans, rivers. I believe Meido is mistaken. But I don't want to fight him and win. Yet, nor must we simply fold our arms and give in. Therefore, we must gather all our strength, and simply do what we can. And if it's all to no avail in the end, well, then we lose. We lose, and we relinquish everything. Relinquish the Group. Relinquish the future of the clan. Relinquish our memories of Henro Sensei, mountains, rivers—relinquish it all. Even living as humans. We are extraordinary people, people of the extra-ordinary. And it's only fitting that we of the extra-ordinary should have extraordinariness and absurdity in our souls. You understand, Ai. I'll say no more. As I've already decided in discussion with the Aunts and Uncles, I'm handing my leadership over to you. You are now the third Parent. Understood?"

Ai held Tenro's gaze. In her eyes a dark flame flickered. "Yes," she answered. Then she nodded firmly. "I accept."

Tenro wordlessly got to his feet. There was a spring in his motion that belied his age. "Yugaku, announce this to our companions," he ordered. "At five o'clock tomorrow morning there will be a ceremony of 'Parent Transmission' for the Futakami Fraternity. Prepare the leader's *umegai* knife."

Yugaku bowed and rose. Gazing at Ai's dark face with its firm chin, Taku felt he had never seen anyone more beautiful.

30

It took seventeen nights from their departure from Izu for the Company of Fifty-Five to complete their *Great Nori* and arrive at the final destination, the base camp at the foot of the Katsuragi Range. All along the way, they had added time to the journey by meeting with Group members and performing *connections* to bid farewell to Tenro.

Now in the Yamato region at last, they had been invited to spend the night at the house of a builder who was particularly dedicated to working for the Group. Here everyone took their first bath of the journey and washed away the dust of travel, was treated to a hotpot meal and sweet potato wine, and sank into deep sleep.

Settled in the corridor leading off from the living room on the second floor, Taku found he couldn't sleep despite his weariness, so he got up again and went downstairs. Every room overflowed with fellow pilgrims. The exhaustion of the *Great Nori* seemed to have suddenly overcome them, and they slept like the dead.

Taku was hunting about in the kitchen for the remains of the wine when he sensed someone at the door. The tall figure in pilgrim's *happi* coat and leggings slipped silently into the kitchen, and whispered in a low, soft voice, "I'm off to climb Mount Nijo right now. Will you come with me?"

It was Ai's voice. She put out a hand and grasped his shoulder. Something like an electrical current ran through him. "Yes," he replied. "Wait while I go get ready."

"I'll be in the back yard." Ai disappeared out the door, while Taku went upstairs and donned his coat and leggings. For his feet he chose, instead of the pilgrim's straw sandals, the hiking boots he'd used throughout the *Great Nori*. Then he went out to the yard. It was still dark. Somewhere in the distance a dog barked.

"For some reason I just can't sleep," Ai said. "You too?"

"I guess we're overexcited from having completed the long journey."

"Yes, I guess so." Ai nodded with a little smile. "That shape there is Mount Nijo. Can you see it?"

Taku strained his eyes in the direction she was pointing. He could just make out the ridgeline, like the outline of a sleeping animal, against the night sky. "I can. That's the female peak, right?"

"That's right. I was out here staring up at it, and I suddenly just had to go. The mountain must be calling me. Let's go."

With these words she shot off into the darkness, Taku following.

She was heading north. He guessed she was aiming for Taima Temple.

"What route will we take to the mountain?" Taku asked as he strode behind her.

Ai was traveling at speed through the darkness. "There are various ways, just as there've always been many routes crossing these mountains to link Kawachi and Yamato. There's the Takenouchi Road that crosses Takenouchi Pass to the south of Nijo. Then there's the Osaka Road that follows the Anamushi Pass area. And Iwaya Road that crosses from Taima via Iwaya Pass. Then on the north side of Mount Nijo you've got the old Sekiya Road, that crosses via Tajiri Pass. In the north there's also Tatsuta Road that runs south of Mount Ikoma, and the Thirteen Pass Road that cuts across Mount Ikoma. The most direct route between Nara and Osaka, Kurakoshi Road, goes over Kuragari Pass. Then going south into southern Kawachi there are ways crossing Hiraishigoe and Mizugoe Pass. And everything I've mentioned so far just amounts to the ones that have been known from the old days. Besides these there used to be the hidden, secret paths, made by roaming tramps and beggars, woodsmen, animals. The paths the Kenshi used to use were often these hidden ways. We're taking one of them up Mount Nijo tonight."

Ai's pace quickened further. Taku could detect a strange hum in the air, as if the night air that flowed about her was faintly singing. He too walked faster, keeping pace.

At length they arrived at the end of the plain with its scattering of houses, and began to climb. The path was densely overgrown, and so narrow that one had to turn side-on to make one's way along it. They crossed streams and clambered up rocky slopes, Ai making her way up the steep mountainside as easily and lithely as a frolicking child. The wind roared, tossing the valley trees. As they went higher, the cold intensified. Almost nothing was visible around them—all that could be seen were the brightly glittering stars beyond the treetops.

"Roughly where are we now?" Taku asked the rapidly advancing back ahead of him.

"We're about to come out onto the saddleback ridge. There, see it over there?"

Taku was concentrating all his strength into his knees as he scrambled up the slope. For an instant he thought he'd lost her, then suddenly his field of vision cleared, and the sky opened like a curtain before him. He was standing on the watershed between the male and female peaks.

Ai turned to him. "Look, Kawachi's down on that side, and Yamato's on the other." He stood beside her, gazing down over what seemed a distant, black sea. The wind had suddenly died, and a sense of impending dawn began to fill the sky. Yet despite the hour, lights still glowed here and there on the plain to east and west.

"Over there is the Nintoku Tomb. And the Takenouchi Highway is…"

Ai paused, and ran her fingers through her short-cropped hair. Taku followed her gaze, searching for the old road he had walked before. But night still shrouded it from sight.

So where would the work camp have been, the one where the Kenshi were held while they worked on the highway? he wondered. In his mind's eye he saw the hut surrounded by its fence. He imagined the eight men being led from it into the night by Nawagi's henchmen.

Ai turned to him. "This is where you and I first met, isn't it, Taku?"

He nodded. Everything had begun from that meeting in the mist. He recalled watching Ai climb up the slope of the female peak at an impossible speed.

"You were amazing, Ai," he said, half to himself. "You climbed through a beam like a spotlight, vibrating like a wonderful golden bee as you went. I could only stand there watching in astonishment, feeling as if I was in some dream..."

"If it was now, you'd have been following me in no time."

"No, there's no way."

"Not so," Ai said firmly, gazing into his eyes. "No one can perform a *nori* by themselves, you know. But if they walk with a companion with whom they have a true rapport, they'll find they have double the power. If you walk with fifty-five companions, you'll be still stronger. And if you can be at one with a whole clan, its ancestors, and people even further back in time, what a magnificent world will open to you. But even that's not enough, in fact. It's when we can unite ourselves with lives beyond the human—with this mountain, the night, the wind, the trees, rocks, plants, birds, with all this—that we'll experience the true *nori*. I haven't got that far yet. But I want to. Would you come with me, Taku?"

Taku nodded silently. His great grandfather Henro must have been seeking the same sort of thing back in the days of his youth when he lived the life of a beggar monk on Mount Nijo and performed the mountain circuit austerities. And the early mountain monk En no Ozunu, who was accused of using magical powers to fly through the air and was exiled to Izu— he too must have been able to become one with the rocks, trees, wind, animals and birds of Mount Nijo.

He peered into the night, which seemed all the darker for hovering on the edge of dawn. Then suddenly he found himself recalling that poem, almost like a spell, that he'd seen carved onto the stone pillar near Yusenji on the path up the mountain.

Ayashiya tare ka Futakami no yama.

He felt now that he could understand those puzzling words, *Ayashiya tare ka*, not through reason but through intuition. '*Tis most*

strange, who can it be?—Futakami Mountain. Mount Nijo, or Futakami
as it was called of old, had long been a place where people had
come together in spirit, where the ghosts of the dead dwelt. This
was surely why Prince Otsu's sister had written that poignant poem
after his execution, longing to embrace this mountain in her heart
as the soul of her dead brother.

"Ai, do you remember that poem?" he said. "You know,
the famous one written by Prince Otsu's sister—what was her
name?—mourning his death after he was buried on the male peak
up there. I read it once in a guide book, but I can't remember how
it begins."

> *"Mortal of this transient world,*
> *yet will I from tomorrow*
> *turn these eyes to Futakami*
> *seeing that mountain*
> *as my brother,"*

she murmured. Then she laid her hand on his shoulder, and went
on, "But it's not because I'm particularly interested in ancient
poetry that I know this poem. We Kenshi have our own poems,
and our own clan history's oral traditions. When we look down like
this on the Yamato Plain, we don't see it through the ancient poetry
anthologies or the early history chronicles that everyone knows
about and identifies with the place. The drama of all those bloody
struggles for power that took place down there have virtually
nothing to do with wanderers like ourselves."

Taku nodded. He understood exactly what she was saying. Aware
of the warmth of her hand on his shoulder, he asked, "So then why
do you remember the Princess's poem so well, Ai?"

For a moment she didn't speak. Then finally, she whispered
quietly, "There's a reason. Do you want to hear it? It concerns you
too."

"Me? The long-ago murder of Prince Otsu concerns me?"

Ai nodded solemnly. For a moment her eyes seemed to shine
blue in the darkness.

"Yes, please, you must tell me."

"All right." She drew her face closer to his. She was so close that he almost felt her hot breath at his ear. "Prince Otsu was executed on the grounds that he'd plotted against the throne, but to prove to the world that he'd planned a coup d'état, they had to capture his co-conspirators and the men he'd secretly assembled for the task. A group of so-called 'insurgents' was caught as well as various people connected with the plot. In fact, they were a group of winnower-making Kenshi who happened to be napping on the bank of a nearby river. Outrageously, they were accused of being a gang of hoodlums who'd conspired with Otsu and been set up as a conscripted band of rebels to carry out the insurrection, and they were dragged through the streets of the capital and then condemned to hard labor for life. They weren't 'goodmen,' see— they weren't cultivators, they had no fixed address or citizenship, so there was no need to treat them as fully human. Their leader was exiled to Izu. His name is recorded as Toki no Mitsukuri— '*Mitsukuri*' is written to mean 'road-maker'—but the real meaning of the name was 'winnower-maker' or 'winnower.' He lived and died in the mountains of Izu. His name is still memorialized in a place below Basara Pass in Kamo."

History repeats itself, Taku thought as he listened. How often had the same thing happened since that first Kenshi roundup in 686?

"So this band of completely irrelevant vagabonds ended up being implicated in Prince Otsu's plot, and used as evidence against him. But the leader who was exiled to Izu, he does actually have a connection with it." She turned to him. "What was the original name of your great-grandfather Henro, do you remember, Taku?"

"The Katsuragi Monkey, wasn't it?"

"I mean before that."

"Er, Henro Basara?"

"That's right. And the only family with the name Basara are the descendants of Toki no Mitsukuri, who lived around Basara Pass. This is the history passed down to us by word of mouth."

"Wait a minute." Taku shook his head. Putting together all Ai had just said, he understood that his own great-grandfather was a distant descendant of the Kenshi leader who had been exiled to Izu back in the seventh century for his supposed part in Prince Otsu's rebellion. A light suddenly flashed in the darkness of his mind. So this was why when Henro Katsuragi led his fellow prisoners in escaping from the work camp under Mount Nijo, he'd made the long journey to Izu seeking the support of his clan. And this was why the Group headquarters were in the mountains near Basara Pass. So the Futakami Pilgrimage was not simply made in memory of those who had died in the Meiji incident at the Nintoku Tomb. It was also a pilgrimage back to the clan's original home, from which they'd been exiled back in the seventh century. His mind was beginning to confuse Prince Otsu and Toki no Mitsukuri now.

"So the man in the grave up there and my family…" He looked up to the dark peak, feeling that invisible history snaking suddenly through him till his body almost shook. He went on, murmuring half to himself, "If the oral traditions are right, I really do have some weird connection to the Prince Otsu incident. But only as a descendent of a victim who was caught up in the supposed plot. That really is all it is, right?"

"The Kenshi have always been on the dark side of history," said Ai, "always caught up in it as victims." She raised a finger. "Right, I'm going up to the male peak."

The instant after she spoke, she was already climbing up the dark path from the saddleback ridge at terrific speed. Taku followed. Unlike the last time, he now kept her in view ahead of him. He barely glanced at his feet. He slid through the wind, climbing in the dark with the sensation of her warmth and rhythm on his skin leading him.

At length they arrived at the top. After huddling together a little to rest, Ai wordlessly beckoned Taku to a hollow a little way below the summit. Beneath the trees that glowed faintly with dew, she removed her coat and slowly took off her leggings. Then, with an unaffected gesture, she slipped off the rest of her clothes. Taku gazed astonished at the naked body lying quietly there on the grass, white as a shining stone, so different from her dark face.

"Come. This is why I've come to the mountain." Ai stretched out her arms as she spoke. At that moment, the sun finally slid above the horizon. He gazed at her breasts, now crimson in the sun's rays. One seemed to lie a little flatter than the other, and to his eyes they rose like the male and female peaks of the mountain. Taku knelt in the grass and buried his head between them.

As he did so, the images of Mount Nijo and the Nintoku Tomb coalesced in his mind. That flattened female peak and the high round male peak—it came to him that the authorities who had once built the tomb in the form of a flatter front and rounded back had surely wanted to build a version of Futakami. Nijo was the only volcano in the area. It had given birth to the Yamato plateau and the Kawachi plain. The ancients must indeed have had special feelings for this mountain. And Nijo was a mountain of stone. The huge tomb was likewise sealed with a glittering layer of stones. It was truly a man-made Mount Nijo. There was no question. Those strangely-shaped tombs, sometimes called "keyhole tombs" for their shape when viewed from the air, were modeled after the mountain. He saw a vision of countless tombs rising like waves against the backdrop of Mount Nijo.

Closing his eyes, Taku quietly slipped off his clothes.

31

A mist flowed around them—dense, heavy, almost solid to the touch.

Darkness had begun to invade the air. With each gust of wind, the branches sighed sorrowfully.

On the round, tumulus-shaped summit of the female peak, people had silently begun to gather, clad in the traditional pilgrim's leggings, knee breeches and *happi* coat. Some had crossed over from the male peak, others were even now climbing up from the saddleback ridge between. There were figures clambering up the steep slope from the Iwaya path, while others again were arriving at the summit from the direction of Iwaya itself. There were old folks and women among them. All were hastening at marvelous speed, along the ridges and up through the trees to gather on the summit, their coats fluttering as they went. On every coat were the words "Tenmu Jinshin Group" and "Company of Fifty-Five."

Below them, the lights of Kawachi, Izumi and Sakai were visible through gaps in the mist. It was past dusk, and they were the only people on Mount Nijo.

With the overweight Aunt of the Fifth House, Taku had made his way up to the saddleback ridge from the Takenouchi Highway. All the Uncles had already arrived. Taku also saw among the crowd the faces of teachers such as Rokotsu Sarashino, Hokuyo Hachimai, and Shirabe Yusurido, as well as Shuso Kariya, one of the Wayfarer managers.

The last to arrive were Ai and Yugaku. They came climbing up with the slight figure of an old man clad in white *happi* between them.

It was the Group leader, Tenro Katsuragi. His step belied the fact that he was in his late seventies.

"I've kept you all waiting." A smile wrinkled the skin around his eyes. "I've been enjoying myself walking all over the mountain, that's why I'm late, I'm afraid." With this apology, he spoke a few short words and bowed to each in turn, finally arriving before Taku.

"And you too, Taku. Please look after the Group." He bowed. Then he leaned forward. "And Ai," he added quietly. "Well then," he continued, looking about him at the assembled people with a smile. "It's time for me to *go down*."

"The year of Japan's defeat in the war, Henro Sensei *went down* in this mountain. He did it well, as one would expect from a man who had performed the mountain circuit austerity between the male and female peaks thirty thousand times. He requested Meido Ikarino and myself to assist. Through his death, he cautioned the Group and Wayfarers of the period never to forget the wanderer's spirit. I have lived my life in accordance with these words. And yet I must blame myself for the fact that the Group and Wayfarers' League today seem to be on the verge of forgetting our Sensei's aim." He paused, then continued solemnly.

"Please spread the word to everyone on your return: Tenro *went down* with defeat on his lips. He had reached the end of his wisdom and endurance, and felt that the only way he could spur the Group on was to die. Tell them that henceforward also, if the Group and the Wayfarers seem bent on choosing the wrong path, the leader must speak to them through his or her death."

"Well, I don't want to make a fuss over this parting," he finished. "Let's get on with it." He beckoned Ai to his side. Then he gestured to Yugaku and Taku.

"Three is too many really, but never mind. I'm going to teach you the true Dwelling of the Dead. So you'll know for the next time someone *goes down*."

Tenro nodded to everyone.

Shuso Kariya, the Wayfarer manager, now spoke. "I'll stake everything I have to pass on your last wishes to the Wayfarers, Sensei," she said, her voice so soft she seemed almost to be talking to herself. "Your words will strike our members a painful blow to the heart, I know. But these words of censure, embodied in your self-sacrifice, will not be fruitless. We'll prove it to you. We'll join with the Group, and follow your urging by returning the Wayfarers to Henro Sensei's original impulse."

"I'm afraid I won't be around in this world to have anything proven to me," Tenro responded with chuckle.

"Oh, Sensei," the Aunt of the Fifth House murmured, wiping away a tear, "You always did love a joke."

"I'll go now," Tenro said simply. He turned, and led the way down the female peak. Mist shrouded the white-robed old man as he went. Behind him walked Taku, Ai, and Yugaku.

How far had they walked? Tenro seemed almost to be flying as he strode on along some invisible path through the head-high grasses and between the trees. Ai and Yugaku followed close behind, while Taku ran desperately through the mist trying to keep them in sight ahead of him.

Finally, Tenro came to a halt. "Here will do," he announced. "This looks like a good hole."

He was pointing to a deep crack where the rock face had crumbled, a place like a deep, dark split in the earth itself. Tenro knelt and put his head in. "Yes," he murmured, "this is the place." Then he turned to the others. "This is one of the entrances to the Great Wind Cave that extends everywhere under Mount Nijo. This mountain's like Mount Fuji—deep inside there are vast holes no one knows about, that run the length and breadth of the mountain. Henro Basara, the man who became our founder, came to the mountain having learned of them from the legends of Toki no Mitsukuri that were handed down in Mitsukuri in Izu in the early days of Meiji. Henro still sleeps down there in the deeps, in the great limestone cave. Indeed I can only feel he still lives. So now I will make my pilgrimage down the dark road below Nijo to call on him. I believe I'll meet him there, sometime, somewhere."

Tenro put out a hand and touched Ai's cheek. Then he touched the cheeks of Yugaku and Taku in turn, and nodded firmly.

"Now, once I'm inside and call out to you, you must pile rocks over the entrance. Gather those rocks round about in preparation to block up the hole."

The three of them set about doing as instructed. Then Tenro wriggled down into the hole, twisting his arms and legs to get through until at last he disappeared inside. After a pause there came a call from within. Silently, the three began to fill the hole with rocks.

"Make sure you make a good solid pile," came the muffled voice from inside. "And if you have a chance to meet Meido," it continued, "tell him I said to say I'll be waiting on the other side."

The pile of rocks, wet from the mist, slipped suddenly to the ground, but Taku carefully gathered them up again and piled them in the entrance once more. When he turned around, he found Ai weeping silently. She continued to pile up the rocks, face averted.

"That should be enough," Yugaku said finally. He stood, and so did Ai. Taku remained on his knees, gazing at the now-sealed place where the dark crack in the mountain had been.

Henro, his own forebear, had also *gone down* like this somewhere into the earth below. The thought sent an incomprehensibly fierce flood of emotion coursing through him.

Suddenly he collapsed, and threw himself face down on the earth. "AU AU AU," he wailed, flinging out his arms as if to embrace the whole mountain, and burying his face between earth and rock.

"AU AU AU," came a distant voice as if in response. He raised his head, surprised. It was like an echo from some far place, and was also the cry that rose from the top of the female peak as the Uncles, Aunts, and Family raised their final call to Tenro.

32

Taku was walking with Ai along the old highway at the foot
of the Katsuragi Range. They were moving slowly. Ancient
shrines, white-washed earthen store houses, stone walls,
and temple roofs rose in turn before them, then slipped away as
they walked on.

Yugaku walked a little ahead. His arm was still far from healed,
but while he walked he seemed oblivious to any wounds.

Last night's thick mist seemed a dream now, with Mount Nijo
beautiful in the limpid morning light. The camel-like hump of the
female peak and the somewhat steeper male peak stood out in
strong relief, as if carved into the sky.

The three had spent the night on Mount Nijo, unable to bring
themselves to leave despite the mist and cold that made them
shiver.

Even once they had descended the mountain the next morning,
a strange warmth continued to glow deep within them. They were
tired, but they couldn't stay still. Driven by the urge to keep moving,
they began to walk again.

Ai had barely spoken since the night before. Her sunken eyes
were dark as the narrow cave into which Tenro had *gone down*. But
it was clear that once she set off walking, her body found its natural
rhythm once more.

Yes, Taku said to himself, it's all about walking. What Ai needed
now was not words of comfort, it was to walk and to go on walking.
This is what would help her recover from the trauma of the night's
events. He strode a little faster, and felt her pace unconsciously
quicken in response.

Before them on their right, Katsuragi and Mount Kongo towered violet. As they advanced, Taku could see how astonishingly steeply the mountainside rose out of the Yamato Plain. The plan Ai had come up with was to walk along the old highway under the mountain as far as Kazenomori Pass, then return a ways to cross Mizugoe Pass, and head for the Nintoku Tomb via Tondabayashi. The southern flank of Katsuragi was immediately ahead. From there a number of old roads wound on—the Kujira village road, the Handa foothills road, the Nagara road, the Asazuma village road, the road along the Takamiya foothills, and the Kamogami village road. At Kazenomori they would come upon the little shrine to the god of the wind that blew across the boundary between Katsuragi and Kii beyond.

Walking a little faster, Taku suddenly recalled the postcard he'd received last week from Kyoko Shimamura. "I'm 'tramping' along the road to Rikuzen Takada right now," she wrote. "I haven't walked much in this area before, so it's all fresh and new to me. This Tohoku area fascinates me with its faint whiff of the ancient Jomon culture. Hanada, Kozo Hayashi and quite a few other people have quit Meteor, one way or another, as well as me. Hanada says he's determined to run a yakitori bar. Will he succeed, I wonder? Me, I'm doing another circuit of Japan. Too bad I didn't end up a bride. I guess you'll be walking well with Ai now. I have faith we'll meet again somewhere, some day. The Tramp."

Taku smile wryly to himself. Hanada would have a hard time making a go of a yakitori bar, he thought.

Ai suddenly broke the long silence. "What is it?"

Taku shook his head. "Nothing," he replied. "You're the one who looks like you want to say something, actually."

"Yes." She nodded. "It's funny, but when I'm with you I just naturally want to walk slowly. Why should that be?"

"You don't have to drop your pace just to fit in with mine, you know," Taku said, somewhat stung. "I actually want to somehow walk faster when I'm with you."

"Really?" Ai peered up at him, a mischievous twinkle in her eyes. Then her expression stiffened suddenly. "Oh, a *nobori*. Something must have happened," she exclaimed.

Taku's gaze followed hers. Up on Mount Nijo, which until now had stood clear as a picture against the sky, a line of white smoke was snaking up into the morning air.

"What would that be?"

"That smoke's a signal to say the local Group people have something they want to tell us."

"Has something happened to the Group, I wonder?"

"I wonder. Anyway, let's find a phone booth somewhere round here. The sooner the better."

At that moment, Yugaku came hurtling back down the path.

"Ai!" he yelled. "There's a *nobori*! Have you seen it?"

"Yes! We must telephone the Group immediately!"

"Let's go down to the road over there. There's bound to be a phone booth somewhere outside a shop."

"Right."

Yugaku was already rounding the corner onto a side road twenty or thirty meters away, shoulders broad as an eagle's wings as he ran. Taku and Ai followed.

When they arrived at the road, Yugaku was at a public telephone outside a liquor store, tensely clutching the receiver. "Right, I see." He gave a firm nod, and put the phone down. His expression was a strained mixture of powerful excitement and anxiety. He clenched his right fist and struck it into his left palm with an audible blow.

"What's happened? Is it something bad?" Ai asked. Her eyes shone with a fierce anticipation.

"Meido Ikarino's been shot. Five bullets from a .38-caliber revolver pumped into his stomach. He's being operated on right now, they say."

Taku and Ai looked at each other. Somehow Taku knew it was that Smith & Wesson Centennial. Ryuzaki was one of the Group children whom Tenro had personally named, he suddenly recalled.

"He got in first," Yugaku said, regret in his voice.

Ai was gazing fixedly at Mount Nijo. "How stupid," she murmured.

"If Ikarino doesn't recover," Taku asked, "what will happen to the Ikarino Corporation?"

"It's bound to fall apart," said Ai. "There've been problems enough already, heaven knows. Ikarino's held it all together till now by force, through the power of his magnetism."

Yugaku broke in. "And you can be sure the old rival establishment conglomerates that have been longing to do him down will swing into action now. They've already joined forces with American multinationals to harass the Ikarino Corporation." He crossed his arms and groaned. "If the Wayfarers' League gets caught up in all that, it'll be a heavy blow to us as well. It's been thanks to the Wayfarers that our clan has survived these last hundred-odd years. If we're not careful, the whole Group could fall apart."

Taku didn't understand the details of all this, but it was clear that the Group was facing grave difficulties, regardless of whether Ikarino lived or died.

"But that's okay." Ai seemed to be speaking in response to his own thoughts. "Our clan has always valued freedom from possessions, having nothing. We can start from the beginning again, and go back to the principle of *menme-shinogi*. We'll do it ourselves—cut this bulky body back down to size again. Stop pressing forward, and start purposely retreating. We'll give up relying on power, and live as powerless folk again. We're Kenshi, whose motto is 'Live in no place,' after all. A wonderful clan who understands what it is to relinquish, not take. To relinquish land. Relinquish house. Relinquish the security of home. We've always lived this way, with nothing more than our own bodies, so there's no need to panic about what might happen to the Group and the Wayfarers' League now. It's true, isn't it? We are the Wind. The wind must be light, must run. The wind must never stand still. I'm right, aren't I?"

She raised her face and gazed towards Mount Nijo. The ribbon of smoke was now no longer there in the sky.

"When you look from this angle, the two peaks overlap to become one."

It was true. Taku could now see a single summit. As he looked, there flashed for an instant vividly before his eyes a vision of figures in running flight between that beautiful mountain and the sky above.

"A *nori!*" Ai's voice was tense. When he turned, she was no longer beside him. She was disappearing like a trembling bee into the distance, towards the shimmering purple mountain range of Katsuragi. Yugaku also was no longer beside him.

"Right!" Taku breathed deep, drawing in a great draft of rich air. The toes of his feet spread like fingers and kicked down at the earth, sliding his body smoothly forward. The wind whistled past his cheeks.

Taku was no longer a lone walker. He was hurtling, flashing along the old Katsuragi road in company with the visionary flying figures over Mount Nijo. The road to another kingdom, of boundless freedom, a realm without borders, stretched clearly before him. He was Henro. He was Shin'ichi. He was Stone-break Gen, he was Saera Maki's father, he was Yuzo in Mikuni, Kyoko Shimamura. He was aware of everyone overlapping within him, just as Nijo's two peaks had now merged to become one. *I'm Ai Katsuragi*, he thought, *I'm the Fifty-Five of the Eight Houses.* He trembled with a fierce joy. His eyes saw nothing around him, but his feet had become eyes. He was flashing lightly over the old Katsuragi road, with a speed he'd never before experienced.

The wind was invisible. Yet it existed. The Kingdom of the Wind was now before him. *I am the wind*, his body said, as with terrific speed he *flew* through the morning light that flooded down over shining Katsuragi.